Praise for #1 *New York Times* bestselling author

NORA ROBERTS

"When Roberts puts her expert fingers on the pulse of romance, legions of fans feel the heartbeat."

—*Publishers Weekly*

"Roberts' bestselling novels are some of the best in the romance genre."

—*USA TODAY*

"With clear-eyed, concise vision and a sure pen, Roberts nails her characters and settings with awesome precision, drawing readers into a vividly rendered world of family-centered warmth and unquestionable magic."

—*Library Journal*

"You can't bottle wish fulfillment, but Nora Roberts certainly knows how to put it on the page."

—*New York Times*

"Nora Roberts is among the best."

—*Washington Post Book World*

NORA ROBERTS

SPOTLIGHT

Silhouette Books

Published by Silhouette Books

America's Publisher of Contemporary Romance

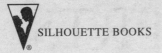

SILHOUETTE BOOKS

Spotlight

ISBN-13: 978-0-373-28245-6

Copyright © 2017 by Harlequin Books S.A.

The publisher acknowledges the copyright holder
of the individual works as follows:

Untamed
Copyright © 1983 by Nora Roberts

Dance of Dreams
Copyright © 1983 by Nora Roberts

Visit Silhouette Books at www.Harlequin.com

Printed in U.S.A.

CONTENTS

UNTAMED

For my sons.
Life's a circus.
Go for it!

Chapter 1

At the crack of the whip, twelve lions stood on their haunches and pawed the air. On command, they began to leap from pedestal to pedestal in a quick, close-formation, figure eight pattern. This required split-second timing. With voice and hand commands the trainer kept the tawny, springing bodies moving.

"Well done, Pandora."

At her name and the signal, the muscular lioness leaped to the ground and lay down on her side. One by one the others followed suit, until, snarling and baring their teeth, they stretched across the tanbark. A male was positioned beside each female; at a sharp reproof from the trainer, Merlin ceased nibbling on Ophelia's ear.

"Heads up!" They obeyed as the trainer walked briskly in front of them. The whip was tossed aside with a flourish, then, with apparent nonchalance, the trainer reclined lengthwise across the warm bodies. The center cat, a full-maned African, let out a great, echoing bellow. As a reward for his response to the cue, his ear was given a good scratching. The trainer rose from the feline couch, clapped hands and brought the lions to their feet. Then, with a hand signal, each was called by name and sent through the chute and into their cages. One stayed behind, a huge, black-maned cat who, like an ordinary tabby, circled and rubbed up against his trainer's legs.

Deftly, a rope was attached to a chain that was hidden under his mane. Then, with swift agility, the trainer mounted the lion's back. As the door of the big cage opened, lion and rider passed through for a tour of the practice ring. When they reached the back door of the ring barn, Merlin, the obliging lion, was transferred to a wheel cage.

"Well, Duffy." Jo turned after the cage was secured. "Are we ready for the road?"

Duffy was a small, round man with a monk's fringe of chestnut hair and a face that exploded with ginger freckles. His open smile and Irish blue eyes gave him the look of an aging choirboy. His mind was sharp, shrewd and scrappy. He was the best manager Prescott's Circus Colossus could have had.

"Since we open in Ocala tomorrow," he replied in a raspy voice, "you'd better be ready." He shifted his fat cigar stump from the right side of his mouth to the left.

Jo merely smiled, then stretched to loosen muscles grown taut during the thirty minutes in the cage. "My cats are ready, Duffy. It's been a long winter. They need to get back on the road as much as the rest of us."

Duffy frowned. As circumstances had it, he stood only inches higher than his animal trainer. Widely spaced, almond-shaped eyes stared back at him. They were as sharp and green as emeralds, surrounded by thick, inky lashes. At the moment they were fearless and amused, but Duffy had seen them frightened, vulnerable and lost. He shifted his cigar again and took two quick puffs as Jo gave a cage hand instructions.

He remembered Steve Wilder, Jo's father. He had been one of the best cat men in the business. Jo was as good with the cats as Wilder had been. In some ways, Duffy acknowledged, even better. But she had the traits of her mother: delicate build; dark, passionate looks. Jolivette Wilder was as slender as her aerialist mother had been, with bold green eyes and straight, raven black hair that fell to just below her waist. Her brows were delicately arched, her nose small and straight, her cheekbones high and elegant, while her mouth was full and soft. Her skin was tawny from the Florida sun; it added to her gypsy-like appearance. Confidence added spark to the beauty.

Finishing her instructions, Jo tucked her arm through Duffy's. She had seen that frown before. "Somebody quit?" she asked as they began to walk toward Duffy's office.

"Nope."

His monosyllabic reply caused Jo to lift a brow. It was not often Duffy answered any question briefly. Years of experience told her to hold her tongue as they moved across the compound.

Rehearsals were going on everywhere. Vito the wire walker informally sharpened his act on a cable stretched between two trees. The Mendalsons called out to each other as they tossed their juggling pins high in the air, while the equestrian act led their horses into the ring barn. She saw one of the Stevenson girls walking on stilts. She'd be six now, Jo mused, tossing the hair from her eyes as she watched the young girl's wavering progress. Jo remembered the year she had been born. It had been that same year that she had been allowed to work the big cage alone. She had been sixteen, and it had been another full year before she had been permitted to work an audience.

For Jo, there had never been any home but the circus. She had been born during the winter break, had been tucked into her parents' trailer the following spring to spend her first year and each subsequent one of her life thereafter on the road. She had inherited both her fascination and her flair with animals from her father, her style and grace of movement from her mother. Though she had lost both parents fifteen years before, they continued to influence her. Their legacy to her had been a world of restlessness, a world of fantasies. She had grown up playing with lion cubs, riding elephants, wearing spangles and traveling like a gypsy.

Jo glanced down at a cluster of daffodils growing by the side of Prescott's winter office and smiled. She remembered planting them when she had been thirteen and in love with a tumbler. She remembered, too, the man who had stooped beside her, offering advice on bulb planting and broken hearts. As Jo thought of Frank Prescott, her smile grew sad.

"I still can't believe he's gone," she murmured as she and Duffy moved inside.

Duffy's office was sparsely furnished with a wooden desk, metal filing cabinets and two spindly chairs. A collage of posters adorned the walls. They promised the amazing, the astounding, the incredible: elephants that danced, men who flew through the air, beautiful girls who spun by their teeth, raging tigers that rode horseback. Tumblers, clowns, lions, strong men, fat ladies, boys who could balance on their forefingers; they brought the magic of the circus into the drab little room.

As Jo glanced over at a narrow pine door, Duffy followed her gaze. "I keep expecting him to come busting through there with some crazy new idea," he mumbled as he began to fiddle with his prize possession, an automatic coffeemaker.

"Do you?" With a sigh Jo straddled a chair, then rested her chin on its back. "We all miss him. It's not going to seem the same without him this year." She looked up suddenly, and her eyes were angry. "He wasn't an old man, Duffy. Heart attacks should be for old men." She brooded into space, touched again with the injustice of Frank Prescott's death.

He had been barely into his fifties and full of laughter and simple kindness. Jo had loved him and trusted him without reservation. At his death she had grieved for him more acutely than she had for her own parents. In her longest memory he had been the core of her life.

"It's been nearly six months," Duffy said gruffly as he studied her face. When Jo glanced up, he stuck out a mug of coffee.

"I know." She took the mug, letting it warm her hands in the chilly March morning. Resolutely, she shook off the mood. Frank would not have wanted to leave sadness behind. Jo studied the coffee, then sipped. It was predictably dreadful. "Rumor has it we're following last year's route to the letter. Thirteen states." Jo smiled, watching Duffy wince over his coffee before he downed it. "Not superstitious, are you?" She grinned, knowing he kept a four-leaf clover in his billfold.

"Pah!" he said indignantly, coloring under his freckles. He set down his empty cup, then moved around his desk and sat behind it. When he folded his hands on the yellow blotter, Jo knew he was getting down to business. Through the open window she could hear the band rehearsing. "We should be in Ocala by six tomorrow," he began. Dutifully, Jo nodded. "Should have the tents up before nine."

"The parade should be over by ten, and the matinee will start at two," Jo finished with a smile. "Duffy, you're not going to ask me to work the menagerie in the sideshow again, are you?"

"Should be a good crowd," he replied, adroitly skirting her question. "Bonzo predicts clear skies."

"Bonzo should stick with pratfalls and unicycles." She watched as Duffy chewed on the stub of a now dead cigar. "Okay," she said firmly, "let's have it."

"Someone's going to be joining us in Ocala, at least temporarily." He pursed his lips as his eyes met Jo's. His were blue, faded with age. "I don't know if he'll finish out the season with us."

"Oh, Duffy, not some first of mayer we have to break in this late?" Jo demanded, using the circus term for novice. "What is he, some energetic writer who wants an epic on the vanishing tent circus? He'll spend a few weeks as a roustabout and swear he knows all there is to know about it."

"I don't think he'll be working as a roustabout," Duffy muttered. Striking a match, he coaxed the cigar back to life. Jo frowned, watching the smoke struggle toward the ceiling.

"It's a bit late to work in a new act now, isn't it?"

"He's not a performer." Duffy swore lightly under his breath, then met Jo's eyes again. "He owns us."

For a moment Jo said nothing. She sat unmoving, as Duffy had seen her from time to time when she trained a young cat. "No!" She rose suddenly, shaking her head. "Not him. Not now. Why does he have to come? What does he want here?"

"It's his circus," Duffy reminded her. His voice was both rough and sympathetic.

"It'll never be his circus," Jo retorted passionately. Her eyes lit and glowed with a temper she rarely let have sway. "It's Frank's circus."

"Frank's dead," Duffy stated in a quiet, final tone. "Now the circus belongs to his son."

"Son?" Jo countered. She lifted her fingers to press them against her temple. Slowly, she moved to the window. Outside, the sun was pouring over the heads of troupers. She watched the members of the trapeze act, in thick robes worn over their tights, head toward the ring barn. The chatter of mixed languages was so familiar she failed to notice it. She placed her palms on the windowsill and with a little sigh, steadied her temper. "What sort of son is it who never bothers to visit his father? In thirty years he never came to see Frank. He never wrote. He didn't even come to the funeral." Jo swallowed the tears of anger that rose to her throat and thickened her voice. "Why should he come now?"

"You've got to learn that life's a two-sided coin, kiddo," Duffy said briskly. "You weren't even alive thirty years ago. You don't know why Frank's wife up and left him or why the boy never visited."

"He's not a boy, Duffy, he's a man." Jo turned back, and he saw that she again had herself under control. "He's thirty-one, thirty-two years old now, a very successful attorney with a fancy Chicago office. He's very wealthy, did you know?" A small smile played on her lips but failed to reach her eyes. "And not just from court cases and legal fees. There's quite a lot of money on his mother's side. Nice, quiet, old money. I can't understand what a rich city lawyer would want with a tent circus."

Duffy shrugged his broad, round shoulders. "Could be he wants a tax shelter. Could be he wants to ride an elephant. Could be anything. He might want to take inventory and sell us off, piece by piece."

"Oh, Duffy, no!" Emotion flew back into Jo's face. "He couldn't do that."

"The heck he couldn't," Duffy muttered as he stubbed out his cigar. "He can do as he pleases. If he wants to liquidate, he liquidates."

"But we have contracts through October…"

"You're too smart for that, Jo." Duffy frowned, scratching his rim of hair. "He can buy them off or let them play through. He's a lawyer. He can figure the way out of a contract if he wants to. He can wait till August

when we start to negotiate again and let them all lapse."
Seeing Jo's distress, he backpedaled. "Listen, kiddo, I
didn't say he was going to sell, I said he *could.*"

Jo ran a hand through her hair. "There must be something we can do."

"We can show a profit by the end of the season,"
Duffy said wryly. "We can show the new owner what
we have to offer. I think it's important that he sees we're
not just a mud show but a profitable three-ring circus
with class acts. He should see what Frank built, how
he lived, what he wanted to do. I think," Duffy added,
watching Jo's face, "that you should be in charge of
his education."

"Me?" Jo was too incredulous to be angry. "Why?
You're better qualified in the public relations department than I am. I train lions, not lawyers." She could
not keep the hint of scorn from her voice.

"You were closer to Frank than anyone. And there
isn't anyone here who knows this circus better than
you." Again he frowned. "And you've got brains. Never
thought much use would come of all those fancy books
you read, but maybe I was wrong."

"Duffy." Her lips curved into a smile. "Just because
I like to read Shakespeare doesn't mean I can deal with
Keane Prescott. Even thinking about him makes me
furious. How will I act when I meet him face to face?"

"Well." Duffy shrugged before he pursed his lips.
"If you don't think you can handle it…"

"I didn't say I *couldn't* handle it," Jo muttered.

"Of course, if you're afraid…"

"I'm not afraid of anything, and I'm certainly not
afraid of some Chicago lawyer who doesn't know saw-

dust from tanbark." Sticking her hands in her pockets, she paced the length of the small room. "If Keane Prescott, attorney-at-law, wants to spend his summer with the circus, I'll do my best to make it a memorable one."

"Nicely," Duffy cautioned as Jo moved to the door.

"Duffy—" She paused and gave him an innocent smile. "You know what a gentle touch I have." To prove it, Jo slammed the door behind her.

Dawn was hovering over the horizon as the circus caravan drew up in a large grassy field. Colors were just a promise in a pale gray sky. In the distance was grove upon grove of orange trees. As Jo stepped from the cab of her truck, the fragrance met her. It's a perfect day, she decided, then took a long, greedy breath. To her, there was no more beautiful sight than dawn struggling to life.

The air was vaguely chilly. She zipped up her gray sweat jacket as she watched the rest of the circus troupe pouring out of their trucks and cars and trailers. The morning quiet was soon shattered by voices. Work began immediately. As the Big Top canvas was being unrolled out of the spool truck, Jo went to see how her lions had fared the fifty-mile journey.

Three handlers unloaded the traveling cages. Buck had been with Jo the longest. He had worked for her father, and during the interim between his death and Jo's professional debut, he had worked up a small act with four male lions. His shyness had made his retirement from performing a relief. To Buck, two people were a crowd. He stood six foot four, and his build was powerful enough for him to pad the sideshow from time to time as Hercules the Strong Man. He had an impressive head of wild blond hair and a full, curling beard. His hands were wide, with thick, strong fingers, but Jo remembered their gentleness when the two of them had delivered a lioness of a pair of cubs.

Pete's small frame seemed puny beside Buck's. He was of indeterminable age. Jo guessed between forty and fifty, but she was never certain. He was a quiet man with skin like polished mahogany and a rich, low-pitched voice. He had come to Jo five years before, asking for a job. She had never asked where he had come from, and he had never told her. He wore a fielder's cap and was never seen without a wad of gum moving gently in his teeth. He read Jo's books and was the undisputed king of the poker table.

Gerry was nineteen and eager. He was nearly six feet and still carried the lankiness of his youth. His mother sewed, and his father was a souvenir salesman, or a candy butcher, as circus jargon had it. Working the big cage was Gerry's dream, and because it had been hers, Jo had finally agreed to tutor him.

"How are my babies?" she demanded as she approached. At each cage she paused and soothed a nervous cat, calling each by name until they had settled. "They've traveled well. Hamlet's still edgy, but it's his first year on the road."

"He's a mean one," Buck muttered, watching Jo move from cage to cage.

"Yes, I know," she replied absently. "He's smart, too." She had twisted her hair into one thick braid and now tossed it to her back. "Look, here come some towners." A few cars and a smattering of bikes drew into the field.

These were the people from the outlying towns who wanted to see a Big Top raised, who wanted to see the circus, if only for a moment, from the other side. Some would watch while others would lend a hand with tent poles, stretching canvas and rigging. They would earn a show pass and an unforgettable experience.

"Keep them clear of the cages," Jo ordered, nodding to Pete before she moved toward the still-flaccid canvas. Buck lumbered beside her.

The field was alive with ropes and wire and people. Six elephants were harnessed but idle, with their handlers standing by the stake line. As workers pulled on guy ropes, the dusky brown canvas billowed up like a giant mushroom.

The poles were positioned—side, quarter, center— while the canvas muffled the sounds of scrambling workers. In the east the sun was rising fast, streaking the sky with pink. There were shouted instructions from the head canvas man, laughter from adventuresome boys and an occasional oath. As the quarter poles were driven into the sag of canvas, Jo signaled Maggie, the large African elephant. Obligingly, Maggie lowered her trunk. Jo stepped nimbly into the U, then scrambled onto the wide, gray back.

The sun grew higher by the second, shooting the first streams of light onto the field. The scent of orange blossoms mingled with the odor of leather harnesses. Jo had watched the canvas rise under a lightening sky countless times. Each time it was special, and the first raising each season was the most special of all. Maggie lifted her head and trumpeted as if pleased to be around for another season. With a laugh Jo reached back and swatted her rough, wrinkled rump. She felt free and fresh and incredibly alive. *If there were a moment,* she thought suddenly, *that I could capture and bottle, it would be this one. Then, when I'm very old, I could take it out and feel young again.* Smiling, she glanced down at the people swarming below her.

Her attention was caught by a man who stood by a coil of cable. Typically, she noted his build first. A well-proportioned body was essential to a performer. He was lean and stood straight. She noted he had good shoulders but doubted if there was much muscle in his arms. Though he was dressed casually in jeans, *city* stood out all over him. His hair was a dark, rich blond, and the early breeze had disturbed it so that it teased his forehead. He was clean-shaven, with a narrow, firm-jawed face. It was an attractive face. It was not, Jo mused, smoothly handsome like Vito the wire walker's but more aware, more demanding. Jo liked the face, liked the shape of the long, unsmiling mouth, liked the hint of bone beneath his tawny skin. Most of all she liked the directness of the amber eyes that stared back at her. They're like Ari's, she observed, thinking of her favorite lion. She was certain that he had been watching her long before she had looked down. Knowing this, Jo was impressed with his unselfconsciousness. He continued to stare, making no effort to camouflage his interest. She laughed, unperturbed, and tossed her braid from her shoulder.

"Want a ride?" she called out. Too many strangers had walked in and out of her world for her to be aloof.

She watched his brow lift in acknowledgment of her offer. She would see if it was only his eyes that were like Ari's. "Maggie won't hurt you. She's gentle as a lamb, just bigger." Instantly, she saw he had understood the challenge. He walked across the grass until he stood beside her. He moved well, she noted. Jo tapped Maggie's side with the bull hook she carried. Wearily, the elephant knelt down on her trunklike front legs. Jo held out her hand. With an agility that surprised her, the man mounted the elephant and slid into place behind her.

For a moment she said nothing, a bit stunned by the trembling that had coursed up her arm as her palm had met his. The contact had been brief. Jo decided she had imagined it. "Up, Maggie," she said, giving her mount another tap. With an elephantine sigh, Maggie obeyed, rocking her passengers gently from side to side.

"Do you always pick up strange men?" the voice behind her inquired. It was a smooth, well-keyed voice, a good pitchman's voice.

Jo grinned over her shoulder. "Maggie's doing the picking up."

"So she is. Are you aware that she's remarkably uncomfortable?"

Jo laughed with genuine enjoyment. "You should try riding her a few miles in a street parade while keeping a smile on your face."

"I'll pass. Are you in charge of her?"

"Maggie? No, but I know how to handle her. You have eyes like one of my cats," she told him. "I like them. And since you seemed to be interested in Maggie and me, I asked you up."

This time it was he who laughed. Jo twisted her head,

wanting to see his face. There was humor in his eyes now, and his teeth were white and straight. Liking his smile, she answered with one of her own. "Fascinating. You asked me to take a ride on an elephant because I have eyes like your cat's. And no offense to the lady beneath me, but I was looking at you."

"Oh?" Jo pursed her lips in thought. "Why?"

For several seconds he studied her in silence. "Strange, I believe you really don't know."

"I wouldn't ask if I did," she returned, shifting her weight slightly. "It would be a waste of time to ask a question if I knew the answer." She shifted again and turned away from him. "Hold on now. Maggie's got to earn her bale of hay."

The poles hung between the canvas and the ground at forty-five-degree angles. Quickly the elephant's chains were hooked to the metal rings at the base of the quarter poles. Jo urged Maggie forward in unison with her coworkers. Poles skidded along the ground, then up into place, pushing the canvas with it. The Big Top billowed to life under the early-morning sky.

Her job done, Maggie moved through the flaps and into the light. "Beautiful, isn't it?" Jo murmured. "It's born fresh every day."

Vito walked by, calling out to Jo in Italian. Sending him a wave, she called back in his own language, then signaled to Maggie to kneel again. Jo waited until her passenger had dismounted before she slid off. It surprised her, when they stood face to face, that he was so tall. Tilting back her head, she judged him to be only two inches shy of Buck.

"You looked shorter when I was up on Maggie," she told him with her usual candor.

"You looked taller."

Jo chuckled, patting Maggie behind the ear. "Will you see the show?" She knew that she wanted him to, knew as well that she wanted to see him again. She found this both strange and intriguing. Men had always taken a second place to her cats, and towners had never interested her.

"Yes, I'm going to see the show." There was a slight smile on his face, but he was studying her thoughtfully. "Do you perform?"

"I have an act with my cats."

"I see. Somehow I pictured you in an aerial act, flying from the trapeze."

She sent him an easy smile. "My mother was an aerialist." Someone called her name, and looking, Jo saw Maggie was needed for raising the sideshow tent. "I have to go. I hope you like the show."

He took her hand before she could lead Maggie away. Jo stood still, again surprised by a trembling up her arm. "I'd like to see you tonight."

Glancing up, she met his eyes. They were direct and unselfconscious. "Why?" The question was sincere. Jo knew she wanted to see him as well but was unsure why.

This time he did not laugh. Gently, he ran a finger down the length of her braid. "Because you're beautiful, and you intrigue me."

"Oh." Jo considered. She had never thought of herself as beautiful. Striking, perhaps, in her costume, surrounded by her cats, but in jeans, without makeup, she doubted it. Still, it was an interesting thought. "All right, if there's no trouble with the cats. Ari hasn't been well."

A smile played at the corners of his mouth. "I'm sorry to hear that."

There was another loud summons for Jo, and both looked toward it. "I see you're needed," he said with a nod. "Perhaps you could point out Bill Duffy for me before you go."

"Duffy?" Jo repeated, surprised. "You can't be looking for a job?" There was incredulity in her voice, and he grinned.

"Why can't I?"

"Because you don't fit any of the types."

"Are there types?" he asked, both interested and amused. Jo shook her head in annoyance.

"Yes, of course, and you don't fit into any of them."

"Actually, I'm not looking for a job, so to speak," he told her, still smiling. "But I am looking for Bill Duffy."

It was against Jo's nature to probe. Privacy was both guarded and respected in the circus. Shielding her eyes with her hand, Jo looked around until she spotted Duffy supervising the raising of the cookhouse tent. "There," she said, pointing. "Duffy's the one with the red checked jacket. He still dresses like an outside talker."

"A what?"

"You'd call it a barker, I imagine." With easy grace she mounted the patient Maggie. "That's a towner's term, not a circus one." She smiled at him, then urged Maggie into a walk. "Tell Duffy Jo said to give you a pass," she called over her shoulder, then waved and turned away.

Dawn was over, and it was morning.

Chapter 2

Jo stood at the back door of the Big Top waiting for her cue. Beside her was Jamie Carter, alias Topo. He was a third generation clown and wore his bright face and orange wig naturally. He was young and limber and used these traits as well as his makeup to bring enthusiasm to his craft. To Jo, Jamie was more brother than friend. He was tall and thin, and under his greasepaint his face was mobile and pleasant. He and Jo had grown up together.

"Did she say anything?" Jamie demanded for the third time. With a sigh, Jo tossed closed the flap of the tent. Inside, clowns were performing around the hippodrome track while hands set up the big cage.

"Carmen said nothing. I don't know why you waste your time." Her voice was sharp, and Jamie bristled.

"I don't expect you to understand," he said with great

dignity. His thin shoulders drew straight under his red-polka-dot shirt. "After all, Ari's the closest you've come to being involved with the opposite sex."

"That's very cute," Jo replied, unoffended by the jibe. Her annoyance stemmed from seeing Jamie make a fool of himself over Carmen Gribalti, the middle sister of the flying Gribaltis. She was darkly beautiful, grace-ful, talented, selfish and sublimely indifferent to Jamie. Looking into his happy, painted face and moody eyes, Jo's irritation dissipated. "She probably hasn't had a chance to answer the note you sent her," she soothed. "The first day of a new season's always wild."

"I suppose," Jamie muttered with a grudging shrug. "I don't know what she sees in Vito."

Jo thought of the wire walker's dark, cocky looks and rippling muscles. Wisely, she refrained from mention-ing them. "Who can account for taste?" She gave him a smacking kiss on his round, red nose. "Personally, I get all wobbly when I see a man with thick, orange hair."

Jamie grinned. "Proves you know what to look for in a man."

Turning, Jo lifted the flap again, noting Jamie's cue was nearly upon them. "Did you happen to notice a towner hanging around today?"

"Only a couple dozen of them," Jamie answered drily as he lifted the pail of confetti he used to finish the gag now being performed inside.

Jo shot him a half-hearted glare. "Not the usual type. About thirty, I think," she continued. "Wearing jeans and a T-shirt. He was tall, six-one, six-two," she went on as laughter poured out of the open flap to drown out her words. "He had dark blond straight hair."

"Yeah, I saw him." Jamie nudged her out of his way and prepared to make his entrance. "He was going into the red wagon with Duffy." With a wild, high-pitched scream, Topo the clown bounded into the Big Top in size fifteen tennis shoes, brandishing his bucket of confetti.

Thoughtfully, Jo watched Jamie chase three other clowns around the track. It was odd, she thought, for Duffy to take a towner into the administration trailer. He had said he wasn't looking for a job. He wasn't a drifter; there was an unmistakable air of stability about him. He wasn't a circus hand from another show, either. His palm had been too smooth. And, her mind added as she vaulted onto Babette, a pure white mare, there had been an undeniable aura of urbanity about him. Success, as well, she thought. And authority. No, he had not been looking for a job.

Jo shrugged, annoyed that a stranger was crowding into her thoughts. It irritated her further that she had scanned the crowds for him during the parade and that even now she wondered if he sat somewhere in the circular arena. He hadn't been at the matinee. Jo patted the mare's neck absently, then straightened as she heard the ringmaster's whistle.

"Ladies and gentlemen," he called in deep, musical tones. "Presenting the most spectacular exhibition of animal subjugation under the Big Top. Jovilette, Queen of the Jungle Cats!"

Jo nudged Babette with her heels and raced into the arena. The applause rose to meet her as the audience appreciated the dashing figure she cut. Swathed in a black cape, raven hair flying free under a glittering tiara, she galloped bareback on the snow-white mare. In each hand she held a long, thin whip, which she cracked alternately overhead. At the entrance to the big cage she leaped from the still-racing horse. While Babette galloped out of the back door and into the care of a handler, Jo shifted both whips into one hand, then removed the cape with a flourish. Her costume was a close-fitting, one-piece jumpsuit, dazzling in white and spangled with gold sequins. In dramatic contrast, her hair hung straight and severe down her back.

Make an entrance, Frank had always said. And Jo-vilette made an entrance.

The twelve cats were already in the cage, banding its inside edge as they perched on blue and white pedestals. Entering the main cage appeared routine to the audience, but Jo knew it was one of the most dangerous moments of the act. To enter, she had to pass directly between two cats as she moved from the safety cage to the main arena. She always stationed her best behaved cats there, but if one was irritated, or even playful, he could easily strike out with a powerful paw. Even with sharp claws retracted, the damage could be deadly.

She entered swiftly and was surrounded by cats on all sides. Her spangles and tiara caught the lights and played with them as she began to move around the cage, cracking the whip for showmanship while using her voice to command the cats to rise on their haunches. She moved them through their routine, adjusting the timing to compensate for any feline reluctance, letting one trick begin where the last ended.

Jo disliked overdone propping, preferring action and movement. The contrast of the big, tawny cats and the small white and gold woman were the best props available to her. She used them well. Hers was a *picture act*, relying on style and flash, rather than a *fighting act*, which emphasized the ferocity of the big cats by employing blank-bulleted guns and rehearsed charges, or *bounces*. Her confidence transmitted itself to the audience, making her handling of the cats appear effortless. In truth, her body was coiled for any danger, and her mind was focused so intently on her cats, there might have been no audience at all.

She stood between two high pedestals as the cats leaped over her head from both directions. They set up a light breeze, which stirred her hair. They roared when she cued them, setting up an echoing din. Now and then one reached out to paw at the stock of her whip, and she stopped him with a quick command. She sent her best leaper through a hoop of flame and coaxed her best balancer to walk on a glistening silver ball. She ended to waves of applause by trotting Merlin around the hippodrome track.

At the back door Merlin jumped into a wheel cage and was turned over to Pete. "Nice show," he said as he handed her a long chenille robe. "Smooth as silk."

"Thanks." Cold, she bundled into the robe. The spring night was frigid in contrast to the hot lights and heat in the big cage. "Listen, Pete, tell Gerry he can feed the cats tonight. They're behaving themselves."

Pete snapped his gum and chuckled. "Won't he be riding high tonight." As he moved to the truck that would pull the cage to the cat area, Jo called after him.

"Pete." She bit her lip, then shrugged when he twisted his head. "You'll keep an eye on him, won't you?"

Pete grinned and climbed into the cab of the truck. "Who you worried about, Jo? Those big cats or that skinny boy?"

"Both," she answered. The rhinestones in her tiara sparkled as she tossed her head and laughed. Knowing she had nearly an hour before the finale parade, Jo walked away from the Big Top. She thought of wandering to the cookhouse for some coffee. Mentally, she began replaying every segment of her act. It had gone well, she thought, pleased with the timing and the flow. If Pete had said it had been smooth, Jo knew it had. She had heard his criticisms more than once over the past five years. True, Hamlet had tested her once or twice, but no one knew that but Jo and the cat. She doubted if anyone but Buck would have seen that he had given her trouble. Closing her eyes a moment, Jo rolled her shoulders, loosening tight, tensed muscles.

"That's quite an act you have."

Jo whirled around at the sound of the voice. She could feel her heart rate accelerate. Though she wondered at her interest in a man she barely knew, Jo was aware that she had been waiting for him. There was a quick surge of pleasure as she watched him approach, and she allowed it to show on her face.

"Hello." She saw that he smoked a cigar, but unlike Duffy's, his was long and slim. Again she admired the elegance of his hands. "Did you like the show?"

He stopped in front of her, then studied her face with a thoroughness that made her wonder if her makeup had smeared. Then he gave a small, surprised laugh and shook his head. "Do you know," he began, "when you told me this morning that you did an act with cats, I had Siamese in mind rather than African."

"Siamese?" Jo repeated blankly, then laughed. "House cats?" He brushed her hair behind her back while Jo giggled at the thought of coaxing a Siamese to jump through a flaming hoop.

"From my point of view," he told her as he let a strand of her hair linger between his fingers, "it made more sense than a little thing like you walking into a cage with a dozen lions."

"I'm not little," Jo corrected good-naturedly. "Besides, size hardly matters to twelve lions."

"No, I suppose it doesn't." He lifted his eyes from her hair and met hers. Jo continued to smile, enjoying looking at him. "Why do you do it?" he asked suddenly.

Jo gave him a curious look. "Why? Because it's my job."

By the way he studied her, Jo could see that he was not satisfied with the simplicity of her answer. "Perhaps I should ask *how* you became a lion tamer."

"Trainer," Jo corrected automatically. To her left, she could hear the audience's muffled applause. "The Beirots are starting," she said with a glance toward the sound. "You shouldn't miss their act. They're first-rate acrobats."

"Don't you want to tell me?" His voice was soft.

She lifted a brow, seeing that he truly wanted to know. "Why, it's not a secret. My father was a trainer, and I have a knack for working with cats. It just followed." Jo had never thought about her career past this point, and she shrugged it aside. "You shouldn't waste your ticket standing out here. You can stand by the back door and watch the rest of the act." Jo turned to lead the way to the performers' entrance but stopped when his hand took hers.

He stepped forward until their bodies were nearly touching. Jo could feel the heat from his as she watched his face. Her heart was thudding in a quick, steady rhythm. She could hear it vibrate through her the same way it did when she approached a new cat for the first time. Here was something new, something untested. She tingled with the excitement of the unknown when he lifted his hand to touch her cheek. She did not move but let the warmth spread while she watched him carefully, gauging him. Her eyes were wide, curious and unafraid.

"Are you going to kiss me?" she asked in a tone that expressed more interest than desire.

His eyes lit with humor and glittered in the dim light. "I had given it some thought," he answered. "Do you have any objections?"

Jo considered a moment, dropping her eyes to his mouth. She liked its shape and wondered how it would feel against hers. He brought her no closer. One hand still held hers while the other slid around to cradle her neck. Jo shifted her gaze until their eyes met again. "No," she decided. "I haven't any objections."

The corners of his mouth twitched as he tightened his hold slightly on the base of her neck. Slowly, he lowered his head toward hers. Curious and a bit wary, Jo kept her eyes open, watching his. She knew from experience that you could tell more about people and about cats from the eyes. To her surprise, his remained open as well, even as their lips met.

It was a gentle kiss, without pressure, only a whisper

of a touch. Amazed, Jo thought she felt the ground trem-ble under her feet. Dimly, she wondered if the elephants were being led by. But it can't be time, she thought in confusion. His lips moved lightly over hers, and his eyes remained steady. Jo's pulse drummed under her skin. They stood, barely touching, as the Big Top throbbed with noise behind them. Lazily, he traced her lips with the tip of his tongue, teasing them open. Still there was no demand in the kiss, only testing. Unhurried, con-fident, he explored her mouth while Jo felt her breath accelerating. A soft moan escaped her as her lids flut-tered down.

For an instant she surrendered utterly to him, to the new sensations swimming through her. She leaned against him, straining toward pleasure, sighing with it as the kiss lingered.

He drew her away, but their faces remained close. Dizzily, Jo realized that she had risen to her toes to compensate for their difference in height. His hand was still light on the back of her neck. His eyes were gold in the darkening night.

"What an incredible female you are, Jovilette," he murmured. "One surprise after another."

Jo felt stunningly alive. Her skin seemed to tingle with new feelings. She smiled. "I don't know your name."

He laughed, releasing her neck to take her other hand in his. Before he could speak, Duffy called out from the direction of the Big Top. Jo turned to watch as he moved toward them in his quick, rolling walk.

"Well, well, well," he said in his jolly, rough voice. "I didn't know you two had met. Has Jo been showing you around already?" Reaching them, he squeezed Jo's shoulder. "Knew I could count on you, kiddo." Jo glanced at him in puzzlement, but he continued before she could form a question. "Yes, sir, this little girl puts on quite a show, doesn't she? Always a grabber. And she knows this circus like the back of her hand. Born and raised to it," he continued. Jo relaxed. She recognized that Duffy was into one of his spiels, and there was no stopping him. "Yessiree, any questions you got, you just ask our Jo, and she'll tell you. 'Course, I'm always at your disposal, too. Anything I can tell you about the books or accounts or contracts and the like, you just let me know." Duffy puffed twice on his cigar as Jo felt her first hint of unease.

Why was Duffy rambling about books and contracts? Jo glanced at the man who still held her hands in his. He was watching Duffy with an easy, amused smile.

"Are you a bookkeeper?" Jo asked, perplexed. Duffy laughed and patted her head.

"You know Mr. Prescott's a lawyer, Jo. Don't miss your cue." He gave them both a friendly nod and toddled off.

Jo had stiffened almost imperceptibly at Duffy's offhand information, but Keane had felt it. His brows lowered as he studied her. "Now you know my name."

"Yes." All warmth fled from Jo. Her voice was as cool as her blood. "Would you let go of my hands, Mr. Prescott?"

After a brief hesitation Keane inclined his head and obliged. Jo stuffed her hands quickly into the pockets of her robe. "Don't you think we've progressed to the first name stage of our relationship, Jo?"

"I assure you, Mr. Prescott, if I had known who you were, we wouldn't have progressed at all." Jo's words were stiff with dignity. Inside, though she tried to ignore it, she felt betrayal, anger, humiliation. All pleasure had died from the evening. Now the kiss that had left her feeling clean and alive seemed cheap and shabby. No, she would not use his first name, she vowed. She would never use it. "If you'll excuse me, I have some things to do before my cue."

"Why the turnaround?" he asked, halting her with a hand on her arm. "Don't you like lawyers?"

Coldly, Jo studied him. She wondered how it was possible that she had completely misjudged the man she had met that morning. "I don't categorize people, Mr. Prescott."

"I see." Keane's tone became detached, his eyes assessing. "Then it would appear that you have an aversion to my name. Should I assume you hold a grudge against my father?"

Jo's eyes glittered with quick fury. She jerked her arm from his hold. "Frank Prescott was the most generous, the kindest, most unselfish man I've ever known. I don't even associate you with Frank, Mr. Prescott. You have no right to him." Though it was nearly impossible, Jo forced herself to speak in a normal tone of voice. She would not shout and draw anyone's attention. This would be kept strictly between Keane Prescott and herself. "It would have been much better if you had told me who you were right away, then there would have been no mix-up."

"Is that what we've had?" he countered mildly. "A mix-up?"

His cool tone was nearly Jo's undoing. He watched her with a dispassionate curiosity that tempted her to slap him. She fought to keep her fury from spilling over into her voice. "You have no right to Frank's circus, Mr. Prescott," she managed quietly. "Leaving it to you is the only thing I've ever faulted him for." Knowing her control was slipping, Jo whirled, running across the grass until she merged with the darkness.

Chapter 3

The morning was surprisingly warm. There were no trees to block the sun, and the smell of the earth was strong. The circus had moved north in the early hours. All the usual scents merged into the aroma of circus: canvas, leather, sweating horses, greasepaint and powder, coffee and oilcloth. The trailers and trucks sat in the accustomed spots, forming the "backyard" that would always take the same formation each time the circus made a stop along the thousands of miles it traveled. The flag over the cookhouse tent signaled that lunch was being served. The Big Top stood waiting for the matinee.

Rose hurried along the midway toward the animal cages. Her dark hair was pinned neatly in a bun at the back of her neck. Her big brown eyes darted about searchingly, while her mouth sat softly in a pout. She was wrapped in a terry cloth robe and wore tennis shoes over her tights. When she saw Jo standing in front of Ari's cage, she waved and broke into a half run. Watching her, Jo shifted her attention from Ari. Rose was always a diversion, and Jo felt in need of one.

"Jo!" She waved again as if Jo had not seen her the first time, then came to a breathless halt. "Jo, I only have a few minutes. Hello, Ari," she added out of politeness. "I was looking for Jamie."

"Yes, I gathered." Jo smiled, knowing Rose had set her heart on capturing Topo's alter ego. And if he had any sense, she thought, he'd let himself be caught instead of pining over Carmen. Silly, she decided, dismissing all affairs of the heart. Lions were easier to understand. "I haven't seen him all morning, Rose. Maybe he's rehearsing."

"Drooling over Carmen, more likely," Rose muttered, sending a sulky glare in the direction of the Gribalti trailer. "He makes a fool of himself."

"That's what he's paid for," Jo reminded her, but Rose did not respond to the humor. Jo sighed. She had a true affection for Rose. She was bright and fun and without pretensions. "Rose," she said, keeping her voice both light and kind. "Don't give up on him. He's a little slow, you know," she explained. "He's just a bit dazzled by Carmen right now. It'll pass."

"I don't know why I bother," she grumbled, but Jo saw the dark mood was already passing. Rose was a creature of quick passions that flared and soon died. "He's not so very handsome, you know."

"No," Jo agreed. "But he has a cute nose."

"Lucky for him I like red," Rose returned and

grinned. "Ah, now we're speaking of handsome," she murmured as her eyes drifted from Jo. "Who is this?"

At the question, Jo glanced over her shoulder. The humor fled from her eyes. "That's the owner," she said colorlessly.

"Keane Prescott? No one told me he was so handsome. Or so tall," she added, admiring him openly as he crossed the backyard. Jo noted that Rose always became more Mexican around men. "Such shoulders. Lucky for Jamie I'm a one-man woman."

"Lucky for you your mama can't hear you," Jo muttered, earning an elbow in the ribs.

"But he comes here, *amiga*, and he looks at you. La, la, my papa would have Jamie to the altar pronto if he looked at me that way."

"You're an idiot," Jo snapped, annoyed.

"Ah, Jo," Rose said with mock despair. "I am a romantic."

Jo was helpless against the smile that tugged at her lips. Her eyes were laughing when she glanced up and met Keane's. Hastily, she struggled to dampen their brilliance, turning her mouth into a sober line.

"Good morning, Jovilette." He spoke her name too easily, she thought, as if he had been saying it for years.

"Good morning, Mr. Prescott," she returned. Rose gave a loud, none-too-subtle cough. "This is Rose Sanches."

"It's a pleasure, Mr. Prescott." Rose extended a hand, trying out a smile she had been saving for Jamie. "I heard you were traveling with us."

Keane accepted the hand and smiled in return. Jo noticed with annoyance that it was the same easy, disarming smile of the stranger she had met the morning before. "Hello, Rose, it's nice to meet you."

Seeing her friend's Mexican blood heat her cheeks, Jo intervened. She would not permit Keane Prescott to make a conquest here. "Rose, you only have ten minutes to get back and into makeup."

"Holy cow!" she said, forgetting her attempt at sophistication. "I've got to run." She began to do so, then called over her shoulder, "Don't tell Jamie I was looking for him, the pig!" She ran a little farther, then turned and ran backward. "I'll look for him later," she said with a laugh, then turned back and streaked toward the midway.

Keane watched her dart across the compound while holding up the long skirts of her robe in one hand. "Charming."

"She's only eighteen," Jo offered before she could stop herself.

When Keane turned to her, his look was one of amusement. "I see," he said. "I'll take that information under advisement. And what does the eighteen-year-old Rose do?" he asked, slipping his thumbs into the front pockets of his jeans. "Wrestle alligators?"

"No," Jo returned without batting an eye. "Rose is Serpentina, your premier sideshow attraction. The snake charmer." She was pleased with the incredulous look that passed over his face. It was replaced quickly, however, with one of genuine humor.

"Perfect." He brushed Jo's hair from her cheek before she could protest by word or action. "Cobras?" he asked, ignoring the flash in her eyes.

"And boa constrictors," she returned sweetly. Jo

brushed the dust from the knees of her faded jeans. "Now, if you'll excuse me…"

"No, I don't think so." Keane's voice was cool, but she recognized the underlying authority. She did her best not to struggle against it. He *was* the owner, she reminded herself.

"Mr. Prescott," she began, banking down hard on the urge to mutiny. "I'm very busy. I have to get ready for the afternoon show."

"You've got an hour and a half until you're on," he countered smoothly. "I think you might spare me a portion of that time. You've been assigned to show me around. Why don't we start now?" The tone of the question left room for only one answer. Jo's mind fidgeted in search of a way out.

Tilting her head back, she met his eyes. He won't be easy to beat, she concluded, studying his steady, measuring gaze. I'd better study his moves more carefully before I start a battle. "Where would you like to begin?" she asked aloud.

"With you."

Keane's easy answer brought a deep frown to Jo's brows. "I don't understand what you mean."

For a moment Keane watched her. There was no coyness or guile in her eyes as they looked into his. "No, I can see you don't," he agreed with a nod. "Let's start with your cats."

"Oh." Jo's frown cleared instantly. "All right." She watched as he pulled out a thin cigar, waiting until the flame of his lighter licked the tip before speaking. "I have thirteen—seven males, six females. They're all African lions between four-and-a-half and twenty-two years."

"I thought you worked with twelve," Keane commented as he dropped his lighter into his pocket.

"That's right, but Ari's retired." Turning, Jo indicated the large male lion dozing in a cage. "He travels with me because he always has, but I don't work him anymore. He's twenty-two, the oldest. My father kept him, even though he was born in captivity, because he was born the same day I was." Jo sighed, and her voice became softer. "He's the last of my father's stock. I couldn't sell him to a zoo. It seemed like shoving an old relative into a home and abandoning him. He's been with this circus every day of his life, just as I have. His name is Hebrew for *lion*." Jo laughed, forgetting the man beside her as she sifted through memories. "My father always gave his cats names that meant lion somehow or other. Leo, Leonard, Leonara. Ari was a first-class leaper in his prime. He could climb, too. Some cats won't. I could teach Ari anything. Smart cat, aren't you, Ari?" The altered tone of her voice caused the big cat to stir. Opening his eyes, he stared back at Jo. The sound he made was more grumble than roar before he dozed again. "He's tired," Jo murmured, fighting a shaft of gloom. "Twenty-two's old for a lion."

"What is it?" Keane demanded, touching her shoulder before she could turn away. Her eyes were drenched with sadness.

"He's dying," she said unsteadily. "And I can't stop it." Stuffing her hands in her pockets, Jo moved away to the main group of cages. To steady herself, she took two deep breaths while waiting for Keane to join her. Regaining her composure, she began again. "I work with these twelve," she told him, making a sweeping gesture. "They're fed once a day, raw meat six days a week and eggs and milk on the seventh. They were all imported directly from Africa and were cage broken when I got them."

The faint sound of a calliope reached them, signaling the opening of the midway. "This is Merlin, the one I ride out on at the finish. He's ten, and the most even-tempered cat I've ever worked with. Heathcliff," she continued as she moved down the line of cages, "he's six, my best leaper. And this is Faust, the baby at four and a half." The lions paced their cages as Jo walked Keane down the line. Unable to prevent herself, Jo gave Faust a signal by raising her hand. Obediently, he sent out a huge, deafening roar. To Jo's disappointment, Keane did not scramble for cover.

"Very impressive," he said mildly. "You put him in the center when you lie down on them, don't you?"

"Yes." She frowned, then spoke her thoughts candidly. "You're very observant—and you've got steady nerves."

"My profession requires them, too, to an extent," he returned.

Jo considered this a moment, then turned back to the lions. "Lazareth, he's twelve and a natural ham. Bolingbroke, he's ten, from the same lioness as Merlin. Hamlet," she said stopping again, "he's five. I bought him to replace Ari in the act." Jo stared into the tawny eyes. "He has potential, but he's arrogant. Patient, too. He's just waiting for me to make a mistake."

"Why?" Keane glanced over at Jo. Her eyes were cool and steady on Hamlet's.

"So he can get a good clean swipe at me," she told him without altering her expression. "It's his first season in the big cage. Pandora," Jo continued, pointing out the females. "A very classy lady. She's six. Hester, at seven, my best all-around. And Portia. It's her first year, too. She's mostly a seat warmer."

"Seat warmer?"

"Just what it sounds like," Jo explained. "She hasn't mastered any complicated tricks yet. She evens out the act, does a few basics and warms the seat." Jo moved on. "Dulcinea, the prettiest of the ladies. Ophelia, who had a litter last year, and Abra, eight, a bit bad-tempered but a good balancer."

Hearing her name, the cat rose, stretched her long, golden body, then began to rub it against the bars of the cage. A deep sound rumbled in her throat. Jo scowled and jammed her hands into her pockets. "She likes you," she muttered.

"Oh?" Lifting a brow, Keane studied the three-hundred-pound Abra more carefully. "How do you know?"

"When a lion likes you, it does exactly what a house cat does. It rubs against you. Abra's rubbing against the bars because she can't get any closer."

"I see." Humor touched his mouth. "I must admit, I'm at a loss on how to return the compliment." He drew on his cigar, then regarded Jo through a haze of smoke. "Your choice of names is fascinating."

"I like to read," she stated, leaving it at that. "Is there anything else you'd like to know about the cats?" Jo was determined to keep their conversation on a professional level. His smile had reminded her all too clearly of their encounter the night before.

"Do you drug them before a performance?"

Fury sparked Jo's eyes. "Certainly not."

"Was that an unreasonable question?" Keane countered. He dropped his cigar to the ground, then crushed it out with his heel.

"Not for a first of mayer," Jo decided with a sigh. She tossed her hair carelessly behind her back. "Drugging is not only cruel, it's stupid. A drugged animal won't perform."

"You don't touch the lions with that whip," Keane commented. He watched the light breeze tease a few strands of her hair. "Why do you use it?"

"To get their attention and to keep the audience awake." She smiled reluctantly.

Keane took her arm. Instantly, Jo stiffened. "Let's walk," he suggested. He began to lead her away from the cages. Spotting several people roaming the backyard, Jo refrained from pulling away. The last thing she wanted was the story spreading that she was having a tiff with the owner. "How do you tame them?" he asked her.

"I don't. They're not tame, they're trained." A tall blonde woman walked by carrying a tiny white poodle. "Merlin's hungry today," Jo called out with a grin.

The woman bundled the dog closer to her breast in mock alarm and began a rapid scolding in French. Jo laughed, telling her in the same language that Fifi was too tough a mouthful for Merlin.

"Fifi can do a double somersault on the back of a moving horse," Jo explained as they began to walk again. "She's trained just as my cats are trained, but she's also domesticated. The cats are wild." Jo turned her face up to Keane's. The sun cast a sheen over her hair and threw gold flecks into her eyes. "A wild thing can never be tamed, and anyone who tries is foolish. If you take something wild and turn it into a pet, you've stolen its character, blanked out its spark. And still, there's always an essence of the wild that can come back to life. When a dog turns on his master, it's ugly. When a lion turns, it's lethal." She was beginning to become accustomed to his hand on her arm, finding it easy to talk to him because he listened. "A full-grown male stands three feet at the shoulder and weighs over five hundred pounds. One well-directed swipe can break a man's neck, not to mention what teeth and claws can do." Jo gave a smile and a shrug. "Those aren't the virtues of a pet."

"Yet you go into a cage with twelve of them, armed with a whip?"

"The whip's window dressing." Jo discounted it with a gesture of her hand. "It would hardly be a defense against even one cat at full charge. A lion is a very tenacious enemy. A tiger is more bloodthirsty, but it normally strikes only once. If it misses, it takes it philosophically. A lion charges again and again. Do you know the line Byron wrote about a tiger's spring? 'Deadly, quick and crushing.'" Jo had completely forgotten her animosity and began to enjoy her walk and conversation with this handsome stranger. "It's a true description, but a lion is totally fearless when he charges, and stubborn. He's not the razzle-dazzle fighter the tiger is, just accurate. I'd bet on a lion against a tiger any day. And a man simply hasn't a prayer against one."

"Then how do you manage to stay in one piece?"

The calliope music was just a hint in the air now. Jo turned, noting with surprise that they had walked a good distance from camp. She could see the trailers and tents, hear occasional shouts and laughter, but she felt oddly separated from it all. She sat down cross-legged on the grass and plucked a blade. "I'm smarter than they are. At least I make them think so. And I dominate them, partly by a force of will. In training, you have to develop a rapport, a mutual respect and, if you're lucky, a certain affection. But you can't trust them to the point where you grow careless. And above all," she added, glancing over as he sat down beside her, "you have to remember the basic rule of poker. Bluff." Jo grinned, leaning back on her elbows. "Do you play poker?"

"I've been known to." Her hair trailed out along the grass, and he lifted a strand. "Do you?"

"Sometimes. My assistant handler, Pete…" Jo scanned the backyard, then smiled and pointed. "There he is, by the second trailer, sitting with Mac Stevenson, the one with the fielder's cap. Pete organizes a game now and then."

"Who's the little girl on stilts?"

"That's Mac's youngest, Katie. She wants to walk on them in the street parade. She's getting pretty good. There's Jamie," she said, then laughed as he did a pratfall and landed at Katie's wooden stilts.

"Rose's Jamie?" Keane asked, watching the impromptu show in the backyard.

"If she has her way. He's currently dazzled by Carmen Gribalti. Carmen won't give Jamie the time of day. She bats her lashes at Vito, the wire walker. He bats his at everyone."

"A complicated state of affairs," Keane commented. He twisted Jo's hair around his fingers. "Romance seems to be very popular in circus life."

"From what I read," she countered, "it's popular everywhere."

"Who dazzles you, Jovilette?" He gave her hair a tug to bring her face around to his.

Jo hadn't realized he was so close. She need do no more than sway for her mouth to touch his. Her eyes measured his while she waited for her pulse to calm. It was odd, she thought, that he had such an effect on her. With sudden clarity, she could smell the grass, a clean, sweet scent, and feel the sun. The sounds of the circus were muted in the background. She could hear birds call out with an occasional high-pitched trill. She remembered the taste of his mouth and wondered if it would be the same.

"I've been too busy to be dazzled," she replied. Her voice was steady, but her eyes were curious.

For the first time, Jo truly *wanted* to be kissed by a man. She wanted to feel again what she had felt the night before. She wanted to be held, not lightly as he had held her before, but close, with his arms tight around her. She wanted to renew the feeling of weightlessness. She had never experienced a strong physical desire, and for a moment she explored the sensation. There was a quiver in her stomach which was both pleasant and disturbing. Throughout her silent contemplations Keane watched her, intrigued by the intensity of her eyes.

"What are you thinking of?"

"I'm wondering why you make me feel so odd," she told him with simple frankness. He smiled, and she noticed that it grew in his eyes seconds before it grew on his mouth.

"Do I?" He appeared to enjoy the information. "Did you know your hair catches the sunlight?" Keane took a handful, letting it spill from between his fingers. "I've never seen another woman with hair like this. It's a temptation all in itself. In what way do I make you feel odd, Jovilette?" he asked as his eyes trailed back up to hers.

"I'm not sure yet." Jo found her voice husky. Abruptly, she decided it would not do to go on feeling odd or to go on wanting to be kissed by Keane Prescott. She scrambled up and brushed off the seat of her pants.

"Running away?" As Keane rose, Jo's head snapped up.

"I never run away from anything, Mr. Prescott." Ice sharpened her voice. She was annoyed that she had allowed herself to fall under his charm again. "I certainly won't run from a city-bred lawyer." Her words were laced with scorn. "Why don't you go back to Chicago and get someone thrown in jail?"

"I'm a defense attorney," Keane countered easily. "I get people out of jail."

"Fine. Go put a criminal back on the streets, then."

Keane laughed, bringing Jo's temper even closer to the surface. "That covers both sides of the issue, doesn't it? You dazzle me, Jovilette."

"Well, it's strictly unintentional." She took a step back from the amusement in his eyes. She would not tolerate him making fun of her. "You don't belong here," she blurted out. "You have no business here."

"On the contrary," he disagreed in a cool, untroubled voice. "I have every business here. I own this circus."

"Why?" she demanded, throwing out her hands as if to push his words aside. "Because it says so on a piece of paper? That's all lawyers understand, I imagine— pieces of paper with strange little words. Why did you come? To look us over and calculate the profit and loss? What's the liquidation value of a dream, Mr. Prescott? What price do you put on the human spirit? Look at it!" she demanded, swinging her arm to encompass the lot behind them. "You only see tents and a huddle of trailers. You can't possibly understand what it all means. But Frank understood. He loved it."

"I'm aware of that." Keane's voice was still calm but had taken on a thin edge of steel. Jo saw that his eyes had grown dark and guarded. "He also left it to me."

"I don't understand why." In frustration, Jo stuffed her hands in her pockets and turned away.

"Neither do I, I assure you, but the fact remains that he did."

"Not once in thirty years did you visit him." Jo whirled back around. Her hair followed in a passionate arch. "Not once."

"Quite true," Keane agreed. He stood with his weight even on both legs and watched her. "Of course, some might look at it differently. Not once in thirty years did he visit me."

"Your mother left him and took you to Chicago—"

"I won't discuss my mother," Keane interrupted in a tone of clipped finality.

Jo bit off a retort, spinning away from him again. Still she could not find the reins to her control. "What are you going to do with it?" she demanded.

"That's my business."

"Oh!" Jo spun back, then shut her eyes and muttered in a language he failed to understand. "Can you be so arrogant? Can you be so dispassionate?" Her lashes fluttered up, revealing eyes dark with anger. "Do the lives of all those people mean nothing to you? Does Frank's dream mean nothing? Haven't you enough money already without hurting people to get more? Greed isn't something you inherited from Frank."

"I'll only be pushed so far," Keane warned.

"I'd push you all the way back to Chicago if I could manage it," she snapped.

"I wondered how much of a temper there was behind those sharp green eyes," Keane commented, watching her passion pour color into her cheeks. "It appears it's a full-grown one." Jo started to retort, but Keane cut her off. "Just hold on a minute," he ordered. "With or without your approval, I own this circus. It might be easier for you if you adjusted to that. Be quiet," he added when her mouth opened again. "Legally, I can do with my—" he hesitated a moment, then continued in a mordant tone "—inheritance as I choose. I have no obligation or intention of justifying my decision to you."

Jo dug her nails into her palms to help keep her voice from shaking. "I never knew I could grow to dislike someone so quickly."

"Jovilette." Keane dipped his hands into his pockets, then rocked back on his heels. "You disliked me before you ever saw me."

"That's true," she replied evenly. "But I've learned to dislike you in person in less than twenty-four hours. I have a show to do," she said, turning back toward the lot. Though he did not follow, she felt his eyes on her until she reached her trailer and closed the door behind her.

Thirty minutes later Jamie sprang through the back door of the Big Top. He was breathless after a lengthy routine and hooked one hand through his purple suspenders as he took in gulps of air. He spotted Jo standing beside the white mare. Her eyes were dark and stormy, her shoulders set and rigid. Jamie recognized the signs. Something or someone had put Jo in a temper, and she had barely ten minutes to work her way out of it before her cue.

He crossed to her and gave a tug on her hair. "Hey."

"Hello, Jamie." Jo struggled to keep her voice pleasant, but he heard the traces of emotion.

"Hello, Jo," he replied in precisely the same tone.

"Cut it out," she ordered before taking a few steps away. The mare followed docilely. Jo had been trying for some time to put her emotions back into some semblance of order. She was not succeeding.

"What happened?" Jamie asked from directly behind her.

"Nothing," Jo snapped, then hated herself for the short nastiness of the word.

Jamie persisted, knowing her too well to be offended. "Nothing is one of my favorite topics of conversation." He put his hands on her shoulders, ignoring her quick, bad-tempered jerk. "Let's talk about it."

"There's nothing to talk about."

"Exactly." He began massaging the tension in her shoulders with his white gloved hands.

"Oh, Jamie." His good-heartedness was irresistible. Sighing, she allowed herself to be soothed. "You're an idiot."

"I'm not here to be flattered."

"I had an argument with the owner." Jo let out a long breath and shut her eyes.

"What're you doing having arguments with the owner?"

"He infuriates me." Jo whirled around. Her cape whipped and snapped with the movement. "He shouldn't be here. If he were back in Chicago…"

"Hold it." With a slight shake of her shoulders, Jamie halted Jo's outburst. "You know better than to get yourself worked up like this right before a show. You can't afford to have your mind on anything but what you're doing when you're in that cage."

"I'll be all right," she mumbled.

"Jo." There was censure in his voice mixed with affection and exasperation.

Reluctantly, Jo brought her gaze up to his. It was impossible to resist the grave eyes in the brightly painted face. With something between a sigh and a moan, she dropped her forehead to his chest. "Jamie, he makes me so mad! He could ruin everything."

"Let's worry about it when the time comes," Jamie suggested, patting her hair.

"But he doesn't understand us. He doesn't understand anything."

"Well, then it's up to us to make him understand, isn't it?"

Jo looked up and wrinkled her nose. "You're so logical."

"Of course I am," he agreed and struck a pose. As he wiggled his orange eyebrows, Jo laughed. "Okay?" he asked, then picked up his prop bucket.

"Okay," she agreed and smiled.

"Good, 'cause there's my cue."

When he disappeared behind the flap, Jo leaned her cheek against the mare and nuzzled a moment. "I don't think I'm the one to make him understand, though."

I wish he'd never come, she added silently as she vaulted onto the mare's back. *I wish I'd never noticed how his eyes are like Ari's and how nice his mouth is when he smiles*, she thought. Jo ran the tip of her tongue gingerly over her lips. *I wish he'd never kissed me. Liar.* Her conscience spoke softly in her ear: *Admit it, you're glad he kissed you. You've never felt anything like that before, and no matter what, you're glad he kissed you last night. You even wanted him to kiss you again today.*

She forced her mind clear, taking deep, even breaths until she heard the ringmaster announce her. With a flick of her heels, she sent the mare sprinting into the tent.

It did not go well. The audience cheered her, oblivious to any problem, but Jo was aware that the routine was far from smooth. And the cats sensed her preoccupation. Again and again they tested her, and again and again Jo was forced to alter her timing to compensate. When the act was over, her head throbbed from the strain of concentration. Her hands were clammy as she turned Merlin over to Buck.

The big man came back to her after securing the cage. "What's the matter with you?" he demanded without preamble. By the underlying and very rare anger in his voice, Jo knew he had observed at least a portion of her act. Unlike the audience, Buck would note any deviation. "You go in the cage like that again, one of those cats is going to find out what you taste like."

"My timing was a little off, that's all." Jo fought against the trembling in her stomach and tried to sound casual.

"A little?" Buck glowered, looking formidable behind the mass of blond beard. "Who do you think you're fooling? I've been around these ugly cats since before you were born. When you go in the cage, you've got to take your brain in with you."

Only too aware that he was right, Jo conceded. "I know, Buck. You're right." With a weary hand she pushed back her hair. "It won't happen again. I guess I was tired and a little off-balance." She sent him an apologetic smile.

Buck frowned and shuffled. Never in his forty-five years had he managed to resist feminine smiles. "All right," he muttered, then sniffed and made his voice firm. "But you go take a nap right after the finale. No coffee. I don't want to see you around again until dinnertime."

"Okay, Buck." Jo kept her voice humble, though she was tempted to grin. The weakness was going out of her legs, and the dull buzz of fear was fading from between her temples. Still she felt exhausted and agreeable to Buck's uncharacteristic tone of command. A nap, she decided as Buck drove Merlin away, was just what she needed, not to mention that it was as good a way as any to avoid Keane Prescott for the rest of the day. Shooing this thought aside, Jo decided to while away the time until the finale in casual conversation with Vito the wire walker.

Chapter 4

It rained for three days. It was a solid downpour, not heavy but insistent. As the circus wound its way north, the rain followed. Nevertheless, canvas men pitched the tents in soggy fields and muddy lots while straw was laid on the hippodrome track and performers scurried from trailers to tents under dripping umbrellas.

The lot near Waycross, Georgia, was scattered with puddles under a thick, gray sky. Jo could only be grateful that no evening show had been scheduled. By six, it was nearly dark, with a chill teasing the damp air. She hustled from the cookhouse after an early supper. She would check on the cats, she decided, then closet herself in her trailer, draw the curtains against the rain and curl up with a book. Shivering, she concluded that the idea was inspired.

She carried no umbrella but sought questionable

shelter under a gray rolled-brim hat and thin wind-breaker. Keeping her head lowered, she jogged across the mud, skimming around or hopping over puddles. She hummed lightly, anticipating the simple pleasures of an idle evening. Her humming ended in a muffled gasp as she ran into a solid object. Fingers wrapped around her upper arms. Even before she lifted her head, Jo knew it was Keane who held her. She recognized his touch. Through some clever maneuvering, she had managed to avoid being alone with him since they had walked together and looked back on the circus.

"Excuse me, Mr. Prescott. I'm afraid I wasn't looking where I was going."

"Perhaps the weather's dampened your radar, Jo-vilette." He made no move to release her. Annoyed, Jo was forced to hold her hat steady with one hand as she tilted her head to meet his eyes. Rain fell cool on her face.

"I don't know what you mean."

"Oh, I think you do," Keane countered. "There's not another soul around. You've been careful to keep yourself in a crowd for days."

Jo blinked rain from her lashes. She admitted rue-fully that it had been foolish to suppose he wouldn't notice her ploy. She saw he carried no umbrella either, nor did he bother with a hat. His hair was darkened with rain, much the same color that one of her cats would be if caught in an unexpected shower. It was difficult, in the murky light, to clearly make out his features, but the rain could not disguise his mockery.

"That's an interesting observation, Mr. Prescott," Jo said coolly. "Now, if you don't mind, I'm getting wet." She was surprised when she remained in his hold after a strong attempt on her part to pull away. Frowning, she put both hands against his chest and pushed. She discovered that she had been wrong; under the lean frame was an amazing amount of strength. Infuriated that she had misjudged him and that she was outmatched, Jo raised her eyes again. "Let me go," she demanded between clenched teeth.

"No," Keane returned mildly. "I don't believe I will."

Jo glared at him. "Mr. Prescott, I'm cold and wet and I'd like to go to my trailer. Now, what do you want?"

"First, I want you to stop calling me Mr. Prescott." Jo pouted but she kept silent. "Second, I'd like an hour of your time for going over a list of personnel." He paused. Through her windbreaker Jo could feel his fingers unyielding on her arms.

"Is there anything else?" she demanded, trying to sound bored.

For a moment there was only the sound of rain drumming on the ground and splashing into puddles. "Yes," Keane said quietly. "I think I'll just get this out of my system."

Jo's instincts were swift but they were standing too close for her to evade him. And he was quick. Her protest was muffled against his mouth. Her arms were pinioned to her sides as his locked around her. Jo had felt a man's body against her own before—working out with the tumblers, practicing with the equestrians—but never with such clarity as this. She was aware of Keane in every fiber of her being. His body was whipcord lean and hard, his arms holding the strength she had discounted the first time she had seen him. But more, it was his mouth that mystified her. Now it was not gentle or testing; it took and plundered and demanded more before she could withhold a response.

Jo forgot the rain, though it continued to fall against her face. She forgot the cold. The warmth spread from inside, where her blood flowed fast, as her body was molded to Keane's. She forgot herself, or the woman she had thought herself to be, and discovered another. When he lifted his mouth, Jo kept her eyes closed, savoring the lingering pleasures, inviting fresh ones.

"More?" he murmured as his hand trailed up, then down her spine. Heat raced after it. "Kissing can be a dangerous pastime, Jo." He lowered his mouth again, then nipped at her soft bottom lip. "But you know all about danger, don't you?" He kissed her hard, leaving her breathless. "How courageous are you without your cats?"

Suddenly her heart raced to her throat. Her legs became rubbery, and a tingle sprinted up her spine. Jo recognized the feeling. It was the way she felt when she experienced a close call with the cats. Reaction would set in after the door of the safety cage locked behind her and the crisis had passed. It was then that fear found her. She studied Keane's bold, amber eyes, and her mouth went dry. She shuddered.

"You're cold." His voice was abruptly brisk. "Small wonder. We'll go to my trailer and get you some coffee."

"No!" Jo's protest was sharp and instantaneous. She knew she was vulnerable and she knew as well that she did not yet possess the experience to fight him. To be alone with him now was too great a risk.

Keane drew her away, but his grip remained firm. She could not read his expression as he searched her face. "What happened just now was personal," he told her. "Strictly man to woman. I'm of the opinion that lovemaking should be personal. You're an appealing armful, Jovilette, and I'm accustomed to taking what I want, one way or another."

His words were like a shot of adrenaline. Jo's chin thrust forward, and her eyes flamed. "No one *takes* me, one way or another." She spoke with the deadly calm of fury. "If I make love with anyone, it's only because I want to."

"Of course," Keane agreed with an easy nod. "We're both aware you'll be willing when the time comes. We could make love quite successfully tonight, but I think it best if we know each other better first."

Jo's mouth trembled open and closed twice before she could speak. "Of all the arrogant, outrageous…"

"Truthful," Keane supplied, tossing her into incoherency again. "But for now, we have business, and while I don't mind kissing in the rain, I prefer to conduct business in a drier climate." He held up a hand as Jo started to protest. "I told you, the kiss was between a man and a woman. The business we have now is between the owner of this circus and a performer under contract. Understood?"

Jo took a long, deep breath to bring her voice to a normal level. "Understood," she agreed. Without another word she let him lead her across the slippery lot.

When they reached Keane's trailer, he hustled Jo inside without preliminaries. She blinked against the change in light when he hit the wall switch. "Take off your coat," he said briskly, pulling down her zipper before she could perform the task for herself. Instinctively, her hand reached for it as she took a step backward. Keane merely lifted a brow, then stripped off his own jacket. "I'll get the coffee." He moved down the length of the narrow trailer and disappeared around the corner where the tiny kitchen was set.

Slowly, Jo pulled off her dripping hat, letting her hair tumble free from where it had been piled under its confinement. With automatic movements she hung both her hat and coat on the hooks by the trailer door. It had been almost six months since she had stood in Frank's trailer, and like a woman visiting an old friend, she searched for changes.

The same faded lampshade adorned the maple table lamp that Frank had used for reading. The shade sat straight now, however, not at its usual slightly askew angle. The pillow that Lillie from wardrobe had sewn for him on some long-ago Christmas still sat over the small burn hole in the seat cushion of the couch. Jo doubted that Keane knew of the hole's existence. Frank's pipe stand sat, as always, on the counter by the side window. Unable to resist, Jo crossed over to run her finger over the worn bowl of his favorite pipe.

"Never could pack it right," she murmured to his well-loved ghost. Abruptly, her senses quivered. She twisted her head to see Keane watching her. Jo dropped her hand. A rare blush mantled her cheeks as she found herself caught unguarded.

"How do you take your coffee, Jo?"

She swallowed. "Black," she told him, aware that he was granting her the privacy of her thoughts. "Just black. Thank you."

Keane nodded, then turned to pick up two steaming

mugs. "Come, sit down." He moved toward the Formica table that sat directly across from the kitchen. "You'd better take off your shoes. They're wet."

After squeaking her way down the length of the trailer, Jo sat down and pulled at the damp laces. Keane set both mugs on the table before disappearing into the back of the trailer. When he returned, Jo was already sipping at the coffee.

"Here." He offered her a pair of socks.

Surprised, Jo shook her head. "No, that's all right. I don't need…"

Her polite refusal trailed off as he knelt at her feet. "Your feet are like ice," he commented after cupping them in his palms. Briskly, he rubbed them while Jo sat mute, oddly disarmed by the gesture. The warmth was spreading dangerously past her ankles. "Since I'm responsible for keeping you out in the rain," he went on as he slipped a sock over her foot, "I'd best see to it you don't cough and sneeze your way through tomorrow's show. Such small feet," he murmured, running his thumb over the curve of her ankle as she stared wordlessly at the top of his head.

Raindrops still clung to and glistened in his hair. Jo found herself longing to brush them away and feel the texture of his hair beneath her fingers. She was sharply aware of him and wondered if it would always be this way when she was near him. Keane pulled on the second sock. His fingers lingered on her calf as he lifted his eyes. Hers were darkened with confusion as they met his. The body over which she had always held supreme control was journeying into frontiers her mind had not yet explored.

"Still cold?" Keane asked softly.

Jo moistened her lips and shook her head. "No. No, I'm fine."

He smiled a lazy, masculine smile that said as clearly as words that he was aware of his effect on her. His eyes told her he enjoyed it. Unsmiling, Jo watched him rise to his feet.

"It doesn't mean you'll win," she said aloud in response to their silent communication.

"No, it doesn't." Keane's smile remained as his gaze roamed possessively over her face. "That only makes it more interesting. Open and shut cases are invariably boring, hardly worth the trouble of going on if you've won before you've finished your opening statement."

Jo lifted her coffee and sipped, taking a moment to settle her nerves. "Are we here to discuss the law or circus business, Counselor?" she asked, letting her eyes drift to his again as she set the mug back on the table. "If it's law, I'm afraid I'm going to disappoint you. I don't know much about it."

"What do you know about, Jovilette?" Keane slid into the chair beside hers.

"Cats," she said. "And Prescott's Circus Colossus. I'll be glad to let you know whatever I can about either."

"Tell me about you," he countered, and leaning back, pulled a cigar from his pocket.

"Mr. Prescott—" Jo began.

"Keane," he interrupted, flicking on his lighter. He glanced at the tip of his cigar, then back up at her through the thin haze of smoke.

"I was under the impression you wanted to be briefed on the personnel."

"You are a member of this circus, are you not?" Casually, Keane blew smoke at the ceiling. "I have every intention of being briefed on the entire troupe and see no reason why you shouldn't start with yourself." His eyes traveled back to hers. "Humor me."

Jo decided to take the line of least resistance. "It's a short enough story," she said with a shrug. "I've been with the circus all my life. When I was old enough, I started work as a generally useful."

"A what?" Keane paused in the action of reaching for the coffeepot.

"Generally useful," Jo repeated, letting him freshen her cup. "It's a circus term that means exactly what it says. Rose's parents, for instance, are generally usefuls. We get a lot of drifters who work that way, too. It's also written into every performer's contract, after the specific terms, that they make themselves generally useful. There isn't room in most circuses, and certainly not in a tent circus, for performers with star complexes. You do what's necessary, what's needed. Buck, my handler, fills in during a slump at the sideshow, and he's one of the best canvas men around. Pete is the best mechanic in the troupe. Jamie knows as much about lighting as most shandies—electricians," she supplied as Keane lifted a brow. "He's also a better-than-average tumbler."

"What about you?" Keane interrupted the flow of Jo's words. For a moment she faltered, and the hands that had been gesturing became still. "Besides riding a galloping horse without reins or saddle, giving orders to elephants and facing lions?" He lifted his cup, watching her as he sipped. A smile lurked in his eyes. Jo frowned, studying him.

"Are you making fun of me?"

His smile sobered instantly. "No, Jo, I'm not making fun of you."

She continued. "In a pinch, I run the menagerie in the sideshow or I fill in the aerial act. Not the trap," she explained, relaxing again. "They have to practice together constantly to keep the timing. But sometimes I fill in on the Spanish Web, the big costume number where the girls hang from ropes and do identical moves. They're using butterfly costumes this year."

"Yes, I know the one." Keane continued to watch her as he drew on his cigar.

"But mostly Duffy likes to use girls who are more curvy. They double as showgirls in the finale."

"I see." A smile tugged at the corners of Keane's mouth. "Tell me, were your parents European?"

"No." Diverted, Jo shook her head. "Why do you ask?"

"Your name. And the ease with which I've heard you speak both French and Italian."

"It's easy to pick up languages in the circus," Jo said.

"Your accent was perfect in both cases."

"What? Oh." She shrugged and absently shifted in her chair, bringing her feet up to sit cross-legged. "We have a wide variety of nationalities here. Frank used to say that the world could take a lesson from the circus. We have French, Italian, Spanish, German, Russian, Mexican, Americans from all parts of the country and more."

"I know. It's like a traveling United Nations." He tipped his cigar ash in a glass tray. "So you picked up some French and Italian along the way. But if you've traveled with the circus all your life, what about the rest of your schooling?"

The hint of censure in his voice brought up her chin. "I went to school during the winter break and had a tutor on the road. I learned my ABC's, Counselor, and a bit more, besides. I probably know more about geography and world history than you, and from more interesting sources than textbooks. I imagine I know more about animals than a third-year veterinary student and have more practical experience healing them. I can speak seven languages and—"

"Seven?" Keane interrupted. "Seven languages?"

"Well, five fluently," she corrected grudgingly. "I still have a bit of trouble with Greek and German, unless I can really take my time, and I can't read Greek yet at all."

"What else besides French, Italian and English?"

"Spanish and Russian." Jo scowled into her coffee. "The Russian's handy. I use it for swearing at the cats during the act. Not too many people understand Russian cursing, so it's safe."

Keane's laughter brought Jo's attention from her coffee. He was leaning back in his chair, his eyes gold with their mirth. Jo's scowl deepened. "What's so funny?"

"You are, Jovilette." Stung, she started to scramble up, but his hands on her shoulders stopped her. "No, don't be offended. I can't help but find it amusing that you toss out so offhandedly an accomplishment that any language major would brag about." Carelessly, he ran a finger over her sulky mouth. "You continually amaze me." He brushed a hand through her hair. "You mumbled something at me the other day. Were you swearing at me in Russian?"

"Probably."

Grinning, Keane dropped his hand and settled into his chair again. "When did you start working with the cats?"

"In front of an audience? When I was seventeen. Frank wouldn't let me start any earlier. He was my legal guardian as well as the owner, so he had me both ways. I was ready when I was fifteen."

"How did you lose your parents?"

The question caught her off guard. "In a fire," she said levelly. "When I was seven."

"Here?"

She knew Keane was not referring to their locale but to the circus. Jo sipped her cooling coffee. "Yes."

"Didn't you have any other family?"

"The circus is a family," she countered. "I was never given the chance to be an orphan. And I always had Frank."

"Did you?" Keane's smile was faintly sarcastic. "How was he as a father figure?"

Jo studied him for a moment. Was he bitter? she wondered. Or amused? Or simply curious? "He never took my father's place," she replied quietly. "He never tried to, because neither of us wanted it. We were friends, as close as I think it's possible for friends to be, but I'd already had a father, and he'd already had a child. We weren't looking for substitutes. You look nothing like him, you know."

"No," Keane replied with a shrug. "I know."

"He had a comfortable face, all creases and folds."

Jo smiled, thinking of it while she ran a finger absently around the rim of her mug. "He was dark, too, just beginning to gray when…" She trailed off, then brought herself back with a quick shake of her head. "Your voice is rather like his, though. He had a truly beautiful voice. I'll ask you a question now."

Keane's expression became attentive, then he gestured with the back of his hand. "Go ahead."

"Why are you here? I lost my temper when I asked you before, but I do want to know." It was against her nature to probe, and some of her discomfort found its way into her voice. "It must have caused you some difficulty to leave your practice, even for a few weeks."

Keane frowned at the end of his cigar before he slowly crushed it out. "Let's say I wanted to see firsthand what had fascinated my father all these years."

"You never came when he was alive." Jo gripped her hands together under the table. "You didn't even bother to come to his funeral."

"I would've been the worst kind of hypocrite to attend his funeral, don't you think?"

"He was your father." Jo's eyes grew dark and her tone sharp in reproof.

"You're smarter than that, Jo," Keane countered calmly. "It takes more than an accident of birth to make a father. Frank Prescott was a complete stranger to me."

"You resent him." Jo felt suddenly torn between loyalty for Frank and understanding for the man who sat beside her.

"No." Keane shook his head thoughtfully. "No, I believe I actively resented him when I was growing up, but…" He shrugged the thought aside. "I grew rather ambivalent over the years."

"He was a good man," Jo stated, leaning forward as she willed him to understand. "He only wanted to give people pleasure, to show them a little magic. Maybe he wasn't made to be a father—some men aren't—but he was kind and gentle. And he was proud of you."

"Of me?" Keane seemed amused. "How?"

"Oh, you're hateful," Jo whispered, hurt by his careless attitude. She slipped from her chair, but before she could step away, Keane took her arm.

"No, tell me. I'm interested." His hold on her arm was light, but she knew it would tighten if she resisted.

"All right." Jo tossed her head to send her hair behind her back. "He had the Chicago paper delivered to his Florida office. He always looked for any mention of you, any article on a court case you were involved in or a dinner party you attended. Anything. You have to understand that to us a write-up is very important. Frank wasn't a performer, but he was one of us. Sometimes he'd read me an article before he put it away. He kept a scrapbook."

Jo pulled her arm away and strode past Keane into the bedroom. The oversize wooden chest was where it had always been, at the foot of Frank's bed. Kneeling down, Jo tossed up the lid. "This is where he kept all the things that mattered to him." Jo began to shift through papers and mementos quickly; she had not been able to bring herself to sort through the chest before. Keane stood in the doorway and watched her. "He called it his memory box." She pushed at her hair with an annoyed hand, then continued to search. "He said memories were the rewards for growing old. Here it is." Jo pulled out a dark green scrapbook, then sat back on her heels. Silently, she held it out to Keane. After a moment he crossed the room and took it from her. Jo could hear the rain hissing on the ground outside as their eyes held. His expression was unfathomable as he opened the book. The pages rustled to join the quiet sound of the rain.

"What an odd man he must have been," Keane murmured, "to keep a scrapbook on a son he never knew." There was no rancor in his voice. "What was he?" he asked suddenly, shifting his eyes back to Jo.

"A dreamer," she answered. "His watch was always five minutes slow. If he hung a picture on the wall, it was always crooked. He'd never straighten it because he'd never notice. He was always thinking about tomorrow. I guess that's why he kept yesterday in this box." Glancing down, she began to straighten the chaos she had caused while looking for the book. A snatch of red caught her eye. Reaching for it, her fingers found a familiar shape. Jo hesitated, then drew the old doll out of the chest.

It was a sad piece of plastic and faded silk with its face nearly washed away. One arm was broken off, leaving an empty sleeve. The golden hair was straggled but brave under its red cap. Ballet shoes were painted on the dainty feet. Tears backed up behind Jo's eyes as she made a soft sound of joy and despair.

"What is it?" Keane demanded, glancing down to see her clutching the battered ballerina.

"Nothing." Her voice was unsteady as she scrambled quickly to her feet. "I have to go." Though she tried, Jo could not bring herself to drop the doll back into the box. She swallowed. She did not wish to reveal her emotions before his intelligent, gold eyes. Perhaps he would be cynical, or worse, amused. "May I have this, please?" She was careful with the tone of the request.

Slowly, Keane crossed the distance between them, then cradled her chin in his hand. "It appears to be yours already."

"It was." Her fingers tightened on the doll's waist. "I didn't know Frank had kept it. Please," she whispered. Her emotions were already dangerously heightened. She could feel a need to rest her head against his shoulder. The evening had been a roller coaster for her feelings, climaxing now with the discovery of her most prized childhood possession. She knew that if she did not escape, she would seek comfort in his arms. Her own weakness frightened her. "Let me by."

For a moment, Jo read refusal in his eyes. Then he stepped aside. Jo let out a quiet, shaky breath. "I'll walk you back to your trailer."

"No," she said quickly, too quickly. "It isn't necessary," she amended, moving by him and into the kitchen. Sitting down, she pulled on her shoes, too distraught to remember she still wore his socks. "There's no reason for us both to get wet again." She rambled on, knowing he was watching her hurried movement, but unable to stop. "And I'm going to check on my cats before I go in, and…"

She stopped short when he took her shoulders and pulled her to her feet. "And you don't want to take the chance of being alone in your trailer with me in case I change my mind."

A sharp denial trembled on her lips, but the knowledge in his eyes crushed it. "All right," she admitted. "That, too."

Keane brushed her hair from her neck and shook his head. He kissed her nose and moved down to pluck her hat and coat from their hooks. Cautiously, Jo followed him. When he held out her coat, she turned and slipped her arms into the sleeves. Before she could murmur her thanks, he turned her back and pulled up the zipper. For a moment his fingers lingered at her neck, his eyes on hers. Taking her hair into his hand, he piled it atop her head, then dropped on her hat. The gestures were innocent, but Jo was rocked by a feeling of intimacy she had never experienced.

"I'll see you tomorrow," he said, pulling the brim of her hat down further over her eyes.

Jo nodded. Holding the doll against her side, she pushed open the door. The sound of rain was amplified through the trailer. "Good night," she murmured, then moved quickly into the night.

Chapter 5

The morning scent was clean. In the new lot rainbows glistened in puddles. At last the sky was blue with only harmless white puffs of clouds floating over its surface. In the cookhouse a loud, crowded breakfast was being served. Finding herself without appetite, Jo skipped going to the cookhouse altogether. She was restless and tense. No matter how she disciplined her mind, her thoughts wandered back to Keane Prescott and to the evening they had spent together. Jo remembered it all, from the quick passion of the kiss in the rain to the calmness of his voice when he had said good-night. It was odd, she mused, that whenever she began to talk to him, she forgot he was the owner, forgot he was Frank's son. Always she was forced to remind herself of their positions.

Deep in thought, Jo slipped into tights and a leotard. It was true, she admitted, that she had failed to keep their relationship from becoming personal. She found it difficult to corral her urge to laugh with him, to share a joke, to open for him the doorway to the magic of the circus. If he could feel it, she thought, he would understand. Though she could admit her interest in him privately, she could not find a clear reason for his apparent interest in her.

Why me? she wondered with a shake of her head. Turning, she opened her wardrobe closet and studied herself in the full-length glass on the back of the door. There she saw a woman of slightly less-than-average height with a body lacking the generous curves of Duffy's showgirls. The legs, she decided, were not bad. They were long and well-shaped with slim thighs. The hips were narrow, more, she thought with a pout, like a boy's than a woman's; and the bustline was sadly inadequate. She knew many women in the troupe with more appeal and a dozen with more experience.

Jo could see nothing in the mirror that would attract a sophisticated Chicago attorney. She did not note the honesty that shone from the exotically shaped green eyes or the strength in her chin or the full promise of her mouth. She saw the touch of gypsy in the tawny complexion and raven hair but remained unaware of the appeal that came from the hint of something wild and untamed just under the surface. The plain black leotard showed her firm, lithe body to perfection, but Jo thought nothing of the smooth satiny sheen of her skin. She was frowning as she pulled her hair back and began to braid it.

He must know dozens of women, she thought as her hands worked to confine her thick mane of hair. He probably takes a different one to dinner every night. They wear beautiful clothes and expensive perfume, she mused, torturing herself with the thought. They have names like Laura and Patricia, and they have low, sophisticated laughs. Jo lifted a brow at the reflection in the mirror and gave a light, low laugh. She wrinkled her brow at the hollowness of the sound. They discuss mutual friends, the Wallaces or the Jamesons, over candlelight and Beaujolais. And when he takes the most beautiful one home, they listen to Chopin and drink brandy in front of the fire. Then they make love. Jo felt an odd tightening in her stomach but pursued the fantasy to the finish. The lovely lady is experienced, passionate and worldly. Her skin is soft and white. When he leaves, she is not devastated but mature. She doesn't even care if he loves her or not.

Jo stared at the woman in the glass and saw her cheeks were wet. On a cry of frustration, she slammed the door shut. *What's wrong with me?* she demanded, brushing all traces of tears from her face. *I haven't been myself for days! I need to shake myself out of this—this...whatever it is that I'm in.* Slipping on gymnastic shoes and tossing a robe over her arm, Jo hustled from the trailer.

She moved carefully, avoiding puddles and any further speculation on Keane Prescott's romantic life. Before she was halfway across the lot, she saw Rose. From the expression on her face, Jo could see she was in a temper.

"Hello, Rose," she said, strategically stepping aside as the snake charmer splashed through a puddle.

"He's hopeless," Rose tossed back. "I tell you," she

continued, stopping and wagging a finger at Jo, "I'm through this time. Why should I waste my time?"

"You've certainly been patient," Jo agreed, deciding that sympathy was the wisest course. "It's more than he deserves."

"Patient?" Rose raised a dramatic hand to her breast. "I have the patience of a saint. Yet even a saint has her limits!" Rose tossed her hair behind her shoulders. She sighed heavily. "Adios. I think I hear Mama calling me."

Jo continued her walk toward the Big Top. Jamie walked by, his hands in his pockets. "She's crazy," he muttered. He stopped and spread his arms wide. His look was that of a man ill-used and innocent. Jo shrugged. Shaking his head, Jamie moved away. "She's crazy," he said again.

Jo watched him until he was out of sight, then darted to the Big Top.

Inside, Carmen watched adoringly while Vito practiced a new routine on the incline wire. The tent echoed with the sounds of rehearsals: voices and thumps, the rattle of rigging, the yapping of clown dogs. In the first ring Jo spotted the Six Beirots, an acrobatic act that was just beginning its warm-ups. Pleased with her timing, Jo walked the length of the arena. A raucous whistle sounded over her head, and she glanced up to shake a friendly fist at Vito. He called from fifteen feet above her as he balanced on a slender wire set at a forty-five-degree angle.

"Hey, chickie, you have a nice rear view. You're almost as cute as me."

"No one's as cute as you, Vito," she called back.

"Ah, I know." With a weighty sigh, he executed a

neat pivot. "But I have learned to live with it." He sent down a lewd wink. "When you going into town with me, chickie?" he asked as he always did.

"When you teach my cats to walk the wire," Jo answered as she always did. Vito laughed and began a light-footed cha-cha. Carmen fired Jo a glare. She must have it bad, Jo decided, if she takes Vito's harmless flirting seriously. Stopping beside her, Jo leaned close and spoke in a conspirator's whisper. "He'd fall off his wire if I said I'd go."

"I'd go," Carmen said with a lovely pout, "if he'd just ask me."

Jo shook her head, wondering why romances were invariably complicated. She was lucky not to have the problem. Giving Carmen an encouraging pat on the shoulder, Jo set off toward the first ring.

The Six Beirots were brothers. They were all small-statured, dark men who had immigrated from Belgium. Jo worked out with them often to keep herself limber and to keep her reflexes sharp. She liked them all, knew their wives and children, and understood their unique blending of French and English. Raoul was the oldest, and the stockiest of the six brothers. Because of his build and strength, he was the under-stander in their human pyramid. It was he who spotted Jo and first lifted a hand in greeting.

"Halo." He grinned and ran his palm over his receding hairline. "You gonna tumble?"

Jo laughed and did a quick handspring into the ring. She stuck out her tongue when the unanimous critique was "sloppy." "I just need to warm up," she said, assuming an air of injured dignity. "My muscles need tuning."

For the next thirty minutes Jo worked with them, doing muscle stretches and limbering exercises, rib stretches and lung expanders. Her muscles warmed and loosened, her heart pumped steadily. She was filled with energy. Her mind was clear. Because of her lightened mood, Jo was easily cajoled into a few impromptu acrobatics. Leaving the more complicated feats to the experts, she did simple ts, handsprings or twists at Raoul's command. She did a brief, semisuccessful thirty seconds atop the rolling globe and earned catcalls from her comrades at her dismount.

She stood back as they began the leaps. One after another they lined up to take turns running along a ramp, bounding upon a springboard and flying up to do flips or twists before landing on the mat. There was a constant stream of French as they called out to each other.

"Hokay, Jo." Raoul gestured with his hand. "Your turn."

"Oh, no." She shook her head and reached for her robe. "Uh-uh." There was a chorus of coaxing, teasing French. "I've got to give my cats their vitamins," she told them, still shaking her head.

"Come on, Jo. It's fun." Raoul grinned and wiggled his eyebrows. "Don't you like to fly?" As she glanced at the ramp, Raoul knew she was tempted. "You take a good spring," he told her. "Do one forward somersault, then land on my shoulders." He patted them to show their ability to handle the job.

Jo smiled and nibbled pensively on her lower lip. It

had been a long while since she had taken the time to go up on the trapeze and really fly. It did look like fun. She gave Raoul a stern look. "You'll catch me?"

"Raoul never misses," he said proudly, then turned to his brothers. *"N'est-ce pas?"* His brothers shrugged and rolled their eyes to the ceiling with indistinguishable mutters. "Ah." He waved them away with the back of his hand.

Knowing Raoul was indeed a top flight understander, Jo approached the ramp. Still she gave him one last narrow-eyed look. "You catch me," she ordered, shaking her finger at him.

"Cherie." He took his position with a stylish movement of his hand. "It's a piece of pie."

"Cake," Jo corrected, took a deep breath, held it and ran. When she came off the springboard, she tucked into the somersault and watched the Big Top turn upside down. She felt good. As the tent began to right itself, she straightened for her landing, keeping herself loose. Her feet connected with Raoul's powerful shoulders, and she tilted only briefly before he took her ankles in a firm grip. Straightening her poor posture, Jo styled elaborately with both arms while she received exaggerated applause and whistles. She leaped down nimbly as Raoul took her waist to give her landing bounce.

"When do you want to join the act?" he asked her, giving her a friendly pat on the bottom. "We'll put you up on the sway pole."

"That's okay." Grinning, Jo again reached for her robe. "I'll stick with the cats." After a cheerful wave, she slipped one arm into a sleeve and started back down the hippodrome track. She pulled up short when she spotted Keane leaning up against the front seat rail.

"Amazing," he said, then straightened to move to her. "But then, the circus is supposed to be amazing, isn't it?" He lifted the forgotten sleeve to her robe, then slipped her other arm into it. "Is there anything here you can't do?"

"Hundreds of things," Jo answered, taking him seriously. "I'm only really proficient with animals. The rest is just show and play."

"You looked amazingly proficient to me for the last half hour or so," he countered as he pulled out her braid from where it was trapped by her robe.

"Have you been here that long?"

"I walked in as Vito was commenting on your rear view."

"Oh." Jo laughed, glancing back to where Vito now stood flirting with Carmen. "He's crazy."

"Perhaps," Keane agreed, taking her arm. "But his eyesight's good enough. Would you like some coffee?"

Jo was reminded instantly of the evening before. Leery of being drawn to his charms again, she shook her head. "I've got to change," she told him, belting her robe. "We've got a show at two. I want to rehearse the cats."

"It's incredible how much time you people devote to your art. Rehearsals seem to run into the beginning of a show, and a show seems to run into more rehearsals."

Jo softened when he referred to circus skills as art. "Performers always look for just a bit more in themselves. It's a constant struggle for perfection. Even when a performance goes beautifully and you know it, you start thinking about the next time. How can I do it better or bigger or higher or faster?"

"Never satisfied?" Keane asked as they stepped out into the sunlight.

"If we were, we wouldn't have much of a reason to come back and do it all over again."

He nodded, but there was something absent in the gesture, as if his mind was elsewhere. "I have to leave this afternoon," he said almost to himself.

"Leave?" Jo's heart skidded to a stop. Her distress was overwhelming and so unexpected that she was forced to take an extra moment to steady herself. "Back to Chicago?"

"Hmm?" Keane stopped, turning to face her. "Oh, yes."

"And the circus?" Jo asked, thoroughly ashamed that it had not been her first concern. She didn't want him to leave, she suddenly realized.

Keane frowned a moment, then continued to walk. "I see no purpose in disrupting this year's schedule." His voice was brisk now and businesslike.

"This year's?" Jo repeated cautiously.

Keane turned and looked at her. "I haven't decided its ultimate fate, but I won't do anything until the end of the summer."

"I see." She let out a long breath. "So we have a reprieve."

"In a manner of speaking," Keane agreed.

Jo was silent for a moment but could not prevent herself from asking, "Then you won't—I mean, you'll be staying in Chicago now. You won't be traveling with us?"

They negotiated their way around a puddle before Keane answered. "I don't feel I can make a judicious decision about the circus after so brief an exposure. There's a complication in one of my cases that needs my personal attention, but I should be back in a week or two."

Relief flooded through her. He would be back, a voice shouted in her ear. *It shouldn't matter to you*, another whispered. "We'll be in South Carolina in a couple of weeks," Jo said casually. They had reached her trailer, and she took the handle of her door before she turned to face him. *It's just that I want him to understand what this circus means*, she told herself as she looked up into his eyes. *That's the only reason I want him to come back.* Knowing she was lying to herself made it difficult to keep her gaze steady.

Keane smiled, letting his eyes travel over her face. "Yes, Duffy's given me a route list. I'll find you. Aren't you going to ask me in?"

"In?" Jo repeated. "Oh, no, I told you, I have to change, and..." He stepped forward as she talked. Something in his eyes told her a firm stand was necessary. She had seen a similar look in a lion's eyes while he contemplated taking a dangerous liberty. "I simply don't have time right now. If I don't see you before you go, have a good trip." She turned and opened the door. Aware of a movement, she turned back, but not before he had nudged her through the door and followed. As it closed at his back, Jo bristled with fury. She did not enjoy being outmaneuvered. "Tell me, Counselor, do you know anything about a law concerning breaking and entering?"

"Doesn't apply," he returned smoothly. "There was no lock involved." He glanced around at the attractive simplicity of Jo's trailer. The colors were restful earth tones without frills. The beige-and-brown-flecked linoleum floor was spotlessly clean. It was the same basic floorplan as Frank's trailer, but here there were softer touches. There were curtains rather than shades at the windows; large, comfortable pillows tossed onto a forest green sofa; a spray of fresh wildflowers tucked into a thin, glass vase. Without comment Keane wandered to a black lacquer trunk that sat directly opposite the door. On it was a book that he picked up while Jo fumed. *"The Count of Monte Cristo,"* he read aloud and flipped it open. "In French," he stated, lifting a brow.

"It was written in French," Jo muttered, pulling it from his hand. "So I read it in French." Annoyed, she lifted the lid on the trunk, preparing to drop the book inside and out of his reach.

"Good heavens, are those all yours?" Keane stopped the lid on its downswing, then pushed books around with his other hand. "Tolstoy, Cervantes, Voltaire, Steinbeck. When do you have time in this crazy, twenty-four-hour world you live in to read this stuff?"

"I make time," Jo snapped as her eyes sparked. "My *own* time. Just because you're the owner doesn't mean you can barge in here and poke through my things and demand an account of my time. This is my trailer. I own everything in it."

"Hold on." Keane halted her rushing stream of words. "I wasn't demanding an account of your time, I was simply astonished that you could find enough of it to do this type of reading. Since I can't claim to be an expert on your work, it would be remarkably foolish of me to criticize the amount of time you spend on it. Second," he said, taking a step toward her—and though Jo stiffened in anticipation, he did not touch her, "I apologize for 'poking through your things,' as you put it. I was interested for several reasons. One being I have quite an extensive library myself. It seems we have a common interest, whether we like it or not. As for barging into your trailer, I can only plead guilty. If you choose to prosecute, I can recommend a couple of lousy attorneys who overcharge."

His last comment forced a smile onto Jo's reluctant lips. "I'll give it some thought." With more care than she had originally intended, Jo lowered the lid of the trunk. She was reminded that she had not been gracious. "I'm sorry," she said as she turned back to him.

His eyes reflected curiosity. "What for?"

"For snapping at you." She lifted her shoulders, then let them fall. "I thought you were criticizing me. I suppose I'm too sensitive."

Several seconds passed before he spoke. "Unnecessary apology accepted if you answer one question."

Mystified, Jo frowned at him. "What question?"

"Is the Tolstoy in Russian?"

Jo laughed, pushing loose strands of hair from her face. "Yes, it is."

Keane smiled, enjoying the two tiny dimples that flickered in her cheeks when she laughed. "Did you know that though you're lovely in any case, you grow even more so when you smile?"

Jo's laughter stilled. She was unaccustomed to this sort of compliment and studied him without any idea of how to respond. It occurred to her that any of the sophisticated women she had imagined that morning would have known precisely what to say. She would have been able to smile or laugh as she tossed back the appropriate comment. That woman, Jo admitted, was not Jovilette Wilder. Gravely, she kept her eyes on his. "I don't know how to flirt," she said simply.

Keane tilted his head, and an expression came and went in his eyes before she could analyze it. He stepped toward her. "I wasn't flirting with you, Jo, I was making an observation. Hasn't anyone ever told you that you're beautiful?"

He was much too close now, but in the narrow confines of the trailer, Jo had little room to maneuver. She was forced to tilt back her head to keep her eyes level with his. "Not precisely the way you did." Quickly, she put her hand to his chest to keep the slight but important distance between them. She knew she was trapped, but that did not mean she was defeated.

Gently, Keane lifted her protesting hand, turning it palm up as he brought it to his lips. An involuntary breath rushed in and out of Jo's lungs. "Your hands are exquisite," he murmured, tracing the fine line of blue up the back. "Narrow-boned, long-fingered. And the palms show hard work. That makes them more interesting." He lifted his eyes from her hand to her face. "Like you."

Jo's voice had grown husky, but she could do nothing to alter it. "I don't know what I'm supposed to say when you tell me things like that." Beneath her robe her breasts rose and fell with her quickening heart. "I'd rather you didn't."

"Do you really?" Keane ran the back of his hand

along her jawline. "That's a pity, because the more I look at you, the more I find to say. You're a bewitching creature, Jovilette."

"I have to change," she said in the firmest voice she could muster. "You'll have to go."

"That's unfortunately true," he murmured, then cupped her chin. "Come, then, kiss me goodbye."

Jo stiffened. "I hardly think that's necessary…"

"You couldn't be more wrong," he told her as he lowered his mouth. "It's extremely necessary." In a light, teasing whisper, his lips met hers. His arms encircled her, bringing her closer with only the slightest pressure. "Kiss me back, Jo," he ordered softly. "Put your arms around me and kiss me back."

For a moment longer she resisted, but the lure of his mouth nibbling at hers was too strong. Letting instinct rule her will, Jo lifted her arms and circled his neck. Her mouth grew mobile under his, parting and offering. Her surrender seemed to lick the flames of his passion. The kiss grew urgent. His arms locked, crushing her against him. Her quiet moan was not of protest but of wonder. Her fingers found their way into his hair, tangling in its thickness as they urged him closer. She felt her robe loosen, then his hands trail up her rib cage. At his touch, she shivered, feeling her skin grow hot, then cold, then hot again in rapid succession.

When his hand took her breast, she shied, drawing in her breath quickly. "Steady," he murmured against her mouth. His hands stroked gently, coaxing her to relax again. He kissed the corners of her mouth, waiting until she quieted before he took her deep again. The thin leotard molded her body. It created no barrier against the warmth of his searching fingers. They moved slowly, lingering over the peak of her breast, exploring its softness, wandering to her waist, then tracing her hip and thigh.

No man had ever touched her so freely. Jo was helpless to stop him, helpless against her own growing need for him to touch her again. Was this the passion she had read of so often? The passion that drove men to war, to struggle against all reason, to risk everything? She felt she could understand it now. She clung to him as he taught her—as she learned—the demands of her own body. Her mouth grew hungrier for the taste of him. She was certain she remained in his arms while seasons flew by, while decades passed, while worlds were destroyed and built again.

But when he drew away, Jo saw the same sun spilling through her windows. Eternity had only been moments.

Unable to speak, she merely stared up at him. Her eyes were dark and aware, her cheeks flushed with desire. But somehow, though it still tingled from his, her mouth maintained a youthful innocence. Keane's eyes dropped to it as his hands loitered at the small of her back.

"It's difficult to believe I'm the first man to touch you," he murmured. His eyes roamed to hers. "And quite desperately arousing. Particularly when I find you've passion to match your looks. I think I'd like to make love with you in the daylight first so that I can watch that marvelous control of yours slip away layer by layer. We'll have to discuss it when I get back."

Jo forced strength back into her limbs, knowing she was on the brink of losing her will to him. "Just because I let you kiss me and touch me doesn't mean I'll let you make love to me." She lifted her chin, feeling her confidence surging back. "If I do, it'll be because it's what I want, not because you tell me to."

The expression in Keane's eyes altered. "Fair enough," he agreed and nodded. "It'll simply be my job to make it what you want." He took her chin in his hand and lowered his mouth to hers for a brief kiss. As she had the first time, Jo kept her eyes open and watched him. She felt him grin against her mouth before he raised his head. "You are the most fascinating woman I've ever met." Turning, he crossed to the door. "I'll be back," he said with a careless wave before it closed behind him. Dumbly, Jo stared into empty space.

Fascinating? she repeated, tracing her still-warm lips with her fingertips. Quickly, she ran to the window, and kneeling on the sofa below it, watched Keane stride away.

She realized with a sudden jolt that she missed him already.

Chapter 6

Jo learned that weeks could drag like years. During the second week of Keane's absence she had searched each new lot for a sign of him. She had scanned the crowds of towners who came to watch the raising of the Big Top, and as the days stretched on and on, she balanced between anger and despair at his continued absence. Only in the cage did she manage to isolate her concentration, knowing she could not afford to do otherwise. But after each performance Jo found it more and more difficult to relax. Each morning she felt certain he would be back. Each night she lay restless, waiting for the sun to rise.

Spring was in full bloom. The high grass lots smelled of it. Often there were wildflowers crushed underfoot, leaving their heavy fragrances in the air. Even as the circus caravan traveled north, the days grew warm, sunlight lingering further into evening. While other troupers enjoyed the balmy air and providentially sunny skies, Jo lived on nerves.

It occurred to her that after returning to his life in Chicago, Keane had decided against coming back. In Chicago he had comfort and wealth and elegant women. Why should he come back? Jo closed her mind against the ultimate fate of the circus, unwilling to face the possibility that Keane might close the show at the end of the season. She told herself the only reason she wanted him to come back was to convince him to keep the circus open. But the memory of being in his arms intruded too often into her thoughts. Gradually, she grew resigned, filling the strange void she felt with her work.

Several times each week she found time to give the eager Gerry more training. At first she had only permitted him to work with the two menagerie cubs, allowing him, with the protection of leather gloves, to play with them and to feed them. She encouraged him to teach them simple tricks with the aid of small pieces of raw meat. Jo was as pleased as he when the cats responded to his patience and obeyed.

Jo saw potential in Gerry, in his genuine affection for animals and in his determination. Her primary concern was that he had not yet developed a healthy fear. He was still too casual, and with casualness, Jo knew, came carelessness. When she thought he had progressed far enough, Jo decided to take him to the next step of his training.

There was no matinee that day, and the Big Top was scattered with rehearsing troupers. Jo was dressed in boots and khakis with a long-sleeved blouse tucked into the waist. She studied Gerry as she ran the stock of her whip through her hand. They stood together in the safety cage while she issued instructions.

"All right, Buck's going to let Merlin through the chute. He's the most tractable of the cats, except for Ari." She paused a moment while her eyes grew sad. "Ari isn't up to even a short practice session." She pushed away the depression that threatened and continued. "Merlin knows you, he's familiar with your voice and your scent." Gerry nodded and swallowed. "When we go in, you're to be my shadow. You move when I move, and don't speak until I tell you. If you get frightened, don't run." Jo took his arm for emphasis. "That's *important*, understand? Don't run. Tell me if you want out, and I'll get you to the safety cage."

"I won't run, Jo," he promised and wiped hands, damp with excitement, on his jeans.

"Are you ready?"

Gerry grinned and nodded. "Yeah."

Jo opened the door leading to the big cage and let Gerry through behind her before securing it. She walked to the center of the arena in easy, confident strides. "Let him in, Buck," she called and heard the immediate rattle of bars. Merlin entered without hurry, then leaped onto his pedestal. He yawned hugely before looking at Jo. "A solo today, Merlin," she said as she advanced toward him. "And you're the star. Stay with me," she ordered as Gerry merely stood still and stared at the big cat. Merlin gave Gerry a disinterested glance and waited.

With an upward move of her arm, she sent Merlin into a sit-up. "You know," she told the boy behind her, "that teaching a cat to take his seat is the first trick. The audience won't even consider it one. The sit-up," she

continued while signaling Merlin to bring his front paws
back down, "is usually next and takes quite a bit of time.
It's necessary to strengthen the cat's back muscles first."
Again she signaled Merlin to sit up, then, with a quick
command, she had him pawing the air and roaring.
"Marvelous old ham," she said with a grin and brought
him back down. "The primary move of each cue is always given from the same position with the same tone
of voice. It takes patience and repetition. I'm going to
bring him down off the pedestal now."

Jo flicked the whip against the tanbark, and Merlin
leaped down. "Now I maneuver him to the spot in the
arena where I want him to lie down." As she moved, Jo
made certain her student moved with her. "The cage is
a circle, forty feet in diameter. You have to know every
inch of it inside your head. You have to know precisely
how far you are from the bars at all times. If you back up
into the bars, you've got no room to maneuver if there's
trouble. It's one of the biggest mistakes a trainer can
make." At her signal Merlin laid down, then shifted to
his side. "Over, Merlin," she said briskly, sending him
into a series of rolls. "Use their names often—it keeps
them in tune with you. You have to know each cat and
their individual tendencies."

Jo moved with Merlin, then signaled him to stop.
When he roared, she rubbed the top of his head with
the stock of her whip. "They like to be petted just like
house cats, but they are not tabbies. It's essential that
you never give them your complete trust and that you
remember always to maintain your dominance. You
subjugate not by poking them or beating or shouting,
which is not only cruel but makes for a mean, unde-

pendable cat, but with patience, respect and will. Never humiliate them. They have a right to their pride. You bluff them, Gerry," she said as she raised both arms and brought Merlin up on his hind legs. "Man is the unknown factor. That's why we use jungle-bred rather than captivity-bred cats. Ari is the exception. A cat born and raised in captivity is too familiar with man, so you lose your edge." She moved forward, keeping her arms raised. Merlin followed, walking on his hind legs. He spread seven feet into the air and towered over his trainer. "They might have a sense of affection for you, but there's no fear and little respect. Unfortunately, this often happens if a cat's been with a trainer a long time. They don't become more docile the longer they're in an act, but they become more dangerous. They test you constantly. The trick is to make them believe you're indestructible."

She brought Merlin down, and he gave another yawn before she sent him back to his seat. "If one swipes at you, you have to stop it then and there, because they try again and again, getting closer each time. Usually, if a trainer's hurt in the cage, it's because he's made a mistake. The cats are quick to spot them. Sometimes they let them pass, sometimes they don't. This one's given me a good smack on the shoulder now and again. He's kept his claws retracted, but there's always the possibility that one time he'll forget he's just playing. Any questions?"

"Hundreds," Gerry answered, wiping his mouth with the back of his hand. "I just can't focus on one right now."

Jo chuckled and again scratched Merlin's head when he roared. "They'll come to you later. It's hard to absorb anything the first time, but it'll come back to you when you're relaxed again. All right, you know the cue. Make him sit up."

"Me?"

Jo stepped to the side, giving Merlin a clear view of her student. "You can be as scared as you like," she said easily. "Just don't let it show in your voice. Watch his eyes."

Gerry rubbed his palm on the thighs of his jeans, then lifted it as he had seen Jo do hundreds of times. "Up," he told the cat in a passably firm voice.

Merlin studied him a moment, then looked at Jo. This, his eyes told her clearly, was an amateur and beneath his notice. Carefully, Jo kept her face expressionless. "He's testing you," she told Gerry. "He's an old hand and a bit harder to bluff. Be firm and use his name this time."

Gerry took a deep breath and repeated the hand signal. "Up, Merlin."

Merlin glanced back at him, then stared with measuring, amber eyes. "Again," Jo instructed and heard Gerry swallow audibly. "Put some authority into your voice. He thinks you're a pushover."

"Up, Merlin!" Gerry repeated, annoyed enough by Jo's description to put some dominance into his voice. Though his reluctance was obvious, Merlin obeyed. "He did it," Gerry whispered on a long, shaky breath. "He really did it."

"Very good," Jo said, pleased with both the lion and her student. "Now bring him down." When this was accomplished, Jo had him bring Merlin from the seat. "Here." She handed Gerry the whip. "Use the stock to scratch his head. He likes it best just behind the ear."

She felt the faint tremble in his hand as he took the whip, but he held it steady, even as Merlin closed his eyes and roared.

Because he had performed well, Jo afforded Merlin the liberty of rubbing against her legs before she called for Buck to let him out. The rattle of the bars was the cat's cue to exit, and like a trouper, he took it with his head held high. "You did very well," she told Gerry when they were alone in the cage.

"It was great." He handed her back the whip, the stock damp from his sweaty palms. "It was just great. When can I do it again?"

Jo smiled and patted his shoulder. "Soon," she promised. "Just remember the things I've told you and come to me when you remember all those questions."

"Okay, thanks, Jo." He stepped through the safety cage. "Thanks a lot. I want to go tell the guys."

"Go ahead." Jo watched him scramble away, leaping over the ring and darting through the back door. With a grin, she leaned against the bars. "Was I like that?" she asked Buck, who stood at the opposite end of the cage.

"The first time you got a cat to sit up on your own, we heard about it for a week. Twelve years old and you thought you were ready for the big show."

Jo laughed, and wiping the damp stock of her whip against her pants, turned. It was then she saw him standing behind her. "Keane!" She used the name she had sworn not to use as pleasure flooded through her. It shone on her face. Just as she had given up hope of seeing him again, he was there. She took two steps toward him before she could check herself. "I didn't know you were back." Jo gripped the stock of the whip with both hands to prevent herself from reaching out to touch him.

"I believe you missed me." His voice was as she remembered, low and smooth.

Jo cursed herself for being so naive and transparent. "Perhaps I did, a little," she admitted cautiously. "I suppose I'd gotten used to you, and you were gone longer than you said you'd be." He looks the same, she thought rapidly, exactly the same. She reminded herself that it had only been a month. It had seemed like years.

"*Mmm*, yes. I had more to see to than I had expected. You look a bit pale," he observed and touched her cheek with his fingertip.

"I suppose I haven't been getting much sun," she said with quick prevarication. "How was Chicago?" Jo needed to turn the conversation away from personal lines until she had an opportunity to gauge her emotions; seeing him suddenly had tossed them into confusion.

"Cool," he told her, making a long, thorough survey of her face. "Have you ever been there?"

"No. We play near there toward the end of the season, but I've never had time to go all the way into the city."

Nodding absently, Keane glanced into the empty cage behind her. "I see you're training Gerry."

"Yes." Relieved that they had lapsed into a professional discussion, Jo let the muscles of her shoulders ease. "This was the first time with an adult cat and no bars between. He did very well."

Keane looked back at her. His eyes were serious and probing. "He was trembling. I could see it from where I stood watching you."

"It was his first time—" she began in Gerry's defense.

"I wasn't criticizing him," Keane interrupted with a tinge of impatience. "It's just that he stood beside you, shaking from head to foot, and you were totally cool and in complete control."

"It's my job to be in control," Jo reminded him.

"That lion must have stood seven feet tall when he went up on his hind legs, and you walked under him without any protection, not even the traditional chair."

"I do a picture act," she explained, "not a fighting act."

"Jo," he said so sharply she blinked. "Aren't you ever frightened in there?"

"Frightened?" she repeated, lifting a brow. "Of course I'm frightened. More frightened than Gerry was—or than you would be."

"What are you talking about?" Keane demanded. Jo noted with some curiosity that he was angry. "I could see that boy sweat in there."

"That was mostly excitement," Jo told him patiently. "He hasn't the experience to be truly frightened yet." She tossed back her hair and let out a long breath. Jo did not like to talk of her fears with anyone and found it especially difficult with Keane. Only because she felt it necessary that he understand this to understand the circus did she continue. "Real fear comes from knowing them, working with them, understanding them. You can only speculate on what they can do to a man. I *know*. I know exactly what they're capable of. They have an incredible courage, but more, they have an incredible guile. I've seen what they can do." Her eyes were calm and clear as they looked into his. "My father almost lost a leg once. I was about five, but I remember it perfectly. He made a mistake, and a five-hundred-pound Nubian sunk into his thigh and dragged him around the arena. Luckily, the cat was diverted by a female in season. Cats are unpredictable when they have sex on their minds, which is probably one of the reasons he attacked my father in the first place. They're fiercely jealous once they've set their minds on a mate. My father was able to get into the safety cage before any of the other cats took an interest in him. I can't remember how many stitches he had or how long it was before he could walk properly again, but I do remember the look in that cat's eyes. You learn quickly about fear when you're in the cage, but you control it, you channel it or you find another line of work."

"Then why?" Keane demanded. He took her shoulders before she could turn away. "Why do you do it? And don't tell me because it's your job. That's not good enough."

It puzzled Jo why he seemed angry. His eyes were darkened with temper, and his fingers dug into her shoulders. As if wanting to draw out her answer, he gave her one quick shake. "All right," Jo said slowly, ignoring the ache in her flesh. "That is part of it, but not all. It's all I've ever known, that's part of it, too. It's what I'm good at." While she spoke, she searched his face for a clue to his mood. She wondered if perhaps he had felt it wrong of her to take Gerry into the cage. "Gerry's going to be good at it, too," she told him. "I imagine everyone needs to be good—really good—at something. And I enjoy giving the people who come to see me the best show I can. But over all, I suppose it's because I love them. It's difficult for a layman to understand a trainer's feeling for his animals. I love their intelligence, their really awesome beauty, their strength, the unquenchable streak of wildness that separates them from well-trained horses. They're exciting, challenging and terrifying."

Keane was silent for a moment. She saw that his eyes were still angry, but his fingers relaxed on her shoulders. Jo felt a light throbbing where bruises would certainly show in the morning. "I suppose excitement becomes addicting—difficult to live without once it's become a habit."

"I don't know," Jo replied, grateful that his temper was apparently cooling. "I've never thought about it."

"No, I suppose you'd have little reason to." With a nod, he turned to walk away.

Jo took a step after him. "Keane." His name raced through her lips before she could prevent it. When he turned back to her, she realized she could not ask any of the dozens of questions that flew through her mind. There was only one she felt she had any right to ask. "Have you thought any more about what you're going to do with us…with the circus?"

For an instant she saw temper flare again into his eyes. "No." The word was curt and final. As he turned his back on her again, she felt a spurt of anger and reached for his arm.

"How can you be so callous, so unfeeling?" she demanded. "How is it possible to be so casual when you hold the lives of over a hundred people in your hands?"

Carefully, he removed her hand from his arm. "Don't

push me, Jo." There was warning in his eyes and in his voice.

"I'm not trying to," she returned, then ran a frustrated hand through her hair. "I'm only asking you to be fair, to be…kind," she finished lamely.

"Don't ask me anything," he ordered in a brisk, authoritative tone. Jo's chin rose in response. "I'm here," he reminded her. "You'll have to be satisfied with that for now."

Jo battled with her temper. She could not deny that in coming back he had proved himself true to his word. She had the rest of the season if nothing else. "I don't suppose I have any choice," she said quietly.

"No," he agreed with a faint nod. "You don't."

Frowning, Jo watched him stride away in a smooth, fluid gait she was forced to admire. She noticed for the first time that her palms were as damp as Gerry's had been. Annoyed, she rubbed them over her hips.

"Want to talk about it?"

Jo turned quickly to find Jamie behind her in full clown gear. She knew her preoccupation had been deep for her to be caught so completely unaware. "Oh, Jamie, I didn't see you."

"You haven't seen anything but Prescott since you stepped out of the cage," Jamie pointed out.

"What are you doing in makeup?" she asked, skirting his comment.

He gestured toward the dog at her feet. "This mutt won't respond to me unless I'm in my face. Do you want to talk about it?"

"Talk about what?"

"About Prescott, about the way you feel about him."

The dog sat patiently at Jamie's heels and thumped his tail. Casually, Jo stopped and ruffled his gray fur.

"I don't know what you're talking about."

"Look, I'm not saying it can't work out, but I don't want to see you get hurt. I know how it is to be nuts about somebody."

"What in the world makes you think I'm nuts about Keane Prescott?" Jo gave the dog her full attention.

"Hey, it's me, remember?" Jamie took her arm and pulled her to her feet. "Not everybody would've noticed, maybe, but not everybody knows you the way I do. You've been miserable since he went back to Chicago, looking for him in every car that drove on the lot. And just now, when you saw him, you lit up like the midway on Saturday night. I'm not saying there's anything wrong with you being in love with him, but—"

"In love with him?" Jo repeated, incredulous.

"Yeah." Jamie spoke patiently. "In love with him."

Jo stared at Jamie as the realization slid over her. "In love with him," she murmured, trying out the words. "Oh, no." She sighed, closing her eyes. "Oh, no."

"Didn't you have enough sense to figure it out for yourself?" Jamie said gently. Seeing Jo's distress, he ran a hand gently up her arm.

"No, I guess I'm pretty stupid about this sort of thing." Jo opened her eyes and looked around, wondering if the world should look any different. "What am I going to do?"

"Heck, I don't know." Jamie kicked sawdust with an oversize shoe. "I'm not exactly getting rave notices myself in that department." He gave Jo a reassuring pat. "I just wanted you to know that you always have a sympathetic ear here." He grinned engagingly before he turned to walk away, leaving Jo distracted and confused.

Jo spent the rest of the afternoon absorbed with the idea of being in love with Keane Prescott. For a short time she allowed herself to enjoy the sensation, the novel experience of loving someone not as a friend but as a lover. She could feel the light and the power spread through her, as if she had caught the sun in her hand. She daydreamed.

Keane was in love with her. He'd told her hundreds of times as he'd held her under a moonlit sky. He wanted to marry her, he couldn't bear to live without her. She was suddenly sophisticated and worldly enough to deal with the country club set on their own ground. She could exchange droll stories with the wives of other attorneys. There would be children and a house in the country. How would it feel to wake up in the same town every morning? She would learn to cook and give dinner parties. There would be long, quiet evenings when they would be alone together. There would be candlelight and music. When they slept together, his arms would stay around her until morning.

Idiot. Jo dragged herself back sternly. As she and Pete fed the cats, she tried to remember that fairy tales were for children. None of those things are ever going to happen, she reminded herself. I have to figure out how to handle this before I get in any deeper.

"Pete," she began, keeping her voice conversational as she put Abra's quota of raw meat on a long stick. "Have you ever been in love?"

Pete chewed his gum gently, watching Jo hoist the

meat through the bars. "Well, now, let's see." Thrusting out his lower lip, he considered. "Only 'bout eight or ten times, I guess. Maybe twelve."

Jo laughed, moving down to the next cage. "I'm serious," she told him. "I mean *really* in love."

"I fall in love easy," Pete confessed gravely. "I'm a pushover for a pretty face. Matter of fact, I'm a pushover for an ugly face." He grinned. "Yes, sir, the only thing like being in love is drawing an ace-high flush when the pot's ripe."

Jo shook her head and continued down the line. "Okay, since you're such an expert, tell me what you do when you're in love with a person and the person doesn't love you back and you don't want that person to know that you're in love because you don't want to make a fool of yourself."

"Just a minute." Pete squeezed his eyes tight. "I got to think this one through first." For a moment he was silent as his lips moved with his thoughts. "Okay, let's see if I've got this straight." Opening his eyes, he frowned in concentration. "You're in love—"

"I didn't say *I* was in love," Jo interrupted hastily.

Pete lifted his brows and pursed his lips. "Let's just use *you* in the general sense to avoid confusion," he suggested. Jo nodded, pretending to absorb herself with the feeding of the cats. "So, you're in love, but the guy doesn't love you. First off, you've got to be sure he doesn't."

"He doesn't," Jo murmured, then added quickly, "Let's say he doesn't."

Pete shot her a look out of the corner of his eye, then

shifted his gum to the other side of his mouth. "Okay, then the first thing you should do is change his mind."

"Change his mind?" Jo repeated, frowning at him.

"Sure." Pete gestured with his hand to show the simplicity of the procedure. "You fall in love with him, then he falls in love with you. You play hard to get, or you play easy to get. Or you play flutter and smile." He demonstrated by coyly batting his lashes and giving a winsome smile. Jo giggled and leaned on the feeding pole. Pete in fielder's cap, white T-shirt and faded jeans was the best show she'd seen all day. "You make him jealous," he continued. "Or you flatter his ego. Girl, there're so many ways to get a man, I can't count them, and I've been gotten by them all. Yes, sir, I'm a real pushover." He looked so pleased with his weakness, Jo smiled. *How easy it would be*, she thought, *if I could take love so lightly.*

"Suppose I don't want to do any of those things. Suppose I don't really know how and I don't want to humiliate myself by making a mess of it. Suppose the person isn't—well, suppose nothing could ever work between us, anyway. What then?"

"You got too many supposes," Pete concluded, then shook his finger at her. "And I got one for you. Suppose you ain't too smart because you figure you can't win even before you play."

"Sometimes people get hurt when they play," Jo countered quietly. "Especially if they aren't familiar with the game."

"Hurting's nothing," Pete stated with a sweep of his hand. "Winning's the best, but playing's just fine. This whole big life, it's a game, Jo. You know that.

And the rules keep changing all the time. You've got nerve," he continued, then laid his rough, brown hand on her shoulder. "More raw nerve than most anybody I've ever known. You've got brains, too, hungry brains. You going to tell me that with all that, you're afraid to take a chance?"

Meeting his eyes, Jo knew hypothetical evasions would not do. "I suppose I only take calculated risks, Pete. I know my turf, I know my moves. And I know exactly what'll happen if I make a mistake. I take a chance that my body might be clawed, not my emotions. I've never rehearsed for anything like this, and I think playing it cold would be suicide."

"I think you've got to believe in Jo Wilder a little more," Pete countered, then gave her cheek a quick pat.

"Hey, Jo." Looking over, Jo saw Rose approaching. She wore straight-leg jeans, a white peasant blouse and a six-foot boa constrictor over her shoulders.

"Hello, Rose." Jo handed Pete the feeding pole. "Taking Baby out for a walk?"

"He needed some air." Rose gave her charge a pat. "I think he got a little carsick this morning. Does he look peaked to you?"

Jo looked down at the shiny, multicolored skin, then studied the tiny black eyes as Rose held Baby's head up for inspection. "I don't think so," she decided.

"Well, it's a warm day," Rose observed, releasing Baby's head. "I'll give him a bath. That might perk him up."

Jo noticed Rose's eyes darting around the compound. "Looking for Jamie?"

"Hmph." Rose tossed her black curls. "I'm not wast-

ing my time on that one." She stroked the latter half of Baby's anatomy. "I'm indifferent."

"That's another way to do it," Pete put in, giving Jo a nudge. "I forgot about that one. It's a zinger."

Rose frowned at Pete, then at Jo. "What's he talking about?"

With a laugh, Jo sat down on a water barrel. "Catching a man," she told her, letting the warm sun play on her face. "Pete's done a study on it from the male point of view."

"Oh." Rose threw Pete her most disdainful look. "You think I'm indifferent so he'll get interested?"

"It's a zinger," Pete repeated, adjusting his cap. "You get him confused so he starts thinking about you. You make him crazy wondering why you don't notice him."

Rose considered the idea. "Does it usually work?"

"It's got an eighty-seven percent success average," Pete assured her, then gave Baby a friendly pat. "It even works with cats." He jerked his thumb behind him and winked at Jo. "The pretty lady cat, she sits there and stares off into space like she's got important things occupying her mind. The boy in the next cage is doing everything but standing on his head to get her attention. She just gives herself a wash, pretending she doesn't even know he's there. Then, maybe after she's got him banging his head against the bars, she looks over, blinks her big yellow eyes and says, 'Oh, were you talking to me?'" Pete laughed and stretched his back muscles. "He's hooked then, brother, just like a fish on a line."

Rose smiled at the image of Jamie dangling from her own personal line. "Maybe I won't put Baby in Carmen's trailer after all," she murmured. "Oh, look, here comes Duffy and the owner." An inherent flirt, Rose instinctively fluffed her hair. "Really, he is the most handsome man. Don't you think so, Jo?"

Jo's eyes had already locked on Keane's. She seemed helpless to release herself from the gaze. Gripping the edge of the water barrel tightly, she reminded herself not to be a fool. "Yes," she agreed with studied casualness. "He's very attractive."

"Your knuckles are turning white, Jo," Pete muttered next to her ear.

Letting out a frustrated breath, Jo relaxed her hands. Straightening her spine, she determined to show more restraint. Control, she reminded herself, was the basic tool of her trade. If she could train her emotions and outbluff a dozen lions, she could certainly outbluff one man.

"Hello, Duffy." Rose gave the portly man a quick smile, then turned her attention to Keane. "Hello, Mr. Prescott. It's nice to have you back."

"Hello, Rose." He smiled into her upturned face, then lifted a brow as his eyes slid over the reptile around her neck and shoulders. "Who's your friend?"

"Oh, this is Baby." She patted one of the tan-colored saddle marks on Baby's back.

"Of course." Jo noticed how humor enhanced the gold of his eyes. "Hello, Pete." He gave the handler an easy nod before his gaze shifted and then lingered on Jo.

As on the first day they had met, Keane did not bother to camouflage his stare. His look was cool and assessing. He was reaffirming ownership. It shot through Jo that yes, she was in love with him, but she was also afraid of him. She feared his power over her, feared his capacity to hurt her. Still, her face registered none of her thoughts. Fear, she reminded herself as her eyes remained equally cool on his, was something she understood. Love might cause impossible problems, but fear could be dealt with. She would not cower from him, and she would honor the foremost rule of the arena. She would not turn and run.

Silently, they watched each other while the others looked on with varying degrees of curiosity. There was the barest touch of a smile on Keane's lips. The battle of wills continued until Duffy cleared his throat.

"Ah, Jo."

Calmly, without hurry, she shifted her attention. "Yes, Duffy?"

"I just sent one of the web girls into town to see the local dentist. Seems she's got an abscess. I need you to fill in tonight."

"Sure."

"Just for the web and the opening spectacular," he continued. Unable to prevent himself, he cast a quick look at Keane to see if he was still staring at her. He was. Duffy shifted uncomfortably and wondered what the devil was going on. "Take your usual place in the finale. We'll just be one girl shy in the chorus. Wardrobe'll fix you up."

"Okay." Jo smiled at him, though she was very much aware of Keane's eyes on her. "I guess I'd better go practice walking in those three-inch heels. What position do I take?"

"Number four rope."

"Duffy," Rose chimed in and tugged on his sleeve. "When are you going to let me do the web?"

"Rose, how's a pint-sizer like you going to stand up with that heavy costume on?" Duffy shook his head at her, keeping a respectable distance from Baby. After thirty-five years of working carnies, sideshows and circuses, he still was uneasy around snakes.

"I'm pretty strong," Rose claimed, stretching her spine in the hope of looking taller. "And I've been practicing." Anxious to demonstrate her accomplishments, Rose deftly unwound Baby. "Hold him a minute," she requested and dumped several feet of snake into Keane's arms.

"Ah…" Keane shifted the weight in his arms and looked dubiously into Baby's bored eyes. "I hope he's eaten recently."

"He had a nice breakfast," Rose assured him, going into a fluid backbend to show Duffy her flexibility.

"Baby won't eat owners," Jo told Keane. She did not bother to suppress her grin. It was the first time she had seen him disconcerted. "Just a stray towner, occasionally. Rose keeps him on a strict diet."

"I assume," Keane began as Baby slithered into a more comfortable position, "that he's aware I'm the owner."

Grinning at Keane's uncomfortable expression, Jo turned to Pete. "Gee, I don't know. Did anybody tell Baby about the new owner?"

"Haven't had a chance, myself," Pete drawled, taking out a fresh stick of gum. "Looks a lot like a towner, too. Baby might get confused."

"They're just teasing you, Mr. Prescott," Rose told him as she finished her impromptu audition with a full split. "Baby doesn't eat people at all. He's docile as a lamb. Little kids come up and pet him during a demonstration." She rose and brushed off her jeans. "Now, you take a cobra…"

"No, thank you," Keane declined, unloading the six-foot Baby back into Rose's arms.

Rose slipped the boa back around her neck. "Well, Duffy, I'm off. What do you say?"

"Get one of the girls to teach you the routine," he said with a nod. "Then we'll see." Smiling, he watched Rose saunter away.

"Hey, Duffy!" It was Jamie. "There's a couple of towners looking for you. I sent them over to the red wagon."

"Fine. I'll just go right on along with you." Duffy winked at Jo before turning to catch up with Jamie's long stride.

Keane was standing very close to the barrels. Jo knew getting down from her perch was risky. She knew, too, however, that her pulse was beginning to behave erratically despite her efforts to control it. "I've got to see about my costume." Nimbly, she came down, intending to skirt around him. Even as her boots touched the ground, his hands took her waist. Exercising every atom of willpower, she neither jerked nor struggled but lifted her eyes calmly to his.

His thumbs moved in a lazy arch. She could feel the warmth through the fabric of her blouse. With her entire being she wished he would not hold her. Then, perversely, she wished he would hold her closer. She struggled not to weaken as her lips grew warm under the kiss of his eyes. Her heart began to hammer in her ears.

Keane ran a hand down the length of her long, thick braid. Slowly, his eyes drifted back to hers. Abruptly, he released her and backed up to let her pass. "You'd best go have wardrobe take a few tucks in that costume."

Deciding she was not meant to decipher his changing moods, Jo stepped by him and crossed the compound. If she spent enough time working, she could keep her thoughts from dwelling on Keane Prescott. Maybe.

Chapter 7

The Big Top was packed for the evening show. Jo watched the anticipation in the range of faces as she took her temporary position in the opening spectacular. The band played jumpy, upbeat music, leaning heavily on brass as the theme parade marched around the hippodrome track. As the substitute Bo Peep, Jo wore a demure mobcap and a wide crinoline skirt and led a baby lamb on a leash. Because her act came so swiftly on the tail of the opening, she rarely participated in the spectacular. Now she enjoyed a close-up look at the audience. In the cage, she blocked them out almost completely.

They were, she decided, a well-mixed group: young babies, older children, parents, grandparents, teenagers. They gave the pageant enthusiastic applause. Jo smiled and waved as she performed the basic choreography with hardly a thought.

After a quick costume change, she took her cue as Queen of the Jungle Cats. After that followed another costume change that transformed her into one of the Twelve Spinning Butterflies.

"Just heard," Jamie whispered in her ear as she took the customary pose by the rope. "You got the job for the next week. Barbara won't be able to handle the teeth grip."

Jo shifted her shoulders to compensate for the weight of her enormous blue wings. "Rose is going to learn the routine," she mumbled back, smiling in the flood of the sunlight. "Duffy's giving her the job if she can stand up under this blasted costume." She made a quick, annoyed sound and smiled brightly. "It weighs a ton."

Slowly, to the beat of the waltz the band played, Jo climbed hand over hand up the rope. "Ah, showbiz," she heard Jamie sigh. She vowed to poke him in the ribs when she took her bow. Then, hooking her foot in the hoop, she began the routine, imitating the other eleven Spinning Butterflies.

She was able to share a cup of coffee with Rose's mother when she returned the butterfly costume to wardrobe and changed into her own white and gold jumpsuit. Her muscles complained a bit due to the unfamiliar weight of the wings, and she gave a passing thought to a long, luxurious bath. That was a dream for September, she reminded herself. Showers were the order of the day on the road.

Jo's last duty in the show was to stand on the head of Maggie, the key elephant in the finale's long mount.

Sturdy and dependable, Maggie stood firm while four elephants on each side of her rose on their hind legs, resting their front legs on the back of the one in front. Atop Maggie's broad head, Jo stood glittering under the lights with both arms lifted in the air. It was here, more than any other part of the show, that the applause washed over her. It merged with the music, the ringmaster's whistle, the laughter of children. Where she had been weary, she was now filled with energy. She knew the fatigue would return, so she relished the power of the moment all the more. For those few seconds there was no work, no long hours, no predawn drives. There was only magic. Even when it was over and she slid from Maggie's back, she could still feel it.

Outside the tent, troupers and roustabouts and shandies mingled. There were anecdotes to exchange, performances to dissect, observations to be made. Gradually, they drifted away alone, in pairs or in groups. Some would change and help strike the tents, some would sleep, some would worry over their performances. Too energized to sleep, Jo planned to assist in the striking of the Big Top.

She switched on a low light as she entered her trailer, then absently braided her hair as she moved to the tiny bath. With quick moves she creamed off her stage makeup. The exotic exaggeration of her eyes was whisked away, leaving the thick fringe of her lashes and the dark green of her irises unenhanced. The soft bloom of natural rose tinted her cheeks again, and her mouth, unpainted, appeared oddly vulnerable. Accustomed to the change, Jo did not see the sharp contrast between Jovilette the performer and the small, somewhat fragile woman in the glittering jumpsuit. With her face naked and the simple braid hanging down her back, the look of the wild, of the gypsy, was less apparent. It remained in her movements, but her face rinsed of all artifice and unframed, was both delicate and young, part ingenue, part flare. But Jo saw none of this as she reached for her front zipper. Before she could pull it down, a knock sounded on her door.

"Come in," she called out and flicked her braid behind her back as she started down the aisle. She stopped in her tracks as Keane stepped through the door.

"Didn't anyone ever tell you to ask who it is first?" He shut the door behind him and locked it with a careless flick of his wrist. "You might not have to lock your door against the circus people," he continued blandly as she remained still, "but there are several dozen curious towners still hanging around."

"I can handle a curious towner," Jo replied. The offhand quality of his dominance was infuriating. "I never lock my door."

There was stiffness and annoyance in her voice. Keane ignored them both. "I brought you something from Chicago."

The casual statement succeeded in throwing Jo's temper off the mark. For the first time, she noticed the small package he carried. "What is it?" she asked.

Keane smiled and crossed to her. "It's nothing that bites," he assured her, then held it out.

Still cautious, Jo lifted her eyes to his, then dropped her gaze back to the package. "It's not my birthday," she murmured.

"It's not Christmas, either," Keane pointed out.

The easy patience in the tone caused Jo to lift her eyes again. She wondered how it was he understood her hesitation to accept presents. She kept her gazed locked on his. "Thank you," she said solemnly as she took the gift.

"You're welcome," Keane returned in the same tone.

The amenities done, Jo recklessly ripped the paper. "Oh! It's Dante," she exclaimed, tearing off the remaining paper and tossing it on the table. With reverence she ran her palm over the dark leather binding. The rich scent drifted to her. She knew her quota of books would have been limited to one a year had she bought a volume so handsomely bound. She opened it slowly, as if to prolong the pleasure. The pages were heavy and rich cream in color. The text was Italian, and even as she glanced over the first page, the words ran fluidly through her mind.

"It's beautiful," she murmured, overcome. Lifting her eyes to thank him again, Jo found Keane smiling down at her. Shyness enveloped her suddenly, all the more intense because she had so rarely experienced it. A lifetime in front of crowds had given her a natural confidence in almost any situation. Now color began to surge into her cheeks, and her mind was a jumble of words that would not come to order.

"I'm glad you like it." He ran a finger down her cheek. "Do you always blush when someone gives you a present?"

Because she was at a loss as to how to answer his question, Jo maneuvered around it. "It was nice of you to think of me."

"It seems to come naturally," Keane replied, then watched Jo's lashes flutter down.

"I don't know what to say." She was able to meet his eyes again with her usual directness, but he had again touched her emotions. She felt inadequate to deal with her feelings or with his effect on her.

"You've already said it." He took the book from Jo's hand and paged through it. "Of course, I can't read a word of it. I envy you that." Before Jo could ponder the idea of a man like Keane Prescott envying her anything, he looked back up and smiled. Her thoughts scattered like nervous ants. "Got any coffee?" he asked and set the book back down on the table.

"Coffee?"

"Yes, you know, coffee. They grow it in quantity in Brazil."

Jo gave him a despairing look. "I don't have any made. I'd fix you a cup, but I've got to change before I help strike the tents. The cookhouse will still be serving."

Keane lifted a brow as he let his eyes wander over her face. "Don't you think that between Bo Peep, lions and butterflies, you've done enough work tonight? By the way, you make a very appealing butterfly."

"Thank you, but—"

"Let's put it this way," Keane countered smoothly. He took the tip of her braid in his fingers. "You've got the night off. I'll make the coffee myself if you show me where you keep it."

Though she let out a windy sigh, Jo was more amused than annoyed. Coffee, she decided, was the least she could do after he had brought her such a lovely present. "I'll make it," she told him, "but you'll probably wish you'd gone to the cookhouse." With this dubious invitation, Jo turned and headed toward the kitchen. He made no sound, but she knew he followed her. For the first time, she felt the smallness of her kitchen.

Setting an undersized copper kettle on one of the two burners, Jo flicked on the power. It was a simple matter to keep her back to him while she plucked cups from the cupboard. She was well aware that if she turned around in the compact kitchen, she would all but be in his arms.

"Did you watch the whole show?" she asked conversationally as she pulled out a jar of instant coffee.

"Duffy had me working props," Keane answered. "He seems to be making me generally useful."

Amused, Jo twisted her head to grin at him. Instantly, she discovered her misstep in strategy. Keane's face was only inches from hers, and in his eyes she read his thoughts. He wanted her, and he intended to have her. Before she could shift her position, Keane took her shoulders and turned her completely around. Jo knew she had backed up against the bars.

Leisurely, he began to loosen her hair, working his fingers through it until it pooled over her shoulders. "I've wanted to do that since the first time I saw you. It's hair to get lost in." His voice was soft as he took a generous handful. The gesture itself seemed to stake his claim. "In the sun it shimmers with red lights, but in the dark it's like night itself." It came to her that each time she was close to him, she was less able to resist him. She became more lost in his eyes, more beguiled by his power. Already her mouth tingled with the memory of his kiss, with the longing for a new one. Behind them the kettle began a feverish whistle.

"The water," she managed and tried to move around him. With one hand in her hair, Keane kept her still as he turned off the burner. The whistle sputtered peevishly, then died. The sound echoed in Jo's head.

"Do you want coffee?" he murmured as his fingers trailed to her throat.

Jo's eyes clung to his. Hers were enormous and direct, his quiet and searching. "No," she whispered, knowing she wanted nothing more at that moment than to belong to him. He circled her throat with his hand and pressed his fingers against her pulse. It fluttered wildly.

"You're trembling." He could feel the light tremor of her body as he brought her closer. "Is it fear?" he demanded as his thumbs brushed over her lips. "Or excitement?"

"Both," she answered in a voice thickened with emotion. She made a tiny, confused sound as his palm covered her heart. Its desperate thudding increased. "Are you…" She stopped a moment because her voice was breathless and unsteady. "Are you going to make love to me?" *Did his eyes really darken?* she wondered dizzily. *Or is it my imagination?*

"Beautiful Jovilette," he murmured as his mouth lowered to hers. "No pretentions, no evasions…irresistible." The quality of the kiss altered swiftly. His mouth was hungry on hers, and her response leaped past all caution. If loving him was madness, her heart reasoned, could making love take her further beyond sanity? Past wisdom and steeped in sensation, she let her heart rule her will. When her lips parted under his, it was not in surrender but in equal demand.

Keane gentled the kiss. He kept her shimmering on the razor's edge of passion. His mouth teased, promised, then fed her growing need. He found the zipper at the base of her throat and pulled it downward slowly. Her skin was warm, and he sought it, giving a low sound of pleasure as her breast swelled under his hand. He explored without hurry, as if memorizing each curve and plane. Jo no longer trembled but became pliant as her body moved to the rhythm he set. Her sigh was spontaneous, filled with wonder and delight.

With a suddenness that took her breath away, Keane crushed her mouth beneath his in fiery urgency. Jo's instincts responded, thrusting her into a world she had only imagined. His hands grew rougher, more insistent. Jo realized he had relinquished control. They were both riding on the tossing waves of passion. This sea had no horizon and no depth. It was a drowning sea that pulled the unsuspecting under while promising limitless pleasure. Jo did not resist but dived deeper.

At first she thought the knocking was only the sound of her heart against her ribs. When Keane drew away, she murmured in protest and pulled him back. Instantly, his mouth was avid, but as the knocking continued, he swore and pulled back again.

"Someone's persistent," he muttered. Bewildered, Jo stared up at him. "The door," he explained on a long breath.

"Oh." Flustered, Jo ran a hand through her hair and tried to collect her wits.

"You'd better answer it," Keane suggested as he

pulled the zipper to her throat in one quick move. Jo broke the surface into reality abruptly. For a moment Keane watched her, taking in her flushed cheeks and tousled hair before he moved aside. Willing her legs to carry her, Jo walked to the front of the trailer. The door handle resisted, then she remembered that Keane had locked it, and she turned the latch.

"Yes, Buck?" she said calmly enough when she opened the door to her handler.

"Jo." His face was in shadows, but she heard the distress in the single syllable. Her chest tightened. "It's Ari."

He had barely finished the name before Jo was out of the trailer and running across the compound. She found both Pete and Gerry standing near Ari's cage.

"How bad?" she demanded as Pete came to meet her.

He took her shoulders. "Really bad this time, Jo."

For a moment she wanted to shake her head, to deny what she read in Pete's eyes. Instead, she nudged him aside and walked to Ari's cage. The old cat lay on his side as his chest lifted and fell with the effort of breathing. "Open it," she ordered Pete in a voice that revealed nothing. There was the jingle of keys, but she did not turn.

"You're not going in there." Jo heard Keane's voice and felt a restraining grip on her shoulders. Her eyes were opaque as she looked up at him.

"Yes, I am. Ari isn't going to hurt me or anyone else. He's just going to die. Now, leave me alone." Her voice was low and toneless. "Open it," she ordered again, then pulled out of Keane's loosened hold. The bars rattled as he slid the door open. Hearing it, Jo turned, then hoisted herself into the cage.

Ari barely stirred. Jo saw, as she knelt beside him, that his eyes were open. They were glazed with weariness and pain. "Ari." She sighed, seeing there would be no tomorrow for him. His only answer was a hollow wheezing. Putting a hand to his side, she felt the ragged pace of his breathing. He made an effort to respond to her touch, to his name, but managed only to shift his great head on the floor. The gesture tore at Jo's heart. She lowered her face to his mane, remembering him as he had once been: full of strength and a terrifying beauty. She lifted her face again and took one long, steadying breath. "Buck." She heard him approach but kept her eyes on Ari. "Get the medical kit. I want a hypo of pentobarbital." She could feel Buck's brief hesitation before he spoke.

"Okay, Jo."

She sat quietly, stroking Ari's head. In the distance were the sounds of the Big Top going down, the call of men, the rattle of rigging, the clang of wood against metal. An elephant trumpeted, and three cages down, Faust roared half-heartedly in response.

"Jo." She turned her head as Buck called her and pushed her hair from her eyes. "Let me do it."

Jo merely shook her head and held out her hand.

"Jo." Keane stepped up to the bars. His voice was gentle, but his eyes were so like the cat's at her knees, Jo nearly sobbed aloud. "You don't have to do this yourself."

"He's my cat," she responded dully. "I said I'd do it when it was time. It's time." Her eyes shifted to Buck. "Give me the hypo, Buck. Let's get it done." When the syringe was in her hand, Jo stared at it, then closed her fingers around it. Swallowing hard, she turned back to

Ari. His eyes were on her face. After more than twenty years in captivity there was still something not quite tamed in the dying cat. But she saw trust in his eyes and wanted to weep. "You were the best," she told him as she passed a hand through his mane. "You were always the best." Jo felt a numbing cold settling over her and prayed it would last until she had finished. "You're tired now. I'm going to help you sleep." She pulled the safety from the point of the hypodermic and waited until she was certain her hands were steady. "This won't hurt, nothing is going to hurt you anymore."

Involuntarily, Jo rubbed the back of her hand over her mouth, then, moving quickly, she plunged the needle into Ari's shoulder. A quiet whimper escaped her as she emptied the syringe. Ari made no sound but continued to watch her face. Jo offered no words of comfort but sat with him, methodically stroking his fur as his eyes grew cloudy. Gradually, the effort of his breathing lessened, becoming quieter and quieter until it wasn't there at all. Jo felt him grow still, and her hand balled into a fist inside the mass of his mane. One quick, convulsive shudder escaped her. Steeling herself, she moved from the cage, closing the door behind her. Because her bones felt fragile, she kept them stiff, as though they might shatter. Even as she stepped back to the ground, Keane took her arm and began to lead her away.

"Take care of things," he said to Buck as they moved past.

"No." Jo protested, trying and failing to free her arm. "I'll do it."

"No, you won't." Keane's tone held a quiet finality. "Enough's enough."

"Don't tell me what to do," she said sharply, letting her grief take refuge in anger.

"I *am* telling you," he pointed out. His hand was firm on her arm.

"You *can't* tell me what to do," she insisted as tears rose treacherously in her throat. "I want you to leave me alone."

Keane stopped, then took her by the shoulders. His eyes caught the light of a waning moon. "There's no way I'm going to leave you alone when you're so upset."

"My emotions have nothing to do with you." Even as she spoke, he took her arm again and pulled her toward her trailer. Jo wanted desperately to be alone to weep out her grief in private. The mourning belonged to her, and the tears were personal. As if her protests were nonexistent, he pulled her into the trailer and closed the door behind them. "Will you get out of here?" she demanded, frantically swallowing tears.

"Not until I know you're all right." Keane's answer was calm as he walked back to the kitchen.

"I'm perfectly all right." Her breath shuddered in and out quickly. "Or I will be when you leave me alone. You have no right to poke your nose in my business."

"So you've told me before," Keane answered mildly from the back of the trailer.

"I just did what had to be done." She held her body rigid and fought against her own quick, uneven breathing. "I put a sick animal out of his misery. It's as simple as that." Her voice broke, and she turned away, hugging her arms. "For heaven's sake, Keane, go away!"

Quietly, he walked back to her carrying a glass of water. "Drink this."

"No." She whirled back to him. Tears spilled out of her eyes and trickled down her cheeks despite her efforts to banish them. Hating herself, she pressed the heel of her hand between her brows and closed her eyes. "I don't want you here." Keane set down the glass, then gathered her into his arms. "No, don't. I don't want you to hold me."

"Too bad." He ran a hand gently up and down her back. "You did a very brave thing, Jo. I know you loved Ari. I know how hard it was to let him go. You're hurting, and I'm not leaving you."

"I don't want to cry in front of you." Her fists were tight balls at his shoulders.

"Why not?" The stroking continued up and down her back as he cradled her head in the curve of his shoulder.

"Why won't you let me be?" she sobbed as her control slipped. Her fingers gripped his shirt convulsively. "Why am I always losing what I love?" She let the grief come. She let his arms soothe her. As desperately as she had protested against it, she clung to his offer of comfort.

She made no objection as he carried her to the couch and cradled her in his arms. He stroked her hair, as she had stroked Ari, to ease the pain of what couldn't be changed. Slowly, her sobbing quieted. Still she lay with her cheek against his chest, with her hair curtaining her face.

"Better?" he asked as the silence grew calmer. Jo nodded, not yet trusting her voice. Keane shifted her as he reached for the glass of water. "Drink this now."

Gratefully, Jo relieved her dry throat, then went without resistance back against his chest. She closed her eyes, thinking it had been a very long time since she had been held in anyone's lap and soothed. "Keane," she murmured. She felt his lips brush over the top of her head.

"Hmm?"

"Nothing." Her voice thickened as she drifted toward sleep. "Just Keane."

Chapter 8

Jo felt the sun on her closed lids. There was the summer-morning sound of excited birds. Her mind, levitating slowly toward the surface, told her it must be Monday. Only on Monday would she sleep past sunrise. That was the enroute day, the only day in seven the circus held no show. She thought lazily of getting up. She would set aside two hours for reading. *Maybe I'll drive into town and see a movie. What town are we in?* With a sleepy sigh she rolled onto her stomach.

I'll give the cats a good going-over, maybe hose them down if it gets hot enough. Memory flooded back and snapped her awake. *Ari.* Opening her eyes, Jo rolled onto her back and stared at the ceiling. Now she recalled vividly how the old cat had died with his eyes trusting on her face. She sighed again. The sadness was still there, but not the sharp, desperate grief of the night before.

Acceptance was settling in. She realized that Keane's insistence on staying with her during the peak of her mourning had helped her. He had given her someone to rail at, then someone to hold on to. She remembered the incredible comfort of being cradled in his lap, the solid dependability of his chest against her cheek. She had fallen asleep with the sound of his heart in her ear.

Turning her head, Jo looked out the window, then at the patch of white light the sun tossed on the floor. *But it isn't Monday*, she remembered suddenly. *It's Thursday.* Jo sat up, pushing at her hair, which seemed to tumble everywhere at once. What was she doing in bed on a Thursday when the sun was up? Without giving herself time to work out the answer, she scrambled out of bed and hurried from the room. She gave a soft gasp as she ran headlong into Keane.

His hand ran down the length of her hair before he took her shoulder. "I heard you stirring," he said easily, looking down into her stunned face.

"What are you doing here?"

"Making coffee," he answered as he gave her a critical study. "Or I was a moment ago. How are you?"

"I'm all right." Jo lifted her hand to her temple as if to gain her bearings. "I'm a bit disoriented, I suppose. I overslept. It's never happened before."

"I gave you a sleeping pill," Keane told her matter-of-factly. He slipped an arm around her shoulder as he turned back to the kitchen.

"A pill?" Jo's eyes flew to his. "I don't remember taking a pill."

"It was in the water you drank." On the stove the kettle began its piercing whistle. Moving to it, Keane finished making the coffee. "I had my doubts as to whether you'd take it voluntarily."

"No, I wouldn't have," Jo agreed with some annoyance. "I've never taken a sleeping pill in my life."

"Well, you did last night." He held out a mug of coffee. "I sent Gerry for it while you were in the cage with Ari." Again he gave her a quick, intense study. "It didn't seem to do you any harm. You went out like a light. I carried you to bed, changed your clothes—"

"Changed my…" All at once Jo became aware that she wore only a thin white nightshirt. Her hand reached instinctively for the top button that nestled just above her bosom. Thinking hard, she found she could recall nothing beyond falling asleep in his arms.

"I don't think you'd have spent a very comfortable night in your costume," Keane pointed out. Enjoying his coffee, he smiled at the nervous hand she held between her breasts. "I've had a certain amount of experience undressing women in the dark." Jo dropped her hand. It was an unmistakable movement of pride. Keane's eyes softened. "You needed a good night's sleep, Jo. You were worn-out."

Without speaking, Jo lifted her coffee to her lips and turned away. Walking to the window, she could see that the backyard was deserted. Her sleep must indeed have been deep to have kept her unaware of camp breaking.

"Everyone's gone but a couple of roustabouts and a generator truck. They'll take off when you don't need power anymore."

The vulnerability Jo felt was overwhelming. Several times in the course of the evening before, she had lost control, which had always been an essential part of her. Each time, it had been Keane who had been there. She wanted to be angry with him for intruding on her privacy but found it impossible. She had needed him, and he had known it.

"You didn't have to stay behind," she said, watching a crow swoop low over the ground outside.

"I wasn't certain you'd be in any shape to drive fifty miles this morning. Pete's driving my trailer."

Her shoulders lifted and fell before she turned around. Sunlight streamed through the window at her back and poured through the thin folds of her night-shirt. Her body was a slender shadow. When she spoke, her voice was low with regret. "I was horribly rude to you last night."

Keane shrugged and lifted his coffee. "You were upset."

"Yes." Her eyes were an open reflection of her sorrow. "Ari was very important to me. I suppose he was an ongoing link with my father, with my childhood. I'd known for some time he wouldn't make it through the season, but I didn't want to face it." She looked down at the mug she held gripped in both hands. A faint wisp of steam rose from it and vanished. "Last night was a relief for him. It was selfish of me to wish it otherwise. And I was wrong to strike out at you the way I did. I'm sorry."

"I don't want your apology, Jo." Because he sounded annoyed, she looked up quickly.

"I'd feel better if you'd take it, Keane. You've been very kind."

To her astonishment, he swore under his breath and turned back to the stove. "I don't care for your gratitude any more than your apology." He set down his mug and poured in more coffee. "Neither of them is necessary."

"They are to me," Jo replied, then took a step toward him. "Keane…" She set down her coffee and touched his arm. When he turned, she let impulse guide her. She rested her head on his shoulder and slipped her arms around his waist. He stiffened, putting his hands to her shoulders as if to draw her away. Then she heard his breath come out in a long sigh as he relaxed. For an instant he brought her closer.

"I never know precisely what to expect from you," he murmured. He lifted her chin with his finger. In automatic response, Jo closed her eyes and offered her mouth. She felt his fingers tighten on her skin before his lips brushed hers lightly. "You'd better go change." His manner was friendly but cool as he stepped away. "We'll stop off in town, and I'll buy you some breakfast."

Puzzled by his attitude but satisfied he was no longer annoyed, Jo nodded. "All right."

Spring became summer as the circus wound its way north. The sun stayed longer, peeking into the Big Top until well after the evening show began. Heavy rain came infrequently, but there were quick summer storms with thunder and lightning. Through June, Prescott's Circus Colossus snaked through North Carolina and into western Tennessee.

During the long weeks while spring tripped over into summer, Jo found Keane's attitude a paradox. His friendliness toward her was offhand. He laughed if she said something amusing, listened if she had a complaint and to her confusion, slipped a thin barrier between them. At times she wondered if the passion that had flared between them the night he had returned from Chicago had truly existed. Had the desire she had tasted on his lips been a fantasy? The closeness she had felt blooming between them had withered and blown away. They were only owner and trouper now.

Keane flew back to Chicago twice more during this period, but he brought no surprise presents back with him. Not once during those long weeks did he come by her trailer. Initially, his altered manner confused her. He was not angry. His mood was neither heated nor icy with temper but fell into an odd middle ground she could not understand. Jo ached with love. As days passed into weeks, she was forced to admit that Keane did not seem to be interested in a close relationship.

On the eve of the July 4 show, Jo sat sleepless in her bed. In her hand she held the volume of Dante, but the book was only a reminder of the emptiness she felt. She closed it, then stared at the ceiling. *It's time to snap out of it*, she lectured herself. *It's time to stop pretending he was ever really part of my life. Loving someone only makes him a part of your wishes. He never talked about love, he never promised anything, never offered anything but what he gave to me. He's done nothing to hurt me.* Jo squeezed her eyes shut and pressed the book between her fingers. *How I wish I could hate him for showing me what life could be like and then turning away*, she thought.

But I can't. Jo let out a shaky breath and relaxed her grip on the book. Gently, she ran a finger down its smooth, leather binding. *I can't hate him, but I can't love him openly, either. How do I stop? I should be grateful he stopped wanting me. I would have made love with him. Then I'd hurt a hundred times more. Could I hurt a hundred times more?* For several moments she lay still, trying to quiet her thoughts.

It's best not to know, she told herself sternly. *It's best to remember he was kind to me when I needed him and that I haven't a right to make demands. Summer doesn't last forever. I may never see him again when it's over. At least I can keep the time we have pleasant.*

The words sounded hollow in her heart.

Chapter 9

The Fourth of July was a full day with a run to a new lot, the tent raising, a street parade and two shows. But it was a holiday. Elephants wore red, white and blue plumes atop their massive heads. The evening performance would be held an hour earlier to allow for the addition of a fireworks display. Traditionally, Prescott's circus arranged to spend the holiday in the same small town in Tennessee. The license and paperwork for the display were seen to in advance, and the fireworks were shipped ahead to be stored in a warehouse. The procedure had been precisely the same for years. It was one of the circus's most profitable nights. Concessions thrived.

Jo moved through the day with determined cheerfulness. She refused to permit the distance between her and Keane to spoil one of the highlights of the summer. Brooding, she decided, would not change things. The mood of the crowd helped to keep her spirits light.

Between shows came the inevitable lull. Some troupers sat outside their trailers exchanging small talk and enjoying the sun. Others got in a bit more practice or worked out a few kinks. Bull hands washed down the elephants, causing a minor flood in the pen area.

Jo watched the bathing process with amusement. She never ceased to enjoy this particular aspect of circus life, especially if there were one or two inexperienced bull hands involved. Invariably, Maggie or one of the other veteran bulls would spray a trunkful of water over the new hands to initiate them. Though Jo knew the other hands encouraged it, they always displayed remarkable innocence.

Spotting Duffy, Jo moved away from the elephant area and wandered toward him. She could see he was deep in discussion with a towner. He was as short as Duffy but wider, with what she had once heard Frank call a successful frame. His stomach started high and barreled out to below his waist. He had a ruddy complexion and pale eyes that squinted hard against the sun. Jo had seen his type before. She wondered what he was selling and how much he wanted for it. Since Duffy was puffing with annoyance, Jo assumed it was quite a lot.

"I'm telling you, Carlson, we've already paid for storage. I've got a signed receipt. And we pay fifteen bucks delivery, not twenty."

Carlson was smoking a small, unfiltered cigarette and dropped it to the ground. "You paid Myers for storage, not me. I bought the place six weeks ago." He shrugged his wide shoulders. "Not my problem you paid in advance."

Looking over, Jo saw Keane approaching with Pete. Pete was talking rapidly, Keane nodding. As Jo watched, Keane glanced up and gave Carlson a quick study. She had seen that look before and knew the older man had been assessed. Keane caught her eye, smiled and began to move past her. "Hello, Jo."

Unashamedly curious, Jo fell into step beside him. "What's going on?"

"Why don't we find out?" he suggested as they stopped in front of Duffy and Carlson. "Gentlemen," Keane said in an easy tone. "Is there a problem?"

"This character," Duffy spouted, jerking a scornful thumb at Carlson's face, "wants us to pay twice for storage on the fireworks. Then he wants twenty for delivery when we agreed on fifteen."

"Myers agreed on fifteen," Carlson pointed out. He smiled without humor. "I didn't agree on anything. You want your fireworks, you gotta pay for them first—cash," he added, then spared Keane a glance. "Who's this guy?"

Duffy began to wheeze with indignation, but Keane laid a restraining hand on his shoulder. "I'm Prescott," he told him in untroubled tones. "Perhaps you'd like to fill me in."

"Prescott, huh?" Carlson stroked both his chins as he studied Keane. Seeing youth and amiable eyes, he felt closer to success. "Well, now we're getting somewhere," he said jovially and stuck out his hand. Keane accepted it without hesitation. "Jim Carlson," he continued as he gave Keane's hand a brisk pump. "Nice circus you got here, Prescott. Me and the missus see it every year. Well, now," he said again and hitched up his belt. "Seeing as you're a businessman, too, I'm sure we can straighten all this out. Problem is, your fireworks've been stored in my warehouse. Now, I gotta make a living, they can't just sit there for free. I bought the place off Myers six weeks ago. I can't be held responsible for a deal you made with him, can I?" Carlson gave a stretched-lip smile, pleased that Keane listened so politely. "And as for delivery, well…" He made a helpless gesture and patted Keane's shoulder. "You know about gas prices these days, son. But we can work that out after we settle this other little problem."

Keane nodded agreeably. "That sounds reasonable." He ignored Duffy's huffing and puffing. "You do seem to have a problem, Mr. Carlson."

"I don't have a problem," Carlson countered. His smile suffered a fractional slip. "You've got the problem, unless you don't want the fireworks."

"Oh, we'll have the fireworks, Mr. Carlson," Keane corrected with a smile Jo thought more wolfish than friendly. "According to paragraph three, section five, of the small business code, the lessor is legally bound by all contracts, agreements, liens and mortgages of the previous lessor until such time as all aforesaid contracts, agreements, liens and mortgages are expired or transferred."

"What the…" Carlson began with no smile at all, but Keane continued blandly.

"Of course, we won't pursue the matter in court as long as we get our merchandise. But that doesn't solve your problem."

"My problem?" Carlson sputtered while Jo looked

on in frank admiration. "I haven't got a problem. If you think…"

"Oh, but you do, Mr. Carlson, though I'm sure there was no intent to break the law on your part."

"Break the law?" Carlson wiped damp hands on his slacks.

"Storing explosives without a license," Keane pointed out. "Unless, of course, you obtained one after your purchase of the warehouse."

"Well, no, I…"

"I was afraid of that." Keane lifted his brow in pity. "You see, in paragraph six of section five of the small business code it states that all licenses, permits and warrants shall be nontransferable. Authorization for new licenses, permits or warrants must be requested in writing by the current owner. Notarized, naturally." Keane waited a bit to allow Carlson to wrestle with the idea. "If I'm not mistaken," he continued conversationally, "the fine's pretty hefty in this state. Of course, sentencing depends on—"

"Sentencing?" Carlson paled and mopped the back of his neck with a handkerchief.

"Look, tell you what." Keane gave Carlson a sympathetic smile. "You get the fireworks over here and off your property. We don't have to bring the law in on something like this. Just an oversight, after all. We're both businessmen, aren't we?"

Too overwrought to detect sarcasm, Carlson nodded.

"That was fifteen on delivery, right?"

Carlson didn't hesitate but stuck the damp handkerchief back in his pocket and nodded again.

"Good enough. I'll have the cash for you on delivery. Glad to help you out."

Relieved, Carlson turned and headed for his pickup. Jo managed to keep her features grave until he pulled off the lot. Simultaneously, Pete and Duffy began to hoot with laughter.

"Was it true?" Jo demanded and took Keane's arm.

"Was what true?" Keane countered, merely lifting a brow over the hysterics that surrounded him.

"'Paragraph three, section five, of the small business code,'" Jo quoted.

"Never heard of it," Keane answered mildly, nearly sending Pete into orbit.

"You made it up," Jo said in wonder. "You made it all up!"

"Probably," Keane agreed.

"Smoothest con job I've seen in years," Duffy stated and gave Keane a parental slap on the back. "Son, you could go into business."

"I did," Keane told him and grinned.

"I ever need a lawyer," Pete put in, pushing his cap farther back on his head, "I know where to go. You come on by the cookhouse tonight, Captain. We're having ourselves a poker game. Come on, Duffy, Buck's gotta hear about this."

As they moved off, Jo realized that Keane had been officially accepted. Before, he had been the legal owner but an outsider, a towner. Now he was one of them. Turning, she lifted her face to his. "Welcome aboard."

"Thank you." She saw he understood precisely what had been left unsaid.

"I'll see you at the game," she said before her smile became a grin. "Don't forget your money."

She turned away, but Keane touched her arm, bring-

ing her back to him. "Jo," he began, puzzling her by the
sudden seriousness of his eyes.

"Yes?"

There was a brief hesitation, then he shook his head.
"Nothing, never mind. I'll see you later." He rubbed his
knuckles over her cheek, then walked away.

Jo studied her hand impassively. On the deal, she
had missed a heart flush by one card and now waited
for someone to open. Casually, she moved her glance
around the table. Duffy was puffing on a cigar, apparently unconcerned with the dwindling chips in front
of him. Pete chewed his gum with equal nonchalance.
Amy, the wife of the sword swallower, sat beside him,
then Jamie, then Raoul. Directly beside Jo was Keane,
who, like Pete, was winning consistently.

The pot grew. Chips clinked on the table. Jo discarded and was pleased to exchange a club for the fifth
heart. She slipped it into her hand without blinking.
Frank had taught her the game. Before the second round
of betting, Jamie folded in disgust. "Should never have
taken Buck's seat," he muttered and frowned when Pete
raised the bet.

"You got out cheap, kiddo," Duffy told him dolefully
as he tossed in chips. "I'm only staying in so I don't
change my standard of living. Money'll do that to you,"
he mumbled obscurely.

"Three kings," Pete announced when called, then
spread his cards. Amid a flutter of complaints cards
were tossed down.

"Heart flush," Jo said mildly before Pete could rake in
the pot. Duffy leaned back and gave a hoot of laughter.

"Attagirl, Jo. I hate to see him win all my money."

During the next two hours the cookhouse tent grew hot and ripe with the scents of coffee and tobacco and beer. Jamie's luck proved so consistently poor that he called for Buck to relieve him.

Jo found herself with an indifferent pair of fives. Almost immediately the betting grew heavy as Keane raised Raoul's opening. Curiosity kept Jo in one round, but practicality had her folding after the draw. Divorced from the game, she watched it with interest. Leaning on her elbows, she studied each participant. Keane played a good game, she mused. His eyes gave nothing away. They never did. Casually, he nursed the beer beside him while Duffy, Buck and Amy folded. Studying him closely, Pete chewed his gum. Keane returned the look, keeping the stub of his cigar clamped between his teeth. Raoul muttered in French and scowled at his cards.

"Could be bluffing," Pete considered, seeing Keane's raise. "Let's raise it five more and see what's cooking." Raoul swore in French, then again in English, before he tossed in his hand. Taking his time, Keane counted out the necessary chips and tossed them into the pot. It was a plastic mountain of red, white and blue. Then, he counted out more.

"I'll see your five," he said evenly, "and raise it ten."

There was mumbling around the table. Pete looked into his hand and considered. Shifting his eyes, he took in the generous pile of chips in front of him. He could afford to risk another ten. Glancing up, he studied Keane's face while he fondled his chips. Abruptly, he broke into a grin.

"Nope," he said simply, turning his cards face down. "This one's all yours."

Setting down his cards, Keane raked in a very sweet pot. "Gonna show 'em?" Pete asked. His grin was affable.

Keane pushed a stray chip into the pile and shrugged. With his free hand he turned over the cards. The reaction ranged from oaths to laughter.

"Trash," Pete mumbled with a shake of his head. "Nothing but trash. You've got nerve, Captain." His grin grew wide as he turned over his own cards. "Even I had a pair of sevens."

Raoul gnashed his teeth and swore elegantly in two languages. Jo grinned at his imaginative choice of words. She rose on a laugh and snatched off the soft felt hat Jamie wore. Deftly, she scooped her chips into it. "Cash me in later," she requested, then gave him a smacking kiss on the mouth. "But don't play with them."

Duffy scowled over at her. "Aren't you cashing in early?"

"You've always told me to leave 'em wanting more," she reminded him. With a grin and a wave, she swung through the door.

"That Jo," said Raoul, chuckling as he shuffled the cards. "She's one smart cracker."

"Cookie," Pete corrected, opening a fresh stick of gum. He noticed that Keane's gaze had drifted to the door she had closed behind her. "Some looker, too," he commented and watched Keane's eyes wander back to his. "Don't you think, Captain?"

Keane slipped his cards into a pile as they were dealt to him. "Jo's lovely."

"Like her mother," Buck put in, frowning at his cards. "She was a beaut, huh, Duffy?" Duffy grunted in agreement and wondered why Lady Luck refused to smile on him. "Always thought it was a crime for her to die that way. Wilder, too," he added with a shake of his head.

"A fire, wasn't it?" Keane asked as he picked up his cards and spread them.

"Electrical fire." Buck nodded and lifted his beer. "A short in their trailer's wiring. What a waste. If they hadn't been in bed asleep, they'd probably still be alive. The trailer was halfway gone before anybody set up an alarm. Just plain couldn't get to the Wilders. Their side of the trailer was like a furnace. Jo's bedroom was on the other side, and we nearly lost her. Frank busted in the window and pulled her out. Poor little tyke. She was holding onto this old doll like it was the last thing she had left. Kept it with her for I don't know how long. Remember, Duffy?" He glanced into his hand and opened for two. "It only had one arm." Duffy grunted again and folded. "Frank sure knew how to handle that little girl."

"She knew how to handle him, more likely," Duffy mumbled. Raoul bumped the pot five, and Keane folded.

"Deal me out the next hand," he said as he rose and moved to the door. One of the Gribalti brothers took the chair Jo had vacated, and Jamie slipped into Keane's. Curious, he lifted the tip of the cards. He saw a jack-high straight. With a thoughtful frown, he watched the door swing shut.

Outside, Jo moved through the warm night. With a glance at the sky, she thought of the fireworks. They had been wonderful, she mused, stirring up the stars with exploding color. Though it was over and a new day hovered, she felt some magic remained in the night. Far from sleepy, she wandered toward the Big Top.

"Hello, pretty lady."

Jo looked into the shadows and narrowed her eyes. She could just barely make out a form. "Oh, you're Bob, aren't you?" She stopped and gave him a friendly smile. "You're new."

He stepped toward her. "I've been on for nearly three weeks." He was young, Jo guessed about her own age, with a solid build and sharp-featured face. Just that afternoon she had watched Maggie give him a shower.

Jo pushed her hands into the pockets of her cut-offs and continued to smile. It appeared he thought his tenure made him a veteran. "How do you like working with the elephants?"

"It's okay. I like putting up the tent."

Jo understood his feeling. "So do I. There's a game in the cookhouse," she told him with a gesture of her arm. "You might like to sit in."

"I'd rather be with you." As he moved closer, Jo caught the faint whiff of beer. *He's been celebrating*, she thought and shook her head.

"It's a good thing tomorrow's Monday," she commented. "No one's going to be in any shape to pitch a tent. You should go to bed," she suggested. "Or get some coffee."

"Let's go to your trailer." Bob weaved a little, then took her arm.

"No." Firmly, Jo turned in the opposite direction. "Let's go to the cookhouse." His advances did not trouble her. She was close enough to the cookhouse tent that if she called out, a dozen able-bodied men would come charging. But that was precisely what Jo wanted to avoid.

"I want to go with you," he said, stumbling over the words as he veered away from the cookhouse again. "You look so pretty in that cage with those lions." He put both arms around her, but Jo felt it was as much for balance as romance. "A fella needs a pretty lady once in a while."

"I'm going to feed you to my lions if you don't let me go," Jo warned.

"Bet you can be a real wildcat," he mumbled and made a fumbling dive for her mouth.

Though her patience was wearing thin, Jo endured the kiss that landed slightly to the left of bull's-eye. His hands, however, had better aim and grabbed the firm roundness of her bottom. Losing her temper, Jo pushed away but found his hold had taken root. In a quick move, she brought up her fist and caught him square on the jaw. With only a faint sound of surprise, Bob sat down hard on the ground.

"Well, so much for rescuing you," Keane commented from behind her.

Turning quickly, Jo pushed at her hair and gave an annoyed sigh. She would have preferred no witnesses. Even in the dim light, she could see he was furious. Instinctively, she stepped between him and the man who sat on the ground fingering his jaw and shaking the buzzing from his ears.

"He—Bob just got a bit overenthusiastic," she said hastily and put a restraining hand on Keane's arm. "He's been celebrating."

"I'm feeling a bit enthusiastic myself," Keane stated.

As he made to brush her aside, Jo clung with more fervor.

"No, Keane, please."

Looking down, he fired a glare. "Jo, would you let go so that I can deal with this?"

"Not until you listen." The faint hint of laughter in her eyes only enraged him further, and Jo fought to suppress it. "Keane, please, don't be hard on him. He didn't hurt me."

"He was attacking you," Keane interrupted. He barely resisted the urge to shake her off and drag the still-seated Bob by the scruff of the neck.

"No, he was really more just leaning on me. His balance is a trifle impaired. He only tried to kiss me," she pointed out, wisely deleting the wandering hands. "And I hit him much harder than I should have. He's new, Keane, don't fire him."

Exasperated, he stared at her. "Firing was the least of what I had in mind for him."

Jo smiled, unable to keep the gleam from her eyes. "If you were going to avenge my honor, he really didn't do much more than breathe on it. I don't think you should run him through for that. Maybe you could just put him in the stocks for a couple of days."

Keane swore under his breath, but a reluctant smile tugged at his mouth. Seeing it, Jo loosened her hold. "Miss Wilder wants to give you a break," he told the dazed Bob in a tough, no-nonsense voice that Jo decided he used for intimidating witnesses. "She has a softer heart than I do. Therefore, I won't knock you down several more times or kick you off the lot, as I had entertained doing." He paused, allowing Bob time to consider this possibility. "Instead, I'll let you sleep off your—enthusiasm." In one quick jerk, he pulled Bob to his feet. "But if I ever hear of you breathing uninvited on Miss Wilder or any other of my female employees, we'll go back to the first choice. And before I kick you out," he added with low menace, "I'll let it be known that you were decked by one punch from a hundred-pound woman."

"Yes, sir, Mr. Prescott," said Bob as clearly as possible.

"Go to bed," Jo said kindly, seeing him pale. "You'll feel better in the morning."

"Obviously," Keane commented as Bob lurched away, "you haven't done much drinking." He turned to Jo and grinned. "The one thing he's not going to feel in the morning is better." Jo smiled, pleased to have Keane talk to her without the thin shield of politeness. "And where," he asked and took her hand for examination, "did you learn that right jab?"

Jo laughed, allowing Keane's fingers to interlock with hers. "It would hardly have knocked him down if he hadn't already been tilting in that direction." Her face turned up to his and sparkled with starlight. In his eyes an expression she couldn't comprehend came and went. "Is something wrong?"

For a moment he said nothing. In her breast her heart began to hammer as she waited to be kissed. "No, nothing," he said. The moment was shattered. "Come on, I'll walk you back to your trailer."

"I wasn't going there." Wanting to put him back into an easy mood, she linked her arm with his. "If you come with me, I'll show you some magic." Her smile slanted invitingly. "You like magic, don't you, Keane? Even a sober, dedicated lawyer must like magic."

"Is that how I strike you?" Jo almost laughed at the trace of annoyance in his voice. "As a sober, dedicated lawyer?"

"Oh, not entirely, though that's part of you." She enjoyed feeling that for the moment she had him to herself. "You've also got a streak of adventure and a rather nice sense of humor. And," she added with generous emphasis, "there's your temper."

"You seem to have me all figured out."

"Oh, no." Jo stopped and turned to him. "Not at all. I only know how you are here. I can only speculate on how you are in Chicago."

His brow lifted as she caught his attention. "Would I be different there?"

"I don't know." Jo's forehead wrinkled in thought. "Wouldn't you be? Circumstances would. You probably have a house or a big apartment, and there's a housekeeper who comes in once—no, twice—a week." Caught up in the picture, she gazed off into the distance and built it further. "You have an office with a view of the city, a very efficient secretary and a brilliant law clerk. You go to business lunches at the club. In court you're deadly and very successful. You have your own tailor and work out at the gym three times a week. There's the theater on the weekends, along with something physical. Tennis maybe, not golf. No, handball."

Keane shook his head. "Is this the magic?"

"No." Jo shrugged and began to walk again. "Just guesswork. You don't have to have a great deal of money to know how people who do behave. And I know you take the law seriously. You wouldn't choose a career that wasn't very important to you."

Keane walked in silence. When he spoke, his voice was quiet. "I'm not certain I'm comfortable with your little outline of my life."

"It's very sketchy," Jo told him. "I'd have to understand you better to fill in the gaps."

"Don't you?"

"What?" Jo asked, pausing. "Understand you?" She laughed, tickled at the absurdity of his question. "No, I don't understand you. How could I? You live in a different world." With this, she tossed aside the flap of the Big Top and stepped into its darkness. When she hit the switch, two rows of overhead lights flashed on. Shadows haunted the corners and fell over the arena seats.

"It's wonderful, isn't it?" Her clear voice ran the length of the tent and echoed back. "It's not empty, you know. They're always here—the troupers, the audience, the animals." She walked forward until she stood beside the third ring. "Do you know what this is?" she asked Keane, tossing out her arms and turning a full circle. "It's an ageless wonder in a changing world. No matter what happens on the outside, this is here. We're the most fragile of circuses, at the mercy of the elephants, of emotions, of mechanics, of public whims. But six days a week for twenty-nine weeks we perform miracles. We build a world at dawn, then disappear into the dark. That's part of it—the mystery." She waited until Keane moved forward to join her.

"Tents pop up on an empty lot, elephants and lions walk down Main Street. And we never grow old, because each new generation discovers us all over again."

She stood slender and exquisite in a circle of light. "Life here's crazy. And it's hard. Muddy lots, insane hours, sore muscles, but when you've finished your act and you get that feeling that tells you it was special, there's nothing else like it in the world."

"Is that why you do it?" Keane asked.

Jo shook her head and moved out of the circle of light into the dark and into another ring. "It's all part of the same thing. We all have our own reasons, I suppose. You've asked me that before. I'm not certain I can explain. Maybe it's that we all believe in miracles." She turned under the light, and it shimmered around her. "I've been here all my life. I know every trick, every illusion. I know how Jamie's dad gets twenty clowns into a two-seater car. But each time I see it, I laugh and I believe it. It's not just the excitement, Keane, it's the anticipation of the excitement. It's knowing you're going to see the biggest or the smallest or the fastest or the highest." Jo ran to the center ring and threw up her arms.

"Ladies and gentlemen," she announced with a toss of her head. "For your amazement and astonishment, for the first time in America, a superabundance of mountainous, mighty pachyderms led in a stupendous exhibition of choreography by the Great Serena." Jo laughed and shifted her hair to her back with a quick movement of her hand. "Dancing elephants!" she said to Keane, pleased that he was smiling. "Or you listen to the talker in the sideshow when he starts his spiel. Step right up. Come a little closer." She curled her fingers in invitation. "See the Amazing Serpentina and her monstrous, slithering vipers. Watch the beautiful young girl charm a deadly cobra. Watch her accept the reptilian embrace of the gargantuan boa. Don't miss the chance to see the enchantress of the evil serpent!"

"I suppose Baby might sue for slander."

Jo laughed and stepped up on the ring. "But when the crowds see little Rose with a boa constrictor wrapped around her shoulders, they've gotten their money's worth. We give them what they come for: color, fantasy, the unique. Thrills. You've seen the audience when Vito does his high wire act without a net."

"A net seems little enough protection when he's balancing on a wire at two hundred feet." Keane stuck his hands in his pockets and frowned. "He risks his life every day."

"So does a police officer or a fire fighter." Jo spoke quietly and rested her hands on his shoulders. It seemed more necessary than ever that she make him understand his father's dream. "I know what you're saying, Keane, but you have to understand us. The element of danger is essential to many of the acts. You can hear the whole audience suck in their breath when Vito does his back somersault on the wire. They'd be impressed if he used a net, but they wouldn't be terrified."

"Do they need to be?"

Jo's sober expression lightened. "Oh, yes! They need to be terrified and fascinated and mesmerized. It's all included in the price of a ticket. This is a world of superlatives. We test the limit of human daring, and every day it changes. Do you know how long it took before the first man accomplished the triple on the trapeze? Now it's nearly a standard." A light of anticipation flared in her eyes. "One day someone will do a quadruple. If a man stands in this ring and juggles three torches today, tomorrow someone will juggle them on horseback and after that there'll be a team tossing them back and forth while swinging on a trap. It's our job to do the incredible, then, when it's done, to do the impossible. It's that simple."

"Simple," Keane murmured, then lifted a hand to caress her hair. "I wonder if you'd think so if you could see it from the outside."

"I don't know." Her fingers tightened on his shoulders as he buried his other hand in her hair. "I never have."

As if his thoughts centered on it, Keane combed his fingers through her hair. Gradually, he pushed it back until only his hands framed her face. They stood in a pool of light that threw their shadows long behind them. "You are so lovely," he murmured.

Jo neither spoke nor moved. There was something different this time in the way he touched her. There was a gentleness and a hesitation she had not felt before. Though they looked directly into hers, she could not read his eyes. Their faces were close, and his breath fluttered against her mouth. Jo slid her arms around his neck and pressed her mouth to his.

Not until that moment had she realized how empty she had felt, how desperately she had needed to hold him. Her lips were hungry for his. She clung while all gentleness fled from his touch. His hands were greedy. The weeks that he had not touched her were forgotten as her skin warmed and hummed with quickening blood. Passion stripped her of inhibitions, and her tongue sought his, taking the kiss into wilder and darker depths.

Their lips parted, only to meet again with sharp new demands. She understood that all needs and all desires were ultimately only one—Keane.

His mouth left hers, and for an instant he rested his cheek against her hair. For that moment Jo felt a contentment more complete than she had ever known. Abruptly, he drew away.

Puzzled, she watched as he drew out a cigar. She lifted a hand to run it through the hair he had just disturbed. He flicked on his lighter. "Keane?" She looked at him, knowing her eyes offered everything.

"You've had a long day," he began in an oddly polite tone. Jo winced as if he had struck her. "I'll walk you back to your trailer."

She stepped off the ring and away from him. Pain seared along her skin. "Why are you doing this?" To her humiliation, tears welled in her eyes and lodged in her throat. The tears acted as a prism, refracting the light and clouding her vision. She blinked them back. Keane's brows drew together at the gesture.

"I'll take you back," he said again. The detached tone of his voice accelerated all Jo's fury and grief.

"How dare you!" she demanded. "How dare you make me…" The word *love* nearly slipped through her lips, and she swallowed it. "How dare you make me want you, then turn away! I was right about you from the beginning. I thought I'd been wrong. You're cold and unfeeling." Her breath came quickly and unevenly, but she refused to retreat until she had said it all. Her face was pale with the passion of her emotions. "I don't know why I thought you'd ever understand what Frank had given you. You need a heart to see the intangible.

I'll be glad when the season's over and you do whatever it is you're going to do. I'll be glad when I never have to see you again. I won't let you do this to me anymore!" Her voice wavered, but she made no attempt to steady it. "I don't want you to ever touch me again."

Keane studied her for a long moment, then took a careful drag on his cigar. "All right, Jo."

The very calmness of his answer tore a sob from her before she turned and ran from the Big Top.

Chapter 10

In July the troupe circled through Virginia, touched the tip of West Virginia on their way into Kentucky, then moved into Ohio. Audiences fanned themselves as the temperatures in the Big Top rose, but they still came.

Since the evening of the Fourth of July, Jo had avoided Keane. It was not as difficult as it might have been, as he spent half the month in Chicago dealing with his business. Jo functioned. She ate because eating was necessary in order to maintain her strength. She slept because rest was essential to remaining alert in the cage. She did not find any enjoyment in food nor was her sleep restful. Because so many in the troupe knew her well, Jo struggled to keep on a mask of normalcy. Above all, she needed to avoid any questions, any advice, any sympathy. It was necessary, because of her profession, to put her emotions on hold a great deal of the time. After some struggle and some failure, Jo achieved a reasonable success.

Her training of Gerry continued, as did his progress. The additional duty of working with him helped fill her small snatches of spare time. On afternoons when no matinee was scheduled, Jo took him into the big cage. As he grew more proficient, she brought other cats in to join Merlin. By the first week in August they were working together with her full complement of lions.

The only others who were rehearsing in the Big Top were the equestrian act. They ran through the Thread the Needle routine in the first ring. Hooves echoed dully on tanbark. Jo supervised while Gerry sent the cats into a pyramid. At his urging, Lazarus climbed up the wide, arched ladder that topped the grouping. Twice he balked, and twice Gerry was forced to reissue the command.

"Good," Jo commented when the pyramid was complete.

"He wouldn't go." Gerry began to complain, but she cut him off.

"Don't be in too much of a hurry. Bring them down." Her tone was brisk and professional. "Make certain they dismount and take their seats in the right order. It's important to stick to routine."

Hands resting on hips, Jo watched. In her opinion, Gerry had true potential. His nerves were good, he had a feeling for the animals, and he was slowly developing patience. Still she balked at the next step in his training: leaving him alone in the arena. Even with only Merlin, she felt it too risky. He was still too casual. Not yet did he possess enough respect for the lion's guile.

Jo moved around the arena, and the lions, used to

her, were not disturbed. As the cats settled onto their pedestals, she once more moved to stand beside Gerry. "Now we'll walk down the line. You make each do a sit-up before we send them out."

One by one the cats rose on their haunches and pawed the air. Jo and Gerry moved down their ranks. The heat was becoming oppressive, and Jo shifted her shoulders, longing for a cool shower and a change of clothes. When they came to Hamlet, he ignored the command with a rebellious snarl.

Bad-tempered brute, thought Jo absently as she waited for Gerry to reissue the command. He did so but moved forward as if to emphasize the words.

"No, not so close!" Jo warned quickly. Even as she spoke, she saw the change in Hamlet's eyes.

Instinctively, she stepped over, nudging Gerry back and shielding his body with hers. Hamlet struck out, claws extended. There was a moment of blind heat in her shoulder as the skin ripped. Swiftly, she was facing the cat, holding tightly on to Gerry's arm as they stood just out of range.

"Don't run," she ordered, feeling his jerk of panic. Her arm was on fire as the blood began to flow freely. Keeping her movements quick but smooth, she took the whip from Gerry's nerveless hand and cracked it hard, using her left arm. She knew that if Hamlet continued his defiance and attacked, it was hopeless. The other cats were certain to join in a melee. It would be over before anything could be done. Already, Abra shifted restlessly and bared her teeth.

"Open the chute," Jo called out. Her voice was cool as ice. "Back toward the safety cage," she instructed

Gerry as she gave the cats their signal to leave the arena. "I've got to get them out one at a time. Move slow, and if I tell you to stop, you stop dead. Understand?"

She heard him swallow as she watched the cats begin to leap off their pedestals and file into the chute. "He got you. Is it bad?" The words were barely a whisper and drenched in terror.

"I said go." Half the cats were gone, and still Hamlet's eyes were locked on hers. There was no time to waste. One part of her brain heard shouting outside the cage, but she blocked it out and focused all her concentration on the cat. "Go now," she repeated to Gerry. "Do as you're told."

He swallowed again and began to back away. Long seconds dragged until she heard the rattle of the safety cage door. When his turn came, Hamlet made no move to leave his seat. Jo was alone with him. She could smell the heat, the scent of the wild and the fragrance of her own blood. Her arm was alive with pain. Slowly, she tested him by backing up. The safety cage seemed hundreds of miles away. The cat tensed immediately, and she stopped. She knew he would not let her cross the arena. Outrunning him was impossible, as the distance between them could be covered in one spring. She had to outbluff him instead.

"Out," she ordered firmly. "Out, Hamlet." As he continued to watch her, Jo felt a trickle of sweat slide down between her shoulder blades. Her skin was clammy with it in contrast to the warmth of the blood that ran down her arm. There was a sudden, vivid picture inside her head of her father being dragged around the cage. Fear tripped inside her throat. There was a lightness fluttering in the top of her head, and she knew that a moment's terror would cause her to faint. She stiffened her spine and pushed it away.

Speed was important. The longer she allowed the cat to remain in the arena after his cue, the more defiant he would become. And the more dangerous. As yet he was unaware that he held her at such a sharp disadvantage. "Out, Hamlet." Jo repeated the command with a crack of the whip. He leaped from the pedestal. Jo's stomach trembled. She locked every muscle, and as the cat hesitated, she repeated the command. He was confused, and she knew this could work as an advantage or a curse. Confused, he might spring or retreat. Her fingers tightened on the stock of the whip and trembled. The cat paced nervously and watched her.

"Hamlet!" She raised her voice and bit off each syllable. "Go out." To the words she added the hand signal she had used before he was fully trained to voice command.

As if rebuffed, Hamlet relaxed his tail and padded into the chute. Before the door slid completely closed, Jo sank to her knees. Her body began to quake fiercely with the aftershock. No more than five minutes had passed since Hamlet had defied Gerry's command, but her muscles bore the strain of hours. For an instant her vision blurred. Even as she shook her head to clear it, Keane was on the ground beside her.

She heard him swear, ripping the tattered sleeve of her blouse from her arm. He fired questions at her, but she could do no more than shake her head and gulp in air. Focusing on him, she noticed his eyes were unusually dark against his face.

"What?" She followed his voice but not the words.

He swore again, sharply enough to penetrate the first layer of her shock. He pulled her to her feet, then continuing the motion smoothly, lifted her into his arms. "Don't." Her mind struggled to break through the fog and function. "I'm all right."

"Shut up," he said harshly as he carried her from the cage. "Just shut up."

Because speaking cost her some effort, Jo obeyed. Closing her eyes, she let the mixture of excited voices whirl around her. Her arm screamed with pain, but the throbbing reassured her. Numbness would have terrified her. Still she kept her eyes shut, not yet having the courage to look at the damage. Being alive was enough.

When she opened her eyes again, Keane was carrying her into the administration wagon. At the sound of the chaos that followed them, Duffy strode through from his office. "What the…" he began, then stopped and paled beneath his freckles. He moved quickly forward as Keane set Jo in a chair. "How bad?"

"I don't know yet," Keane muttered. "Get a towel and the first-aid kit."

Buck had come in behind them and, already having secured the items, handed them to Keane. Then he moved to a cabinet and located a bottle of brandy.

"It's not too bad," Jo managed. Because her voice was tolerably steady, she screwed up her courage and looked down. Keane had fastened a rough bandage from the remains of her sleeve. Though the flow of blood had slowed, there were streaks of it down her arm, and too much spreading from the wound to be certain how extensive the cuts were. Nausea rocked in her stomach.

"How do you know?" Keane demanded between his

teeth as he began to clean the wound. He wrung out the towel in the basin Buck set beside him.

"It's not bleeding that badly." Jo swallowed the queasiness. As her mind began to clear, she frowned at the tone of Keane's voice. Feeling her stare, he glanced up. In his eyes was such fury, she pulled away.

"Be still," he ordered roughly and gave his attention back to her arm.

The cat had delivered only a glancing blow, but even so, there were four long slices in her upper arm. Jo set her jaw as pain ripped through her. Keane's brusqueness brought more hurt, and she fought to show no reaction to either. The aftermath of fear was bubbling through her. She longed to be held, to be soothed by the hands that tended to her wound.

"She's going to need stitches," Keane said without looking at her.

"And an antitoxin shot," Buck added, handing Jo a generous glass of brandy. "Drink this, honey. It'll help settle you."

The gentleness in his voice nearly undid her. He laid his big hand against her cheek, and for a moment she pressed against it.

"Drink now," Buck ordered again. Obediently, Jo lifted the glass and swallowed. The room whirled, then snapped into focus. She made a small sound and pressed the glass to her forehead. "Tell me what happened in there." Buck crouched down beside her as Keane began to apply a temporary bandage.

Jo took a moment to draw air in and out of her lungs. She lowered the glass and spoke steadily. "Hamlet didn't respond, and Gerry repeated a command, but he stepped forward. Too close. I saw Hamlet's eyes, and I knew. I should have moved faster. I should have been watching him more carefully. It was a stupid mistake." She stared into the brandy as she berated herself.

"She stepped between the boy and the cat." Keane bit off the words as he completed the bandaging. Rising, he moved to the brandy and poured. Not once did he turn to look at Jo. Hurt, she stared at his back before looking back at Buck.

"How's Gerry?"

Buck urged the glass back to her lips. A faint tint of pink was creeping into her cheeks. "Pete's with him. Got his head between his knees. He'll be fine."

Jo nodded. "I guess I'll have to go to town and have this seen to." She handed the glass to Buck and wondered if she dare attempt to rise yet. With another deep breath, she glanced at Duffy. "Make sure he's ready to go in when I get back."

Keane turned from the window. "Go in where?" His face was set in hard lines.

In response, Jo's voice was chilled. "In the cage." She turned her eyes to Buck. "We should be able to have a short run-through before the evening show."

"No." Jo's head snapped up as Keane spoke. For a long moment they stared at each other with odd, unreasonable antagonism. "You're not going back in there today." His voice held curt authority.

"Of course I am," Jo countered, managing to keep the combination of pain and anger from her words. "And if Gerry wants to be a cat man, he's going in, too."

"Jo's right," Buck put in, trying to soothe what he sensed was an explosive situation. "It's like falling off a horse. You can't wait too long before you get back up, or you won't ride again."

Keane never took his eyes from Jo. He continued as if Buck hadn't spoken. "I won't permit it."

"You can't stop me." Indignation forced her to her feet. The brisk movement caused her arm to protest, and her struggle against it showed momentarily in her eyes.

"Yes, I can." Keane took a long swallow of brandy. "I own this circus."

Jo's fists tightened at his tone, at his careless use of his authority. Not once since he had knelt beside her in the cage had he given her any sign of comfort or reassurance. She had needed it from him. To masquerade its trembling, she kept her voice low. "But you don't own me, Mr. Prescott. And if you'll check your papers and the legalities, you'll see you don't own the lions or my equipment. I bought them, and I maintain them out of my salary. My contract doesn't give you the right to tell me when I can or can't rehearse my cats."

Keane's face was granite hard. "Neither does it give you the right to set up in the Big Top without my permission."

"Then I'll set up someplace else," she tossed back. "But I *will* set up. That cat will be worked again today. I won't take the risk of losing months of training."

"But you will risk being killed," Keane shot back and slammed down his glass.

"What do you care?" Jo shouted. All control deserted her. The cuts were deep on her emotions as well as her flesh. She had passed through a terror more acute than she had known since the night of her parents' death. More than anything else, she wanted to feel Keane's arms around her. She wanted to know the security she had felt when he had let her weep out her grief for Ari in his arms. "I'm nothing to you!" Her head shook quickly, tossing her hair. There was a bubble of hysteria in her voice, and Buck reached out to lay a hand on her shoulder.

"Jo," he warned in his soft, rumbling voice.

"No!" She shook her head and spoke rapidly. "He hasn't the right. You haven't the right to interfere with my life." She flared at Keane again with eyes vivid with emotion. "I know what I have to do. I know what I *will* do. Why should it matter to you? You aren't legally responsible if I get mauled. No one's going to sue you."

"Hold on, Jo." This time Buck spoke firmly. As he took her uninjured arm, he felt the tremors shooting through her. "She's too upset to know what she's saying," he told Keane.

There was a mask over Keane's face which concealed all emotion. "Oh, I think she knows what she's saying," he disagreed quietly. For a moment there was only the sound of Jo shuddering and the splash of brandy being poured into a glass. "You do what you have to do, Jo," he said after drinking again. "You're perfectly correct that I haven't any rights where you're concerned. Take her into town," he told Buck, then turned back to the window.

"Come on, Jo." Buck urged her to the door, slipping a supportive arm around her waist. Even as they stepped outside, Rose came running from the direction of the midway.

"Jo!" Her face was white with concern. "Jo, I just

heard." She glanced at the bandage with wide, terrified eyes. "How bad is it?"

"Just scratches, really," Jo assured her. She added the best smile she could muster. "Buck's going to take me into town for a couple of stitches."

"Are you sure?" She looked up at the tall man for reassurance. "Buck?"

"Several stitches," he corrected but patted Rose's hand. "But it's not too bad."

"Do you want me to come with you?" She fell into step beside them as Buck began to lead Jo again.

"No. Thank you, Rose." Jo smiled with more feeling. "I'll be fine."

Because of the smile, Rose was able to relax. "I thought when I heard…well, I imagined all sorts of terrible things. I'm glad you're not badly hurt." They had reached Buck's truck, and Rose leaned over to kiss Jo's cheek. "We all love you so."

"I know." Squeezing her hand, Jo let Buck help her into the cab of his truck. As he maneuvered from the lot, Jo rested her head against the back of the seat and shut her eyes. Never could she remember feeling more spent, more battered.

"Hurt bad?" Buck asked as they switched to an asphalt road.

"Yes," she answered simply, thinking of her heart as much as her arm.

"You'll feel better when you're patched up."

Jo kept her eyes shut, knowing some wounds never heal. Or if they did, they left scars that ached at unexpected times.

"You shouldn't have gone off on him that way, Jo." There was light censure in Buck's voice.

"He shouldn't have interfered," Jo retorted. "It's none of his business. *I'm* none of his business."

"Jo, it's not like you to be so hard."

"Hard?" She opened her eyes and turned to Buck. "What about him? Couldn't he have been kinder, shown even the barest trace of compassion? Did he have to speak to me as if I were a criminal?"

"Jo, the man was terrified. You're only looking at this from one side." He scratched his beard and gave a gusty sigh. "You can't know what it's like to be outside that cage, helpless when someone you care about is facing down death. I had to all but knock him unconscious to keep him out of there until we got it through his head that he'd just get you killed for sure. He was scared, Jo. We were all scared."

Jo shook her head, certain Buck exaggerated because of his affection for her. Keane's voice had been hard, his eyes angry. "He doesn't care," she corrected quietly. "Not like the rest of you. You didn't swear at me. You weren't cold."

"Jo, people have different ways—" Buck began, but she interrupted.

"I know he wouldn't want to see me hurt, Buck. He's not heartless or cruel." She sighed as all the force of anger and fear washed out of her body and left her empty. "Please, I don't want to talk about him."

Buck heard the weariness in her voice and patted her hand. "Okay, honey, just relax. We'll have you all fixed up in no time."

Not all fixed up, Jo thought. Far from all fixed up.

Chapter 11

As the weeks passed, Jo's arm lost its stiffness. She healed cleanly. The only traces were thin scars that promised to fade but not disappear. She found, however, that some spark had gone out of her life. Constantly, she fought against a vague dissatisfaction. Nothing— not her work, not her friends, not her books—brought about the contentment she had grown up with. She had become a woman, and her needs had shifted. Jo knew the root of her problem was Keane, but the knowledge was not a solution. He had left the circus again on the very night of her accident. Nearly four weeks later he had not returned.

Three times Jo had sat down to write him, needing to assuage her guilt for the harsh things she had said to him. Three times she had torn up the paper in frustration. No matter how she rearranged the words, they were wrong. Instead, she clung to the hope that he would come back one last time. If, she felt, they could part as friends, without bitterness or hard words, she could accept the separation. Willing this to happen, she was able to return to her routine with some tranquility. She rehearsed, performed, joined in the daily duties of circus life. She waited. The caravan moved closer to Chicago.

Jo stood in the steaming Big Top on a late August afternoon. Dressed in a leotard, she worked on ground exercises with the Beirot Brothers. It was this daily regimentation that had aided in keeping her arm limber. She could now move into a back walk-over without feeling any protest in her injured arm.

"I feel good," Jo told Raoul as they worked out. "I feel really good." She did a quick series of pirouettes.

"You don't keep your shoulder in shape by dancing on your feet," Raoul challenged.

"My shoulder's fine," she tossed back, then proved her point by bending into a handstand. Slowly, she lowered her legs to a forty-five degree angle, bringing one foot to rest on the knee of the opposite leg. "It's perfect." She executed a forward roll and sprang to her feet. "I'm strong as an ox," she claimed and did a quick back handspring followed by a backflip.

She landed at Keane's feet.

The cascade of emotions that raced through her reflected briefly in her eyes before she regained her balance. "I didn't—I didn't know you were back." Instantly, she regretted the inanity of the words but could find no others. The longing was raw in her to hurl herself into his arms. She wondered that he could not feel her need through the pores of her skin.

"I just got in." His eyes continued to search her face after his hands dropped to his sides. "This is my mother," he added. "Rachael Loring, Jovilette Wilder."

At his words, Jo's gaze moved from his face. She saw the woman beside him. If she had seen Rachael Loring in a crowd of two thousand, she would have known her for Keane's mother. The bone structure was the same, though hers was more elegant. Her brows were golden wings, flaring out at the end, as Keane's did. Her hair was smooth, brushed up and away from her face with no gray to mar its tawny perfection. But it was the eyes that sent a jolt through Jo. She had not thought to see them in anyone's face but Keane's. The woman was dressed simply in an unpretentiously tailored suit that bespoke taste and wealth. There was, however, none of the cool, distant polish that Jo had always attributed to the woman who had taken her son and left Frank. There was a charm to the smile that curved in greeting.

"Jovilette, such a lovely name. Keane's told me of you." She extended her hand, and Jo accepted, intending a quick, impersonal shake. Rachael Loring, however, laid her other hand atop their joined ones and added warmth. "Keane tells me you were very close to Frank. Perhaps we could talk."

The affection in her voice confused Jo into a stumbling reply. "I—yes. I—if you'd like."

"I should like very much." She squeezed Jo's hand again before releasing it. "Perhaps you have time to show me around?" She smiled with the question, and Jo found it increasingly difficult to remain aloof. "I'm sure there've been some changes since I was here last. You must have some business to attend to," she said, looking up at Keane. "I'm sure Jovilette will take good care of me. Won't you, dear?" Without waiting for either to respond, Rachael tucked her arm through Jo's and began to walk. "I knew your parents," she said as Keane watched them move away. "Not terribly well, I'm afraid. They came here the same year I left. But I recall they were both thrilling performers. Keane tells me you've followed your father's profession."

"Yes, I…" She hesitated, feeling oddly at a disadvantage. "I did," she finished lamely.

"You're so young." Rachael gave her a gentle smile. "How terribly brave you must be."

"No…no, not really. It's my job."

"Yes, of course." Rachael laughed at some private memory. "I've heard that before."

They were outside now, and she paused to look thoughtfully around her. "I think perhaps I was wrong. It hasn't really changed, not in thirty years. It's a wonderful place, isn't it?"

"Why did you leave?" As soon as the words were spoken, Jo regretted them. "I'm sorry," she said quickly. "I shouldn't have asked."

"Of course you should." Rachael sighed and patted Jo's hand. "It's only natural. Duffy's still here, Keane tells me." At the change in subject, Jo imagined her question had been evaded.

"Yes, I suppose he always will be."

"Could we have some coffee, or some tea, perhaps?" Rachael smiled again. "It's such a long drive from town. Is your trailer nearby?"

"It's just over in the backyard."

"Oh, yes." Rachael laughed and began to walk again. "The neighborhood that never changes over thousands of miles. Do you know the story of the dog and the bones?" she asked. Though Jo knew it well, she said nothing. "One version is that a roustabout gave his dog a bone every night after dinner. The dog would bury the bone under the trailer, then the next day try to dig it back up. Of course, it was fifty miles behind in an empty lot. He never figured it out." Quietly, she laughed to herself.

Feeling awkward, Jo opened the door to her trailer. How could this woman be the one she had resented all of her life? How could this be the cold, heartless woman who had left Frank? Oddly, Rachael seemed totally at ease in the narrow confines of the trailer.

"How efficient these are." She looked around with interest and approval. "You must barely realize you're on wheels." Casually, she picked up the volume of Thoreau which lay on Jo's counter. "Keane told me you have an avid interest in literature. In language, too," she added, glancing up from the book. Her eyes were golden and direct like her son's. Jo was tossed back suddenly to the first morning of the season when she had looked down and found Keane's eyes on her.

It made her uncomfortable to learn Keane had discussed her with his mother. "I have some tea," Jo told her as she moved toward the kitchen. "It's a better gamble than my coffee."

"That's fine," Rachael said agreeably and followed her. "I'll just sit here while you fix it." She settled herself with apparent ease at the tiny table across from the kitchen.

"I'm afraid I haven't anything else to offer you." Jo kept her back turned as she routed through her cupboard.

"Tea and conversation," Rachael answered in mild tones, "will be fine."

Jo sighed and turned. "I'm sorry." She shook her head. "I'm being rude. I just don't know what to say to you, Mrs. Loring. I've resented you for as long as I can remember. Now you're here and not at all as I imagined." She managed to smile, albeit ruefully. "You're not cold and hateful, and you look so much like…" She stopped, horrified that she had nearly blurted out Keane's name. For a moment her eyes were utterly naked.

Rachael smoothed over the awkwardness. "I don't wonder you resented me if you were as close to Frank as Keane tells me. Jovilette," she said softly, "did Frank resent me, too?"

Helpless, Jo responded to the hint of sadness. "No. Not while I knew him. I don't think Frank was capable of resentments."

"You understood him well, didn't you?" Rachael watched as Jo poured boiling water into mugs. "I understood him, too," she continued as Jo brought the mugs to the table. "He was a dreamer, a marvelous free spirit." Absently, she stirred her tea.

Consumed with curiosity, Jo sat across from her and waited for the story she sensed was coming.

"I was eighteen when I met him. I had come to the circus with a cousin. The Colossus was a bit smaller in those days," she added with a reminiscent smile, "but it was all the same. Oh, the magic!" She shook her head and sighed. "We tumbled into love so fast, married against all my family's objections and went on the road. It was exciting. I learned the web routine and helped out in wardrobe."

Jo's eyes widened. "You performed?"

"Oh, yes." Rachael's cheeks tinted a bit with pride. "I was quite good. Then I became pregnant. We were both like children waiting for Christmas. I wasn't quite nineteen when I had Keane, and I'd been with the circus for nearly a year. Things became difficult over the next season. I was young and a bit frightened of Keane. I panicked if he sneezed and was constantly dragging Frank into town to see doctors. How patient he was."

Rachael leaned forward and took Jo's hand. "Can you understand how hard this life is for one not meant for it? Can you see that through the magic of it, the excitement and wonder, there are hardships and fears and impossible demands? I was little more than a child myself, with an infant to care for, without the endurance or vocation of a trouper, without the experience or confidence of a mother. I lived on nerves for an entire season." She let out a little rush of breath. "When it was over, I went home to Chicago."

For the first time, Jo imagined the flight from Rachael's point of view. She could see a girl, younger than herself, in a strange, demanding world with a baby to care for. Over the years Jo had seen scores of people try the life she'd led and last only weeks. Still she shook her head in confusion.

"I think I understand how difficult it must have been

for you. But if you and Frank loved each other, couldn't you have worked it out somehow?"

"How?" Rachael countered. "Should I have taken a house somewhere and lived with him half a year? I would have hated him. Should he have given up his life here and settled down with me and Keane? It would have destroyed everything I loved about him." Rachael shook her head, giving Jo a soft smile. "We did love each other, Jovilette, but not enough. Compromise isn't always possible, and neither of us were capable of adjusting to the needs of the other. I tried, and Frank would have tried had I asked him. But it was lost before it had really begun. We did the wisest thing under the circumstances." Looking into Jo's eyes, she saw youth and confidence. "It seems cold and hard to you, but it was no use dragging out a painful situation. He gave me Keane and two years I've always treasured. I gave him his freedom without bitterness. Ten years after Frank, I found happiness again." She smiled softly with the memory. "I loved Frank, and that love remains as young and sweet as the day I met him."

Jo swallowed. She searched for some way to apologize for a grudge held for a lifetime. "He—Frank kept a scrapbook on Keane. He followed the Chicago papers."

"Did he?" Rachael beamed, then leaned back in her chair and lifted her mug. "How like him. Was he happy, Jovilette? Did he have what he wanted?"

"Yes," Jo answered without hesitation. "Did you?"

Rachael's eyes came back to Jo's. For a moment the look was speculative, then it grew warm. "What a good heart you have, generous and understanding. Yes, I had what I wanted. And you, Jovilette, what do you want?"

At ease now, Jo shook her head and smiled. "More than I can have."

"You're too smart for that," Rachael observed, studying her. "I think you're a fighter, not a dreamer. When the time comes to make your choice, you won't settle for anything less than all." She smiled at Jo's intent look, then rose. "Will you show me your lions? I can't tell you how I'm looking forward to seeing you perform."

"Yes, of course." Jo stood, then hesitated. She held out her hand. "I'm glad you came."

Rachael accepted the gesture. "So am I."

Throughout the rest of the day Jo looked for Keane without success. After meeting and talking with his mother, it had become even more imperative that she speak with him. Her conscience would have no rest until she made amends. By showtime she had not yet found him.

Each act seemed to run on and on as she fretted for the finish. He would be with his mother in the audience, and undoubtedly she would find him after the show. She strained with impatience as the acts dragged.

After the finale she stood at the back door, unsure whether to wait or to go to his trailer. She was struck with both relief and alarm when she saw him approaching.

"Jovilette." Rachael spoke first, taking Jo's hands in hers. "How marvelous you were, and how stunning. I see why Keane said you had an untamed beauty."

Surprised, Jo glanced up at Keane but met impassive amber eyes. "I'm glad you enjoyed it."

"Oh, I can't tell you how much. The day has brought

me some very precious memories. Our talk this afternoon meant a great deal to me." To Jo's surprise, Rachael leaned over and kissed her. "I hope to see you again. I'm going to say goodbye to Duffy before you drive me back, Keane," she continued. "I'll meet you in the car. Goodbye, Jovilette."

"Goodbye, Mrs. Loring." Jo watched her go before she turned to Keane. "She's a wonderful person. She makes me ashamed."

"There's no need for that." He tucked his hands into his pockets and watched her. "We both had our reasons for resentments, and we were both wrong. How's your arm?"

"Oh." Jo's fingers traveled to the wound automatically. "It's fine. There's barely any scarring."

"Good." The word was short and followed by silence. For a moment Jo felt her courage fail her.

"Keane," she began, then forced herself to meet his eyes directly. "I want to apologize for the horrible way I behaved after the accident."

"I told you once before," he said coolly, "I don't care for apologies."

"Please." Jo swallowed her pride and touched his arm. "I've been saving this one for a very long time. I didn't mean those things I said," she added quickly. "I hope you'll forgive me." It wasn't the eloquent apology she had planned, but it was all she could manage. His expression never altered.

"There's nothing to forgive."

"Keane, please." Jo grabbed his arm again as he turned to go. "Don't leave me feeling as if you don't forgive me. I know I said dreadful things. You have every right to be furious, but couldn't you—can't we be friends again?"

Something flickered over his face. Lifting his hand, he touched the back of it to her cheek. "You have a habit of disconcerting me, Jovilette." He dropped his hand, then thrust it into his pocket. "I've left something for you with Duffy. Be happy." He walked away from her while she dealt with the finality of his tone. He was walking out of her life. She watched him until he disappeared.

Jo had thought she would feel something, but there was nothing; no pain, no tears, no desperation. She had not known a human being could be so empty and still live.

"Jo." Duffy lumbered up to her, then held out a thick envelope. "Keane left this for you." Then he moved past her, anxious to see that all straggling towners were nudged on their way.

Jo felt all emotions had been stripped away. Absently, she glanced at the envelope as she walked to her trailer. Without enthusiasm, she stepped inside, then tore it open. She remained standing as she pulled out the contents. It took her several moments to decipher the legal jargon. She read the group of papers through twice before sitting down.

He's given it to me, she thought. Still she could not comprehend the magnitude of it. *He's given me the circus.*

Chapter 12

O'Hare Airport was an army of people and a cacophony of sound. Nearly losing herself in the chaos of it, Jo struggled through the masses and competed for a cab. At first she had merely gawked at the snow like a towner seeing his first sword swallower. Then, though she shivered inside the corduroy coat she had bought for the trip, she began to enjoy it. It was beautiful as it lay over the city, and it helped to turn her mind from the purpose of her journey. Never had she been north so late in the year. Chicago in November was a sensational sight.

She had learned, after the initial shock had worn off, that Keane had not only given her the circus but a responsibility, as well. Almost immediately there had been contracts to negotiate. She had been tossed into a sea of paperwork, forced to rely heavily on Duffy's experience as she tried to regain her balance. As the season had come to a close, Jo had attempted a dozen times to call Chicago. Each time, she had hung up before Keane's number could be dialed. It would be, she had decided, more appropriate to see him in person. Her trip had been postponed a few weeks due to Jamie and Rose's wedding.

It was there, as she had stood as maid of honor, that Jo had realized what she must do. There was only one thing she truly wanted, and that was to be with Keane. Watching Rose's face as their vows had been exchanged, Jo had recalled her unflagging determination to win the man she loved.

And will I stay here? Jo had demanded of herself thousands of miles away from him. No. Her heart had begun to thud as she had mapped out a plan. She would go to Chicago to see him. She would not be turned away. He had wanted her once; she would make him want her again. She would not live out her life without at least some small portion of it being part of his. He didn't have to love her. It was enough that she loved him.

And so, shivering against the unfamiliar cold, Jo scrambled into a cab and headed across town. She brushed her hair free of snow with chilled fingers, thinking how idiotic she had been to forget to buy a hat and gloves. *What if he isn't home?* she thought suddenly. *What if he's gone to Europe or Japan or California?* Panic made her giddy, and she pushed it down. *He has to be home. It's Sunday, and he's sitting at home reading or going over a brief—or entertaining a woman,* she thought, appalled. *I should stop and call. I should tell the driver to take me back to the airport.* Closing her eyes, Jo fought to regain her calm. She took long, deep breaths and stared at the buildings and sidewalks. Gradually, she felt the tiny gurgle of hysteria dissipate.

I won't be afraid, she told herself and tried to believe it. *I won't be afraid.* But Jovilette, the woman who reclined on a living rug of lions, was very much afraid. What if he rejected her? *I won't let him reject me,* she told herself with a confident lift of her chin. *I'll seduce him.* She pressed her fingers to her temples. *I wouldn't know how to begin. I've got to tell the driver to turn around.*

But before she could form the words, the cab pulled up to a curb. With the precision of a robot, Jo paid the fare, overtipping in her agitation, and climbed out.

Long after the cab had pulled away, she stood staring up at the massive glass-girdled building. Snow waltzed around her, sprinkling her hair and shoulders. A jostle from a rushing pedestrian broke the spell. She picked up her suitcases and hurried through the front door of the apartment buildings.

The lobby was enormous, with smoked glass walls and a deep shag carpet. Not knowing she should give her name at the desk, Jo wandered toward the elevators, innocently avoiding detection by merging with a group of tenants. Once inside the car, Jo pushed the button for the penthouse with a nerveless forefinger. The chatter of those in the elevator with her registered only as a distant humming. She never noticed when the car stopped for their departure.

When it stopped a second time and the doors slid open, she stared at the empty space for ten full seconds. Only as the automatic doors began to close did she snap out of her daze. Pushing them open again, she stepped through and into the hall. Her legs were wobbly, but she forced them to move forward in the direction of the penthouse. Panic sped up and down her spine until she set down her bags and leaned her brow against Keane's door. She urged air in and out of her lungs. She remembered that Rachael Loring had called her a fighter. Jo swallowed, lifted her chin and knocked. The wait was mercifully brief before Keane opened the door. She saw surprise light his eyes as he stared at her.

Her hair was dusted with snow as it lay over the shoulders of her coat. Her face glowed with the cold, and her eyes were bright, nearly feverish with her struggle for calm. Only once did her mouth tremble before she spoke.

"Hello, Keane."

He only stared, his eyes running over her in disbelief. He was leaner, she thought as she studied his face. As she filled herself with the sight of him, she saw he wore a sweatshirt and jeans. His feet were bare. He hadn't shaved, and her hand itched to test the roughness of his beard.

"What are you doing here?" Jo felt a resurgence of panic. His tone was harsh, and he had not answered her smile. She strained for poise.

"May I come in?" she asked, her smile cracking.

"What?" He seemed distracted by the question. His brows lowered into a frown.

"May I come in?" she repeated, barely defeating the urge to turn tail and run.

"Oh, yes, of course. I'm sorry." Running a hand through his hair, Keane stepped back and gestured her inside.

Instantly, Jo's shoes sank into the luxurious pile of the buff-colored carpet. For a moment she allowed herself to gaze around the room, using the time for the additional purpose of regaining her composure. It was an open, sweeping room with sharp, contrasting colors. There was a deep brown sectional sofa with a chrome and glass coffee table. There were high-backed chairs in soft creams and vivid slashes of blue in chunky floor pillows. There were paintings, one she thought she recognized as a Picasso, and a sculpture she was certain was a Rodin.

On the far right of the room there was an elevation of two steps. Just beyond was a huge expanse of glass that featured a spreading view of Chicago. Jo moved toward it with undisguised curiosity. Now, inexplicably, fear had lessened. She found that once she had stepped over the threshold she had committed herself. She was no longer afraid.

"It's wonderful," she said, turning back to him. "How marvelous to have a whole city at your feet every day. You must feel like a king."

"I've never thought of it that way." With half the room between them, he studied her. She looked small and fragile with the bustling city at her back.

"I would," she said, and now her smile came easily. "I'd stand at the window and feel regal and pompous."

At last she saw his lips soften and curve. "Jovilette," he said quietly. "What are you doing in my world?"

"I needed to talk to you," she answered simply. "I had to come here to do it."

He moved to her then, but slowly, with his eyes on hers. "It must be important."

"I thought so."

His brow lifted, then he shrugged. "Well, then, we'll talk. But first, let's have your coat."

Jo's cold fingers fumbled with the buttons and caused Keane to frown again. "Good heavens, you're frozen." He captured her hands between his and swore. "Where are your gloves?" he demanded like an irate parent. "It must be all of twelve degrees outside."

"I forgot to buy any," Jo told him as she dealt with the heavenly feeling of his hands restoring warmth to hers.

"Idiot. Don't you know better than to come to Chicago in November without gloves?"

"No." Jo responded to his anger with a cheerful smile. "I've never been to Chicago in November before. It's wonderful."

His eyes lifted from her hands to her face. He watched her for a long moment, then she heard him sigh. "I'd nearly convinced myself I could be cured."

Jo's eyes clouded with concern. "Have you been ill?"

Keane laughed with a shake of his head, then he pushed away the question and became brisk again. "Here, let's have your coat. I'll get you some coffee."

"You needn't bother," she began as he undid the buttons on the coat himself and drew it from her shoulders.

"I'd feel better if I was certain your circulation was restored." He paused and looked down at her as he laid her coat over his arm. She wore a green angora sweater with pearl buttons and a gray skirt in thin wool. The soft fabric draped softly at her breasts and over her hips and thighs. Her shoes were dainty and impractical sling-back heels.

"Is something wrong?"

"I've never seen you wear anything but a costume or jeans."

"Oh." Jo laughed and combed her fingers through her damp hair. "I expect I look different."

"Yes, you do." His voice was low, and there was a frown in his eyes. "Right now you look as if you've come from college for the holidays." He touched the ends of her hair, then turned away. "Sit down. I'll get the coffee."

A bit puzzled by his mercurial moods, Jo wandered about the room, finally ignoring a chair to kneel beside one of the pillows near the picture window. Though the carpet swallowed Keane's footsteps, she sensed his return.

"How wonderful to have a real winter, if just for the snow." She turned a radiant face his way. "I've always wondered what Christmas is like with snow and icicles." Images of snowflakes danced in her eyes. Seeing he carried two mugs of coffee, she rose and took one. "Thank you."

"Are you warm enough?" he asked after a moment.

Jo nodded and sat in one of the two chairs opposite the sofa. The novelty of the city made her mission seem like a grand adventure. Keane sat beside her, and for a moment they drank in companionable silence.

"What did you want to talk to me about, Jo?"

Jo swallowed, ignoring the faint trembling in her chest. "A couple of things. The circus, for one." She shifted in her chair until she faced him. "I didn't write because I felt it too important. I didn't phone for the same reason. Keane..." All her carefully thought-out speeches deserted her. "You can't just give something like that away. I can't take it from you."

"Why not?" He shrugged and sipped his coffee. "We both know it's always been yours. A piece of paper doesn't change that one way or the other."

"Keane, Frank left it to you."

"And I gave it to you."

Jo made a small sound of frustration. "Perhaps if I could pay you for it…"

"Someone asked me once what was the value of a dream or the price of a human spirit." Jo shifted her eyes to his helplessly. "I didn't have an answer then. Do you have one now?"

She sighed and shook her head. "I don't know what to say to you. 'Thank you' is far from adequate."

"It's not necessary, either," Keane told her. "I simply gave back what was yours in any case. What else was there, Jo? You said there were a couple of things."

This was it, Jo's brain told her. Carefully, she set down the coffee and rose. Waiting for her stomach to settle, she walked a few feet out into the room, then turned. She allowed herself a deep breath before she met Keane's eyes.

"I want to be your mistress," she said with absolute calm.

"What?" Both Keane's face and voice registered utter shock.

Jo swallowed and repeated. "I want to be your mistress. That's still the right term, isn't it, or is it antiquated? Is *lover* right? I've never done this before."

Slowly, Keane set his mug beside hers and rose. He

did not move toward her but watched her with probing eyes. "Jo, you don't know what you're saying."

"Oh, yes, I do," she cut him off and nodded. "I might not have the terminology exactly right, but I do know what I mean, and I'm sure you do, too. I want to be with you," she continued and took a step toward him. "I want you to make love to me. I want to live with you if you'll let me, or at least close by."

"Jo, you're not talking sensibly." Sharply, Keane broke into her speech. Turning away, he thrust his hands into his pockets and balled them into fists. "You don't know what you're asking."

"Don't I appeal to you anymore?"

Keane whirled, infuriated with the trace of curiosity in her voice. "How can you ask me that?" he demanded. "Of course you appeal to me! I'm not dead or in the throes of senility!"

She moved closer to him. "Then if I want you, and you want me, why can't we be lovers?"

Keane swore violently and grabbed her shoulders. "Do you think I could have you for a winter and then blithely let you go? Do you think I could untangle myself at the start of the season and watch you stroll out of my life? Haven't you the sense to see what you do to me?" He shook her hard with the question, stealing any breath she might have used to answer him.

"You make me crazy!" Abruptly, he dragged her against him. His mouth bruised hers, his fingers dug into her flesh. Jo's head spun with confusion and pain and ecstasy. It seemed centuries since she had tasted his mouth on hers. She heard him groan as he tore himself away. He turned, leaving her to find her own balance as the room swayed. "What do I have to do to be rid of you?" His words came in furious undertones.

Jo blew out a breath. "I don't think kissing me like that is a very good start."

"I'm aware of that," he murmured. She watched the rise and fall of his shoulders. "I've been trying to avoid doing it since I opened the door."

Quietly, Jo walked to him and put a hand on his arm. "You're tense," she discovered and automatically sought to soothe the muscles. "I'm sorry if I'm going about this the wrong way. I thought telling you outright would be better than trying to seduce you. I don't think I'd be very good at that."

Keane made a sound somewhere between a laugh and a moan. "Jovilette," he murmured before he turned and gathered her into his arms. "How do I resist you? How many times must I pull away before I'm free of you? Even the thought of you drives me mad."

"Keane." She sighed and shut her eyes. "I've wanted you to hold me for so long. I want to belong to you, even for just a little while."

"No." He pulled away, then forced her chin up with his thumb and forefinger. "Don't you see that once would be too much and a lifetime wouldn't be enough? I love you too much to let you go and enough to know I have to." Shock robbed her of speech. She only stared as he continued. "It was different when I didn't know, when I thought I was—how did you put it? 'Dazzled.'" He smiled briefly at the word. "I was certain if I could make love to you, I could get you out of my system. Then, the night Ari died, I held you while you slept. I realized I was in love with you, had been in love with you right from the beginning."

"But you…" Jo shook her head as if to clear it. "You never told me, and you seemed so cold, so distant."

"I couldn't touch you without wanting more." He pulled her close again and for a moment buried his face in her hair. "But I couldn't stay away. I knew if I wanted to have you, to really have you, one of us had to give up what we did, what we were. I wondered if I could give up the law. It was really all I ever wanted to do. I discovered I wanted you more."

"Oh, Keane." She shook her head, but he put her from him suddenly.

"Then I found out that wouldn't work, either." Keane turned, paced to the window and stared out. The snow was falling heavily. "Every time you walked into that cage, I walked into hell. I thought perhaps I'd get used to it, but it only got worse. I tried leaving, coming back here, but I could never shake you loose. I kept coming back. The day you were hurt…" Keane paused. Jo heard him draw in his breath, and when he continued, his voice was deeper. "I watched you step in front of that boy and take the blow. I can't tell you what I felt at that moment. There aren't words for it. All I could think of was getting to you. I wonder if Pete ever told you that I decked him before Buck got to me. He took it very well, considering. Then I had to—to just stand there and watch while that cat stalked you. I've never known that kind of fear before. The kind that empties you out, body and soul."

He lapsed into silence. "Then it was over," he continued, "and I got to you. You were so white, and you were bleeding in my arms." He muttered an oath, then was silent again. He shook his head. "I wanted to burn the place down, get you away, strangle the cats with my bare hands. Anything. I wanted to hold you, but I couldn't get past the fear and the unreasonable anger at having been helpless. Before my hands stopped shaking, you were making plans to go back into that damnable cage. I wanted to kill you myself then and be done with it."

Slowly, Keane turned and walked back to her. "I saw it happen again every time I closed my eyes for weeks afterward. I can show you exactly where the scars are." He lifted a finger and traced four lines on her upper arm precisely where the claws had ripped her skin. He dropped his hand and shook his head. "I can't watch you go in the cage, Jo." He lifted his hand again and let it linger over her hair. "If I let you stay with me now, I wouldn't be able to let you go back to your own life. And I can't ask you to give it up."

"I wish you would." Solemn eyed, Jo watched him. "I very much wish you would."

"Jo." Shaking his head, he turned away. "I know what it means to you."

"No more than the law means to you, I imagine," she said briskly. "But you said you were willing to give that up."

"Yes, but…"

"Oh, very well." She pushed back her hair. "If you won't ask me, I'll have to ask you. Will you marry me?"

Keane turned back, giving her his lowered brow frown. "Jo, you can't…"

"Of course I can. This is the twentieth century. If

I want to ask you to marry me, then I will. I did," she pointed out.

"Jo, I don't…"

"Yes or no, please, Counselor. This isn't an easy question." She stepped forward until they stood toe to toe. "I'm in love with you, and I want to marry you and have several babies. Is that agreeable?"

Keane's mouth opened and closed. He gave her an odd smile and lifted his hands to her shoulders. "This is rather sudden."

Jo felt a wild surge of joy. "Perhaps it is," she admitted. "I'll give you a minute to think about it. But I might as well tell you, I won't take no for an answer."

Keane's fingers traced the curve of her neck. "It seems I have little choice."

"None at all," she corrected. Boldly, she locked her arms around him and pulled his mouth down to hers. The kiss was instantly urgent, instantly searching. Joined, they lowered to the rug and clung. For a long, long moment, their lips were united in a language too complex for words. Then, as if to reassure himself she was real, Keane searched the familiar curves of her body, tasted the longed-for flavor of her skin.

"Why did I think I could live without you?" he whispered. His mouth came desperately back to hers. "Be sure, Jo, be sure." Roughened with emotion, his voice was low while the words were spoken against her lips. "I'll never be able to let you go. I'm asking you for everything."

"No. No, it's not like that. Hold me tighter. Kiss me again," she demanded as his lips roamed her face. "Kiss me." She wondered if the sound of pleasure she heard

was his or her own. She had not known a kiss could be
so intimate, so terrifyingly exciting. No, she thought
as she soared with the knowledge that he loved her. He
wasn't asking everything, he was giving it.

"I'm leaving something behind," she told him when
their lips parted, "and replacing it with something in-
finitely more important." She buried her face in the
curve of his neck. "When you realize how much I love
you, you'll understand."

Keane drew away and stared down at her. At last he
spoke, but it was only her name. It was a soft sigh of a
sound. She smiled at it and lifted a hand to his cheek.
"If there's a way to compromise…"

"No." She shook her head, remembering his mother's
words. "Sometimes there can't be a compromise. We
love each other enough not to need one. Please, don't
think I'm making a sacrifice. I'm not." She smiled a
little and rubbed her palm experimentally over the stub-
ble of his neglected beard. "I don't regret one minute
of my life in the circus, and I don't regret changing it.
You've given me the circus, so I'll always be a part of
it." Her smile faded, and her eyes grew serious. "Will
you belong to me, Keane?"

He took her hand from his cheek and pressed it to
his lips. "I already do. I love you, Jovilette. I'll spend a
lifetime loving you."

"That's not long enough," she said as their lips met
again. "I want more. I want forever."

With slow, building passion, his hands moved over
her. Taking his time, he loosened the buttons on her
sweater. "So beautiful," he murmured as his lips trailed
down her throat and found the gentle swell. Jo's breath

caught at the new intimacy. "You're trembling. I love knowing I can make your skin tremble under my hands." His lips roamed back to hers before he cradled her in his arms. "I've wanted to be with you, to hold you, just hold you, for so long. I can't remember not wanting it."

With a sigh washed with contentment, Jo snuggled against him. "Keane," she murmured.

"Hmm?"

"You never answered me."

"About what?" He kissed her closed lids, then tangled his fingers in her hair.

Jo opened her eyes. Her brows arched over them. "Are you going to marry me or not?"

Keane laughed, rolled her onto her back and planted a long, lingering kiss on her mouth. "Is tomorrow soon enough?"

* * * * *

DANCE OF DREAMS

For Cora Spasibo.

Chapter 1

The cat lay absolutely still on his back, eyes closed, front paws resting on his white chest. The last rays of the sun slanted through the long vertical blinds and shone on his orange fur. He was undisturbed by the sound of a key in the lock that broke the silence of the apartment. He half opened his eyes when he heard his mistress's voice but closed them again, just as lazily, when he noted she was not alone. She'd brought that man home with her again, and the cat had no liking for him. He went back to sleep.

"But Ruth, it's barely eight o'clock. The sun's still up."

Ruth dropped her keys on the dainty Queen Anne table beside the door, then turned with a smile. "Donald, I told you I had to make it an early evening. Dinner was lovely. I'm glad you talked me into going out."

"In that case," he said, taking her into his arms in a practiced move, "let me talk you into extending the evening."

Ruth accepted the kiss, enjoyed the gentle surge of warmth just under her skin. But when he pulled her closer, she drew away. "Donald." Her smile was the same easy one she had worn before the kiss. "You really have to go."

"A nightcap," he murmured, kissing her again, lightly, persuasively.

"Not tonight." She moved firmly out of his arms. "I have an early class tomorrow, Donald, plus a full day of rehearsals and fittings."

He gave her a quick kiss on the forehead. "It'd be easier for me if it were another man, but this passion for dancing..." He shrugged before reluctantly turning to leave. Was he losing his touch? he wondered.

Ruth Bannion was the first woman in over ten years who had held him off so consistently and successfully. Why, he asked himself, did he keep coming back? She opened the door for him, giving him one last, lingering smile as she urged him through. A glimpse of her silhouette in the dim light before she shut the door on him answered his question. She was more than beautiful—she was unique.

Ruth was still smiling as she hooked the chain and security lock. She enjoyed Donald Keyser. He was tall and dark and stylishly handsome, with an acerbic humor and exquisite taste. She respected his talents as a designer, wore a number of his creations herself and was able to relax in his company—when she found the time. Of course, she was aware that Donald would have preferred a more intimate relationship.

It had been a simple matter for Ruth to decide against it. She was attracted to Donald and was fond of him. But he simply did not stir her emotions. While she knew he could make her laugh, she doubted very much that he could make her cry. Turning into the darkened apartment, Ruth felt a twinge of regret. She felt abruptly, unexpectedly alone.

Ruth turned to study herself in the gilt-framed, rectangular mirror that hung in the hallway. It was one of the first pieces she had bought when she had moved into the apartment. The glass was old, and she had paid a ridiculous price for it, despite the dark spots near the top right-hand corner. It had meant a great deal to Ruth to be able to hang it on the wall of her own apartment, her own home. Now, as the light grew dim, she stared at her reflection.

She had left her hair down for the evening, and it flowed over her shoulders to swing past her elbows. With an impatient move, she tossed it back. It lifted, then settled behind her, black and thick. Her face, like her frame, was small and delicate, but her features weren't even. Her mouth was generous, her nose small and straight, her chin a subtle point. Though the bones in her face were elegant, the deep brown eyes were huge and slanted catlike. The brows over them were dark and straight. An exotic face, she had been told, yet she saw no beauty in it. She knew that with the right makeup and lighting she could look stunning, but that was different. That was an illusion, a role, not Ruth Bannion.

With a sigh, Ruth turned away from the mirror and crossed to the plush-covered Victorian sofa. Knowing she was now alone, Nijinsky rolled over, stretched and yawned luxuriously, then padded over to curl in her lap. Ruth scratched his ears absently. Who was Ruth Bannion? she wondered.

Five years before, she had been a very green, very eager student beginning a new phase of her training in New York. *Thanks to Lindsay*, Ruth remembered with a smile. Lindsay Dunne, teacher, friend, idol—the finest classical ballerina Ruth had ever seen. She had convinced Uncle Seth to let her come here. It warmed Ruth to think of them now, married, living in the Cliff House in Connecticut with their children. Every time she visited them, the love and happiness lingered with her for weeks afterward. She had never seen two people more right for each other or more in love. Except perhaps her own parents.

Even after six years, thinking of her parents brought on a wave of sadness—for herself and for the tragic loss of two bright, warm people. But in a strange way Ruth knew it had been their death that had brought her to where she was today.

Seth Bannion had become her guardian, and their move to the small seacoast town in Connecticut had brought them both to Lindsay. It had been through Lindsay that Seth had been made to see Ruth's need for more training. Ruth knew it hadn't been easy for her uncle to allow her to make the move to New York when she had been only seventeen. She had, of course, been well cared for by the Evanstons, but it had been difficult for Seth to give her up to a life he knew to be so difficult and demanding. It was love that had made him hesitate and love that had ultimately ruled his decision. Her life had changed forever.

Or perhaps, Ruth reflected, it had changed that first

time she had walked into Lindsay's school to dance. It had been there that she had first danced for Davidov.

How terrified she had been! She had stood there in front of a man who had been heralded as the finest dancer of the decade. A master, a legend. Nikolai Davidov, who had partnered only the most gifted ballerinas, including Lindsay Dunne. Indeed, he had come to Connecticut to convince Lindsay to return to New York as the star in a ballet he had written. Ruth had been overwhelmed by his presence and almost too stunned to move when he had ordered her to dance for him. But he had been charming. A smile touched Ruth's mouth as she leaned her head back on the cushions. And who, she thought lazily, could be more charming than Nick when he chose to be? She had obeyed, losing herself in the movement and the music. Then he had spoken those simple, stunning words.

"When you come to New York, come to me."

She had been very young and had thought of Nikolai Davidov as a name to be whispered reverently. She would have danced barefoot down Broadway if he had told her to.

She had worked hard to please him, terrified of the sting of his temper, unable to bear the coldness of his disapproval. And he had pushed her. Ruth remembered how he had been constantly, mercilessly demanding. There had been nights she had curled up in bed, too exhausted to even weep. But then he would smile or toss off a compliment, and every moment of pain would vanish.

She had danced with him, fought with him, laughed with him, watching the gradual changes in him over the years, and still, there was an elusive quality about him.

Perhaps that was the secret of his attraction for
women, she thought: the subtle air of mystery, his
foreign accent, his reticence about his past. She had
gotten over her infatuation with him years ago. She
smiled, remembering the intensity of her crush on
him. He hadn't appeared to even notice it. She had
been scarcely eighteen. He'd been nearly thirty and
surrounded by beautiful women. *And still is*, she reminded herself, smiling in rueful amusement as she
stood to stretch. The cat, now dislodged from her lap,
stalked huffily away.

My heart's whole and safe, Ruth decided. Perhaps
too safe. She thought of Donald. Well, it couldn't be
helped. She yawned and stretched again. And there was
that early class in the morning.

Sweat dampened Ruth's T-shirt. Nick's choreography
for *The Red Rose* was complicated and strenuous. She
took a much-needed breather at the barre. The remain-
der of the cast was scattered around the rehearsal hall,
either dancing under Nick's unflagging instructions or
waiting, as she did, for the next summons.

It was only eleven, but Ruth had already worked
through a two-hour morning class. The long, loose
T-shirt she wore over her tights was darkened by patches
of perspiration; a few tendrils of her hair had escaped
from her tightly secured bun. Still, watching Nick demonstrate a move, any thought of fatigue drained from
her. He was, she thought as she always did, absolutely
fabulous.

As artistic director of the company and as established
creator of ballets, he no longer had to dance to remain
in the limelight. He danced, Ruth knew, because he was

born to do so. He skimmed just under six feet, but his lean, wiry build gave an illusion of more height. His hair was like gold dust and curled carelessly around a face that had never completely lost its boyish charm. His mouth was beautiful, full and finely sculpted. And when he smiled...

When he smiled, there was no resisting him. Fine lines would spread out from his eyes, and the large irises would become incredibly blue.

Watching him demonstrate a turn, Ruth was grateful that at thirty-three, with all his other professional obligations, he still continued to dance.

He stopped the pianist with a flick of his hand. "All right, children," he said in his musically Russian-accented voice. "It could be worse."

This from Davidov, Ruth mused wryly, was close to an accolade.

"Ruth, the pas de deux from the first act."

She crossed to him instantly, giving an absent brush at the locks of hair that danced around her face. Nick was a creature of moods—varied, mercurial, unexplained moods. Today he appeared to be all business. Ruth knew how to match his temperament with her own. Facing, they touched right hands, palm to palm. Without a word, they began.

It was an early love scene, more a duel of wits than an expression of romance. But Nick hadn't written a fairy tale ballet this time. He had written a passionate one. The characters were a prince and a gypsy, each fiercely flesh and blood. To accommodate them the dances were exuberant and athletic. They challenged each other; he demanded, she defied. Now and then a toss of the head or a gesture of the wrist was employed to accent the mood.

The late summer sun poured through the windows, patterning the floor. Drops of sweat trickled unheeded, unfelt, down Ruth's back as she turned in, then out of Nick's arms. The character of Carlotta would enrage and enrapture the prince throughout the ballet. The mood for their duel of hearts was set during their first encounter.

It was at times like this, when Ruth danced with Nick, that she realized she would always worship him, the dancer, the legend. To be his partner was the greatest thrill of her life. He took her beyond herself, beyond what she had ever hoped to be. On her journey from student to the corps de ballet to principal dancer, Ruth had danced with many partners, but none of them could touch Nick Davidov for sheer brilliance and precision. And endurance, she thought ruefully as he ordered the pas de deux to begin again.

Ruth took a moment to catch her breath as the pianist turned back the pages of the score. Nick turned to her, lifting his hand for hers. "Where is your passion today, little one?" he demanded.

It was a salutation Ruth detested, and he knew it. The grin shot across his face as she glared at him. Saying nothing, she placed her palm to his.

"Now, my gypsy, tell me to go to the devil with your body as well as your eyes. Again."

They began, but this time Ruth stopped thinking of her pleasure in dancing with him. She competed now, step for step, leap for leap. Her annoyance gave Nick precisely what he wanted. She dared him to best her. She spun into his arms, her eyes hot. Poised only a moment, she spun away again and with a grand jeté, challenged him to follow her.

They ended as they had begun, palm to palm, with her head thrown back. Laughing, Nick caught her close and kissed her enthusiastically on both cheeks.

"There, now, you're wonderful! You spit at me even while you offer your hand."

Ruth's breath was coming quickly after the effort of the dance. Her eyes, still lit with temper, remained on Nick's. A swift flutter raced up her spine, distracting her. She saw that Nick had felt it, too. She saw it in his eyes, felt it in the fingers he pressed into the small of her back. Then it was gone, and Nick drew her away.

"Lunch," he stated and earned a chorus of approval. The rehearsal hall began to clear immediately. "Ruth." Nick took her hand as she turned to join the others. "I want to talk to you."

"All right, after lunch."

"Now. Here."

Her brows drew together. "Nick, I missed breakfast—"

"There's yogurt in the refrigerator downstairs, and Perrier." Releasing her hand, Nick walked to the piano. He sat and began to improvise. "Bring some for me, too."

Hands on her hips, Ruth watched him play. *Of course*, she thought wrathfully, *he'd never consider I'd say no. He'd never think to ask me if I had other plans. He expects I'll run off like a good little girl and do his bidding without a word of complaint.*

"Insufferable," she said aloud.

Nick glanced up but continued to play. "Did you speak?" he asked mildly.

"Yes," she answered distinctly. "I said, you're insufferable."

"Yes." Nick smiled at her good-humoredly. "I am."

Despite herself, Ruth laughed. "What flavor?" she demanded and was pleased when he gave her a blank look. "Yogurt," she reminded him. "What flavor yogurt, Davidov."

In short order Ruth's arms were ladened with cartons of yogurt, spoons, glasses and a large bottle of Perrier. There was the sound of chatter from the canteen below her mingling with Nick's playing the piano from the hall above. She climbed the stairs, exchanging remarks with two members of the corps and a male soloist. The music Nick played was a low, bluesy number. Because she recognized the style, Ruth knew it to be one of his own compositions. *No, not a composition*, she corrected as she paused in the doorway to watch him. *A composition you write down, preserve. This is music that comes from the heart.*

The sun's rays fell over his hair and his hands—long, narrow hands with fluid fingers that could express more with a gesture than the average person could with a speech.

He looks so alone!

The thought sped into her mind unexpectedly, catching her off balance. *It's the music*, she decided. *It's only because he plays such sad music.* She walked toward him, her ballet shoes making no sound on the wood floor.

"You look lonely, Nick."

From the way his head jerked up, Ruth knew she had broken into some deep, private thought. He looked at her oddly a moment, his fingers poised above the piano keys. "I was," he said. "But that's not what I want to talk to you about."

Ruth arched a brow. "Is this going to be a business lunch?" she asked him as she set cartons of yogurt on the piano.

"No." He took the bottle of Perrier, turning the cap. "Then we'd argue, and that's bad for the digestion, yes? Come, sit beside me."

Ruth sat on the bench, automatically steeling herself for the jolt of electricity. To be where he was was to be in the vortex of power. Even now, relaxed, contemplating a simple dancer's lunch, he was like a circuit left on hold.

"Is there a problem?" she asked, reaching for a carton of yogurt and a spoon.

"That's what I want to know."

Puzzled, she turned her head to find him studying her face. He had bottomless blue eyes, clear as glass, and the dancer's ability for complete stillness.

"What do you mean?"

"I had a call from Lindsay." The blue eyes were fixed unwaveringly on hers. His lashes were the color of the darkest shade of his hair.

More confused, Ruth wrinkled her brow. "Oh?"

"She thinks you're not happy." He was still watching her steadily: the pressure began to build at the base of her neck. Ruth turned away, and it lessened immediately. There had never been anyone else who could unnerve her with a look.

"Lindsay worries too much," she said lightly, dipping the spoon into the yogurt.

"Are you, Ruth?" Nick laid his hand on her arm,

and she was compelled to look back at him. "Are you unhappy?"

"No," she said immediately, truthfully. She gave him the slow half smile that was so much a part of her. "No."

He continued to scan her face as his hand slid down to her wrist. "Are you happy?"

She opened her mouth, prepared to answer, then closed it again on a quick sound of frustration. Why must those eyes be on hers, so direct, demanding perfect honesty? They wouldn't accept platitudes or pat answers. "Shouldn't I be?" she countered. His fingers tightened on her wrist as she started to rise.

"Ruth." She had no choice but to face him again. "Are we friends?"

She fumbled for an answer. A simple yes hardly covered the complexities of her feelings for him or the uneven range of their relationship. "Sometimes," she answered cautiously. "Sometimes we are."

Nick accepted that, though amusement lit his eyes. "Well said," he murmured. Unexpectedly, he gathered both of her hands in his and brought them to his lips. His mouth was soft as a whisper on her skin. Ruth didn't pull away but stiffened, surprised and wary. His eyes met hers placidly over their joined hands, as if he were unaware of her would-be withdrawal. "Will you tell me why you're not happy?"

Carefully, coolly, Ruth drew her hands from his. It was too difficult to behave in a contained manner when touching him. He was a physical man, demanding physical responses. Rising, Ruth walked across the room to a window. Manhattan hustled by below.

"To be perfectly honest," she began thoughtfully, "I haven't given my happiness much thought. Oh, no."

She laughed and shook her head. "That sounds pomp-ous." She spun back to face him, but he wasn't smil-ing. "Nick, I only meant that until you asked me, I just hadn't thought about being unhappy." She shrugged and leaned back against the windowsill. Nick poured some fizzing water and, rising, took it to her.

"Lindsay's worried about you."

"Lindsay has enough to worry about with Uncle Seth and the children and her school."

"She loves you," he said simply.

He saw it—the slow smile, the darkening warmth in her eyes, the faintly mystified pleasure. "Yes, I know she does."

"That surprises you?" Absently, he wound a loose tendril of her hair around his finger. It was soft and slightly damp.

"Her generosity astonishes me. I suppose it always will." She paused a moment, then continued quickly before she lost her nerve. "Were you ever in love with her?"

"Yes," he answered instantly, without embarrassment or regret. "Years ago, briefly." He smiled and pushed one of Ruth's loosened pins back into her hair. "She was always just out of my reach. Then before I knew it, we were friends."

"Strange," she said after a moment. "I can't imagine you considering anything out of your reach."

Nick smiled again. "I was very young, the age you are now. And it's you we're speaking of, Ruth, not Lind-say. She thinks perhaps I push you too hard."

"Push too hard?" Ruth cast her eyes at the ceiling. "*You*, Nikolai?"

He gave her his haughtily amused look. "I, too, was astonished."

Ruth shook her head, then moved back to the piano. She exchanged Perrier for yogurt. "I'm fine, Nick. I hope you told her so." When he didn't answer, Ruth turned, the spoon still between her lips. "Nick?"

"I thought perhaps you've had an unhappy...relationship."

Her brows lifted. "Do you mean, am I unhappy over a lover?"

It was instantly apparent that he hadn't cared for her choice of words. "You're very blunt, little one."

"I'm not a child," she countered testily, then slapped the carton onto the piano again. "And I don't—"

"Do you still see the designer?" Nick interrupted her coolly.

"The designer has a name," she said sharply. "Donald Keyser. You make him sound like a label on a dress."

"Do I?" Nick gave her a guileless smile. "But you don't answer my question."

"No, I don't." Ruth lifted the glass of Perrier and sipped calmly, though a flash of temper leaped into her eyes.

"Ruth, are you still seeing him?"

"That's none of your business." She made her voice light, but the steel was beneath it.

"You are a member of the company." Though his eyes blazed into hers, he enunciated each word carefully. "I am the director."

"Have you also taken over the role of Father Confessor?" Ruth tossed back. "Must your dancers check out their lovers with you?"

"Be careful how you provoke me," he warned.

"I don't have to justify my social life to you, Nick," she shot back without a pause. "I go to class, I'm on time for rehearsals. I work hard."

"Did I ask you to justify anything?"

"Not really. But I'm tired of you playing the role of stern uncle with me." A frown line ran down between her brows as she stepped closer to him. "I have an uncle already, and I don't need you to look over my shoulder."

"Don't you?" He plucked a loose pin from her hair and twirled it idly between his thumb and forefinger while his eyes pierced into hers.

His casual tone fanned her fury. "No!" She tossed her head. "Stop treating me like a child."

Nick gripped her shoulders, surprising her with the quick violence. She was drawn hard against him, molded to the body she knew so well. But this was different. There were no music or steps or storyline. She could feel his anger—and something more, something just as volatile. She knew he was capable of sudden bursts of rage, and she knew how to deal with them, but now...

Her body was responding, astonishing her. Their hearts beat against each other. She could feel his fingertips digging into her flesh, but there was no pain. The hands she had brought up to shove him away with were now balled loosely into fists and held motionlessly aloft.

He dropped his eyes to her lips. A sharp pang of longing struck her—sharper, sweeter than anything she had ever experienced. It left her dazed and aching.

Slowly, knowing only that what she wanted was a breath away, Ruth leaned forward, letting her lids sink down in preparation for his kiss. His breath whispered on her lips, and hers parted. She said his name once, wonderingly.

Then, with a jerk and a muttered Russian oath, Nikolai pushed her away. "You should know better," he said, biting off the words, "than to deliberately make me angry."

"Was that what you were feeling?" she asked, stung by his rejection.

"Don't push it." Nick tossed off the American slang with a movement of his shoulders. Temper lingered in his eyes. "Stick with your designer," he murmured at length in a quieter tone as he turned back to the piano. "Since he seems to suit you so well."

He sat again and began to play, dismissing her with silence.

Chapter 2

She must have imagined it. Ruth relived the surge of concentrated desire she had experienced in Nick's arms. *No, I'm wrong*, she told herself again. *I've been in his arms countless times and never, never felt anything like that. And*, Ruth reminded herself as she showered off the grime of the day, *I was in his arms a half-dozen times after, when we went back to rehearsal.*

There had been something, she admitted grudgingly as she recalled the crackling tension in the air when they had gone over a passage time and time again. But it had been annoyance, aggravation.

Ruth let the water flow and stream over her, plastering her hair to her naked back. She tried, now that she was alone, to figure out her reaction to Nick's sudden embrace.

Her response had been nakedly physical and shockingly urgent. On the other hand, she could recall the warm pleasure of Donald's kisses—the soft, easily resisted temptation. Donald used quiet words and gentle persuasion. He used all the traditional trappings of seduction: flowers, candlelight, intimate dinners. He made her feel—Ruth grasped for a word. *Pleasant.* She rolled her eyes, knowing no man would be flattered with that description. Yet she had never experienced more than *pleasant* with Donald or any other man she had known. And then, in one brief moment, a man she had worked with for years, a man who could infuriate her with a word or move her to tears with a dance, had caused an eruption inside her. There had been nothing *pleasant* about it.

He never kissed me, she mused, losing herself for a moment in the remembering. *Or even held me, really— not as a lover would, but...*

It was an accident, she told herself and switched off the shower with a jerk of her wrist. A fluke. Just a chain reaction from the passion of the dance and the anger of the argument.

Standing naked and wet, Ruth reached for a towel to dry herself. She began with her hair. Her body was small and delicately built, thin by all but a dancer's standards. She knew it intimately, as only a dancer could. Her limbs were long and slender and supple. It had been her classical dancer's build—and the fateful events of her life—that had brought her to Lindsay years before.

Lindsay. Ruth smiled, remembering vividly her fiery dancing in *Don Quixote*, a ballet Lindsay had starred in before she and Ruth had met. Ruth's smile became wry as she recalled her first face-to-face meeting with the older dancer. It had been years later, in Lindsay's small ballet school. Ruth had been both awed and terrified. She had stated boldly that one day she, too, would dance in *Don Quixote*!

And she had, Ruth remembered, wrapping a towel around her slim body. And Uncle Seth and Lindsay had come, even though Lindsay had been nearly eight months pregnant at the time. Lindsay had cried, and Nick had joked and teased her.

With a sigh, Ruth dropped the towel in a careless heap and reached for her robe. Only Lindsay would have guessed that all was not quite right. Ruth belted the thin fuchsia robe and picked up a comb. She had spoken of Donald, she remembered, playing back their last phone conversation. She had told them about the fabulous little chest she had found in the Village. They had chatted about the children, and Uncle Seth had begged her to come visit them her first free weekend.

And through all the tidbits and family gossip, Lindsay sensed something she hadn't even realized herself. Ruth frowned. That she wasn't happy. Not unhappy, she thought and took the comb smoothly through her long, wet hair. Just dissatisfied. Silly, she decided, annoyed with herself. She had everything she'd ever wanted. She was a principal dancer with the company, a recognized name in the world of ballet. She would be starring in Davidov's latest ballet. The work was hard and demanding, but Ruth craved it. It was the life she had been born for.

But still, sometimes, she longed to break the rules, to race back to the vagabond time she had known as a child. There had been such freedom, such adventure. Her eyes lit with the memories: skiing in Switzerland where the air was so cold and clean it had hurt her throat to breathe it; the smells and colors of Istanbul. The thin, large-eyed children in the streets of Crete; a funny little room with glass doorknobs in Bonn. All those years she had traveled with her journalist parents. Had they ever been more than three months in one place? It had been impossible to form any strong attachments, except to each other. And to the dance. That had been her constant childhood companion, traveling with her in an ever-changing environment. The teachers had spoken with different voices, different accents, in different languages, but the dance had remained there for her.

The years of travel had given Ruth an early maturity; there was no shyness, only self-sufficiency and caution. Then came her life with Seth, then Lindsay, and her years with the Evanston family that had opened her up, encouraging her to offer trust and affection. Still her world remained insular, as only the world of ballet can be. Perhaps because of this she was an inveterate observer. Watching and analyzing people was more than a habit with Ruth; it had become her nature.

And it was this that had led to her further annoyance with Nick. She had watched him that afternoon and sensed disturbances, but she hadn't been able to put a name to them. What he had been thinking and feeling remained a mystery. Ruth didn't care for mysteries.

That's why Donald appeals to me, she mused with a half smile. She toyed with the bottles of powder and scent on her dressing table. *He's so unpretentious, so predictable. His thoughts and feelings are right on the surface. No eddies, no undercurrents. But with a man like Nick...*

She poured lotion into her palm and worked it over her arms. A man like Nick, she thought, was totally unpredictable, a constant source of annoyance and confusion. Volatile, unreasonable, exhausting. Just trying to keep up with him wore her out. And it was so difficult to please him! She had seen many dancers push themselves beyond endurance to give him what he wanted. She did it herself. What was it about him that was endlessly fascinating?

A knock on her door broke into Ruth's thoughts. She shrugged, turning away from the dressing table. It was no use trying to dissect Nikolai Davidov. She flipped on a light in the living room as she rushed through it to the front door. Her glance through the peephole surprised her. She drew the chain from the door.

"Donald, I was just thinking about you."

She was swept up in his arms before she had the chance to offer him a friendly kiss. "*Mmm*, you smell wonderful."

Her laugh was smothered by his lips. The kiss grew long, deeper than the casual greeting Ruth had intended. Yet she allowed the intimacy, encouraging it with her own seeking tongue. She wanted to feel, to experience more than the warm pleasure she was accustomed to. She wanted the excitement, the tingling touch of fear she had felt only that afternoon in another man's arms. But when it was over, her heartbeat was steady, her blood cool.

"Now that," Donald murmured and nuzzled her neck, "is the way to say hello."

Ruth stayed in his arms a moment, enjoying his solidarity, the unspoken offer of protection. Then, pulling away, she smiled into his eyes. "It's also a way of saying it's nice to see you, but what are you doing here?"

"Taking you out," he said and swung her farther into

the room. "Go put on your prettiest dress," he ordered, giving her cheek a brief caress. "One of mine, of course. We're going to a party."

Ruth pushed her still-damp hair away from her face. "A party?"

"*Hmm*—yes." Donald glanced at Nijinsky, who lay sprawled in sleep on Ruth's small, glass-topped dinette table. "A party at Germaine Jones's," he continued as he and the cat ignored each other. "You remember, the designer who's pushing her short, patterned skirts and knee socks."

"Yes, I remember." Ruth had the quick impression of a short, pixie-like redhead with sharp green eyes and thick, mink lashes. "I wish you'd called first."

"I did—or tried to," he put in. "It's a spur-of-the-moment thing, but I did phone the rehearsal hall. I missed you there and you hadn't gotten home yet." He shrugged away the oversight as he drew out his slim, gold cigarette case. "Germaine's throwing the party together at the last minute, but a lot of important people will show. She's hot this season." Donald slipped the case back into the inside pocket of his smartly tailored slate-colored suit jacket, then flicked on his lighter.

"I can't make it tonight."

Lifting a brow, Donald blew out a stream of smoke. "Why not?" He took in her wet hair and thin robe. "You don't have plans, do you?"

Ruth was tempted to contradict him. He was beginning to take too much for granted. "Is that such a remote possibility, Donald?" she asked, masking her annoyance with a smile.

"Of course not." He grinned disarmingly. "But somehow I don't think you do. Now be a good girl and slip into that red slinky number. Germaine's bound to have on one of her famous ensembles. You'll make her look like a misplaced cheerleader."

She studied him a moment, with her dark eyes thoughtful. "You're not always kind, are you, Donald?"

"It's not a kind business, darling." He shrugged an elegant shoulder.

Ruth bit back a sigh. She knew he was fond of her and undeniably attracted, but she wondered if he would be quite so fond or so attracted if he didn't consider her to be an asset when she wore one of his designs. "I'm sorry, Donald, I'm just not up to a party tonight."

"Oh, come on, Ruth." He tapped his cigarette in the ashtray, his first sign of impatience. "All you have to do is look beautiful and speak to a few of the right people."

Ruth banked down on a rising surge of irritation. She knew Donald had never understood the demands and rigors of her profession.

"Donald," she began patiently. "I've been working since eight this morning. I'm bone tired. If I don't get the proper rest, I won't be able to function at top level tomorrow. I have a responsibility to the rest of the company, to Nick and to myself."

Carefully, Donald stubbed out the cigarette. Smoke hung in the air a moment, then wafted out through an open window. "You can't tell me you won't do any socializing, Ruth. That's absurd."

"Not as absurd as you think," she returned, crossing to him. "There're less than three weeks until the ballet opens, Donald. Parties simply have to wait until after."

"And me, Ruth?" He pulled her into his arms. Underneath his calm, civilized exterior, she sensed the anger. "How long do I have to wait?"

"I've never promised you anything, Donald. You've known from the beginning that my work is my first priority. Just as your work is for you."

"Does that mean you have to keep denying that you're a woman?"

Ruth's eyes remained calm, but her tone chilled. "I don't believe I've done that."

"Don't you?" Donald's hold on her tightened, just as Nick's had hours before. She found it interesting that the two men should draw two such differing responses from her. With Nick she had felt equal anger and a sharp attraction. Now she felt only impatience touched with fatigue.

"Donald, I'm hardly denying my womanhood by not going to bed with you."

"You know how much I want you." He pulled her closer. "Every time I touch you, I feel you give up to a certain point. Then it stops, just as if you've thrown up a wall." His voice roughened with frustration. "How long are you going to lock me out?"

Ruth felt a pang of guilt. She knew he spoke the truth, just as she knew there was nothing she could do to alter it. "I'm sorry, Donald."

He read the regret in her eyes and changed tactics. Drawing her close again, he spoke softly, his eyes warming. "You know how I feel about you, darling." His lips took hers quietly, persuasively. "We could leave the party early, bring a bottle of champagne back here."

"Donald. You don't—" she began. Another knock at the door interrupted her. Distracted, she didn't bother with the peephole before sliding the chain. "Nick!" She stared at him foolishly, her mind wiped clean.

"Do you open the door to everyone?" he asked in

mild censure as he entered without invitation. "Your hair's wet," he added, taking a generous handful. "And you smell like the first rain in spring."

It was as if the angry words had never been spoken, as if the simmering, restrained passion had never been. He was smiling down at her, an amused, cocky look in his eyes. Bending, he kissed her nose.

Ruth made a face as she pulled her thoughts into order. "I wasn't expecting you."

"I was passing," he said, "and saw your lights."

At the sound of Nick's voice, Nijinsky leaped from the table to rub affectionate circles around the dancer's ankles. Stooping, Nick stroked him once from neck to tail and laughed when the cat rose on his hind legs to jump at him affectionately. Nick rose, with Nijinsky purring audibly in his arms, then spotted Donald across the room.

"Hello." There was no apparent change in his amiability.

"You remember Donald," Ruth began hurriedly, guilty that for a moment she had completely forgotten him.

"Naturally." Nick continued to lazily scratch Nijinsky's ears. Purring ferociously, the cat stared with glinted amber eyes at the other man. "I saw a dress of your design on a mutual friend, Suzanne Boyer." Nick smiled with a flash of white teeth. "They were both exquisite."

Donald lifted a brow. "Thank you."

"But you don't offer me a drink, Ruth?" Nick commented, still smiling affably at Donald.

"Sorry," she murmured, automatically turning toward the small bar she had arranged on a drop leaf table in a corner. She reached for the vodka and poured. "Donald?"

"Scotch," he said briefly, trying to maintain some distance from Nick's cheerful friendliness.

Ruth handed Donald his Scotch and walked to Nick.

"Thanks." Accepting the glass, Nick sat in an overstuffed armchair and allowed the cat to walk tight circles on his lap. Nijinsky settled back to sleep while Nick drank. "Your business goes well?" he asked Donald.

"Yes, well enough," Donald responded to Nick's inquiry. He remained standing and sipped his Scotch.

"You use many plaids in your fall designs." Nick drank the undiluted vodka with a true Russian disregard for its potency.

"That's right." A hint of curiosity intruded into Donald's carefully neutral voice. "I didn't imagine you'd follow women's fashions."

"I follow women," Nick countered and drank again deeply. "I enjoy them."

It was a flat statement meant to be taken at face value. There were no sexual overtones. Nick enjoyed many women, Ruth knew, on many levels—from warm, pure friendships, as his relationship with Lindsay, to hot, smoldering affairs like that with their mutual friend Suzanne Boyer. His romances were the constant speculation of the tabloids.

"I think," Nick continued, disrupting Ruth's thoughts, "that you, too, enjoy women—and what makes them beautiful, interesting. It shows in your designs."

"I'm flattered." Donald relaxed enough to take a seat on the sofa.

"I never flatter," Nick returned with a quick, crooked

smile. "A waste of words. Ruth will tell you I'm a very frugal man."

"Frugal?" Ruth lifted a brow, pursing her lips as if tasting the word. "No, I think the word is *egocentric*."

"The child had great respect once upon a time," Nick said into his empty glass.

"When I was a child, yes," she retorted. "I know you better now."

Something flashed in his eyes as he looked at her; anger, challenge, amusement—perhaps all three. She wasn't certain. She kept her eyes level.

"Do you?" he murmured, then set the glass aside. "You would think she'd have more awe for men of our age," he said mildly to Donald.

"Donald doesn't demand awe," she returned, hardly realizing how quickly she was becoming heated. "And he doesn't care for me to think of him as aged and wise."

"Fortunate," Nick decided as neither of them so much as glanced at the man they were discussing. "Then he won't have to adjust his expectations." He gently stroked Nijinsky's back. "She has a nasty tongue, as well."

"Only for a select few," Ruth responded.

Nick tilted his head, shooting his disarmingly charming smile. "It's my turn to be flattered, it seems."

Blast him! she thought furiously. Never at a loss for an answer.

Regally, Ruth rose. Her body moved fluidly under the silk of her robe. Donald's gaze flicked down a moment, but Nick's remained on her face. "Like you," she said to him with a cool smile, "I find flattery a waste of time and words. You'll have to excuse me," she continued. "Donald and I are going to a party. I have to change."

There was some satisfaction to be gained from turning her back on him and walking away. She closed her bedroom door firmly. Impatiently, she grabbed the red dress out of her closet, pulled lingerie from her drawers and flung the heap onto the bed. Stripping out of the robe, she started to toss it aside when she heard the doorknob turn. Instinctively she held the robe in front of her, clutching it with both hands at her breasts. Her eyes were wide and astonished as Nick stalked into the room. He shut the door behind him.

"You can't come in here," she began on a rush, too surprised to be outraged or embarrassed.

Ignoring her, Nick crossed the room. "I am in here."

"Well, you can just turn around and get out." Ruth shifted the robe higher, realizing impotently that she was at a dead disadvantage. "I'm not dressed," she pointed out needlessly.

Nick's eyes flicked briefly and without apparent interest over her naked shoulders. "You appear adequately covered." The eyes shot back to her face and locked on hers. "Isn't a twelve-hour day enough for you, Ruth? You have an eight o'clock class in the morning."

"I know what time my class is," she retorted. Cautiously, she took one hand from the robe to push back her hair. "I don't need you to remind me of my schedule, Nick, any more than I need your approval of what I do with my free time."

"You do when it interferes with your performance for me."

She frowned as he stepped onto artistic ground. "You've had no reason to complain about my performance."

"Not yet," he agreed. "But I want your best—and

you can hardly give me that if you exhaust yourself with these silly parties—"

"I have always given you my best, Nick," she tossed back. "But since when has every ounce of effort and sweat been enough for you?" She started to swirl away from him, remembered the robe no longer covered her flank and simmered in frustrated rage. "Would you please go?"

"I take what I need," he shot back, again overlooking her heated request. "Not so many years ago, *milaya*, you were eager to give it to me."

"That's not fair!" The gibe stung. "I still am. When I am working, there's nothing I won't give to you. But my private life is just that—private. Stop playing daddy, Nick. I've grown up."

"Is that all you want?" His burst of fury stunned her, so that she took an automatic step back. "Is being treated as a woman what is important to you?"

"I'm sick of you treating me as if I were still seventeen and ready to bend at the knee when you walk into a room." Her anger grew to match his. "I'm a responsible adult, able to look after myself."

"A responsible adult." His eyes narrowed, and Ruth recognized the danger signals. "Shall I show you how I treat responsible adults who also happen to be women?"

"No!"

But she was already in his arms, already molded close. It wasn't the hard, overpowering kiss she might have expected and fought against. He kissed as if he knew she would respond to him with equal fervor. It was a man's mouth seeking a woman's. There was no need for persuasion or force.

Ruth's lips parted when his did. Their tongues met.

Her thoughts, her body, her world concentrated fully and completely on him. The scent of her bath rose between them. Reaching up to draw him closer, Ruth took her hands from the robe. It dropped unheeded to the floor. Nick ran his hands down her naked back, much as he had done to the cat, in one long, smooth stroke. With a low sound of pleasure, Ruth pressed closer.

And as he ran his hands up her sides to linger there, the kiss grew deeper, beyond what she knew and into the uncharted.

Her head fell back in submission as she tangled her fingers in his hair. She pulled him closer, demanding that he take all she offered. It was a dark, pungent world she had never tasted, and she yearned. Her body quivered with hot need as his hands ran over her. She had felt them on her countless times in the past, steadying her, lifting her, coaching her. But there was no music to bring them together here, no planned choreography, only instinct and desire.

When she felt herself being drawn away from him, Ruth protested, straining closer. But his hands came firmly to her shoulders, and they were separated.

Ruth stood naked before him, making no attempt to cover herself. She knew he had already seen her soul; there was no need to conceal her body. Nick took his eyes down her, slowly, carefully, as if he would memorize every inch. Then his eyes were back on hers, darkened, penetrating. There was fury in them. Without a word, he turned and left the room.

Ruth heard the front door slam, and she knew he had gone.

Chapter 3

And one, and two, and three, and four. Ruth made the moves to the time Nick called. After hours of dancing, her body was beyond pain. She was numb. The scant four hours sleep had not given her time to recharge. It had been her own anger and a need to defy that had kept her at the noisy, smoke-choked party until the early hours of the morning. She knew that, just as she knew her dancing was well below par that day.

There was no scathing comment from Nick, no bout of temper. He simply called out the combinations again and again. He didn't shout when she missed her timing or swear when her pirouettes were shaky. When he partnered her, there were no teases, no taunts in her ear.

It would be easier, Ruth thought as she stretched to a slow arabesque, if he'd shouted or scolded her for doing what he had warned her against. But Nick had simply lowered her into a fish dive without saying a word.

If he had shouted, she could have shouted back and released some of her self-disgust. But he gave her no excuse through the classes and hours of rehearsals to lose her temper. Each time their eyes met, he seemed to look through her. She was only a body, an object moving to his music.

When Nick called a break, Ruth went to the back of the room and, sitting on the floor, brought her knees to her chest and rested her forehead on them. Her feet were cramping, but she lacked the energy to massage them. When someone draped a towel around her neck, she glanced up.

"Francie." Ruth managed a grateful smile.

"You look bushed."

"I am," Ruth returned. She used the towel to wipe perspiration from her face.

Francie Myers was a soloist, a talented, dedicated dancer and one of the first friends Ruth had made in the company. She was small and lean with soft, fawn-colored hair and sharp, black eyes. She was constantly acquiring and losing lovers with perpetual cheerfulness. Ruth admired her unabashed honesty and optimism.

"Are you sick?" Francie asked, slipping a piece of gum into her mouth.

Ruth rested her head against the wall. Someone was idling at the piano. The room was abuzz with conversation and music. "I was at a miserably crowded party until three o'clock this morning."

"Sounds like fun." Francie stretched her leg up to touch the wall behind her, then back. She glanced at Ruth's shadowed eyes. "But I don't think your timing was too terrific."

Ruth shook her head on a sigh. "And I didn't even want to be there."

"Then what were you doing there?"

"Being perverse," Ruth muttered, shooting a quick glance at Nick.

"That takes the fun out of it." Francie's eyes darted across the room and landed on an elegant blonde in a pale blue leotard. "Leah's had a few comments about your style today."

Ruth followed Francie's gaze. Leah's golden hair was pulled back from a beautifully sculptured ivory-skinned face. She was talking to Nick now, gesturing with her long, graceful hands.

"I'm sure she did."

"You know how badly she wanted the lead in this ballet," Francie went on. "Even dancing Aurora hasn't pacified her. Nick isn't dancing in *Sleeping Beauty*."

"Competition keeps the company alive," Ruth said absently, watching Nick smile and shake his head at Leah.

"And jealousy," Francie added.

Ruth turned her head again, meeting the dark, sharp eyes. "Yes," she agreed after a moment. "And jealousy."

The piano switched to a romantic ballad, and someone began to sing.

"Nothing's wrong with a little jealousy." Francie rhythmically circled her ankles one at a time. "It's healthy. But Leah…" Her small, piquant face was abruptly serious. "She's poison. If she wasn't such a beautiful dancer, I'd wish her in another company. Watch her," she added as she rose. "She'll do anything to get what she wants. She wants to be the prima ballerina of this company, and you're in her way."

Thoughtfully, Ruth stood as Francie moved away. The attractive dancer rarely spoke ill of anyone. Perhaps she was overreacting to something Leah had said. Ruth had felt Leah's jealousy. There was always jealousy in the company, as there was in any family. It was a fact of life. Ruth also knew how badly Leah had wanted the part of Carlotta in Nick's new ballet.

They had competed for a great number of roles since their days in the corps. Each had won, and each had lost. Their styles were diverse, so that the roles each created were uniquely individual. Ruth was an athletic, passionate dancer. Leah was an elegant dancer—classic, refined, cool. She had a polished grace that Ruth admired but never tried to emulate. Her dancing was from the heart; Leah's was from the head. In technical skills they were as equal as two dancers could be. Ruth danced in *Don Quixote*, while Leah performed in *Giselle*. Ruth was the Firebird, while Leah was Princess Aurora. Nick used them both to the best advantage. And Ruth would be his Carlotta.

Now, watching her across the room, Ruth wondered if the jealousy was more deeply centered than she had sensed. Though they had never been friends, they had maintained a certain professional respect. But Ruth had detected an increase of hostility over the past weeks. She shrugged, then pulled the towel from her shoulders. It couldn't be helped. They were all there to dance.

"Ruth."

She jolted and spun around at the sound of Nick's voice. His eyes were cool on her face, without expression. A wave of anxiety washed over her. He was cruelest when he controlled his temper. She had been in the wrong and was now prepared to admit it. "Nick," Ruth began, ready to humble herself with an apology.

"Go home."

She blinked at him, confused. "What?"

"Go home," he repeated in the same frigid tone.

Her eyes were suddenly round and eloquent. "Oh, no, Nick, I—"

"I said go." His words fell like an ax. "I don't want you here."

Even as she stared at him, she paled from the hurt. There was nothing, nothing he could have done to wound her more deeply than to send her away. She felt both a rush of angry words and a rush of tears back up in her throat. Refusing to give way to either, she turned and crossed the room. Picking up her bag, Ruth walked to the door.

"Second dancers, please," she heard Nick call out before she shut it behind her.

Ruth slept for three hours with Nijinsky curled into the small of her back. She had closed the blinds in her bedroom, and fresh from a shower, lay across the spread. The room was dim, and the only sound was the cat's gentle snoring. When she woke, she woke instantly and rolled from her stomach to her back. Nijinsky was disturbed enough to pad down to the foot of the bed. Huffily, he began to clean himself.

Nick's words had been the last thing she had thought of before slumber and the first to play in her mind when she awoke. She had been wrong. She had been punished. No one she knew could be more casually cruel than Nikolai Davidov. She rose briskly to open the blinds, determined to put the afternoon's events behind her.

"We can't lie around in the dark all day," she informed Nijinsky, then flopped back on the bed to ruffle his fur. He pretended to be indignant but allowed her to fondle and stroke. At last, deciding to forgive her, he nudged his forehead against hers. The gesture brought Nick hurtling back into Ruth's mind.

"Why do you like him so much?" she demanded of Nijinsky, tilting his head until the unblinking amber eyes were on hers. "What is it about him that attracts you?" Her brows lowered, and she began to scratch under the cat's chin absently as she stared into the distance. "Is it his voice, that musical, appealingly accented voice? Or is it the way he moves, with such fluidly controlled grace? Or how he smiles, throwing his whole self into it? Is it how he touches you, with his hands so sure, so knowing?"

Ruth's mind drifted back to the evening before, when Nick had stood holding her naked in his arms. For the first time since the impulsive, arousing kiss, Ruth allowed herself to think of it. The night before, she had dressed in a frenzy and had rushed off to the party with Donald, not giving herself a chance to think. She had come home exhausted and had fought with fatigue all day. Now rested, her mind clear, she dwelled on the matter of Nick Davidov. There was no question: She had seen desire in his eyes. Ruth curled on the spread again, resting her cheek on her hand. He had wanted her.

Desire. Ruth rolled the word around in her mind. *Is that what I saw in his eyes?* The thought had warmth creeping under her skin. Then, like a splash of ice water, she remembered his eyes that afternoon. No desire, no anger, not even disapproval. Simply nothing.

For a moment Ruth buried her face in the spread. It

still hurt to remember his dismissal of her. She felt as though she had been cast adrift. But her common sense told her that one botched rehearsal wasn't the end of the world, and one kiss, she reminded herself, wasn't the beginning of anything.

The poster on the far wall caught her eye. Her uncle had given it to her a decade before. Lindsay and Nick were reproduced in their roles as Romeo and Juliet. Without a second thought, Ruth reached over, picked up the phone and dialed.

"Hello." The voice was warm and clear.

"Lindsay."

"Ruth!" There was surprise in the voice, followed by a quick rush of affection. "I didn't expect to hear from you before the weekend. Did you get Justin's picture?"

"Yes." Ruth smiled, thinking of the boldly colored abstract her four-year-old cousin had sent to her. "It's beautiful."

"Naturally. It's a self-portrait." Lindsay laughed her warm, infectious laugh. "You've missed Seth, I'm afraid. He's just run into town."

"That's all right." Ruth's eyes were drawn back to the poster. "I really called just to talk to you."

There was only the briefest of pauses, but Ruth sensed Lindsay's quick understanding. "Trouble at rehearsal today?"

Ruth laughed. She tucked her legs under her. "Right. How did you know?"

"Nothing makes a dancer more miserable."

"Now I feel silly." Ruth gathered her hair in her hand and tossed it behind her back.

"Don't. Everyone has a bad day. Did Nick shout at

you?" There was a trace of humor rather than sympathy; that in itself was a balm.

"No." Ruth glanced down at the small pattern of flowers in the bedspread. Thoughtfully, she traced one with her thumbnail. "It'd be so much easier if he had. He told me to go home."

"And you felt as though someone had knocked you down with a battering ram."

"And then ran over me with a truck." Ruth smiled into the phone. "I knew you'd understand. What made it worse, he was right."

"He usually is," Lindsay said drily. "It's one of his less endearing traits."

"Lindsay…" Ruth hesitated, then plunged before she could change her mind. "When you were with the company, were you ever—attracted to Nick?"

Lindsay paused again, a bit longer than she had the first time. "Yes, of course. It's impossible not to be, really. He's the sort of man who draws people."

"Yes, but…" Ruth hesitated again, searching for the right words. "What I meant was—"

"I know what you meant," Lindsay said, sparing her. "And yes, I was once very attracted."

Ruth glanced back up at the poster again, studying the star-crossed lovers. She dropped her eyes. "You're closer to him, I think, than anyone else."

"Perhaps," Lindsay considered a moment, weighing Ruth's tone and her own choice of words. "Nick's a very private person."

Ruth nodded. The statement was accurate. Nick could give of himself to the company, at parties, to the press and to his audience. He could flatter the individual with personal attention, but he was amazingly reticent about his personal life. Yes, he was careful about who he let inside. Suddenly Ruth felt alone.

"Lindsay, please, will you and Uncle Seth come to the opening? I know it's difficult, with the children and the school and Uncle Seth's work, but... I need you."

"Of course," Lindsay agreed without hesitation, without questions. "We'll be there."

Hanging up a few moments later, Ruth sat in silence. *I feel better*, she decided, just talking to her, making contact. *She's more than family, she's a dancer, too. And she knows Nick.*

Lindsay had been a romantically lovely Juliet to Nick's Romeo. It was a ballet Ruth had never danced with him. Keil Lowell had been her Romeo; a dark whip of a dancer who loved practical jokes. Ruth had danced with Nick in *Don Quixote*, in *The Firebird* and in his ballet *Ariel*, but in her mind, Juliet had remained Lindsay's role. Ruth had searched for one of her own. She believed she had found it in Carlotta of *The Red Rose*.

It was hers, she thought suddenly. And she had better not forget it. Jumping from the bed, she pulled tights from her dresser drawer and began to tug them on.

When Ruth entered the old, six-story building that housed the company, it was past seven, but there were still some members of the troupe milling about. Some hailed her, and she waved in return but didn't stop. Newer members of the corps watched her pass. Someday, they thought. Ruth might have felt their dreams rushing past her if she hadn't been so impatient to begin.

She took the elevator up, her mind already forming the moves she would demand of her body. She wanted to work.

She heard the music before she pushed open the door of the studio. It always seemed larger without the dancers. She stood silently by the door and watched.

Nikolai Davidov's leaps were like no one else's. He would spring as if propelled, then pause and hang impossibly suspended before descending. His body was as fluid as a waterfall, as taut as a bow string. He had only to command it. And there was more, Ruth knew, just as mesmerized by him as she had been the first time she'd seen him perform; there was his precision timing, his strength and endurance. And he could act—an essential part of ballet. His face was as expressive as his body.

Davidov was fiercely concentrating. His eyes were fixed on the mirrored wall as he searched for faults. He was perfecting, refining. Sweat trickled down his face despite the sweatband he wore. There was virility as well as poetry in his moves. Ruth could see the rippling, the tightening of muscles in his legs and arms as he threw himself into the air, twisting and turning his body, then landing with perfect control and precision.

Oh, God, she thought, forgetting everything but sheer admiration. *He is magnificent.*

Nick stopped and swore. For a moment he scowled at himself in the glass, his mind on his own world. When he walked back to the CD player to replay the selection, he spotted Ruth. His eyes drifted over her, touching on the bag she had slung over her shoulder.

"So, you've rested." It was a simple statement, without rancor.

"Yes." She took a deep breath as they continued to watch each other. "I'm sorry I wasn't any good this morning." When he didn't speak, she walked to a bench to change her shoes.

"So, now you come back to make up?" There was a hint of amusement in his voice.

"Don't make fun of me."

"Is that what I do?" The smile lingered at the corners of his mouth.

Her eyes were wide and vulnerable. She dropped them to the satin ribbons she crossed at her ankles. "Sometimes," she murmured.

He moved softly. Ruth wasn't aware he had come to her until he crouched down, resting his hands on her knees. "Ruth." His eyes were just below hers now, his tone gentle. "I don't make fun of you."

She sighed. "It's so difficult when you're so often right." She made a face at him. "I wasn't going to that silly party until you made me so mad."

"Ah." Nick grinned, squeezing her knee companionably. "So, it's my fault, then."

"I like it better when it's your fault." She pulled the towel from her bag and used it to dry his damp face. "You work too hard, Davidov," she said. Nick lifted his hands lightly to her wrists.

"Do you worry about me, *milaya*?"

His eyes were thoughtful on hers. *They're so blue*, Ruth thought, *like the sea from a distance or the sky in summer.* "I never have before," she mused aloud. "Wouldn't it be strange if I started now? I don't suppose you need anyone to worry about you."

He continued to look at her, then the smile slid into his eyes. "Still, it's a comfortable feeling, yes?"

"Nick." He had started to rise, but Ruth put a hand to his shoulder. She found herself speaking quickly while the courage was with her. "Last night—why did you kiss me?"

He lifted a brow at the question, and though his eyes never left hers, she felt the rest of her body grow warm from them. "Because I wanted to," he told her at length. "It's a good reason." He rose then, and she got up with him.

"But you never wanted to before."

The smile was quick, speeding across his face. "Didn't I?"

"Well, you never kissed me before, not like that." She turned away, pulling off the T-shirt she wore over her bone-colored leotard.

He studied the graceful arch of her back. "And do you think I should do everything I want?"

Ruth shrugged. She had come to dance, not to fence. "I imagined you did," she tossed back as she approached the barre. As she went into a deep plié, she cast a look back over her shoulder. "Don't you?"

He didn't smile. "Do you mean to be provocative, Ruth, or is it an accident?"

She sensed the irritation in his voice but shrugged again. Perhaps she did. "I haven't tried it very often before," she said carelessly. "It might be fun."

"Be careful where you step," he said quietly. "It's a long fall."

Ruth laughed, enjoying the smooth response of her muscles to her commands. "Being safe isn't my goal in life, Nikolai. You'd understand if you'd known my parents. I'm a born adventurer."

"There are different kinds of danger," he pointed out, moving back to the CD player. "You might not find them all pleasurable?"

"Do you want me to be afraid of you?" she asked, turning.

The player squawked when he pressed the fast-forward button. "You would be," he told her simply, "if it were what I wanted."

Their eyes met in the mirror. It took all of Ruth's concentration to complete the leg lift. *Yes*, she admitted silently, keeping her eyes on his. *I would be. There's no emotion he can't rip from a person. That, along with his technical brilliance, makes him a great dancer. But I won't be intimidated.* She dipped to the ground again, her back straight.

"I don't frighten easily, Nick." In the glass, her eyes challenged.

He pushed the button, stopping the machine. The room was thrown into silence while the last of the sun struggled into the window.

"Come." Nick again pressed a button on the player. Music swelled into the room. Walking to the center, Nick held out a hand. Ruth crossed to him, and without speaking they took their positions for the grand pas de deux.

Nick was not only a brilliant dancer, he was a demanding teacher. He would have each detail perfect, each minute gesture exact. Again and again they began the movement, and again and again he stopped to correct, to adjust.

"No, the head angle is wrong. Here." He moved her head with his hands until he was satisfied. "Your hands here, like so." And he would position her as he chose.

His hands were professional, adjusting her shoulders, skimming lightly at her waist as she spun, gripping her thigh for a lift. She was content to be molded by him. Yet it seemed she could not please him. He grew impatient, she frustrated.

"You must *look* at me!" he demanded, stopping her again.

"I was," she tossed back, frowning.

With a quick Russian oath he walked over and punched the button to stop the music. "With no feeling! You feel nothing. It's no good."

"You keep stopping," she began.

"Because it's wrong."

She glared at him briefly. "All right," she muttered and wiped the sweat from her brow with her forearm. "What do you want me to feel?"

"You're in love with me." Ruth's eyes flew up, but he was already involved with the CD player. "You want me, but you have pride, spirit. You won't be taken, do you see? Equal terms or nothing." He turned back, his eyes locking on hers. "But the desire is there. Passion, Ruth. It smolders. *Feel* it. You tell me you're a woman, not a child. Show me, then."

He crossed back to her. "Now," he said, putting a hand to her waist. "Again."

This time Ruth allowed her imagination to move her. She was a gypsy in love with a prince, fiercely proud, deeply passionate. The music was fast, building the mood. It was an erotic dance, with a basic sexuality in the steps and gestures. There was a great deal of close work, bodies brushing, eyes locking. She felt the very real pull of desire. Her blood began to hum with it.

Eagerly, as if to burn out what she was feeling, she executed the *soubresauts* trapped somewhere between truth and fantasy. She did want him and was no longer sure that she was feeling only as Carlotta. He touched her, drew her, and always she retreated—not running away but simply standing on her own.

The music built. They spun farther and farther away from each other, each rejecting the attraction. They leaped apart, but then, as if unable to resist, they came back full circle. Back toward each other and past, then, with a final turn, they were in each other's arms. The music ended with the two wrapped close together, face to face, heart to heart.

The silence came as a shock, leaving Ruth dazed between herself and the role. Both she and Nick were breathing quickly from the demands of the dance. She could feel the rapid beat of his heart against hers. Her eyes, as she stood on pointe were almost level with his. He looked into hers as she did into his—searching, wondering. Their lips met; the time for questions was passed.

This time she felt the hunger and impatience she had only sensed before. He seemed unable to hold her close enough, unable to taste all he craved. His mouth was everywhere, running wildly over her face and throat. White heat raced along her skin in its wake. She could smell the muskiness of his sweat, taste the salty dampness on his face and throat as her own lips wandered. Then his mouth came back to hers, and they joined in mutual need.

He murmured something, but she couldn't understand. Even the language he spoke was a mystery. Their bodies fused together. Only the thin fabric of her leotard and tights came between his hands and her skin. They pressed here, touched there, lingered and aroused. His lips were at her ear, his teeth catching and tugging at the lobe. He murmured to her in Russian, but she had no need to understand the words.

His mouth found hers again, hotter this time, more insistent. Ruth gave and took with equal urgency, shuddering with pleasure as he slid a hand to her breast for a rough caress while her mouth, ever searching, ever questing, clung to his.

When he would have drawn her away, Ruth buried her face in his shoulder and strained against him. Nothing had ever prepared her for the rapid swing of strength to weakness. Even knowing she was losing part of herself, she was unable to stop it.

"Ruth." Nick drew her away, his hands gentle now. He looked at her, deep into the cloudy depths of her eyes. She was too moved by what was coursing through her to read his expression. "I didn't mean that to happen."

She stared at him. "But it did." It seemed so simple. She smiled. But when she lifted a hand to touch his cheek, he stopped her by taking her wrist.

"It shouldn't have."

She watched him, and her smile faded. Her eyes became guarded. "Why not?"

"We've a ballet to do in less than three weeks." Nick's voice was brisk now, all business. "This isn't the time for complications."

"Oh, I see." Ruth turned away so that he wouldn't see the hurt. Walking back to the bench, she began to untie her shoes. "I'm a complication."

"You are," he agreed and moved to the player again. "I haven't the time or the inclination to indulge you romantically."

"Indulge me romantically," she repeated in a low, incredulous voice.

"There are women who need a candlelight courtship," he continued, his back still to her. "You're one of them. At this point I haven't the time."

"Oh, I see. You only have time for more basic relationships," she said sharply, tying her tennis shoes with trembling fingers. How easily he could make her feel like a fool!

Nick turned to her now, watchful. "Yes."

"And there are other women who can provide that."

He gave a slight shrug. "Yes. I apologize for what happened. It's easy to get caught up in the dance."

"Oh, please." She tossed her toe shoes into the bag. "There's no need to apologize. I don't need you to indulge me romantically, Nick. Like you, I know others."

"Like your designer?"

"That's right. But don't worry, I won't blow any more rehearsals. I'll give you your ballet, Nick." Her voice was thickening with tears, but she was helpless to prevent it. "They'll rave above it, I swear it. It's going to make me the most important prima ballerina in the country." The tears came, and though she despised them, she didn't brush them aside. They rolled silently down her cheeks. "And when the season's over, I'll never dance with you again. *Never!*"

She turned and ran from the studio without giving him a chance to respond.

Chapter 4

The backstage cacophony penetrated Ruth's closed dressing room door. It was closed, uncharacteristically, for only one reason: she wanted to avoid Nick.

He was always everywhere before a performance—popping into dressing rooms, checking costumes and makeup, calming preperformance jitters. No detail was too insignificant to merit his attention, no problem too small for him to seek the solution. He always had and always would involve himself.

In the past Ruth had cherished his brief, explosive visits. His energy was an inspiration and settled her own anxieties. Now, however, she wanted as much distance between herself and the company star and artistic director as possible. During the past weeks of rehearsal that hadn't been possible physically, but she would attempt an emotional distance nevertheless.

She felt reasonably certain that although Nick wouldn't normally respect a closed door, he would, in this case, take her point. The small gesture satisfied her.

Perhaps because of her turmoil and needs, Ruth had worked harder on the role of Carlotta than on any other role in her career. She was determined not just to make it a success, but to make it an unprecedented triumph. It was a gesture of defiance, a bid for independence. These days the character of the sultry gypsy suited her mood exactly.

In the three weeks since her last informal rehearsal with Nick, both dancers had kept their relationship stringently professional. It hadn't always been easy, given the roles they were portraying, but they had exchanged no personal comments, indulged in none of their usual banter. When she had felt his eyes follow her, as she had more than once, Ruth forced herself not to flinch. When she felt his desire draw her, she remembered his last private words to her. That had been enough to stiffen her pride. She had clamped down on her habit of speculating what was in his mind. She'd told herself she didn't need to know, didn't want to know. All she had to do was dance.

Now, dressed in a plain white terry robe, she sat at her dressing table and sewed the satin ribbons onto her toe shoes. The simple dancer's chore helped to relax her.

The heat of the bright, round bulbs that framed her mirror warmed her skin. Already in stage makeup, she had left her hair loose and thick. It was to fly around her in the first scene, as bold and alluring as her character. Her eyes had been darkened, accentuating their shape and size, her lips painted red. The brilliantly colored, full-skirted dress for the first scene hung on the back of her door. Flowers had already begun to arrive, and the room was heavy with scent. On the table at her elbow were a dozen long-stemmed red roses from Donald. She smiled a little, thinking he would be in the audience, then at the reception afterward. She'd keep his roses in her dressing room for as long as they lived. They would help her to remember that not all men were too busy to indulge her romantically.

Ruth pricked her finger on the needle and swore. Even as she brought the wound to her mouth to ease the sting, she caught the glare of her own eyes in the glass.

Serves you right, she told herself silently, for even thinking of him. Indulging her romantically indeed! She picked up her second toe shoe. *He made me sound as though I were sixteen and needed a corsage for the prom!*

Her thoughts were interrupted by a knock on the door. Ruth put down her shoe. She rose and went to the door. If it were Nick, she wanted to meet him on her feet. She lifted her chin as she turned the knob.

"Uncle Seth! Lindsay!" She launched herself into her uncle's arms, then flung herself at the woman beside him. "Oh, I'm so very glad you're here!"

Lindsay found the greeting a bit desperate but said nothing. She only returned the hug and met her husband's eyes over Ruth's head. Their communication was silent and perfectly understood. Ruth turned to give Seth a second hug.

"You both look wonderful!" she exclaimed as she drew them into the room.

Ruth had been close to Seth Bannion during much of her adolescence, but it hadn't been until she'd gone out on her own that she had truly appreciated the changes he had made in his own lifestyle to care for her. He was a highly successful architect and had been a sought-after bachelor and world traveler. He had taken a teenager into his home, adjusted his mode of living and made her his priority. Ruth adored him.

She clasped her hands and admired them both with her eyes. "You look so beautiful, Lindsay," Ruth enthused, turning to take her in. "I never get used to it." Lindsay was small and delicately built. Her pale hair and ivory skin set off her deep blue eyes. She was the warmest person Ruth knew; a woman capable of rich emotions and unlimited love. She wore a filmy smoke-gray dress that seemed to swirl from her shoulders to her feet.

Lindsay laughed and caught Ruth's hands in hers. "What a marvelous compliment. Seth doesn't tell me so nearly enough."

"Only daily," he said, smiling into Lindsay's eyes.

"This is the same dressing room you used for *Ariel,*" Seth commented, glancing around. "It hasn't changed."

"You should know," Lindsay said. "I proposed to you here."

He grinned. "So you did."

"I didn't know that."

They both turned, shifting their attention to Ruth. Lindsay laughed again. "I've never been very good about tradition," she said and wandered over to pick up one of Ruth's toe shoes. "And he didn't ask me soon enough."

The shoes that lined the dressing table stirred memories. What a life, Lindsay thought. *What a world.* She had once been as much a part of it as Ruth was now.

Her eyes lifted and fixed on the dark ones reflected in the glass.

"Nervous?"

Ruth's whole body seemed to sigh. "Oh, yes." She grimaced.

"It's a good ballet," Lindsay said with certainty. She took the quality of Nick's work on faith. She had known him for too long to do otherwise.

"It's wonderful. But…" Ruth shook her head and moved back to her chair. "In the second act there's a passage where I never seem to stop. There are only a few seconds for me to catch my breath before I'm off again."

"Nick doesn't write easy ballets."

"No." Ruth picked up her needle and thread again. "How are the children?"

The quick change of subject was noted. Again Lindsay met Seth's eyes over Ruth's head.

"Justin's a terror," Seth stated wryly with fatherly pride. "He drives Worth mad."

Ruth gave a low, gurgling laugh. "Is Worth maintaining his professional dignity?"

"Magnificently," Lindsay put in. "'Master Justin,'" she quoted, giving a fair imitation of the butler's cultured British tones. "'One must not bring one's pet frog into the kitchen, even when it requires feeding.'" Lindsay laughed, watching Ruth finish the last stitches. "Of course, he dotes on Amanda, though he pretends not to."

"And she's as big a terror as Justin!" Seth commented.

"What a way to describe our children," Lindsay said, turning to him.

"Who dumped the entire contents of a box of fish

food into the goldfish bowl?" he asked her, and she lifted a brow.

"She was only trying to be helpful." A smile tugged at Lindsay's mouth. "Who took them to the zoo and stuffed them with hot dogs and caramel corn?"

"I was only trying to be helpful," he countered, his eyes warm on hers.

Watching them, Ruth felt both a surge of warmth and a shaft of envy. What would it be like to be loved that way? she wondered. *Enduringly.* The word suited them, she decided.

"Shall we clear out?" Lindsay asked her. "And let you get ready?"

"No, please stay awhile. There's time." Ruth fingered the satin ribbons nervously.

Nerves, Lindsay thought, watching her.

"You're coming to the reception, aren't you?" Ruth glanced up again.

"Wouldn't miss it." Lindsay moved over to knead Ruth's shoulders. "Will we meet Donald?"

"Donald?" Ruth brought her thoughts back. "Oh, yes, Donald will be there. Shall we get a table together? You'll like him," she went on without waiting for an answer. Her eyes sought Lindsay's, then her uncle's. "He's very—nice."

"Lindsay!"

Nick stood in the open doorway. His face was alive with pleasure. His eyes were all for Lindsay. She ran into his arms.

"Oh, Nick, it's wonderful to see you! It's always too long."

He kissed her on both cheeks, then on the mouth. "More beautiful every time," he murmured, letting his eyes roam her face. "*Ptichka*, little bird." He used his pet name for her, then kissed her again. "This architect you married—" he shot a quick grin at Seth "—he makes you happy still?"

"He'll do." Lindsay hugged Nick again, fiercely. "Oh, but I miss you. Why don't you come see us more often?"

"When would I find the time?" He kept his arm around Lindsay's waist as he held out a hand to Seth. "Marriage agrees with you. It's good to see you."

Their handshake was warm. Seth knew he shared the two women he loved with the Russian. A part of Lindsay had belonged to Nick before he had known her. Now Ruth was part of his world.

"Are you giving us another triumph tonight?" Seth asked.

"But of course." Nick grinned and shrugged. "It is what I do."

Lindsay gave Nick a squeeze. "He never changes." She rested her head on his shoulder a moment. "Thank God."

Throughout the exchange Ruth said nothing. She observed something rare and special between Lindsay and Nick. It emanated from them so vividly, she felt she could almost touch it. It only took seeing them side by side to remember how perfectly they had moved together on the stage. Unity, precision, understanding. She stopped listening to what they were saying, entranced by their unspoken rapport.

When Nick's eyes met hers, Ruth could only stare. Whatever she had been trying to dissect, to absorb, was forgotten. All she knew was that she had unwittingly allowed the ache to return. His eyes were so blue, so powerful, she seemed unable to prevent him from peeling away the layers and reaching her soul. Marshalling her strength, she pulled herself out of the trance.

It would have been impossible not to have witnessed the brief exchange. Lindsay and Seth silently communicated their concern.

"Nadine will be at the reception, won't she?" Lindsay attempted to ease the sudden tension.

"Hmm?" Nick turned his attention back to her. "Ah, yes, Nadine." He realigned his thoughts and spoke smoothly. "Of course, she will want to bask in the glory before she launches her next fund drive."

"You always were hard on her." Lindsay smiled, remembering how often Nick and Nadine Rothchild, the founder of the company, had disagreed.

"She can take it," he tossed off with a jerk of his shoulder. "I'll see you at the reception?"

"Yes." Lindsay watched his eyes drift back to Ruth's. He hadn't spoken a word to her, nor had Ruth said anything to him. They communicated with their eyes only. He held the contact for several long seconds before turning back to Lindsay.

"I'll see you after the performance," he said, and Ruth quietly let out her breath. "I must go change. *Do svidanya.*"

He was gone before they could answer his goodbye. From down the corridor, they could hear someone calling his name.

Seth walked to Ruth and, putting his hands on her shoulders, bent to kiss the crown of her head. "You'd better be changing."

Ruth tried to pull herself together. "Yes, I'm in the first scene."

"You're going to be terrific." He squeezed her shoulders briefly.

"I want to be." Her eyes lifted to his and held before sweeping to Lindsay. "I have to be."

"You will be," Lindsay assured her, holding out a hand for Seth's even as her eyes stayed on Ruth's. "It's what you were born for. Besides, you were my most gifted pupil."

Ruth turned in the chair and gave Lindsay her first smile since Nick's appearance. She lifted her face to Lindsay's quick kiss. *"Do svidanya!"* Lindsay said, smiling as she and Seth left arm in arm.

Slowly Ruth moved to the door and shut it. For a moment she simply stood, contemplating the colorful costume that would make her Carlotta. She was Ruth Bannion, a little unsure of her emotions, a little afraid of the night ahead. To put on the costume was to put on the role. Carlotta has her vulnerabilities, Ruth mused, fingering the fabric of the skirt, but she cloaks them in boldness and audaciousness. The thought made Ruth smile again. *Oh, yes*, she decided, *she's for me*. Ruth began to dress.

When she left the room fifteen minutes later, she could hear the orchestra tuning up. She was in full costume. Her skirt swayed saucily at her hips, a slash of a red scarf defined her waist. Her hair streamed freely down her back. She hurried past the dancers warming up for the first scene and those idling in the doorways. She spotted Francie sitting cross-legged on the floor in a corner, breaking in her toe shoes with a hammer.

Ruth went to a convenient prop crate and used it for a barre as she began to warm up. She could already smell the sweat and the lights.

Her muscles responded, tightening, stretching, loosening at her command. She concentrated on them purposefully, keeping her back to the stage, the better to concentrate on her own body. Each performance was important to her, but this one was in a class by itself. Ruth had something to prove—to Nick and to herself. She would flaunt her professionalism. Whatever her feelings were for Nick, she would forget them and concentrate only on interpreting Nick's ballet. Nothing would interfere with that.

It had been a bad moment for her in the dressing room when his eyes had pinned hers. Something inside her had wanted to melt and nearly had. Pride had held her aloof, as it had for weeks. He hadn't wanted her— not wholly, not exclusively—the way she had wanted him. The fact that he had so easily agreed that any number of women could give him what he needed had stung.

Scowling, Ruth curled her leg up behind her, pulling and stretching.

It was time someone taught that arrogant Russian a lesson, she thought as she switched legs. Too many women had fallen at his feet. He expected it, just as he expected his dancers to do things his way.

Ruth lifted her chin and found her eyes once again locked tight on Nick's.

He had come out of his dressing room clad in the glittering white-and-gold tunic he would wear in the first act. Spotting Ruth, he had stopped to stand and watch her. He wondered if the passion he saw in her face was her own or, like the costume, assumed for her role as Carlotta. He thought that there, in the dim backstage corridor, with the gypsy costume and smoldering eyes, she had never looked more alluring. It was at that moment that Ruth had lifted her eyes to his.

Each felt the instant attraction; each felt the instant hostility. Ruth tossed her head, glared briefly, then whirled away in a flurry of color and skirts. Her unconscious mimicry of the character she was about to play amused him.

All right, little one, Nick thought with the ghost of a smile. *We'll see who comes out on top tonight. Nick decided he would rather enjoy the challenge.*

He followed Ruth to the wings, dismissing with a wave of his hand one or two who tried to detain him. Reaching Ruth, he spun her around and caught her close, heedless of the backstage audience. She was caught completely off guard. Her reflexes had no time to respond or to reject before his mouth, arrogant and sure, demanded, plundered, then released.

Nick kept his hands on her forearms for a moment, arrogantly smiling. "That should put you in the mood," he said jauntily before turning to stride away.

Furious, Ruth could only stare hotly after his retreating back. There was scattered laughter that her glare did nothing to suppress before she whirled away again and stalked out onto the empty, black stage.

She waited while the stage hands drew the heavy curtain. She waited for the orchestra—strings only, as they played her entrance cue. She waited until she was fully lighted by the single spot before she began to dance.

Her opening solo was short, fast and flamboyant. When she had finished, the stage was lit to show the set of a gypsy camp. The audience exploded into applause.

While the corps and second dancers took over, Ruth was able to catch her breath. She waited, half listening to the praise of Nick's assistant choreographer. Across the long stage she could see Nick waiting in the opposite wing for his entrance.

Top that, Davidov, she challenged silently. Ruth knew she had never danced better in her life. As if he had heard the unspoken dare, Nick grinned at her before he made his entrance.

He was all arrogance, all pride; the prince entering the gypsy camp to buy baubles. He cast aside the trinkets they offered with a flick of the wrist. He dominated the stage with his presence, his talent. Ruth couldn't deny it. It made her only more determined to outdo him. She waited while he dismissed offer after offer, waited for him to make it plain that the gypsies had nothing he desired. Then she glided onstage, her head held high. A red rose was now pinned at her ear.

Their mutual attraction was instant as their eyes met for the first time. The moment was accentuated by the change of lighting and the orchestra's crescendo. Carlotta, seeing the discarded treasures, turned her back on him to join a group of her sisters. The prince, intrigued, approached her for a closer study.

Ruth's mutinous eyes met Nick's again, and she had no trouble jerking her head haughtily away when he took her chin in his hand. Something in Nick's smile made her eyes flare more dramatically as he turned to the dancer who played her father. The prince had found something he desired. He offered his gold for Carlotta.

She defied him with pride and fury. No one could buy her; no one could own her. Taunting him, arousing him, she agreed to sell him a dance for his bag of gold. Enraged yet unable to resist, the prince tossed his gold onto the pile of rejected trinkets. They began their first pas de deux, palm to palm, with heated blood and angry eyes.

The high-level pace was maintained throughout the ballet. The competition between them remained sharp, each spurring the other to excel. They didn't speak between acts, but once, as they danced close, he whispered annoyingly in her ear that her *ballottés* needed polishing.

He lifted her, and she dipped, her head arched down, her feet up, so that he was holding her nearly upside down. Six, seven, eight slow, sustained beats, then she was up like lightning again in an arabesque. Her eyes were like flames as she executed a double turn. When she leaped offstage, leaving him to his solo, Ruth pressed her hand to her stomach, drawing exhausted breaths.

Again and again, the stage burned from their heated dancing. When the ballet finally ended, the two in each other's arms, she managed to pant, "I dislike you intensely, Davidov."

"Dislike all you please," he said lightly as applause and cheers erupted. "As long as you dance."

"Oh, I'll dance, all right," she assured him breathlessly and dipped into a deep, smiling curtsy for the audience.

Only she could have heard his quiet chuckle as he scooped up a rose that had been tossed onstage and presented it to her with a bow.

"My *ballottés* were perfect," she hissed between gritted teeth as he kissed her hand.

"We'll discuss it in class tomorrow." He bowed and presented her to the audience again.

"Go to hell, Davidov," she said, smiling sweetly to the "bravos" that showered over them.

"After the season," he agreed, turning for another bow.

Chapter 5

Nick and Ruth took eleven curtain calls. An hour after the final curtain came down, her dressing room was finally cleared so that she could change from her costume. Now she wore a long white dress with narrow sleeves and a high collar. The only jewelry she added were the sleek gold drop earrings that Lindsay and Seth had given her on her twenty-first birthday. Triumph had made her eyes dark and brilliant and had shot a flush of rose into her cheeks. She left her hair loose and free, as Carlotta's had been.

"Very nice," Donald commented when she met him in the corridor.

Ruth smiled, knowing he spoke of the dress, his design, as much as the woman in it. She slipped her arm through his. "Like it?" Her eyes beamed up into his. "I found it in this little discount dress shop in the clothing district."

He pinched her chin as punishment, then kissed her. "I know I said it before, darling, but you were wonderful."

"Oh, I could never hear that too often." With a laugh she began to lead the way to the stage door. "I want champagne," she told him. "Gallons of it. I think I could swim in it tonight."

"Let's see if it can be arranged."

They moved outside, where his car was waiting. "Oh, Donald," Ruth continued, the moment they had settled into it. "It never felt more *right*. Everything just seemed to come together. The music—the music was so perfect."

"You were perfect," he stated, steering the car into Manhattan traffic. "They were ready to tear the walls down for you."

Much too excited to lean back, Ruth sat on the edge of her seat and turned toward him. "If I could freeze a moment in time, with all its feelings and emotions, it would be this ballet. Tonight. Opening night."

"You'll do it again tomorrow," he told her.

"Yes, and it'll be wonderful, I know. But not like this." Ruth wished he could understand. "I'm not sure it can ever be exactly like this again, or even if it should be."

"I'd think you might get a bit weary of doing the same dance night after night after a couple of weeks."

He pulled over to the curb, and Ruth shook her head. Why did she want him to understand? she wondered as the doorman helped her alight. For all his creative talents as a designer, Donald was firmly rooted to the earth. But tonight she was ready to fly.

"It's hard to explain." She allowed him to lead her

through the wide glass doors and into the hotel lobby. "Something just happens when the lights come on and the music starts. It's always special. Always."

The banquet room was ablaze with light and already crowded with people. Cameras began to click and flash the moment Ruth stepped into the doorway. The applause met her.

"Ruth!" Nadine walked through the crowd with the assurance of a woman who knew people would step aside for her. She was small, with a trim build and grace that revealed her training as a dancer. Her hair was sculptured and palely blond, her skin smooth and pink. The angelic face belied a keen mind. More than she ever had as a dancer, Nadine Rothchild, as company founder, devoted her life to the ballet.

Ruth turned to find herself embraced. "You were beautiful," Nadine said. Ruth knew this to be her highest compliment. Pulling her away, Nadine stared for several long seconds directly into her eyes. It was a characteristic habit. "You've never danced better than you danced tonight."

"Thank you, Nadine."

"I know you want Lindsay and Seth." She began to lead Ruth across the room, leaving Donald to follow in her wake. "We're all sitting together."

Ruth's eyes met Lindsay's first. What she read there was the final gratification. Lindsay held out both her hands, and Ruth extended hers to join them. "I'm so proud of you." Her voice was thick with emotion.

Seth laid his hands on his wife's shoulders and looked at his niece. "Every time I watch you perform, I think you'll never dance any better than you do at that moment. But you always do."

Ruth laughed, still gliding, and lifted her face for a kiss. "It's the most wonderful part I've ever had." She turned then, and taking Donald's arm, made quick introductions.

"I'm a great admirer of your designs." Lindsay smiled up at him. "Ruth wears them beautifully."

"My favorite client. I believe you could easily become my second favorite," Donald returned the compliment. "You have fantastic coloring."

"Thank you." Lindsay recognized the professional tone of the compliment and was more amused than flattered. "You need some champagne," she said, turning to Ruth.

Before they could locate a waiter, the sound of applause had them turning back toward the entrance. Ruth knew before she saw him that it would be Nick. Only he could generate such excitement. He was alone, which surprised her. Where there was Davidov, there were usually women. Ruth knew his eyes would find hers.

Nick quickly dislodged himself from the crowd and slowly, with the perfectly controlled grace of his profession, walked to her, holding a single red rose, which he handed to Ruth. When she accepted it, he took her other hand and lifted it to his lips. He didn't speak, nor did his eyes leave hers, until he turned and walked away.

Just theatrics, she told herself, but she couldn't resist breathing in the scent of the rose. No one knew how to set the stage more expertly than Davidov. Her eyes shifted to Lindsay's. In them Ruth could read both understanding and concern. She barely prevented herself from shaking her head in denial. She forced a bright smile.

"What about that champagne?" she demanded.

Ruth toyed with her dinner, barely eating, too excited for food. It was just as well; she sat at the table with Nadine, and it was a company joke that Nadine judged her dancers by the pound.

Nadine gave Lindsay's dish of chocolate mousse a frowning glance. "You have to watch those rich desserts, dear."

With a laugh Lindsay leaned over and kissed Nadine's cheek. "You're so wonderfully consistent, Nadine. There's too much in the world that's unpredictable."

"You can't dance with whipped cream in your thighs," Nadine pointed out and sipped at her champagne.

"You know," Lindsay said to Ruth, "she caught me once with a bag of potato chips. It was one of the most dreadful experiences of my life." She shot Nadine a grin and licked chocolate from her spoon. "It completely killed my taste for them."

"My dancers look like dancers," Nadine said firmly. "Lots of bone and no bulges. Proper diet is as essential as daily class—"

"And daily class is as essential as breathing," Lindsay finished and laughed again. "Can it really be eight years since I was with the company?"

"You left a hole. It wasn't easy to fill it."

The unexpected compliment surprised Lindsay. Nadine was a pragmatic, brisk woman who took her dancers' talents for granted. She expected the best and rarely considered praise necessary.

"Why, thank you, Nadine."

"It wasn't a compliment but a complaint," Nadine countered. "You left us too soon. You could still be dancing."

Lindsay smiled again. "You seem to have plenty of young talent, Nadine. Your corps is still the best."

Nadine acknowledged this with a nod. "Of course." She paused a moment, looking at Lindsay again as she sipped her wine. "Can you imagine how many Juliets I've watched in my lifetime, Lindsay?"

"Is that a loaded question?" she countered and grinned at Seth. "If I say too many, she'll complain that I'm aging her. Too few, and I'm insulting her."

"Try 'a considerable number,'" he suggested, adding champagne to his wife's glass.

"Good idea." Lindsay shifted her attention back to Nadine. "A considerable number."

"Quite correct." Nadine set down her glass and laid her hands on Lindsay's. Her eyes were suddenly intense. "You were the best. The very best. I wept when you left us."

Lindsay opened her mouth, then shut it again on words that wouldn't come. She swallowed and shook her head.

"Excuse me, please," she murmured. Rising, she hurried across the room.

There were wide glass doors leading to a circling balcony. Lindsay opened them and stepped outside. Leaning on the rail, she took a deep breath. It was a clear night, with stars and moonlight shedding silver over Manhattan's skyline. She looked out blindly.

After all the years, she thought, *and all the distance. I'd have cut off an arm to have heard her say that ten years ago.* She felt a tear run down her cheek and closed her eyes. *Oh, God, how badly I once needed to know what she just told me. And now...*

At the touch of a hand on her shoulder, she started. Lindsay turned into Nick's arms. For a moment she said nothing, letting herself lean on him and remember. She had been his Juliet in that other life, that world she had once been a part of.

"Oh, Nick," she murmured. "How fragile we are, and how foolish."

"Foolish?" he repeated and kissed the top of her head. "Speak for yourself, *ptichka*. Davidov is never foolish."

She laughed and looked up at him. "I forgot."

"Foolish of you." He pulled her back into his arms, and she rose on her toes so that her cheek brushed his. "Nick. You know, no matter how long you're away, no matter how far you go, all of this is still with you. It's more than in your blood, it's in the flesh and muscle." With a sigh, she drew out of his arms and again leaned on the rail. "Whenever I come back, part of me expects to walk into class again or rush to make company calls. It's ingrained."

Nick rested a hip on the rail and studied her profile. There was a breeze blowing her hair back, and he thought again that she was one of the most beautiful women he had ever known. Yet she had always seemed unaware of her physical appeal.

"Do you miss it?" he asked her, and she turned to look at him directly.

"It's not a matter of missing it." Lindsay's brows drew together as she tried to translate emotions into words. "It's more like putting part of yourself in storage. To be honest, I don't think about the company much at home. I'm so busy with the children and my students. And Seth is…" She stopped, and he watched the smile illuminate her face. "Seth is everything." Lindsay turned back to the skyline. "Sometimes, when I come back here to watch Ruth dance, the memories are so vivid, it's almost unreal."

"It makes you sad?"

"A little," she admitted. "But it's a nice feeling all the same. When I look back, I don't think there's anything in my life I'd change. I'm very lucky. And Ruth…" She smiled again, gazing out at New York. "I'm proud of her, thrilled for her. She's so good. She's so incredibly good. Somehow I feel like a part of it all over again."

"You're always a part of it, Lindsay." He caught at the ends of her hair. "Talent like yours is never forgotten."

"Oh, no, no more compliments tonight." She gave a shaky laugh and shook her head. "That's what got me started." Taking a deep breath, she faced him again. "I know I was a good dancer, Nick. I worked hard to be. I treasure the years I was with the company—the ballets I danced with you. My mother still has her scrapbook, and one day my children will look through it." She gave him a puzzled smile. "Imagine that."

"Do you know, I'm always amazed to think of you with two growing children."

"Why?"

He smiled and took her hand. "Because it's so easy to remember you the first time I saw you. You were still a soloist when I came to the company. I watched you rehearsing for *Sleeping Beauty*. You were the flower fairy, and you were dissatisfied with your fouettés."

"How do you remember that?"

Nick lifted a brow. "Because my first thought was how I would get you into my bed. I couldn't ask you— my English was not so good in those days."

Lindsay gave a choked laugh. "You learned quickly enough, as I remember. Though as I recall, you never, in any language, suggested I come into your bed."

"Would you have?" He tilted his head as he studied her. "I've wondered for more than ten years."

Lindsay searched her heart even as she searched his face. She could hear laughter through the windows and the muffled drone of traffic far below. She tried to think of the Lindsay Dunne who had existed ten years before. Ultimately, she smiled and shook her head. "I don't know. Perhaps it's better that way."

Nick slipped an arm around her, and she leaned against his shoulder. "You're right. I'm not sure it would be good to know one way or the other."

They fell silent as their thoughts drifted.

"Donald Keyser seems like a nice man," Lindsay murmured. She felt the fractional stiffening of Nick's arm.

"Yes."

"Ruth's not in love with him, of course, but he isn't in love with her, either. I imagine they're good company for each other." When he said nothing, Lindsay tilted her head and looked at him. "Nick?"

He glanced down and read her unspoken thoughts clearly. "You see too much," he muttered.

"I know you—I know Ruth."

He frowned back out at the skyline. "You're afraid I'll hurt her."

"The thought crossed my mind," Lindsay admitted.

"As it crossed my mind that she might hurt you." Nick looked back at her, and she continued. "It's difficult when I love you both."

After a shrug, he thrust his hands into his pockets and turned to take a few steps away. "We dance together, that's all."

"That's hardly all," Lindsay countered, but as he turned back, annoyed, she continued. "Oh, I don't mean you're lovers, nor is it any of my business if you are. But Nick." She sighed, recognizing the anger in his eyes. "It's impossible to look at the two of you and not see."

"What do you want?" he demanded. "A promise I won't take her to bed?"

"No." Calmly, Lindsay walked to him. "I'm not asking for promises or giving advice. I only hope to give you support if you want it."

She watched the anger die as he turned away again. "She's a child," he murmured.

"She's a woman," Lindsay corrected. "Ruth was barely ever a child. She was grown up in a number of ways when I first met her."

"Perhaps it is safer if I consider her a child."

"You've argued with her."

Nick laughed and faced Lindsay again. "*Ptichka*, I always argue with my partners, yes?"

"Yes," Lindsay agreed and decided to leave it at that. Instead of pressing him, she held out her hand. "We had some great arguments, Davidov."

"The best." Nick took the offered hand in both of his. "Come, let me take you back in. We should be celebrating."

"Did I tell you how wonderful you were tonight or how brilliant your ballet is?"

"Only once." He gave her his charming smile. "And that was hardly enough. I have a very big ego." The creases in his cheeks deepened. "How wonderful was I?"

"Oh, Nick." Lindsay laughed and threw her arms around him. "As wonderful as Davidov can possibly be."

"A suitable compliment," he decided, "as that is a great deal more brilliant than anyone else."

Lindsay kissed him. "I'm so glad you don't change."

They both turned as the door opened. Seth stepped out on the balcony.

"Ah, we're caught," Nick stated, grinning as he kept Lindsay in his arms. "Now your architect will break both my legs."

"Perhaps if you beg for mercy," Lindsay told him, smiling over at Seth.

"Davidov beg for mercy?" Nick rolled his eyes and released her. "The woman is mad."

"Often," Seth agreed. "But I make allowances for it." Lindsay's hand slipped into his. "People are asking for you," he told Nick.

Nick nodded, casting a quick glance toward the dining room. "How long are you staying?"

"Just overnight," Seth answered.

"Then I will say goodbye now." He held out a hand to Seth. *"Do svidanya, priyatel."* He used the Russian term for friend. "You're a man to be envied. *Do svidanya, ptichka."*

"Goodbye, Nick." Lindsay watched him slip back into the dining room. She sighed.

"Feeling better?" Seth asked her.

"How well you know me," she murmured.

"How much I love you," he whispered as he pulled her into his arms.

"Seth. It's been a lovely evening."

"No regrets?"

Lindsay knew he spoke of her career, the choices she had made. "No. No regrets." She lifted her face and met his mouth with hers.

The kiss grew long and deep with a hint of hunger. She heard his quiet sound of pleasure as he drew her closer. Her arms slipped up around his back until her hands gripped his shoulders. *It's always like the first time*, she thought. *Each time he kisses me, it's like the first.*

"Seth," she murmured against his mouth as they changed the angle of the kiss. "I'm much, much too tired for a party tonight."

"Hmm." His lips moved to her ear. "It's been a long day. We should just slip up to our room and get some rest."

Lindsay gave a low laugh. "Good idea." She brought her lips teasingly back to his. "Maybe we could order a bottle of champagne—to toast the ballet."

"A magnum of champagne," Seth decided, drawing her back far enough to smile down into her face. "It was an excellent ballet, after all."

"Oh, yes." Lindsay cast an eye toward the doors that separated them from the crowd of people. She smiled back at her husband. "I don't think we should disturb the party, do you?"

"What party?" Seth asked. Taking her arm, he

walked past the doors. "There's another set of doors on the east side."

Lindsay laughed. "Architects always know the most important things," she murmured.

Chapter 6

By the end of the first week, *The Red Rose* was an established success. The company played to a full house at every performance. Ruth read the reviews and knew it was the turning point of her career. She gave interviews and focused on promoting the ballet, the company and herself. It was a simple matter to engage herself in her work and in her success. It was not so simple to deal with her feelings when she danced, night after night, with Nick.

Ruth told herself they were Carlotta's feelings; that it was merely her own empathy with the role she played. To fall in love with Davidov was impossible.

He was absorbed with ballet. So was she. He was only interested in brief physical relationships. Should she decide to involve herself with a man, she wanted emotions—deep, lasting emotions. The example of her own parents and Lindsay and Seth had spoiled her for anything less. Nick was demanding and selfish and un-reasonable—not qualities she looked for in a lover. He found her foolish and romantic.

She needed to remember that after each performance when her blood was pumping and the need for him was churning inside her. She needed to remind herself of it when she lay awake at night with her mind far too wide awake.

They met onstage almost exclusively, so that when they came together face to face, the temptation was strong to take on the roles of the characters they por-trayed. Whenever Ruth found herself too close to los-ing Carlotta's identity or her distance from Nick, she reviewed his faults. She had plans for her life, both pro-fessionally and personally. She was aware that Nick was the one man who could interfere with them.

She considered herself both self-sufficient and inde-pendent. She had had to be, growing up without an es-tablished home and normal childhood routines. There had been no lasting playmates in her young years, and she had taught herself not to form sentimental attach-ments to the homes her parents had rented, for they had never been homes for long. Ruth's apartment in New York was the first place she had allowed herself to grow attached to. It was hers—paid for with money she earned, filled with the things that were important to her. In the year she had lived there, she had learned that she could make it on her own. She had confidence in herself as a woman and as a dancer. It infuriated her that Nick was the only person on earth who could make her feel insecure in either respect.

Professionally, he could either challenge or intimidate her by a choice of words or with a facial expression. And Ruth was well aware of the confusion he aroused in her as a woman.

The girlhood crush was long over. For years, her passions had been centered on dancing. The men she had dated had been companions, friends. Nick had been the premier danseur, a mentor, a professional partner. It seemed strange to her that her feelings for him could have changed and intensified so quickly.

Perhaps, she thought, it would be easier to fall in love with a stranger rather than be in the embarrassing position of being suddenly attracted to a man she had known and worked with for years. There was no escape from the constant daily contact.

If it had been just a matter of physical attraction, Ruth felt she could have handled it. But it was the emotional involvement that worried her. Her feelings for Nick were complex and deep. She admired him, was fascinated by him, enraged by him, and trusted him without reservation—professionally. Personally, she knew he could, by the sheer force of his personality, overwhelm and devour. She wasn't willing to be the victim. Love, she feared, meant dependence, and that meant a lack of control.

"How far away are you?"

Ruth spun around to see Francie standing in her dressing room doorway. "Oh, miles," she admitted. "Come on in and sit down."

"You seem to have been thinking deep thoughts," Francie commented.

Ruth began to brush her hair back into a ponytail. *"Mmm,"* she said noncommittally. "Wednesdays are the longest. Just the thought of doing two shows makes my toes cramp."

"Seven curtain calls for a matinee isn't anything to sneeze at." Francie sank down on a handy chair. "Poor Nick is at this moment giving another interview to a reporter from *New Trends*."

Ruth gave a half laugh as she tied her hair back with a leather strap. "He'll be absolutely charming, and his accent will get more and more incomprehensible."

"Spasibo." Thank you, Francie said. "One of my few Russian words."

"Where did you learn that?" Ruth turned to face her.

"Oh, I did a bit of Russian cramming a couple of years ago when I thought I might enchant Nick." Grinning, Francie reached in her pocket for a stick of gum. "It didn't work. He'd laugh and pat me on the head now and again. I had delusions of gypsy violins and wild passion." She lifted her shoulders and sighed. "Nick always seems to be occupied, if you know what I mean."

"Yes." Ruth looked at her searchingly. "I never knew you were—interested in Nick that way."

"Honey." Francie gave her a pitying smile. "What female over twelve wouldn't be? And we all know my track record." She laughed and stretched her arms to the ceiling. "I like men. I don't fight it." She dropped her arms into her lap. "I just ended my meaningful relationship with the dermatologist."

"Oh. I'm sorry."

"Don't be sorry. We had fun. I'm considering a new meaningful relationship with the actor I met last week. He's Price Reynolds on *A New Breed*." At Ruth's blank look, she elaborated. "The soap opera."

Ruth shook her head while a smile tugged at her mouth. "I haven't caught it."

"He's tall, with broad shoulders and dark, sleepy eyes. He might just be the one."

Ruth bit her bottom lip in thought. "How do you know when he is?" She met Francie's eyes again. "What makes you think he might be?"

"My palms sweat." She laughed at Ruth's incredulous face. "No, really, they do. Every time. It wouldn't work for you." Francie stopped smiling and leaned forward as she did when she became serious. "It wouldn't be enough for you to think a man *might* be the one. You'd have to *know* he was. I've been in love twice already this year. I was in love at least four or five times last year. How many times have you been in love?"

Ruth looked at her blankly. "Well, I..." Never, she realized. There had been no one.

"Don't look devastated." Francie popped back out of the chair with all the exuberance she showed onstage. "You've never been in love because there's only one meaning of the word for you. You'll know it when it happens." She laid a friendly hand on Ruth's shoulders. "That's going to be it. You're not insecure, like me. You know what you want, what you need. You're not willing to settle for anything less."

"Insecure?" Ruth gave her friend a puzzled smile. "I've never imagined you as insecure."

"I need someone to tell me I'm pretty, I'm clever, I'm loved. You don't." She took a breath. "When we were in the corps, you knew you weren't going to stay there. You never had any doubt." She smiled again. "And neither did anyone else. If you found a man who meant as much to you as dancing does, you'd have it all."

Ruth dropped her eyes. "But he'd have to feel the same about me."

"That's part of the risk. It's like pulling a muscle." Francie grinned again. "It hurts like crazy, but you don't stop dancing. You haven't pulled a muscle yet."

"You're a great one with analogies."

"I only philosophize on an empty stomach," Francie told her. "Want lunch?"

"I can't. I'm meeting Donald." Ruth picked up her watch from the dressing table. "And I'm already late."

"Have fun." Francie headed for the door. "George is picking me up after tonight's show. You can get a look at him."

"George?"

"George Middemeyer." Francie tossed a grin over her shoulder. "Doctor Price Reynolds. He's a neurosurgeon with a failing marriage and a conniving mistress who might be pregnant. Tune in tomorrow."

With that, she was gone. Ruth laughed and grabbed her purse.

The delicatessen where Ruth was to meet Donald was two blocks away. She hurried toward it. She was aware that she was ten minutes late and that Donald was habitually prompt. She had little enough time before she had to report back for company calls.

The rich, strong smells of corned beef and Kosher pickles greeted her the moment she opened the door. The deli wasn't crowded, as the lunch rush was over, but a few people lingered. Two old men played a slow-moving game of checkers at a far table littered with the remnants of their lunch.

Ruth's glance swept over them and found Donald sitting back in his chair, smoking. She walked lightly, with rippling, unconscious confidence through the rows of tiny tables. "I'm sorry, Donald, I know I'm late." She leaned over to give him a quick kiss before she sat. "Have you ordered?"

"No." He tapped his cigarette. "I waited for you."

Ruth lifted a brow. There was something underlying the casual words. Knowing Donald, she told herself to wait. Whatever he had to say he would say in his own time.

She glanced over as the rotund, white-aproned man behind the counter shuffled over to their table. "What'll ya have?"

"Fruit salad and tea, please," Ruth told him, giving him a smile.

"Whitefish and coffee." Donald didn't glance at him. The man gave a little snort before shuffling off again. Ruth grinned at his retreating back.

"Have you ever been in here at lunch time?" she asked Donald. "It's a madhouse. He has a boy helping out during the rush, but they both move at the same pace. *Adagio.*"

"I rarely eat in places like this," Donald commented, taking a last drag before crushing out his cigarette.

Again Ruth detected undercurrents but waited. "It's really all I have time for today, Donald. Today must be pretty frantic for you, too, with your fashion show and reception tonight." She settled her purse strap over the back of her chair, then leaned her elbows on the table. "Is everything going well?"

"It appears to be. Some last-minute mayhem, naturally. Temperamental disagreements between my senior cutter and my head seamstress." He shrugged. "The usual."

"But this show is quite important, isn't it?" She tilted her head at his offhand tone.

"Yes, it's important." He shot her a direct look. "That's why I wanted you there with me."

Ruth met the look but kept her silence as the food was set unceremoniously on the table in front of them. Deliberately, she picked up her spoon but left the salad untouched. "You know why I can't, Donald. We've already discussed it."

He spilled a generous spoonful of sugar into his black coffee. "I also know you've got an understudy. One missed performance wouldn't matter that much."

"An understudy is for serious problems. I can't take a night off because I want to go out on a date."

"It's not quite movies and pizza," he said crossly.

"I know that, Donald." Ruth sipped the tea. A light throbbing had begun behind her eyes. "I'd be there if I could."

"I didn't let you down on opening night."

"That's hardly fair." Ruth set down her cup. She could see by the cool, set look on his face that his mind was already made up. "If you'd had a show scheduled to conflict with mine, you wouldn't have missed it, and I wouldn't have expected you to."

"You're not willing to make adjustments for me or for my work."

Ruth thought of the parties and functions she had attended at his insistence. "I give you what I can, Donald. You knew my priorities when we started seeing each other."

Donald stopped stirring his coffee and set the spoon on the table. "It isn't enough," he said coldly. Ruth felt her stomach tighten. "I want you with me tonight."

Her brow lifted. "An ultimatum?"

"Yes."

"I'm sorry, Donald." Her voice was low but without apology. "I can't."

"You won't," he countered.

"It hardly matters which way you put it," she said wearily.

"I'll be taking Germaine to the showing tonight."

Ruth looked at him. His choice showed a certain shrewdness. His biggest competitor would probably be more useful to him than a dancer.

"I've taken her out a few times recently," he explained. "You've been busy."

"I see." Ruth's response was noncommittal, although his words hurt.

"You've been too self-absorbed lately. There's nothing for you in your life but ballet. You refuse to make room in it for me, for any man. You've a selfish streak, Ruth. Class after class after class, with rehearsals and performances thrown in. Dancing's all you have, all you want."

His words shocked her at first, then cut. Ruth fumbled behind her for her purse, but Donald caught her arm.

"I'm not finished." He held her firmly in her chair. "You stand in front of those mirrors for hours, and what do you see? A body that waits to be told what to do by a choreographer. How often do you move on your own, Ruth? How often do you feel anything that isn't programmed into you? What will you have when the dancing stops?"

"Please." She bit down hard on her lip, trying without success to stop a flow of tears. "That's enough."

He seemed to focus on her face all at once. On a sharp breath, Donald released her arm. "Damn it, Ruth, I'm sorry."

"No." Frantically shaking her head, she pushed back her chair and rose. "Don't say any more." In a flash, she darted out the door.

The steamy summer air struck her like a blast. For a moment she looked up and down the street, confused, before turning toward the studio.

She hurried past the sea of strangers. The barbs that Donald had aimed had struck home—struck deep. Was she just an automaton? An empty body waiting to be filled by the bid of choreographers and composers? Was that how people from the outside saw her—as a ballerina on a music box, pirouetting endlessly until the music stopped?

She wondered how much truth had been in his angry words. Bursting through the front door of the building, she headed straight for her dressing room.

Once inside, she closed her door and leaned back against it. She was shaking from head to foot. A few short remarks from Donald had dehumanized her. Ruth moved slowly to her mirror and switched on all the lights. With hard, searching eyes, she studied her face.

Had her love and devotion for dancing made her selfish and one-dimensional? Was she really unable to feel deeply for a man, to make a positive commitment?

Ruth pressed her hands to her cheeks. The skin was soft, smooth, the scent on her hands was feminine. *But was she?* Ruth could read the panic in her eyes. Where did the dancer end and the woman begin? She shook her head and turned away from her own image.

Too many mirrors, she thought suddenly. There were

too many mirrors in her life, and she was no longer certain what they reflected. What would she be in a decade, when the dancer faced the twilight of her career? Would memories and clippings be all she had?

Closing her eyes, Ruth forced herself to take several long breaths. She had three hours until curtain. There was no time to dwell on problems. She would look for the answers after the performance.

Deciding what she needed was the lunch that had been so recently pushed aside, Ruth went down to the canteen for tea and an apple. The simple familiarity of the place helped level her. There were complaints about strained muscles, impossible dance combinations, Nadine's tight purse strings and the uncertain state of the plumbing on the fourth floor. By the time she was back at her dressing room door, she was steadier.

"Ruth!"

She looked over her shoulder as she placed her hand on the knob.

"Hello, Leah." Ruth tried to drum up some enthusiasm upon seeing the elegant blond dancer.

"Your reviews are marvelous." Leah eased her way into the dressing room as Ruth opened the door and entered. Too well, she knew the blonde's penchant for stirring up trouble. Ruth felt she had had her fair share for one day.

"Roses for the whole ballet," Ruth agreed, walking over to take a seat at her dressing table as Leah settled into a chair. "But I don't imagine you found ballet reviews in there." She let her eyes fall on the tabloid Leah had in her hand.

"You never know whose name's going to pop up in here." She smiled at Ruth, then began thumbing through the paper. "I just happened to see a friend of yours mentioned in here. Let's see now, where…?" She trailed off as she scanned the print. "Oh, yes, here it is. 'Donald Keyser,'" she quoted, "'top designer, has been seen recently escorting his fiery-headed competitor, Germaine Jones. Apparently his interest in ballet has waned.'" Leah lifted her eyes, moving her lips into a sympathetic little smile. "Men are such pigs, aren't they?"

Ruth swallowed her temper. "Aren't they."

"And it's so demeaning to be dumped in print, too."

Ruth's spine snapped straight. Color flowed in, then out of her cheeks. "I was dumped in the flesh, as well," she said with the calm of determination. "So it hardly matters."

"He was terribly good-looking," Leah commented, meticulously folding the paper. "Of course, someone else is bound to come along."

"Haven't I told you about the Texan?" Ruth surprised herself, but the blank, then curious expression on Leah's face was motivation enough to maintain the pretense.

"Texan? What Texan?"

"Oh, we've been keeping a low profile," Ruth ad-libbed airily. "He can't afford to have his name splashed around in print until the divorce is final. Just piles of money, you know, and his second wife's not being very cooperative." She managed a slow smile. "You wouldn't believe the settlement. He offered her the villa in southern Italy, but she's holding out for his art collection. French impressionists."

"I see." Leah narrowed her eyes to a feline slit. "Well, well, aren't you the quiet one."

"Like a sphinx."

"You'll have to be careful how much Nick finds out,"

Leah warned, then ran the tip of her tongue over her top lip. "He really detests nasty publicity. He'll want to be particularly careful now that he's finalizing plans for that big special on cable television."

"Special?" Ruth echoed.

"Didn't you know?" Leah looked pleased again. "Featuring the company, of course, and spotlighting the principal dancers. I'll do Aurora, naturally, probably the wedding scene. I believe Nick plans to do a pas de deux from *Le Corsaire*, and, of course, one from *The Red Rose*. He hasn't chosen his partners yet." She paused deliberately and smiled. "We have two full hours of air time. Nick's very excited about filling it." She slanted Ruth a glance. "Strange he hasn't mentioned it to you, but perhaps he thought you wouldn't be up to it after the strain of these last few weeks."

Leah rose to leave. "Don't worry, darling, he'll be making the announcement in a few days. I'm sure he'll use you somewhere." She dropped the paper into the chair. "Dance well," she said and left, closing the door quietly behind her.

Chapter 7

Ruth sat staring at the closed door for several long minutes. How could Leah know about such an enormously important project and she be left in the dark? *Unless Nick intended to exclude her.*

She knew she and Nick were having their personal problems, but professionally… Professionally, she remembered, she had told him that after this run she'd never dance with him again. Ruth recalled her own words and knew she had meant them, at least at that moment. But did that mean she was not to be partnered by anyone else? Could Nick be so vindictive?

Ruth knew that she was a good dancer. Would Nick drop her for personal reasons? After all, she had threatened him. Ruth closed her eyes and tried to control the rising sickness in her stomach.

He had barely spoken to her since that night. Was

this his way of punishing her for claiming not to want or need him as a partner? Would he let someone else dance Carlotta? The thought was more than Ruth could bear. Over and over she told herself she was a fool to allow herself to grow so attached to a part. Many other women would become Carlotta; she had simply been the first. Yet Ruth knew she had had a hand in creating the role as much as Nick had. She had put her soul into it.

Opening her eyes, Ruth looked directly at the copy of *Keyhole* that was left on the chair. Leah had done her work well, Ruth realized on a long breath. She had wanted to upset Ruth before the performance, and she had succeeded. Everything Donald had said—every feeling of doubt and inadequacy—had been reinforced. Now she feared that Nick would release her from the company when *The Red Rose*'s engagement was finished.

Ruth buried her face in her hands a moment and tried to push it all away. She had a performance to give; nothing could interfere with that. She was a dancer. That couldn't be taken from her.

Less than an hour later Ruth stepped out of her dressing room to warm up backstage. Still shaken, she tried to focus all her power of concentration on the role she was to portray. On another night she would have left Ruth Bannion behind in the dressing room. But not this time. Tonight Carlotta's free-spirited confidence and verve would be difficult to capture.

Ruth loosened her muscles automatically, trying to block out Donald's and Leah's words, but they continued to play through her thoughts.

The sounds of the orchestra tuning brought her

back to the moment. It all felt wrong—the costume, the lights, the whine of strings as they were tested. She was cold, numb. She forgot the first movements of the ballet.

Nick came out of his dressing room. His eyes sought Ruth. It was a habitual practice of his, and it annoyed him. A sign of weakness in himself, however slight, irritated him. Ruth Bannion was becoming a weakness. She was as cool as autumn offstage and as sultry as summer on it. The transition was playing havoc with his nerves. He didn't care for it one bit.

It was difficult to deal with desire that would not abate even when she appeared to be indifferent to him, then challenged him to take her the moment she moved onstage. No woman had made him feel curb and spur at the same time before.

Nick could see the tension in her back, although he couldn't see her face. Her body spoke volumes. "Ruth."

Her already tense shoulders went rigid at the sound of his voice. Slowly, fighting to compose her features, she turned. Something flickered over his face before it became closed and still.

"What's wrong?"

"Nothing." Ruth hoped her voice sounded casual. She didn't flinch when he took her chin in his hand to study her face. Beneath the makeup her skin was pale, her eyes dark and miserable.

"Are you ill?" Had there been concern in his voice, she might have collapsed.

"No."

Nick gave her a long, thorough study before dropping his hand. "Then snap out of it. You have to dance in a moment. If you had a fight with your boyfriend, your tears have to wait."

He heard her sharp intake of breath, saw the simultaneous cloud of hurt in her eyes. "I'll dance, don't worry. No one you've got lined up to replace me will ever dance this part better."

Nick's gaze narrowed as he curled his fingers around her arm. "What are you talking about?"

"Don't." Ruth jerked her arm free. "I've had enough dumped on me tonight. I don't need any more." Her voice broke, and cursing herself, Ruth walked to the wings to wait for her cue. She took long, steadying breaths and forced as much as possible out of her mind.

Her opening dance did not go well. Ruth comforted herself, as she stood again in the wings, that only the sharpest eyes would have detected any flaws. Technically her moves had been perfect, but Ruth knew a dancer had to give more than body to the dance. Her mind and heart had not flowed with her. Her inability to give her best shook her all the more.

She made her second entrance and moments later was dancing with Nick.

"Put some life into it," he demanded in low tones as she spun in a double pirouette. He lifted her into an arabesque. "You dance like a robot."

"Isn't that what you want?" she hissed back. Jeté, jeté, arabesque, and she was back in his arms.

"Be angry," he murmured, lifting her again. "Hate me, but think of me. *Of me.*"

It was difficult to think of anything else. His eyes alone demanded it throughout the performance. Ruth's nerves were stretched to the breaking point by the last act. Emotions were churning inside her until she feared she would be physically sick. Never before had she prayed for a performance to end. Her head pounded desperately, but she fought to the finish. She sagged against Nick when the curtains closed.

"You said you weren't ill." He took her by the shoulders. Ruth shook her head. "Can you take curtain calls?"

"Yes. Yes, of course." She tried to pull out of his arms. He resisted her efforts, then, when her eyes lifted questioningly to his, he released her to take her hand.

The applause was muffled against the heavy curtain, but with a nod from Nick, the drape was lifted. The applause was thunderous. Ruth winced at the volume of noise. Again and again she made her curtsies, hanging on to the knowledge that the long day was almost at an end.

"Enough," Nick said curtly when the applause battered against the curtain yet again. He began to lead her offstage left.

"Nick," Ruth began, confused because her dressing room was in the opposite direction.

"Ms. Bannion is ill," he told the stage manager as they brushed past. "She goes home. She sees no one."

"Nick, I can't," Ruth protested. "I have to change."

"Later." He all but pushed her into the elevator. "We're going up to my office." He punched a button, and the doors slid shut. "We'll talk."

"I can't," Ruth began in rising panic. "I won't."

"You will. For now, be quiet. You're shaking."

Because she knew he wasn't above force to get his own way, Ruth subsided when the doors opened and he propelled her down the hall. The entire floor was dark and deserted. Without the least hesitation, he located the door to his office. Pushing her through, Nick flipped on the lights, then closed and locked the door. "Sit," he ordered shortly, then moved to a low, ornate cabinet.

Ruth had rarely been inside the room. It bespoke a different aspect of Nikolai Davidov, the dancer, the choreographer. This was his executive domain. Here he dealt with the rich, urging money from them to keep the company alive. Ruth could easily imagine him sitting behind the huge, old oak desk, radiating charm and coaxing dollars from patrons. Hadn't she heard Nadine state that Nick was as valuable to the company behind a desk as he was onstage?

Charm. Charisma. That generous, intimate smile that made it impossible to say no. Yes, it was a talent, just as double *tours en l'air* required talent. And style. What was talent without style? Davidov had an abundance of both.

Ruth glanced around the stately office with its old, tasteful furniture and fat, leather chairs. How many thousands of dollars had begun their journey in this office from silk-lined pockets to props, costumes and lights? What elegant balletomane had paid for the costume she was wearing at that moment?

"I said *sit.*"

Nick's curt order broke into Ruth's thoughts. She turned, but before she could speak, she found herself being turned toward the sofa. The unarguable pressure on her shoulder convinced her to sit. A brandy snifter, a quarter full, was thrust into her hands.

"Drink." So saying, Nick moved back to the cabinet for his own brandy. When he was sitting next to her, Nick leaned back into the curve of the sofa arm and watched her. A lift of his brow repeated his order, and Ruth sipped at the brandy.

Silently, he continued to study her while he swirled his own. The quiet was absolute. Ruth drank again, focusing her entire concentration on a scar in the wood of his desk.

"So." The word brought her eyes flying back to his face. He kept his own on hers while he lifted his glass. "Tell me," he ordered.

"There's nothing to tell."

"Ruth." He glanced down at the liquor in his glass as if considering its vintage. "You know at times I am a patient man. This," he said and brought his eyes back to hers, "is not one of those times."

"I'm glad you clarified that." Ruth finished off the brandy recklessly, then set down the snifter. "Well, thanks for the drink." She hadn't even started to rise when his hand clamped over her wrist.

"Don't press your luck," he warned softly. He kept her prisoner while he leisurely sipped his drink. "Answers," he told her. "Now."

"May I have the question first, please?" Ruth kept her voice light, but her pulse betrayed her by beating fitfully against his fingers.

"What was wrong with you tonight?"

"I was a little off." She made an impatient move with her shoulders.

"Why?"

"It was a mood. I have them." She tried, without success, to free her arm. The ease with which he prevented this was infuriating. "Aren't I entitled to any privacy?" she demanded. "Any personal feelings?"

"Not when it interferes with your work."

"I can't dance on automatic." The passion she tried to control slipped into her voice. Her eyes flared with it. "No matter what anyone thinks. I'm not just a body that dances when someone plays the tune. Oh, let me go!" She tugged on her hand again. "I don't want to talk to you."

Ignoring this demand, Nick set down his glass. "Who puts these thoughts into your head?" He took her shoulders, keeping her facing him when she would have turned away. "Your designer?" Her expression gave her away even as she shook her head.

Nick swore quietly in Russian. He increased the pressure of his fingers. "Look at me," he demanded. "Don't you know nonsense when it falls on your ears?"

"He said I had no feelings," she said haltingly, trying to control the tears that thickened her voice and blurred her vision. "That my life, my emotions were all bound up in ballet and without it…" She trailed off and shook her head.

"What does he know?" Nick gave her a quick, exasperated shake. "He's not a dancer. How does he know what we feel? Does he know the difference between jumping and soaring?" There was another quick, concise oath. "He's jealous. He wants to cage you."

"He wants more than I've given him," Ruth countered. "He's entitled to more. I do care about him, but—" She pushed her hair back from her face with both hands.

"You're not in love with him," Nick finished.

"No. No, I'm not. Maybe I'm just not capable of that kind of feeling. Maybe he's right, and I—"

"Stop!" He shook her again, harder than before. Springing up, he prowled the room. Ruth heard him muttering in Russian as he paced. "You're a fool to let anyone make you believe such things. Because you are not in love with a man, you let him convince you you're less than a woman?" He made a sound of disgust and whirled back to her. "What's wrong with you? Where's your spirit? Your temper? If I had said such things to you, you wouldn't have allowed it!"

Ruth pressed her fingers to her temple and tried to rearrange her thoughts. "But you would never have said those things to me."

"No." The answer was quiet. Nick walked back to her. "No, because I know you, understand what's in you. We have this, you see." He took her hand and laced their fingers. Ruth stared at the joined hands. "You have your world and your designer has his. If there was love, you could live in both."

Ruth took a moment, carefully thinking over his words. "Yes, I'd want to," she said slowly. "I'd try to. But—"

"No. No buts. Buts tire me." He sank back down beside her, managing to make the inelegant movement graceful. "So you fought with your designer, and he said stupid things. Is this enough to make you pale and sick?"

"It didn't help to have my replacement shoved down my throat," Ruth shot back. "I didn't care for being taunted with a copy of *Keyhole* chatting about his new relationship an hour before curtain."

"Keyhole?" Nick frowned in confusion. "What is this *Keyhole*? Ah," he said, remembering before Ruth could elaborate. "The silly newspaper with the very bad pictures?"

"The silly newspaper that speculated Donald Keyser had lost interest in the ballet."

"Ah." Nick pressed his fingertips together. "He brought that by your dressing room?"

"No, not Donald…" Ruth broke off, alerted by the sharpening of his eyes. Quickly she moistened her lips and rose. "It doesn't matter. It was stupid to let it upset me."

"Stop." The quiet order froze her. "Who?" Ruth felt the warning feather up her spine. "Who brought the paper to you before the performance?"

"Nick, I—"

"I asked you a question." He rose, too. "It's inexcusable for a member of the company to deliberately set out to disturb another before a performance. I do not permit it."

"I won't tell you. No, I won't," she added firmly as she saw the temper leap into his eyes. "I should've handled it better. I will next time. In any case, there was something more than Donald that upset me tonight." Ruth stood her ground, not so much wanting to protect Leah but more unwilling to subject anyone to the full force of Davidov's temper. She knew he could be brutal.

"I want a name."

"I won't give you one. I can't." She touched his arm and found the muscles rigid. "I just can't," she murmured, using what power she knew her eyes possessed. "There's something more important that we have to settle."

He became very still. Ruth searched his face, but his expression was guarded. Whatever his thoughts, they remained his alone. Feeling the withdrawal, Ruth took her hand from his arm.

"What?"

Ruth caught herself before she moistened her lips

again. Her heart was beginning to pound furiously against her ribs. "I think I'd like another brandy first."

She waited for an angry, impatient refusal, but after a brief hesitation he picked up the snifters and went back to the liquor cabinet. The only sound was the splash of liquid as it hit the glass. She accepted the drink when he offered it, then sipped. She took a deep breath.

"Do you plan to release me from the company?"

Nick's own snifter paused on the way to his lips. "What did you say?"

This time Ruth spoke more firmly. "I said, do you plan to release me from the company?"

"Do I look like a stupid man?" he demanded.

In spite of her tension, the incredulity in his tone made her smile. "No, Davidov."

"*Khorosho.* Good. For once, we agree." He flicked his wrist in angry confusion. "And since I am not a stupid man, why would I release from the company my finest ballerina?"

Ruth stared at him. Shock shot through her body and was plain on her face. "You never said that before," she whispered.

"Said what?"

Shaking her head, she pressed her fingers between her brows, then turned away. "As long as I can remember, I've wanted to dance." Ruth gave a muffled laugh as tears began to flow. "All these years, I've pushed myself—for myself, yes—for the dance and for you. And you never said anything like that to me before." She took a small, shuddering breath. "After a day like this, after tonight's performance, you stand there and very casually tell me I'm the finest ballerina you have." Ruth wiped tears away with a knuckle. "Only you, Nikolai, would choose such a time."

Though she hadn't heard him move, Ruth wasn't surprised when his hands touched her shoulders. "If I hadn't said so before, I should have. But then, I haven't always considered words so very important."

Nick ran his fingers through her hair, watching the light glint on it. "You're very important to me. I will not lose you."

Ruth felt her heart stop beating. Then, like thunder, it began to roar in her ears. We're only speaking of the company, she reminded herself. Of dancing only. She turned.

"Will you replace me as Carlotta for television?"

"For television?" he repeated. He struggled, as he had to do from time to time, to think in precise English. "Do you mean the cable?" Reading the answer in her eyes, he continued. "But that is not yet finalized, how would you…?" He stopped. "So that's what you meant before you went on tonight. And this information, I imagine, came from the same person who brought you the little *Doorknob*?"

"*Keyhole*," Ruth corrected, but he was swearing suddenly in what she recognized as full-blown Russian rage.

"This is not permitted. I will not have my dancers sniping at each other before a performance. I will tell you this—what plans I made, and what casting I do, *I* do." He glared at her, caught up in fury. "My decision. *Mine.* If I chose you to dance Carlotta, then you dance Carlotta."

"I said I wouldn't dance with you again," Ruth began. "But—"

"I care *that* for what you said," Nick said to her with a snap of his fingers. "If I tell you to dance with me, then you do. You have no say in this."

His temper was in full swing, and Ruth's flared to match it. "I have a say in my own life."

"To go or to stay, yes," he agreed. "But if you stay, you do as you're told."

"You haven't told me anything," she reminded him. "I have to hear of your big plans less than an hour before curtain. You've barely spoken to me in weeks."

"I've had nothing to say to you. I don't waste my time."

"You arrogant, insufferable pig! I've poured everything I have into this ballet. I've bled for it. If you think I'm going to let you hand it over to someone else without a fight, you *are* stupid. I don't care if it's a two-minute pas de deux or the whole ballet. It's mine!"

"You think so, little one?" His tone was deceptively gentle.

"I know so," she tossed back. "And don't call me little one. I'm a woman, and Carlotta's mine until I can't dance her anymore." She took a quick breath before continuing. "I'll be dancing her years after you're finished with Prince Stefan."

"Really?" He circled her throat with his hand and squeezed lightly. The meaning pierced through her fury. "And do you forget, *milaya*, who composed the ballet? Who choreographed it and cast you as Carlotta?"

"No. And don't you forget who danced it!"

"You have a lovely, slender neck," he murmured. His fingers caressed it. "Don't tempt me to break it."

"I'm too mad to be frightened of you, Davidov. I

want a simple answer. Do I dance Carlotta on this special or not?"

His eyes roamed over her furious face. "I'll let you know. You've just under a week left in this run. We can discuss future plans when it's finished." He cocked a brow when she let out a furious sigh. "Incentive. Now you'll dance your heart out for me."

"You always know what to say, don't you, Nick?" Ruth started to turn away, but he stopped her.

Very slowly, very deliberately, he lowered his mouth until it hovered an inch above hers. After a long, breathless moment, his lips descended. He heard her draw in her breath at the contact. He could feel her pulse beat against his palm, but still he did not increase the pressure.

Caressingly, the tip of his tongue traced her lips until, with a quiet sigh, they parted and invited him to enter. He had never kissed her with such care before, with such aching tenderness. Was there a defense against such tenderness? Always before, there had been heat and fire and hints of fear. Now she felt nothing but mindless pleasure.

He nipped her bottom lip, stopping just before the point of pain, then he replaced his teeth with his tongue. There was a strong scent of stage makeup and sweat to mix with the taste of brandy. Weak and weightless, she let her head fall back, inviting his complete control.

Their lips clung a few seconds longer as he began to draw her away. Nick felt the quiet release of her breath as she opened heavy eyes to look at him. In them he saw that she was his. He had only to lower her to the couch or pull her to the floor. They were alone, she was willing. He could still taste her, a dark, wild honey flavor that taunted him.

"Little one," he murmured and slid his hand from her throat to stroke her cheek. "What have you eaten today?"

Ruth's thoughts were thrown into instant confusion. "Eaten?" she repeated dumbly.

"Yes, food." There was a hint of impatience in his voice as he scooped up his brandy again. "What food have you had today?"

"I…" Ruth's mind was a total blank. "I don't know," she said finally with a helpless gesture. Her body was still throbbing.

"When's the last time you had a steak?"

"A steak?" Ruth ran a hand through her hair. "Years," she decided with an exasperated laugh.

"Come, you need a good meal." He held out a hand. "I'll take you to dinner."

"Nick, I don't understand you." Bewildered, Ruth ignored his outstretched hand, but he took hers firmly in his and was soon pulling her toward the door.

"Five minutes to change."

"Nick." Ruth stopped in the doorway to study him. "Will I ever understand you?"

His brows lifted and fell at the question. "I'm Davidov," he said with a quick grin. "Is that not enough?"

She laughed shakily. "Too much," she answered. "Too much…"

Chapter 8

Dinner with Nick had been enjoyable but hardly illuminating. Looking back, Ruth realized that they hadn't spoken of ballet at all. After a wild cab ride home, which Nick had apparently enjoyed, he had deposited her at her door with a very quick, passionless kiss.

Ruth had slept until the ring of her alarm clock the following morning. Emotional exhaustion and rich food had proven an excellent tranquilizer.

The next day, routine had taken over. Though her mind still fretted for answers, Ruth knew Nick well enough to realize he intended to make her wait for them. The more she pressed, the more reticent he became.

As the two-week run of *The Red Rose* came to an end, Ruth dealt with the familiar let-down feeling that came with the completion of an engagement. She would be in limbo for a time, waiting for Nick to assign her another role. It was one more unanswered question.

Ruth hung up Carlotta's costume on closing night and felt as though she was losing part of herself. She was in no mood to go to the cast party, though she knew she should at least put in an appearance.

I'd be lousy company, she told herself with a wry smile. No champagne tonight, she decided quickly as she creamed off her makeup. Just a huge glass of milk and an entire bag of cookies, all to myself. No one to share them with but Nijinsky. Ruth pulled on jeans. No brooding, just gorging.

"Come on in!" she called out when there was a knock on her door. She pulled a T-shirt down over her hips as Francie popped her head in.

"Where are you hiding?" she demanded. "They're already into the champagne."

"I'm skipping out," Ruth told her, picking up her purse.

"Oh, but you can't." Francie was still in full costume and make-up. Her darkened lips pouted. "I want you to meet my neurosurgeon."

"Can't tonight." Ruth shot her a grin and a wink. "Big plans."

"Oh?" Francie drew out the word knowingly. "Why didn't you bring him by?"

"I'm not sharing with anyone," she told her. She let out a big, anticipatory sigh. "All mine."

"Wow." Francie's brows shot up. "What's he like?"

"Delicious." Ruth couldn't resist as she swung through the door. "Absolutely delicious."

"Have I seen him?" Francie called out, but Ruth just laughed and dashed for the stage door.

Two hours later Ruth sat in a living room chair. Nijinsky lay sprawled at her feet, belly up, his front paws posed like a fighter's, ready to lead with the left.

Ruth yawned. The old movie on TV wasn't holding her attention. Still she was glad she had slipped out on the party. Her mood had been wrong. The crowds and the laughter and the company jokes would have depressed her, while the solitary time had lifted her spirits. She thought of taking the free hours she would have the next day to go shopping for something useless. Nick would be working her again soon enough. It might be fun to rummage through antique shops for a candle snuffer or pillbox.

Closing her eyes, she stretched luxuriously. Maybe this was the time to steal a couple of days and drive up to see Lindsay and Seth. She frowned when Nick's image flew into her mind.

His quiet, gentle kiss had cracked the very foundations of her defense against him. For days she hadn't allowed herself to think of him in anything but professional terms. He was the main reason, she was finally forced to admit, that she hadn't been able to face the cast party.

She wanted him. No matter how many times, over the past days and weeks, she had refused to accept that thought, her desire simply hadn't changed. But yes, it had—she wanted him more. The longing was difficult enough, but when hints of something else, something more complicated intruded, Ruth tightly closed the door on it.

"I'm too tired to think about that now," she told a totally disinterested Nijinsky. "I'm going to bed." When he made no sign of acknowledgment, Ruth rose and stepped over him to switch off the television. Leaving the plate of cookie crumbs for morning, she flicked off all the lights on her way to bed.

Nick stared up at the dark windows of Ruth's apartment. It's one o'clock in the morning, and she's asleep. *If I had any brains, I'd be asleep, too*, he said fiercely to himself.

He jammed his hands into his pockets and started to walk. *You've no business here, Davidov*, he told himself. You've known that all along. The night was cooling with the first true hint of fall. He hunched his shoulders against it. He'd been an idiot to come. He had told himself that over and over as he had steadily walked the blocks to her apartment building.

If she had been at the party, if he could just have looked at her… Oh, God, he thought desperately, he was long past the time when looking was enough. The nights were driving him mad, and no other woman would do. He needed Ruth.

How long had it been going on? he demanded of himself, never giving a glance as a police car sped by, sirens screaming. A month, a year? Five years? Since that moment in Lindsay's studio when he had first watched Ruth at the barre? He should have known, with that first impossible stir of desire. Good Lord, she'd only been seventeen!

How was he to have known she would taste that way when he kissed her? Or that she would respond as if she had only been sleeping—waiting for him? How was he to have known that the sight of that small, slim body would torment him day after day, night after night? Even when he danced with her, the thought of taking her, of having her melt against him, throbbed through him until he knew he would go mad. He began to walk away.

Nick stopped and turned around. Good God, he wanted her. Now. Tonight.

The banging at her door had Ruth sitting straight up in bed. What was the dream she had been having? *Nick?* She shook her head to clear it. Even as she reached for the clock, the banging started again. Sliding from the bed, she groped for her robe.

"I'm coming!" she called, urged to hurry by the ferocity of the banging. Pulling the robe on as she went, she rushed through the darkened apartment. "For heaven's sake, you're going to wake the neighborhood!" Ruth peered through the peephole, blinked and peered again. She fumbled for the chain; he pounded again.

They stared at each other when the door was opened. Ruth stood bewildered by the traces of temper she saw in his eyes. Her hair was a riot of confusion over the hastily drawn on robe. Her cheeks were still flushed with sleep, her eyes heavy. Nick took a step forward, knowing he had crossed over the line.

"I need you."

Her heart skidded at the three simple words spoken quietly, roughly, as if they fought to be said. Before she knew what she was doing, Ruth held out her arms to him.

Then they were pressed together, mouth to mouth. The hunger was raw, unbelievably strong. It was a devouring kiss—long, desperate, deep. Ruth clung to the wildness of it. She felt his hand tighten its grip on her hair, pulling her head back as if in fury. His mouth left hers only to change angles and probe deeper. There was a hint of brutality, as if he would assuage all his needs by a single kiss.

"I want you." It was a groan from well within him as he drew her away. His eyes were dark and burning. "God, too much."

Ruth gripped the front of his sweater until her fingers hurt. "Not too much," she whispered. She drew him inside.

Her throat was dry with the pounding of her heart as she closed the door and turned to him. They were only silhouettes as they stood, inches apart, in the dark.

She swallowed, sensing his struggle for control. It wasn't control she wanted from him. Not tonight. She wanted him to be driven—for her, by her. The overwhelming need to have him touch her was terrifying. Slowly, hardly conscious of her actions, Ruth reached up to draw the robe from her shoulders. She let it slide soundlessly to the floor as it left her naked.

"Love me," she murmured.

She heard his low groan of surrender as he drew her into his arms. His mouth was hot, his hands rough and possessive. She could feel the urgency of his need.

Ruth tugged at his sweater as they moved toward the bedroom. Somewhere in the hallway she pulled it over his head and threw it to the floor. His muscles flowed under her hands.

They were at the bedroom door when she fumbled with the snap of his jeans. She felt his stomach suck in as her fingers glided over it and heard the hoarse, muffled Russian as his teeth nipped into her shoulder. His hips were narrow, the skin warm. He dug his fingers into her back when she touched him.

"Milenkaya," he said and managed a rough laugh. "Let me get my shoes off."

"I can't." The need was overpowering. She'd already waited so long. "Lie with me." She pulled him toward the bed. "Take me now, Nick. I'll go mad if you don't."

Then they were naked, and he was on top of her. Ruth could hear his heart's desperate race, his ragged breath against her ear. He was trembling, she realized, as he entered her. Her body took over, knowing its own needs, while her mind shuddered with the onslaught of sensations. One moment she was strong, the next weak and spent. Nick lay atop her, his face buried in her hair.

"Sweet God, Ruth." He heaved out the words on labored breaths. "Untouched. Untouched and I take you like a beast!" Nick rolled from her, running a hand through his hair. When he sat up, Ruth could see just the outline of his chest and shoulders, the glimmer of his eyes. "I should have known better. There's no excuse for it. I must have hurt you."

"No." She felt drugged and dizzy, but there was no pain. "No."

"It should never have been like this."

"Are you saying you're sorry this happened?"

"Yes, by God!"

The answer hurt, but she sat up and spoke calmly. "Why?"

"It's obvious, isn't it?" He rose. "I come to your door in the middle of the night and push you into bed without the smallest show of…" He groped for a word, struggling for the English equivalent of his meaning.

"Pushed me into bed?" Ruth repeated. "And of course, I had nothing to do with it." She knelt on the bed and tossed back her hair. Nick saw the glimmer of her angry eyes. "You conceited ass! Who pushed whom into bed? Let's just get the facts straight, Davidov. *I* opened the door, *I* told you what I wanted, *I* took your clothes off. So don't act like this was all your idea. If you want to be sorry you made love with me, go right ahead." She continued to storm before he could open his mouth to speak. "But don't hide behind guilt just because I was a virgin. I was a virgin because I wanted to be. I chose the time to change it. *I* seduced *you*!" she finished furiously.

"Well." Nick spoke again after a long moment of silence. "It seems I've been put in my place."

Ruth gave a short laugh. She was angry and hurt and still throbbing. "That'll be the day."

Nick walked back to the bed and touched her hair with his hand. There were times he thought it would be easier to speak in Russian. His feelings were more clearly articulated in his native tongue.

"Ruth, it is sometimes, when I am upset, difficult to make myself understood." He paused a moment, working out the way to make himself clear. "I'm not sorry to have made love with you. This is something I've wanted for a very long time. I am sorry that your first experience in love had to be so lacking in romance. Do you see?" He cupped her face in his hands and lifted it. "This was not the way to show an innocent the delights of what a man and woman can have."

Ruth looked at him. She could see more clearly now as her eyes grew accustomed to the dark. His face was a pale shadow, but his eyes were vital and alive. She felt the warmth flowing back. She smiled.

"There's another way?" she asked, keeping the smile from her voice.

His fingers traced her cheekbones. "Many other ways."

"Then I think you owe it to me to show me." She slipped her arms around his neck. "Now."

"Ruth—"

"Now," she repeated before she pressed her mouth to his. With a groan, Nick let her taste fill him again. He lingered over the kiss, exciting her with his lips and teeth and tongue. Ruth felt her blood begin to swim.

Gently, so that his thumbs just brushed her nipples, he cupped her breasts. They were small and firm and smooth. The points were taut, and he stroked easily until he heard her breath quicken. Taking his mouth to her ear, he whispered words that meant nothing to her. But the sound of them, the flutter of warm breath, dissolved her. He slid his hands to her back, supporting her as she knelt on the bed. Already she was trembling, but he used only his lips to entice—waiting, waiting.

Slowly, with infinite care, he began to stroke her until her skin was hot against him. He seemed to find the skin on the inside of her thighs irresistible. Again and again he returned there with teasing touches. Once he caressed the triangle between her legs, and her body shuddered as she pressed against his hand. But he retreated to mold her hips and take her deep with a kiss.

The sound of her own breathing was shouting in her ears. As he pressed her back on the bed, she moaned his name.

"There's more, *milaya*," he murmured, feasting on the flavor of her throat. "Much more."

Her breath caught in a gasp and a moan all at once as he took her nipple between his teeth. His tongue became moist as he suckled. Ruth pressed him closer, unaware of the seductive rhythm her body set under his. He took his mouth to her other breast, and shock coursed through her. She called for him mindlessly, steeped in sensation.

His mouth roamed lower and lower as his hands reached for her breasts, still hot and moist from his mouth. He guided her, as he had once guided her to music, setting the pace for their private pas de deux. Again he was the composer, she the dancer, moving to his imagination. Her mind was swept clean. She was utterly his.

She opened for him, and as he entered her, his mouth came greedily down on hers. He moved inside her slowly, ignoring the desperate pressure in his loins for his own release. He took her as though he had a lifetime to savor the ultimate pleasure.

Seconds, minutes, hours, they were joined until both were wild with need. With his mouth still fastened on hers, Nick took them both to the climax.

Drained, aching, Ruth lay tight against him, her head nestled on his chest. He stroked her hair now and then, winding the ends around his fingers. Under her ear Ruth could hear the deep, steady rhythm of his heart. There was no light through the windows. The room was dark and warm and silent.

This, she thought languidly, this is what I've been waiting for. This is the end of my privacy. He knows all my secrets now. Tonight I've given him everything I've ever held inside me. She sighed. "You won't go," she murmured, closing her eyes. "You won't go tonight?"

There was quiet for a moment, their own personal silence. "No," he said softly. "I won't go."

Content, Ruth curled against him and slept.

Chapter 9

Nijinsky leaped onto the bed, wanting his breakfast. He stared, slant-eyed, at Nick for a moment, then calmly padded over his legs and stomach to stand on his chest. Feeling the pressure, Nick stirred and opened his eyes to look straight into the cat's. They regarded each other in silence. Nick brought his hand up and obligingly scratched Nijinsky's ears.

"Well, *priyatel*, you seem to have no objection in finding me here?"

Nijinsky arched his back and stretched, then settled his full length on Nick's chest. Still absently scratching the cat's ears, Nick turned his head to look at Ruth.

She was curled tightly to his side. Indeed, his arm held her firmly there. Her hair looked thick and luxurious spread over the pillowcase. Her breathing was even and deep, her lips slightly parted. She looked impossibly young—too young to feel that wild desire she had shown him. She looked like the sleeping princess, but Nick knew she was more Carlotta than Aurora. She was more fire than flower. He bent down to kiss her.

Ruth awoke to passion, her body tingling into arousal. She sighed and reached for him as his hands began a sure, steady quest. Nijinsky, caught between them, made his disapproval vocal.

Ruth gave a throaty laugh as Nick swore. "He wants his breakfast," she explained. Her eyes were still sleepy as she smiled up at Nick. Experimentally, she lifted her hand to rub his chin with her palm. "I've always wanted to do that," she told him. "Feel a man's beard the first thing in the morning."

Nick slid his hand down to fondle her breast. "I prefer softer things. Your mouth," he specified, lowering his head to nibble at it. "Very soft, very warm."

Nijinsky padded forward to butt his head between theirs. Nick narrowed his eyes at the cat. "My affection for this creature," he stated mildly, "is rapidly fading."

"He likes to keep on schedule," Ruth explained. "He always wakes me right before the alarm goes off." On cue, the clock set off a low, monotonous buzz. "See?" She laughed as Nick reached over her and slammed the button in. "What first?" she asked him. "Shower or coffee?"

He leaned over her still, and his smile was slow. "I had something else in mind."

"Class," she reminded him and slipped quickly from the bed.

Nick watched her walk naked to the closet and pull out a robe. She was slim as a wand, with long legs and no hips—a boyish figure, had it not been for the pure femininity of her gait. As she reached inside the closet, he saw the small thrust of her breast under her outstretched arm. The robe passed over her, and she crossed it in front and belted it. She turned and smiled.

"Well?" she said, flipping her long hair out of the collar of the robe. "Do you want coffee?"

"You are exquisite," he murmured.

Ruth's hands faltered at the knot of the belt. She wondered if she would ever grow used to that tone of voice or that look in his eyes. She knew what would happen if she walked back to the bed. Her body began to tingle, as if his hands were already roaming it. Nijinsky growled.

"Since I'm the first up," she said, casting the cat a rueful glance, "I'll have the shower first." She arched her brows at Nick. "You can make the coffee." As she darted into the bath, she called over her shoulder, "Don't forget to feed the cat."

Ruth turned on the shower and stripped. *Should it feel so right?* she asked as she bundled her hair on top of her head. *When I woke next to him, should I have felt that he simply belonged there?* She had experienced no shyness, none of the awkwardness that she had been certain would have come with the morning after her first time. Ruth stepped under the shower and let the water hit her hot and strong.

But I knew it would be him. Somehow I always knew. Shaking her head, she reached for the soap. *I must be crazy. How could I know it would be like this?* She soaped herself and let her mind drift. They had had meals together between classes and rehearsals. They had been at the same parties. But there had never been any planned, conventional dates between them.

Should there have been? she wondered. Certainly last

night had been no ordinary consummation of a typical relationship. Nick had seen her sweat and swear and rage, seen her weep. His hands had worked pain from her calves and feet. But she knew him only as well as he allowed himself to be known.

Ruth shut off the water. It was too soon, she decided, to explore her heart too deeply. She understood pain, had lived with it, but wouldn't deliberately seek it out. Nick could bring her pain. That, too, she had always known.

After toweling briskly, she slipped back into her robe and walked into the bedroom. She could hear Nick talking to Nijinsky in the kitchen. She smiled and began to pull leotards and tights from her drawer. There was something essentially right about Nick's voice carrying to her through the small apartment. She knew the cat would be much too busy attacking his breakfast to enjoy the conversation, but it pleased her. Another small bond. How many mornings had she held conversations with the disinterested cat?

Nick came into the bedroom with two steaming mugs in his hands. He was naked. His body was glorious; lean and muscled from the rigors of his profession. He strode into the room without the slightest hint of self-consciousness. Another man, Ruth mused, would have pulled on his jeans. Not Davidov.

"It's hot," he stated, setting both mugs down on the dresser before pulling Ruth into his arms. "You smell so good," he murmured against her neck. "The scent of you follows me everywhere."

His chin was raspy against her skin. She laughed, enjoying it.

"I must shave, yes?"

"Yes," Ruth agreed before she turned her mouth into the kiss. "It would hardly do for Davidov to come to class unshaven." They kissed again. His hands went to her hips to bring her closer.

"You have a razor?" He took his mouth to her ear.

"*Hmm.* Yes, in the medicine cabinet." Ruth let her fingers trail up his spine. She gave a muffled shriek when he bit her earlobe.

"The shaving will wait," he decided, drawing her away to pick up his coffee. He sipped and then rose.

"Will you have to go to your apartment for clothes?" Ruth watched the easy rhythm of his muscles before he disappeared into the bath.

"I have things at my office." She heard the shower spurt back to life. "And a fresh razor."

He sang in Russian in the shower. Music was an intrinsic part of him. She found herself humming along as she went into the bath to brush her teeth. "What does it mean?" she asked with a mouthful of toothpaste.

"It's old," he told her. "And tragic. The best Russian songs are old and tragic."

"I was in Moscow once with my parents." Ruth rinsed her mouth. "It was beautiful…the buildings, the snow. You must miss it sometimes."

Ruth didn't have time to scream when he grabbed her and pulled her into the shower with him.

"*Nick!*" Blinded by streaming water, she pushed at her eyes. Her clothes were plastered against her. "Are you crazy?"

"I needed you to wash my back," he explained, drawing her closer. "But now I think there is a better idea."

"Wash your back!" Ruth struggled against him. "You might notice, I'm fully dressed."

"Oh, yes?" He smiled affably. "That's all right, I'll fix that." He pulled the soaked leotard over her shoulders so that her arms were effectively pinned.

"I've already had my shower." Ruth laughed, exasperated, and continued to struggle.

"Now you can have mine. I'm a generous man."

He fastened his mouth on hers as the water poured over them.

"Nick." His hands were wandering, loosening clothes as they went. "We have class." But she had stopped struggling.

"There's time," he murmured, sighing deeply as he found her breast. "We make time."

He drew the tights down over her hips.

Arabesque, pirouette, arabesque, pirouette. Ruth turned and lifted and bent to the commands. The practice was rigorous, as always. Her body, like the bodies of the other students, was drenched with sweat. Every day, seven days a week, they went over and over the basic steps. Professionals. Class was as much a part of a professional dancer's life as shoes and tights.

The small, intimate details were drummed into their minds at the earliest age. Who noticed the two little steps before a jeté? Only a dancer.

Muscles must be constantly tuned. The body must be constantly made to accept the unnatural lines of the dance. Fifth position. Plié. Even a day's respite would cause the body to revolt. Port de bras. The arms and hands must know what to do. A wrong gesture could destroy the line, shatter a mood. Attitude. *Hold it—one, two, three, four...*

"Thank you."

Company class was over. Ruth went for her towel to mop her face. A shower, she thought, wiping the sweat from her neck.

"Ruth."

She glanced up at Nick. He, too, was wet. His hair curled damply around his sweatband.

"Meet me downstairs. Five minutes."

"Five minutes?" Alerted, she slung the towel over her shoulders. "Is something wrong?"

"Wrong?" He smiled, then bent and kissed her, oblivious to the other members of the company. "What should be wrong?"

"Well, nothing." A bit confused, she frowned up at him. "Why, then?"

"You have nothing scheduled for today." It was a statement, not a question, but she still shook her head. "I've seen that I don't, either." He leaned close. "We're going to play."

A smile began to tug at her mouth. "Play?"

"New York is a very entertaining city, yes?"

"So I've heard."

"Five minutes," he repeated and turned away.

Ruth narrowed her eyes at his back. "Fifteen."

"Ten," Nick countered without stopping.

Ruth dived for her bag and dashed for the showers.

In somewhere under ten minutes Ruth came downstairs, freshly washed, clad in jeans and a loose mauve sweater. Her hair was as free as her mood. Nick was already waiting, impatient, parrying questions from two male soloists.

"I'll speak to him tomorrow," he said, moving away

from them when he spotted Ruth. "You're late," he accused, propelling her toward the door.

"Nope. On the minute."

They pushed through the door together.

The noise level was staggering. Somewhere to the left a road crew was tearing up the sidewalk, and the jackhammer shot its machine-gunning sound through the air. Two cabs screeched to a halt in front of them, nose to nose. Their drivers rolled down the windows and swore enthusiastically. Pedestrians streamed by without notice or interest. From a window across the street poured the hot, harsh sounds of punk rock.

"An entertaining city, yes?" Nick slipped his hand through Ruth's arm to clasp hers. Looking down, he gave her a quick grin. "Today, it's ours."

Ruth was suddenly breathless. None of their years together, none of the wild, searing lovemaking, had had the impact of that one intimate, breezy look.

"Where—where are we going?" she managed, struggling to come to terms with what was happening to her.

"Anywhere," Nick told her and pulled her to him for a hard kiss. "Choose." He held her tight a moment, and Ruth found she was laughing.

"That way!" she decided, throwing her hand out to the right.

Summer had vanished overnight. The cooler air made the walking easy, and they walked, Ruth was sure, for miles. They investigated art galleries and bookstores, poking here, prodding there and buying nothing. They sat on the edge of a fountain and watched the crowds passing while they drank hot tea laced with honey.

In Central Park they watched sweating joggers and tossed crumbs to pigeons. There was a world to observe.

In Saks, Ruth modeled a glorious succession of furs while Nick sat, fingers steepled together, and watched.

"No," he said, shaking his head as Ruth posed in a hip-length blue fox, "it's no good."

"No good?" She rubbed her chin against the luxurious collar with an unconscious expression of sensual pleasure. "I like it."

"Not the fur," Nick corrected. "You." He laughed as Ruth haughtily raised her brows. "What model walks with her feet turned out like that?"

Ruth looked down at her feet, then grinned. "I suppose I'm more at home in leotards than furs." She did a quick pirouette that had the sales clerk eyeing her warily. "And it would be hot in class." She slipped it off, letting the satin lining linger over her skin.

"Shall I buy it for you?"

She started to laugh, then saw that he was perfectly serious. "Don't be silly."

"Silly?" Nick rose as Ruth handed the clerk the fur. "Why is this silly? Don't you like presents, little one?"

She knew he used the term to goad her, but she only gave him a dry look. "I live for them," she said throatily, for the clerk's benefit. "But how can I accept it when we've only just met?" With a smoldering glance, she caressed his cheek. "What would you tell your wife?"

"There are some things wives need not know." His voice was suddenly thickly Russian. "In my country, women know their place."

"*Mmm.*" Ruth slipped her arm through his. "Then perhaps you'll show me mine."

"A pleasure." Nick gave the wide-eyed clerk a wolfish grin. "Good day, madam." He swept Ruth away in perfect Cossack style.

"Such wickedness," he murmured as they walked from the store.

"I just love it when you're Russian, Nikolai."

He cocked an eyebrow. "I'm always Russian."

"Sometimes more than others. You can be more American than a Nebraska farmer when you want to be."

"Is this so?" He looked intensely interested for a moment. "I hadn't thought about it."

"That's why you're so fascinating," Ruth told him. "You don't think about it, you just are." Her hand linked with his as they walked. "I've wondered, do you think in Russian and then have to translate yourself?"

"I think in Russian when I am…" He searched for the word. "Emotional."

"That covers a lot of ground." She grinned up at him. "You're often emotional."

"I'm an artist," he returned with a shrug. "We are entitled. When I'm angry, Russian is easier, and Russian curses have more muscle than American."

"I've often wondered what you were saying when you're in a rage." She gave him a hopeful glance, and he laughed, shaking his head. "You spoke to me in Russian last night."

"Did I?" The look he gave her had Ruth's heart in her throat. "Perhaps you could say I was emotional."

"It didn't sound like cursing," she murmured.

His hand was suddenly at the back of her neck, drawing her near. "Shall I translate for you?"

"Not now." Ruth calculated the distance between

Fifth Avenue and her apartment. Too far, she thought. "Let's take a bus." She laughed, her eyes on his.

Nick grinned. "A cab," he countered and hailed one.

Sunlight flooded the bedroom. They hadn't taken the time to draw the blinds. They lay tangled together, naked and quiet after a storm of lovemaking. Content, Ruth drifted between sleep and wakefulness. Beneath her hand, Nick's chest rose and fell steadily; she knew he slept.

Forever, she thought dreamily. I could stay like this forever. She cuddled closer, unconsciously stroking his calf with the bottom of her foot.

"Dancer's feet," he murmured, and she realized that the small movement had awakened him. "Strong and ugly."

"Thanks a lot." She nipped his shoulder.

"A compliment," he countered, then shifted to look down at her. His eyes were sleepy, half-closed. "Great dancers have ugly feet."

She smiled at his logic. "Is that what attracted you to me?"

"No, it was the back of your knees."

Ruth laughed and turned her face into his neck. "Was it really? What about them?"

"When I dance with you, your arms are soft, and I wonder how the back of your knees would feel." Nick leaned up on his elbow to look at her. "How often have I held your legs—for a lift, to ease a cramp? But always there are tights. And what, I say to myself, would it be like to touch?"

Sitting up, he took her calf in his hand. "Here." His fingers slid up to the back of her knees. "And here."

He saw her eyes darken, felt the pulse quicken where his fingers pressed. "So, I am nearly mad from wondering if the softness is everywhere. Soft voice, soft eyes, soft hair."

His voice was low now and quiet. "And I hold your waist to balance you, but there are leotards and costumes. What is the skin like there?" He trailed his hand up over her thigh and stomach to linger at her waist. His fingers followed the contours of her ribcage to reach her breast.

"Small breasts," he murmured, watching her face. "I've felt them pressed against me, seen them lift and fall with your breathing. How would they feel in my hand? What taste would I find there?" He lowered his mouth to let his tongue move lightly over her.

Ruth's limbs felt weighted, as though she had taken some heady drug. She lay still while his hands and mouth explored her, while his voice poured over her. He moved with aching slowness, touching, arousing, murmuring.

"Even onstage, with the lights and the music everywhere, I thought of touching you. Here." His fingers glided over her inner thigh. "And tasting. Here." His mouth moved to follow them. "You would look at me. Such big eyes, like an owl. I could almost see your thoughts and wondered if you could see mine." He pressed his lips against the firm muscles of her stomach and felt her quiver of response. "And what would you do, *milaya*, if you knew how I was aching for you?"

His tongue glided over her navel. She moaned and moved under him. She had never experienced pleasure such as this—a thick, heavy pleasure that made her body hum, that weighed on her mind until even thoughts were sensations.

"So long," he murmured. "Too long, the wanting went on. The wondering."

His hands, though still gentle, became more insistent. They broke through the dark languor that held her. Her body was suddenly fiercely alive. She was acutely aware of her surroundings: the texture of the sheet against her back, the tiny dust motes that spun in the brilliant sunshine, the dull throb of traffic outside the windows. There was an impossible clarity to everything around them. Then it spun into nothing but the hands and mouth that roamed her skin.

She could have been anywhere—in the show, in the desert; Ruth felt only Nick. She heard his breathing, more labored now than it would have been after a strenuous dance. Her own melded with it. With hard, unbridled urgency, he crushed his mouth to hers. His teeth scraped her lips as they parted for him.

The kiss deepened as his hands continued to drive her nearer the edge. Ruth clutched at him, lost in delight. Then he was inside her, and she was catapulted beyond reason into ecstasy.

"Lyubovnitsa." Ruth heard his voice come hoarsely from deep within him. "Look at me."

Her eyes opened heavily as she shuddered again and again with the simultaneous forces of need and delight.

"I have you," he said, barely able to speak. "And still I want you."

She crested on a mountainous peak. Nick buried his face in her hair.

Chapter 10

Francie caught Ruth's arm as they filed in for morning class. "Where'd you disappear to yesterday?" she demanded, pulling Ruth to the barre.

"Yesterday?" Ruth couldn't prevent the smile. "Oh, I went window shopping."

Francie shot her a knowing look. "Sure. Introduce him to me sometime." Her face grew thoughtful at Ruth's quick laugh, but she hurried on. "Have you heard the news?"

Ruth executed her pliés as the room began to fill with other company members. Her eyes drifted to Nick, who was in a far corner with several corps dancers. "What news?" Look how the sun hits his hair, she thought, as if it were drawn to it.

"The television thing." Francie set herself to Ruth's rhythm so that their heads remained level. "Didn't you hear anything?"

"Leah mentioned something." Ruth sought out the blonde as she remembered the preperformance visit. "I was told nothing was definite yet."

"It is now, kiddo." Francie was gratified to see Ruth's attention come full swing back to her.

"It is?"

"Nadine worked a whale of a deal." Francie bent to adjust her leg warmers. "Of course, she had the main man to dangle in front of their noses."

Ruth was fully aware that Francie spoke of Nick. Again her eyes traveled to him. He had his head together with Leah now. The ballerina was using her fluid hands to emphasize her words.

"What sort of deal?"

"Two hours," Francie said with relish. "Prime time. And Nick has virtually a free hand artistically. He has the name, after all, and not only in the ballet world. People who don't know a plié from a pirouette know Davidov. It's some kind of package deal where he agrees to do two more projects. It's him they want. Just think what this could mean to the company!"

Francie rose on her toes. "How many people can we reach in two hours on TV compared to those we reach in a whole season onstage? Oh, God, I hope I get to dance!" She lowered into a plié. "I'd almost be willing to go back into the corps for the chance. You'll do *The Red Rose*." She gave an envious sigh.

Ruth was glad it was time for class to begin.

It was difficult to concentrate. Ruth's body responded to the calls and counts while her mind dashed in a dozen directions. Why hadn't he told her?

Her hand rested on the barre as Madame Maximova

put them through their paces. Ruth was aware that Nick stood directly behind her.

They had been together all day yesterday—and this morning. He had never said a word. Would she dance? Her working leg came up and back in attitude. *Will what's happened between us interfere?*

As she moved out with the class for center practice, Ruth tried to think logically. It had been hardly a week since he had told her things were still unsettled. She struggled to remember what else he had said, what exactly his mood had been. He had been annoyed because her dancing had been below par—concern that she had been upset. He had been furious when she wouldn't divulge the name of the person who had leaked the information.

What had he done? Snapped his fingers and told her *that* was how much he cared for what she said. He played the tune, and she danced. It was as simple as that. Ruth frowned as she did the combination. But why did everyone seem to know about things before her? she wondered. One minute Nick would tell her she was the finest ballerina in the company, and the next, he didn't even bother to fill her in on what could be the most important company project of the year.

How do you figure out such a man? You don't, she reminded herself. Turning her head, she looked him straight in the eye. *He's Davidov.*

Nick met the look a bit quizzically, but the tempo suddenly increased from adagio to allegro and required their attention.

"Thank you," Madame Maximova said to the troupe of dripping bodies thirty minutes later. Her voice, Ruth thought fleetingly, was much more thickly Russian than Nick's, though she had been forty years in America.

"I'd like to see the entire company onstage in fifteen minutes."

Ruth lifted her eyes and caught Nick's in the glass as he made the announcement. The speculative buzzing began immediately. Dancers began to file out in excited groups. Davidov had spoken. Ruth hefted her bag over her shoulder and prepared to join them.

"One moment, Ruth." She stopped obediently at his words. Her training was too ingrained for anything else. He said something to the ballet mistress in quiet Russian that made her chuckle—a formidable achievement. With a brisk nod, she strode from the room as if her bones were a quarter of a century younger than Ruth knew them to be.

Nick crossed to Ruth, absently pulling his towel through his hands. "Your mind was not on class."

"No?"

He recognized her searching look. As usual, it disconcerted him. "Your body moved, but your eyes were very far away. Where?"

Ruth studied him for another moment as she turned over in her mind the best way to broach the subject. She settled on directness. "Why didn't you tell me about the television plans?"

Nick's brow lifted. It was a haughty gesture. "Why should I have?"

"I'm a principal dancer with the company."

"Yes." He waited a beat. "That doesn't answer my question."

"Everyone else seems to know the details." Exasperated, she flared at him. "I'm sure they're avidly discussing it in the corps."

"Very likely," he agreed, slinging the towel over his shoulders. "It's hardly a secret, and secrets are always avidly discussed in the corps."

"You might have told me yourself," she fumed, pricked by his hauteur. "I asked you about it last week."

"Last week it was not finalized."

"It was certainly finalized yesterday, and you never said a word."

She saw his lids lower—a danger signal. When he spoke, his cool tone was another. "Yesterday we were just a man and a woman." He lifted his hands to the ends of the towel, holding them lightly. "Do you think because we are lovers I should give you special treatment as a ballerina?"

"Of course not!" Ruth's eyes widened in genuine surprise at the question. The thought had simply never occurred to her. "How could you think so?"

"Ah." He gave a small nod. "I see. I'm to trust and respect your integrity, while mine is suspect."

"I never meant—" she began, but he cut her off with that imperious flick of the wrist.

"Get your shower. You've only ten minutes now." He strode away, leaving her staring and open-mouthed.

When Ruth dashed into the theater, members of the company were already sitting on the wide stage or pocketed together in corners. Breathless, she settled down next to Francie.

"So." Nick spared her a brief glance. "We seem to be all here now."

He was standing stage center with his hands tucked into the pockets of dull gray sweatpants. His hair was still damp from his shower. Every eye was on him. Nadine sat in a wooden chair slightly to his right in a superbly tailored ice blue suit.

"Most of you seem to know at least the bare details of our plans to do a production for WNT-TV." His eyes swept the group, passing briefly over Ruth, then on. "But Nadine and I will now go over the finer points." He glanced at Nadine, who folded her hands and began.

"The company will do a two-hour presentation of ballet, in vignette style. It will be taped here over a two-week period beginning in one month. Naturally, we plan to include many dances from the ballets in our repertoire. Nick and I, along with Mark and Marianne." She glanced briefly at two choreographers, "have outlined a tentative program. We will, of course, work with the television director and staff on time allowances and so forth." She paused a moment for emphasis. "I needn't tell you how important this is to the company and that I expect the best from every one of you."

Nadine fell silent. Nick turned to pick up a clipboard he had left on a tree stump prop from a forest scene in *Sleeping Beauty.*

"Rehearsals begin immediately," he stated and began to read off the list of dances and roles and rehearsal halls.

It was a diversified program, Ruth concluded, trying not to hold her breath. From Tchaikovsky's *Nutcracker*— Francie gave a muffled squeal when her name was called to dance the Sugar Plum Fairy—to de Mille's *Rodeo.* Obviously, Nick wanted to show the variety and universality of ballet.

Choreographers were assigned, scenes listed. Ruth moistened her lips. Leah was Aurora and Giselle, two plum roles but fully expected. Keil Lowell was to partner Leah both as Prince Charming and as Albrecht. A young corps member began to weep softly as she was given her first solo.

Nick continued to read without glancing up. "Ruth, the grand pas de deux from *The Red Rose* and the second act pas de deux from *Le Corsaire*. I will partner."

Ruth let out her breath slowly and felt the tension ease from her shoulders.

"If time permits, we will also do a scene from *Carnival*."

He continued to read in his quiet, melodious voice, but Ruth heard little more. She could have wept like the young corps dancer. This was what she had worked for. This was the fruit of almost two decades of training. Yet even through the joy, she could feel Nick's temper lick out at her.

He doesn't understand, she thought, frustrated by his quick, volatile moods. *And he's so pigheaded, I'll have to fight my way through to explain*. Drawing her knees up to her chest, she studied him carefully.

Strange, she mused, *for all his generosity of spirit, he doesn't give his trust easily*. She frowned. *Neither do I*, she realized abruptly. *We have a problem*. She rested her chin on her knees. *And I'm not sure yet how to solve it*.

The next few weeks weren't going to be easy, personally or professionally. Personally, Ruth knew she and Nick would have to decide what they wanted from each other and what each could give. She tucked the problem away, a little awed by it.

Professionally, it would be a grueling time. Nick as a choreographer or director was difficult enough, but as a partner, he was the devil himself. He accepted no less

than perfection and had never been gentle about showing his displeasure with anything short of it. Still, Ruth
would have walked over hot coals to dance with him.

Rehearsals would be exhausting for everyone. The
time was short, the expectations high, and a good portion of the company were performing *Sleeping Beauty*
every night for the next two weeks. Tempers and muscles would be strained. They would be limping home at
night to soak their feet in ice or hot baths. They would
pull each other's toes and rub each other's calves and
live on coffee and nerves. But they would triumph; they
were dancers.

Ruth rose with the others when Nick finished. Seeing he was already involved with Nadine, she went to
the small rehearsal hall he had assigned to her. She left
the door open. Company members streamed down the
corridor. There was talk and raised voices. Already the
sound of music flowed out from another room down
the hall. Stravinsky.

Ruth walked to a bench to change to her toe shoes.
She looked at them absently. They would last two or
three more days, she decided. They were barely a week
old. Idly, she wondered how many pairs she had been
through already that year. And how many yards of
satin? She crossed the ribbon over her ankle and looked
up as Nick walked into the room. He closed the door
behind him, and they were cut off from music and
voices.

"We do *Le Corsaire* first," he stated, crossing the
room to sit on the bench. "We work without an accom-
panist for now. They are at a premium, and I have still
to block it out." He pulled down his sweatpants so that
he wore only tights and the unitard.

"Nick, I'd like to talk to you."

"You have a complaint?" He slipped leg warmers over his ankles.

"No. Nick—"

"Then you are satisfied with your assignment? We begin." He rose, and Ruth stood to face him.

"Don't pull your premier danseur pose on me," she said dangerously.

He lifted his brow, studying her with cool blue eyes. "I am premier danseur."

"You're also a human being, but that isn't the point." She could feel the temper she had ordered herself to restrain running away with her.

"And what," he said in a tone entirely too mild, "is the point?"

"What I said this morning had nothing to do with the casting." She put her hands on her hips, prepared to plow her way through the wall he had thrown up between them.

"No? Then perhaps you will tell me what it had to do with. I have a great deal to do."

Her eyes kindled. Her temper snapped. "Go do it then. I'll rehearse alone." She turned away, only to be spun back around.

"I say when and with whom you rehearse." His eyes were as hot as hers. "Now say what you will say so we can work."

"All right, then." Ruth jerked her arm from his hold. "I didn't like being kept in the dark about this. I think I should have heard it from you, straight out. Our being lovers has nothing to do with it. We're dance partners, professional partners. If you can tell half the company, why not me?" She barely paused for breath. "I didn't like the way I had to get tidbits, first from Leah, and then—"

"So, it was Leah," Nick interrupted her tirade with quiet words. Ruth let out a frustrated breath. Temper had betrayed her into telling him what she had promised herself she never would.

"It doesn't matter," she began, but the flick of his wrist stopped her again.

"Don't be stupid," he said impatiently. "There is no excuse for a dancer deliberately disturbing another before a performance. You won't tell me it was not intentional?" He waited, watching her face. Ruth opened her mouth and closed it again. She didn't lie well, even in the best of circumstances. "So don't pretend it doesn't matter," Nick concluded.

"All right," she conceded. "But it's done. There's no use stirring up trouble now."

Nick was thoughtful a moment. Ruth saw that his eyes were hard and distant. She knew very well he was capable of handing out punishment without compassion. "No," he said at length, "I have a need for her at the moment. We have no one who does Aurora so well, but..." His words trailed off, and Ruth knew his mind was fast at work. He would find a way of disciplining Leah and keeping his Aurora dancing. A whip in a velvet glove, Ruth thought ruefully. That was Davidov.

"In any case," she continued, bringing his attention back to her, "Leah isn't the point, either."

Nick focused on her again. "No." He nodded, agreeing to this. "You were telling me what was."

Calmer now, Ruth took a moment to curb her tongue. "I was upset when I heard this morning that things had been arranged. I suppose I felt shut out. We hadn't talked reasonably about dancing since the night we rehearsed together for *The Red Rose*. I was angry then."

"I wanted you," he said simply. "It was difficult."

"For both of us." Ruth took a deep breath. "I had never considered you would treat me differently professionally because we've become lovers. I couldn't stand to think you would. But I was nervous about the casting. I always am."

"That was perhaps an unwise thing for me to say."

Ruth smiled. Such an admission from Davidov was closer to an apology than she had hoped for.

"Perhaps," she agreed with her tongue in her cheek.

His brow lifted. "You still have trouble with respect for your elders."

"How's this?" she asked and stuck out her tongue.

"Tempting." Nick pulled her into his arms and kissed her, long and hard. "Now, I will tell you once so that it is understood." He drew her away again but kept his hands on her shoulders. "I chose you for my partner because I chose to dance with the best. If you were less of a dancer, I would dance with someone else. But it would still be you I wanted at night."

A weight was lifted from her shoulders. She was satisfied that Davidov wanted her for herself and danced with her because he respected her talent.

"Only at night?" she murmured, stepping closer.

Nick gave her shoulders a caress. "We will have little else but the night for ourselves for some time." He kissed her again, briefly, roughly, proprietarily. "Now we dance."

They went to the center of the room, faced the mirrors and began.

Chapter 11

Days passed; long, exhausting days filled with excitement and disappointments. Ruth worked with Nick as he blocked out and tightened their pas de deux from *Le Corsaire*. The choreography must suit the camera, he told her. If the dance was to be recorded by a lens, it had to be played to the lens. This was a different prospect altogether from dancing to an audience. Even during their first improvised rehearsal Ruth realized Nick had done his homework. He worked hand in glove with the television director on angles and sequence.

Ruth's days were filled between classes and rehearsals, but her nights were often empty. Nick's duties as choreographer and artistic director kept him constantly busy. There were other rehearsals to oversee, more dances to be blocked out, budget meetings and late-night sessions with the television staff.

There was little time for the two of them at rehearsals. There they worked as dancer to dancer or dancer to choreographer, fitting movement to music. They argued, they agreed. *The Red Rose* posed little problem, though Nick altered a few details to better suit the new medium. *Le Corsaire* took most of their time. The part suited him perfectly. It was the ideal outlet for his creativity. His verve aroused Ruth's competitiveness. She worked hard.

He criticized tiny details like the spread of her fingers, praised the angle of her head and drove her harder. His vitality seemed to constantly renew itself, and it forced her to keep up or be left behind. At times she wondered how he did it: the endless dancing, the back-to-back meetings.

He had told her they would have the nights for each other, but so far that had not been the case. For the first time since she had moved into her apartment, Ruth was lonely. For as long as she could remember, she had been content with her own company. She walked to the window and opened the blinds to gaze out at the darkness. She shivered.

A knock at the door startled her, then she shook her head. *No, it's not Nick*, Ruth reminded herself as she crossed the room. She knew he had two meetings that night. She glanced through the peephole, then stood for several seconds with her hand on the knob. Taking a breath, she opened the door.

"Hello, Donald."

"Ruth." He smiled at her. "May I come in?"

"Of course." She stepped back to let him enter, then shut the door behind him.

He was dressed casually and impeccably in a leather

jacket and twill trousers. Ruth realized suddenly that it had been weeks since they had last seen each other.

"How are you?" she asked, finding nothing else to say.

"Fine. I'm fine."

She detected a layer of awkwardness under his poise. It put her at ease. "Come, sit down. Would you like a drink?"

"Yes, I would. Scotch, if you have it." Donald moved to a chair and sat, watching Ruth pour the liquor. "Aren't you having one?"

"No." She handed him the glass before taking a seat on the sofa. "I've just had some tea." Absently, she passed her hand over Nijinsky's head.

"I heard your company's doing something for television." Donald swirled the Scotch in his glass, then drank.

"News travels fast."

"You're having some new costumes made," he commented. "Word gets around."

"I hadn't thought of that." She curled her legs under her. "Is your business going well?"

Lifting his eyes from the glass, Donald met hers. "Yes. I'm going to Paris at the end of the month."

"Really?" She gave him a friendly smile. "Will you be there long?"

"A couple of weeks. Ruth…" He hesitated, then set down his glass. "I'd like to apologize for the things I said the last time I saw you."

Her eyes met his, calm, searching. Satisfied, Ruth nodded. "All right."

Donald let out a breath. He hadn't expected such

easy absolution. "I've missed seeing you. I'd hoped we could have dinner."

"No, Donald," she answered just as mildly. She watched him frown.

"Ruth, I was upset and angry. I know I said some hard things, but—"

"It isn't that, Donald."

He studied her, then let out a long breath. "I see. I should've expected there'd be someone else."

"You and I were never more than friends, Donald." There was no apology in her voice, nor anger. "I don't see why that has to change."

"Davidov?" He gave a quick laugh at her surprised expression.

"Yes, Davidov. How did you know?"

"I've eyes in my head," he said shortly. "I've seen the way he looked at you." Donald took another swallow of Scotch. "I suppose you're well suited."

Ruth had to smile. "Is that a compliment or an insult?"

Donald shook his head and rose. "I'm not sure." For a moment he looked at her intensely. She met his gaze without faltering. "Goodbye, Ruth."

Ruth remained where she was. "Goodbye, Donald." She watched him cross the room and shut the door behind him.

After a few moments she took his half-filled glass into the kitchen. Pouring the Scotch down the sink, Ruth thought of the time they had spent together. Donald had made her happy, nothing more, nothing less. Was it true that some women were made for one man? Was she one of them?

Another knock scattered her thoughts. She caught

her bottom lip between her teeth. The last thing she wanted was another showdown with Donald. Resolutely, Ruth went to the door and fixed a smile on her face.

"Nick!"

He carried two boxes, one flat, one larger, and a bottle of wine. *"Privet, milenkaya."* He stepped over the threshold and managed to kiss her over the boxes.

"But you're supposed to be in meetings tonight." Ruth closed the door as he dropped the boxes on her dinette table.

"I cancelled them." He gave her a grin and pulled her against him. "I told you artists are entitled to be temperamental." He made up for his brief first kiss with a lingering one. "You have plans for tonight?" he murmured against her ear.

"Well…" Ruth let the word hang. "I suppose I could alter them—with the right incentive." It felt so good to be held by him, to feel his lips on her skin. "What's in the boxes?"

"Mmm. This and that." Nick drew her away. "That is for later," he said, pointing to the large box. "This is for now." With a flourish, he tossed open the lid of the flat one.

"Pizza!"

Nick leaned over, breathing in its aroma with closed eyes. "It is to die over! Go, get plates before it's cold."

Ruth turned to obey.

"I'll sweat it off you in rehearsal tomorrow." He picked up the wine. "I need a corkscrew."

"What's in the other box?" Ruth called out as she clattered dishes.

"Later. I'm hungry." When she came back, hands filled with plates and glasses, he was still holding the wine while stooping over to greet Nijinsky. "You'll have your share." Watching him, Ruth felt her heart expand.

"I'm so glad you're here."

Nick straightened and smiled. "Why?" He took the corkscrew from her fingers.

"I love pizza," Ruth told him blandly.

"So, I win your heart through your stomach, yes? It's an old Russian custom." The cork came out with a muffled pop.

"Absolutely." Ruth began busily to transfer pizza from box to plates.

"Then you'll bounce onstage like a little round meatball." Nick sat across from her and poured the wine. "It seems time permits for *Carnival*, as well. You do Columbine."

"Oh, Nick!" Ruth, her mouth full of pizza, struggled to swallow and say more.

"The extra rehearsals will help to keep you from getting chubby."

"Chubby!"

"I don't want to strain my back in the lifts." He gave her a wicked smile.

"And what about you?" she asked sweetly. "Who wants to watch Harlequin with a paunch?"

"My metabolism," he told her smugly, "would never permit it." He wolfed down the pizza and reached for his wine. "I've been watching movies," he told her suddenly. "Fred Astaire, Gene Kelly. Such movement. With the right camera work we see all a dancer is. Angles are the key."

"Did you see *An American in Paris*?" Ruth finished off her slice and reached for the wine. "I'd love to do a time step."

"A new set of muscles," Nick mused, looking through her. "It would be interesting."

"What are you thinking?"

His eyes came back to hers and focused. "A new ballet with some of your typically American moves. It's for later." He shook his head as if filing the idea away. "So, have some more." He slid another piece onto Ruth's plate. "When one sins, one should sin magnificently."

"Another old Russian custom?" Ruth asked with a grin.

"But of course." He poured more wine into her glass.

They finished the pizza, giving the cat a whole piece for himself. Nick filled her in on the progress of rehearsals, dropping little bits of company gossip here and there to amuse her. When he began to question her about dance sequences in movies he hadn't seen, Ruth did her best to describe them.

"Are you thinking of writing this new ballet with television in mind?" she asked as they cleared the dishes. "For one of the other two projects you've agreed to do?"

"Perhaps." He was vague. "Nadine would like also a documentary on the company. It's being considered. I learned some when they taped *Ariel* and other ballets, but the cameras were always apart. Ah..." He groped for the word closer to his meaning. "Remote?" Satisfied, he continued. "This time they'll be everywhere, and this director has more knowledge of the dance than others I've worked with. It makes a difference," he concluded and smiled as Ruth handed him a dish to dry. "I've missed you."

Ruth looked up at him. They had been together for hours every day, but she knew what he meant. There was something steadying about standing together in the kitchen. "I've missed you, too."

"We can make a little time when this is over, before new rehearsals begin. A few days." Nick set down the dish and touched her hair. "Will you come with me to California?"

His house in Malibu, she thought and smiled. "Yes." Forgetting the dishes, she slipped her arms around his waist and held him. They were silent a moment, then Nick bent and kissed the top of her head.

"Don't you want to know what's in the other box?"

Ruth groaned. "I can't eat another thing."

"More wine?" he murmured, moving his lips down her temple.

"No." She sighed. "Just you."

"Come, then." Nick drew her away, then offered his hand. "It's been too long."

They walked from the kitchen, but Ruth's eyes fell on the unopened box. "What *is* in there?"

"I thought you weren't interested."

Unable to restrain her curiosity, Ruth lifted the lid. She stared and made no sound.

There, where she had expected some elaborate pastries or a huge cake, was the soft, thick pelt of the blue fox she had modeled in Saks. Touching it with her fingertips, she looked up at Nick.

"It's not fattening," he told her.

"Nick." Ruth made a helpless gesture and shook her head.

"It suited you best. The color is good with your hair." He caught a generous handful of Ruth's hair and let it fall through his fingers. "It's soft. Like you."

"Nick." Ruth took his hand in hers. "I can't."

He lifted a brow. "I'm not allowed to give you presents?"

"Yes, I suppose." She let out a little breath. "I hadn't thought of it." He was smiling at her, making it difficult to explain logically. "But not a present like this."

"I bought you a pizza," he pointed out and brought her hand to his lips. "You didn't object."

"That's not the same thing." She made a small, exasperated sound as his lips brushed her wrist. "And you ate half of it."

"It gave me pleasure," he said simply, "as it will give me pleasure to see you in the fur."

"It's too expensive."

"Ah, I can only buy you cheap presents." He pushed up her sleeve and kissed the inside of her elbow.

Her brows lowered. "Stop making me sound foolish."

"You don't need my help for that." Before she could retort, he pulled her close and silenced her. "Do you find the fur ugly?" he asked.

"No, of course not. It's gorgeous." With a sigh, Ruth rested her head on his shoulder. "But you don't have to buy me anything."

"Have to? No." He ran a hand down her back to the curve of her hip. "The things I have to do, I know. This is what I choose to do." He drew her away, smiling again. "Come, try it on for me."

Ruth studied him carefully. The gesture was generous, impulsive and typically Nick. How could she refuse? "Thank you," she said so seriously that he laughed and hugged her.

"You look at me like an owl again, very sober and wise. Now, please, let me see you wear it."

If Ruth had any doubts, the *please* brushed them aside. She was certain she could count on the fingers of one hand the times he had used the word to her personally. With no more hesitation, she dived into the box. Her fingers sank into fur.

"It is gorgeous, Nick. Really gorgeous."

"Not over your robe, *milaya*." He shook his head as Ruth started to put the coat on. "They don't wear fox with blue terry cloth."

Ruth shot him a look, then undid the knot in her belt. She slipped out of the robe and quickly into the fur. Nick felt his stomach tighten at the brief flashes of her nakedness. Her dark hair fell over the blue-toned white; her eyes shone with excitement.

"I have to see how it looks!" Ruth turned, thinking to dash to the bedroom mirror.

"I love you."

The words stopped her dead. She felt completely winded, as though she had taken a bad fall onstage. Her breath would simply not force its way through her lungs. She closed her eyes. Her fingers were gripping the fur so tightly they hurt. She couldn't relax them. Very slowly, she turned to face him. Her throat was closing, so that when the words came, they were thick. "What did you say?"

"I love you. In English. I've told you in Russian before. *Ya tebya lyublyu.*"

Ruth remembered the words murmured in her ear—words that had jumbled in her brain when he had made love to her, when he had held her close before sleep. Her knees were beginning to shake. "I didn't know what they meant."

"Now you do."

She stared at him, feeling the trembling spread. "I'm afraid," Ruth whispered. "I've waited to hear you say that for so long, and now I'm terrified. Nick." She swallowed as her eyes filled. "I don't think my legs will move."

"Do you want to walk to me or away?"

The question steadied her. Perhaps he was afraid, too. She moved forward. When she stood in front of him, she waited until she thought her voice would be level. "How do I say it in Russian?" she asked him. "I want to say it in Russian first."

"Ya tebya lyublyu."

"Ya tebya lyublyu, Nikolai." She fumbled over the pronunciation. Ruth saw the flash of emotion in his eyes before she was crushed against him. *"Ya tebya lyublyu."* She said again, "I love you."

His mouth was on her hair, her cheeks and eyelids, then bruisingly, possessively on hers. *"Ona-moya,"* he said once, almost savagely. *"She is mine."*

The fur slipped to the floor.

Chapter 12

Ruth knew she had never worked so hard in her life. Performing a full-length ballet was never easy, but dancing for four cameras was very exasperating. Short sequences of step combinations had to be repeated over and over, so that she found it nearly impossible to keep the mood. She was accustomed to the lights, but the technicians' cables and the cameras intruding on the stage were another matter. She felt surrounded by them.

Her muscles cramped from the starting and stopping. Her face had to be remade-up for the closeups and tight shots. The television audience wouldn't care to see beads of perspiration on an elegant ballerina. It was possible, with the distance of a stage performance, to maintain ballet's illusion of effortless fluidity. But the camera was merciless.

Again and again they repeated the same difficult

set of *soubresauts* and pirouettes. Nick seemed inexhaustible. The camera work appeared to fascinate him. He showed no sign of annoyance with minor technical breakdowns but simply stopped, talking with the director as the television crew made ready again. Then he would repeat the steps with renewed energy.

They had been taping what would be no more than a three-minute segment for over two hours. It was an athletic piece, full of passion and spirit—the type of dance that was Nick's trademark. Again Ruth turned in a triple pirouette, felt a flash of pain and went down hard. Nick was crouched beside her in an instant.

"Just a cramp," she managed, trying to get her breath.

"Here?" Taking her calf, he felt the knotted muscle and began to work it.

Ruth nodded, though the pain was acute. She put her forehead on her knees and closed her eyes.

"Ten minutes, please," she heard Nick call out. "Did you hurt anything when you fell?" he murmured, kneading the muscle. Ruth could only shake her head. "It's a bad one," he said, frowning. "It's difficult without warmers."

"I can't do it!" She suddenly banged a fist on the stage and raised her face. "I just can't do it right!"

Nick narrowed his eyes. "What nonsense is this?"

"It's not nonsense. I can't," Ruth continued wildly. "It's impossible. Over and over, back and forth. How can I feel anything when there's no flow to it? People everywhere, practically under my nose, when I'm supposed to be preparing for a leap."

"Ignore them and dance," he said flatly. "It's necessary."

"Necessary?" she tossed back. "I'll tell you what's

necessary. It's necessary to sweat. I'm not even allowed to do that. If that man dusts powder on my face once more, I'll scream." She caught her breath as a cramp shot into her other leg. Her feet were past pain. She lowered her head again. "Oh, Nick, I'm so tired."

"So what do you do? Quit?" His voice was rough as he began to work her other leg. "I need a partner, not a complaining baby."

"I'm not a baby." Her head shot back up. "Nor a machine!"

"You're a dancer." He felt the muscle relaxing under his hand. "So dance."

Her eyes flashed at the curt tone. "Thanks for the understanding." She pushed his hand away and swung to her feet. Her legs nearly buckled under her, but she snapped them straight.

"There's a place for understanding." He rose. "This isn't it. You've work to do. Now, go have the man with the powder fix your face."

Ruth stared at him a moment, then turned and walked offstage without a word.

When she had gone, Nick swore under his breath, then sat down again to work out the pain in his own legs.

"You're a tough man, Davidov."

Nick looked up to see Nadine rise from a chair in the audience. "Yes." He turned his attention back to his leg. "You've told me before."

"It's the way I like you." She walked to the side of the stage and climbed the steps. "But she is still young." Her heels set out an echo as she walked across the stage.

Nadine knelt beside him. She took his leg and began to competently massage the cramp. "Good feet, wonderful legs, very musical." She gave him a quick smile. "She's not yet as tough as we are."

"Better for her."

"More difficult for you because you love her." Nick gave her an inquiring lift of a brow. "There's nothing about my dancers I don't know," Nadine went on. "Often before they do. You've been in love with her for a long time."

"So?" Nick said.

"Dancers often pair up with dancers. They speak the same language, have the same problems." Nadine sat back on her haunches. "But when it's my premier danseur and artistic director involved with my best ballerina, I'm concerned."

"There's no need for it, Nadine." His tone was mild, but there was no mistaking his annoyance.

"Romances can go several ways," she commented. "Believe me, I know very well." Nadine smiled again, a bit ruefully. "Dancers are an emotional species, Nick. I don't want to lose either of you if you have a falling out. This one is destined to be prima ballerina *assoluta*."

Nick's voice was very cool. "Are you suggesting I stop seeing Ruth?" He rose carefully to his feet. His eyes were very direct and very blue.

Nadine studied him thoughtfully. "How long have I known you, Davidov?"

He smiled briefly. "It would only age both of us, Nadine."

She nodded in agreement, then held up her hand. Nick lifted her lightly to her feet. "A long time. Long enough to know better than to suggest to you." Her look became wry. "I've watched your parade of women over the years."

"Spasibo."

"That wasn't praise," she countered. "It was an observation." She paused again, briefly. "Bannion's different."

"Yes," he said simply. "Ruth's different."

"Be careful, Davidov. Falls are dangerous to dancers." She turned as technicians began to wander back toward the stage. "She'll hate you for a while."

"I'll have to deal with that."

"Of course," Nadine agreed, expecting nothing else.

Very erect, face composed, Ruth walked out of the wings. While her makeup was being repaired, she had forced everything out of her mind but the dance she was to perform. Until it was completed and on tape, she would allow herself no emotion but that which her character would feel. She crossed to Nick.

"I'm ready."

He looked down at her. He wanted to ask if there was still pain, wanted to tell her that he loved her. Instead, he said, "Good, then we start again."

Nearly two hours later Ruth stood under the shower. Her body was too numbed for pain. Her thoughts were fuzzy with fatigue. Only two things were clear: she detested dancing for the camera; and when she had needed Nick, he had stepped away. He had spoken to her as though she had been lazy and weak. That she had lost control in public had humiliated her enough. His cold words had added to it.

Her strength and stamina had always been a source of pride for her. It had been an enormous blow to have fallen to the stage, beaten and hurting. She had wanted comfort, and he had given her disdain.

Ruth stepped from the shower and wrapped herself

in a towel just as Leah walked in. Still in street clothes, the blonde leaned against a sink and smiled.

"Hi." She studied Ruth's pale, exhausted face. "Rough day?"

"Rough enough." Ruth walked to her bag to pull out a sweater.

"I heard you had some trouble with your number this afternoon."

Ruth had a moment, as she pulled the sweater over her head, to compose her features. "Nothing major," she said calmly, though the easy words cost her. "*Le Corsaire*'s taping is finished."

"I can't wait to see it." Leah smiled, taking out a brush and pulling it lazily through her baby fine hair. "You're looking pale," she observed as Ruth tugged on her jeans. "Lucky you have a couple of days to rest before they start taping *The Red Rose*."

Ruth pulled up her zipper with a jerk. "You keep up with the schedules."

"I make it my business to know what's going on with everybody in the company."

Ruth sat down and took her sneakers from her bag. She put one on, then threw Leah a long, thoughtful look. "What is it you want?"

"Nick," she answered instantly. Her smile deepened as Ruth's eyes glistened. "Not that way, darling, though it's tempting." She smiled. "It appears that being his lover has its advantages."

Ruth struggled with the desire to hurl her other shoe at the smile. Seething, she slipped it on her foot. "What's between Nick and me is personal and has nothing to do with anyone." Blood pounding, Ruth got to her feet.

"Oh, but there's a connection." Leah reached out

to touch Ruth's arm as she would have swung from the room.

The violent urge surprised Ruth. Her temper had never been so close to being completely, blindly lost. She let her bag drop noisily to the floor.

"What?"

Leah sat on the edge of the sink and crossed her ankles. "I intend to be prima ballerina *assoluta*."

"Is that supposed to be news?" Ruth countered with an arched brow.

"I'm fully aware," Leah continued smoothly, "that to do that and remain with this company, I need Nick for my partner."

"Then you have a problem." Ruth faced her squarely. "Nick is my partner."

"For now," Leah agreed easily. "He'll certainly drop you when he gets tired of sleeping with you."

"That's my concern," Ruth said softly.

"Nick's lovers never last long. We've all witnessed the ebb and flow over the years. Remember that lawyer six or eight months ago? Very elegant. And there was a model before that. He usually avoids picking from the company. Very fastidious, our Nikolai."

"*My* Nikolai." Ruth picked up her bag again. "You'd better satisfy yourself with the partners you're given."

"He won't be dancing much longer than a couple more years. He's already choreographing most of the time. Two years is all I need," Leah returned flatly.

"Two years." Ruth laughed and swung the bag over her shoulder. "I'll be prima ballerina *assoluta* in six months." She let her own fury guide her words. "After the show is aired, everyone in the country will know who I am. If the competition worries you, try another company."

"Competition!" Leah's eyes narrowed. "You barely made it through your first piece." She gave Ruth one of her glittery smiles. "Nick might be persuaded to cut your other two or give them to someone with a bit more stamina."

"Such as you."

"Naturally."

"In a pig's eye," Ruth said mildly, then, shoving Leah aside, she walked out.

Though the small gesture had helped, her nerves were still stretched to the breaking point. The emotional onslaught had taken her mind off her body, and she moved down the steps oblivious to the ache in her calves. She headed for the street, seething with indignation.

"Ruth." Nick took her arm when she failed to respond the first time he called. "Where are you going?"

"Home," she said shortly.

"Fine." He studied her heated face. "I'll take you."

"I know where it is." She turned toward the door again, but his hand remained firm.

"I said I would take you."

"Very well." She shrugged. "Suit yourself."

"I usually do," he answered coolly and drew her outside and into a cab. Ruth sat in her corner with her bag held primly in her lap. Nick sat back against the seat, making no attempt at conversation. His mind was apparently occupied with his own thoughts. Stubbornness prevented Ruth from speaking.

Her scene with Nick onstage replayed in her head,

followed by the scene with Leah. Ruth's anger took the form of stony silence.

When the cab pulled up in front of her apartment, she slid out her side, prepared to bid Nick a cool goodbye. He alighted from the street side, however, and rounding the rear of the cab, took her arm again. His grip was light but unarguable. Making no comment, Ruth walked with him into the building.

She knew she was primed for a fight. It would take only the smallest provocation. Anger was bubbling hot just beneath the surface. She unlocked the door to her apartment. Breezing through, she left Nick to go or come in as he chose.

From his seat on the sofa, Nijinsky rose, arched his back, then leaped soundlessly down. Dutifully, he circled around Ruth's ankles before he moved to Nick. She heard him give the cat a murmured greeting. Staying behind her wall of silence, she went into the bedroom to unpack her bag.

She lingered over the task purposefully. There was no sound from the other room as she carefully placed her toe shoes on her dresser. Meticulously, she took the pins from her hair and let it fall free. A small part of her headache fled with the lack of confinement. She brushed her hair out, letting one long stroke follow the next. The apartment remained absolutely silent.

For a full ten minutes Ruth busied herself around the bedroom, finding a dozen small, meaningless tasks that required her attention. Her nerves began to pound again. Deciding that what she needed was food, Ruth tied her hair back with a ribbon and left the room.

Nick was sound asleep on the couch. He lay on his back with a purring Nijinsky curled in a comfortable ball on his chest. His breathing was slow and even. All her resentment fled.

He's exhausted, she realized. The signs were clear on his face. Why hadn't she noticed them before? Because she had been too involved with her own feelings, she thought guiltily.

The creases were deep in his cheeks. She could see the faint mauve shadows under his eyes. Ruth sighed. She could have wept. *No tears*, she ordered herself firmly.

Taking a mohair afghan from the back of a chair, she spread it up to Nick's waist. He never moved. Nijinsky opened one eye, sent her an accusing glance and settled back to sleep. Ruth sat in a chair and curled her legs under her. She watched her lover sleep.

It was dark when Nick woke. Disoriented, he pressed his fingers to his eyes. There was a weight on his chest. Moving his hand to it, he discovered a warm ball of fur. He let out a long sigh as Nijinsky experimentally dug his claws in. With a halfhearted oath, Nick pushed the cat aside and sat up. A stream of light fell from the kitchen doorway. He sat for some moments longer before rising and walking to it.

Ruth stood at the stove. With her hair pulled back, Nick could study her profile: delicate bones, lifted jaw, the slight slant of her eyes. Her lips were parted in concentration—soft, generous lips he could taste just by looking. She had the slender, arching neck of a classical ballerina. He knew the precise spot where the skin was most sensitive.

She looked very young in the harsh kitchen light, much as she had looked the first time he had seen her—

in the glare of sun on snow in the parking lot of Lindsay's school. Ruth turned suddenly, sensing him. Their eyes locked.

She moistened her lips. "You were stirring. I thought you'd be hungry. Are omelets all right?"

"Yes. Good."

He leaned on the door jamb as she went back to her preparation. A glance at his watch told him it was barely nine o'clock. He had slept for just under two hours. He was as refreshed as if it had been a full night.

"Can I help?"

Ruth kept her eyes on the eggs growing firm in the pan. "You could get out the plates. I'm almost done." Beside her on the counter the percolator began to pop. Nick got out plates and cups. "Do you want anything else?" she asked, hating the strained politeness of her voice.

"No. This is fine."

Expertly, Ruth flipped the first omelet from pan to plate. "Go ahead and get started. I'll just be another minute." Beaten eggs sizzled as she poured them into the pan. "I'll bring the coffee."

Nick took his plate into the dining room. Ruth continued to work, focusing all her concentration on her cooking. The percolator became more lively. She slid the eggs from the pan. Unplugging the coffee, she took it into the dining room.

Nick glanced up as she came in.

"Is it all right?" She set down her plate, then poured coffee into the waiting cups.

"It's good." He forked another mouthful. Ruth avoided his eyes and set the percolator on a trivet. Taking the seat across from him, she began to eat.

"I have to thank you for letting me sleep." Nick watched her push the eggs around on her plate. "I needed it. And this."

"You looked so tired," she murmured. "It never occurred to me that it's difficult for you."

"Ah," he said with light amusement. "Davidov the indestructible."

Ruth lifted her eyes at that. "I suppose that's how I've always seen you. How all of us see you."

His glance was steady. "But then, you are not all of us." He saw the tears spring to her eyes. Something tightened inside his stomach. "You should eat," he said briskly. "It's been a long day."

Ruth picked up her coffee cup, struggling for composure. She'd had enough scenes for one day. "I'm not really hungry."

Nick shrugged and went back to his meal. "Something's burning," he commented. With a cry, Ruth leaped up and dashed into the kitchen.

The omelet pan smoked in a steady column, its surface crackling from the heat. Swearing, she flicked off the flame she had left burning under it and gave the stove an angry kick.

"Careful," Nick said from the doorway. "I can't use a partner with broken toes."

She rounded on him, wanting to vent her anger somewhere. But he smiled. It was as though he had pulled his finger from the dam.

"Oh, Nick!" Ruth threw herself into his arms and clung. "I was so horrible today. I danced so badly."

"No," he corrected, kissing her hair. "You danced beautifully, better when you were angry with me."

Ruth drew her head back and looked at him. She

knew with certainty that he would never lie about her dancing to comfort her. "I shouldn't have been angry with you. I was so wrapped up in myself, in how I was feeling, that I never thought about how difficult it was for you, too. You always make it look so easy."

"You don't like the camera."

"I hate it. It's horrible."

"But valuable."

"I know that. I know it." She drew back to stand away from him. "I hate the way I acted this afternoon, crying in front of all those people, raging at you."

"You're an artist. I've told you, it's expected."

"I don't like public displays." She took a long breath. "I particularly don't like seeing myself as selfish and uncaring."

"You're too hard on yourself, Ruth. The woman I love is not selfish or uncaring."

"I was today." She shook her head. "I didn't stop thinking of myself until I saw you sleeping, looking so utterly exhausted. I know how hard you've been working, not only on our dances but at all the other rehearsals you have to supervise and the meetings and the schedule for the rest of the season. But all I thought about was how I hated those cameras looming everywhere and about how my legs ached." She gave a quiet, shuddering sigh. "I don't like knowing I can be that one-dimensional, too much like what Donald once accused me of."

"Oh, enough." Nick took her shoulders in a firm grip. "We have to think of ourselves, of our own bodies. There's no other way to survive. You're a fool if you believe it makes you less of a person. We're different from others, yes. It's our way."

"Selfish?"

"Must it have a name?" He gave her a little shake, then pulled her against him. "Selfish, if you like. Dedicated. Obsessed. What does it matter? Does it change you? Does it change me?" Suddenly his mouth was on hers.

Ruth moaned with the kiss. His lips were both tender and possessive, sparking small flames deep inside her. He drew her closer, and still closer, until they were molded together.

"This is how I wanted to kiss you when you sat on the stage angry and hurting." His mouth moved over hers with the words. "Do you hate me because I didn't?"

"No. No, but I wanted you to." She held him tighter. "I wanted so badly for you to."

"You would never have finished the dance if I had comforted you then." Nick tilted her head back until their eyes met. "I knew that, because I know you. Does this make me cold and selfish?"

"It makes you Davidov." Ruth sighed and smiled at him. "That's all I want."

"And you are Bannion." He lowered his mouth to hers. "That's all I want."

"You make it sound so simple. Is it simple?"

"Tonight it is simple." He lifted her into his arms.

Chapter 13

Ruth sat six rows back and watched the taping. Her three segments were finished. What would be perhaps nine or ten minutes of air time had taken three grueling days to tape. She had learned to play for the camera, even to tolerate it. But she knew she would never feel the excitement with it that Nick did. He had challenged her to outdo him in their pas de deux from *Carnival*. He had been exuberant, incredibly agile in his Harlequin mask and costume, a teasing, free-spirited soul who infused more vitality into her Columbine than she had believed possible.

He simply glows with energy, she mused, watching him onstage. Even when he's not dancing.

The corps was doing a scene from *Rodeo*. Amid the cowboy hats and gingham, Nick stood in a characteristically drab sweat suit and instructed the dancers. If he had worn gold or silver, he could not have been more of a focal point.

Ruth knew how little relaxation he had allowed himself over the past weeks. Yet as he coached his dancers a last time, he was as vital and alive as a young boy. *How does he do it?* she asked herself.

She thought of what Leah had said and wondered: Would he stop dancing in another two years? Ruth hated to think of it. He looked so young. In most other professions he would be considered young, she reflected. As art director, as choreographer, as composer, he could go on indefinitely. But as danseur *noble*, time was precious.

He knew it, of course. Ruth watched as Davidov stepped out of camera range. How did he feel about it? He'd never told her. There were so many things he'd never told her.

Ruth was aware of how smoothly he changed the subject whenever she probed too deeply about his life in Russia. It wasn't a simple matter of curiosity that prompted her to ask. Yet she didn't know how to explain her questions to him.

It frustrated her that he chose to block off a part of himself from her. Privacy was something Ruth valued deeply and respected in others, but loving Nick wholeheartedly, she had the need to know him completely. Yet he continued to draw back from questions or discussions of his early life or his professional career in his own country. Nor had he spoken with her of his feelings about perhaps coming to the end of his active dancing career.

Too often, she decided, he thought of her as a little

girl. How would she convince him to share his problems with her as well as his joys?

Music filled the theater; the quick, raucously Western American music that set the mood for the dance. Nick watched the corps from behind a cameraman, his hands lightly balled at his hips. Ruth drew in her breath.

Will I always feel like this? she wondered. Moved by him, dazed by him? It was frightening to be in love with a legend. Even in the short time they had been together, career demands had pressured them both. Ballet was both a bond and a strain. The time they spent alone in her apartment was another world. They could be any man and woman then. But the music and the lights called them back. And here, in the world that consumed most of their lives, he was Davidov the master.

"He seems to be handling things well, as usual." Nadine slipped into the seat beside her, and Ruth snapped herself back.

The music had stopped. Nick was talking to the dancers again as the director spoke to some invisible technician on his headset. Ruth let her eyes follow Nick. "Yes, he seems to be."

"Like a boy with a new train set."

Ruth gave Nadine a quizzical look. "Train set?"

"The fresh excitement, the enthusiasm," she explained with a sweeping gesture of her hand. "He's loving this."

"Yes." Ruth looked back at Nick. "I can see that."

"Your dances went well." At Ruth's deprecating laugh, Nadine went on. "Oh, I know you had some adjustments to make. That's life."

"Were you watching?"

"I'm always watching."

"You're not usually kind, Nadine," Ruth commented wryly.

"My dear, I'm never kind. I can't afford to be." The music began again, and though Nadine's eyes were on the stage, she spoke to Ruth. "They did go well, all in all. The tape is magnificent."

"You've seen it?" Ruth was all attention now.

Nadine merely lifted her brow in response. "The program should be all we hoped for. I can say frankly that you and Nick together are the best I've seen in some time. I never thought he'd find a partner to equal Lindsay. Of course, your style and hers are very different. Lindsay took to the air as if she were part of it— effortlessly, almost mystically. You challenge it, as if defying gravity."

Ruth pondered over the description. It seemed to make perfect sense. "Lindsay was the most beautiful ballerina I've ever seen."

"We lost her because she allowed her personal life to interfere," Nadine said flatly.

"She didn't have any choice." Ruth rushed to Lindsay's defense. "When her father was killed and her mother so badly hurt, she had to go."

"We make our own choices." Nadine turned to face Ruth directly. "I don't believe in fate. We make things happen."

"Lindsay did what she had to do."

"What she chose to do," Nadine corrected. "We all do." She studied Ruth's frown. "I've had one priority all my life. I'd like to think all my dancers were the same, but I know better. You have the talent, the youth, the drive to make a very important mark in the world of ballet. Lindsay had just begun to make hers when she left. I wouldn't like to lose you."

"Why should you?" Ruth phrased the question carefully, keeping her eyes on Nadine. She was no longer aware of what was happening onstage.

"Temperaments run high in dancers."

"So I've been told," Ruth said drily. "But that doesn't answer my question."

"I need both you and Nick, Ruth, but I need Nick more." She paused a moment, watching her words sink in. "If the two of you come to a time when things are... no longer as they are, and you can't—or won't—work together, I'd have to make a choice. The company can't afford to lose Nick."

"I see." Ruth turned back to the stage and stared at the dancers.

"I've thought a long time about speaking to you. I felt it best I make my position clear."

"Have you spoken to Nick?"

"No." Nadine looked at Nick as he stood with the technicians. "Not so bluntly. I will, of course, if it becomes necessary. I hope it doesn't."

"Quite a number of dancers in the company become involved with each other," Ruth commented. "Some even marry. Do you make a habit of prying into their private lives?"

"I always thought there was fire behind those scrupulous manners." Nadine smiled thinly. "I'm glad to see it." She paused a moment. "As long as nothing outside interferes with the company, there's no reason to create unhappiness." She gave Ruth another direct look. "But Nick isn't merely one of my dancers. We both know that."

"I don't think you could say that what's between Nick and me has interfered with the company or with our dancing." Ruth sat stiffly.

"Not yet, no. I'm fond of you, Ruth, which is why I spoke. Now I have to go wring a few more dollars out of a patron." Nadine rose and, without another word, moved up the dark aisle and out of the theater.

Onstage, Nick watched his dancers. He saw them both individually and as a group. This one's arm wasn't arched quite right, that one's foot placement was perfect. He kept a close eye on the corps. There were two he planned to make soloists soon. There was a young girl, barely eighteen, whom he observed with special interest. She had an ethereal, otherworldly beauty and great speed. She reminded him a bit of Lindsay. Already he saw her as Carla in *The Nutcracker* the following year. He would have to induce Madame Maximova to work with her individually.

The director stopped the tape, and Nick moved forward to correct a few minor details. They had been working nearly two hours and the hot lights shone without mercy. *Nadine*, he thought as they began again, *is like a hawk hunting chickens when she holds auditions for the corps.* Poor children; were they ever really aware of the drudgery of dance? So few of them would ever go beyond the corps. Again he watched the young girl as she spun into her partner's arms. That one will, he concluded. She'll be chasing after Ruth's heels in two years.

He smiled, remembering Ruth's corps days. She'd been so young and very withdrawn. Only when she had danced had she been truly confident. Even then—yes, even then—he had wanted her, and it had astonished him. He had watched her grow more poised, more open. He'd watched her talent blossom.

Five years, he thought. *Five years, and now, at last, I have her.* Still it wasn't enough. There were nights his duties kept him late, and he was forced to go home to his own empty apartment knowing Ruth slept far away in another bed.

He wondered whether he was more impatient now because he had waited so long for her. It was a daily struggle to keep from hurrying her into a fuller commitment. He hadn't even meant to tell her he loved her, certainly not in that flat, unadorned manner. The moments before she had turned and given the love back to him had left him paralyzed with fear. Fear was a new sensation and one he discovered he didn't care for.

Part of him resented the hold she had on him. No one woman had ever occupied his thoughts so completely. And still she held part of herself aloof from him. It was tantalizing, infuriating.

He wanted her without reserve, without secrets. The longer they went on, the more impossible it became to prevent himself from pressing her for more. Even now, with his mind crammed with his work, he knew she sat out in the darkened theater. He sensed her.

She shouldn't be allowed to pull at him this way, he thought with sudden anger. Yet he wanted her there. Close. The words he had spoken when he had come to her apartment in the night grew more true as time passed. He needed her.

At last the taping session was completed. Nick spoke with the director as dancers filed offstage. They would cool their bodies under showers and nurse their aches. Ruth rose from her seat in the audience and approached the stage. The musicians were talking among themselves, stretching their backs.

"One hour, please," Nick called to them and received a grumbled response.

Technicians shut off the high wattage lights, and the temperature dropped markedly. The crew was talking about the Italian deli down the street and meatball sandwiches. With a laugh, Nick declined joining them. His offer of yogurt in the company canteen was met with unilateral disgust.

"So." He drew Ruth into his arms when she stepped onstage. "What did you think of it?"

"It was wonderful," she answered truthfully. She tried not to think about her conversation with Nadine as Nick gave her a brief kiss. "Apparently, you have a flair for Americana."

"I always thought I'd make a good cowboy." He grinned and picked up one of the abandoned prop hats. With a flourish, he set it on his head. "Now I only need six-guns."

Ruth laughed. "It suits you," she decided, adjusting the hat lower over his forehead. "Did they have cowboys in Russia?"

"Cossacks," he answered. "Not quite the same." He smiled, running his hands down her arms. "Are you hungry? There's an hour before we begin again."

"Yes."

Slipping an arm around her, he tossed off the hat as they crossed the stage. "We'll get something and take it up to my office. I want you alone."

Ten minutes later Nick closed his office door behind them. "We should have music for such an elaborate meal, yes?" He moved to the stereo.

Ruth set down their bowls of fruit salad as he switched on Rimsky-Korsakov. After turning the volume low, he came back to her.

"This first." Nick gathered her into his arms. Ruth lifted her mouth to his, hungry for his kiss.

Her demand fanned the banked fires within him. With a low sound of pleasure, he tangled his fingers in her hair and plundered. Her mouth was avid, seeking, as she let the kiss take her. Desire was a fast-driving force that rocketed inside her. She slipped her hands under his sweat shirt to feel the play of muscles on his back. His mouth began to move wildly over her face; her lips ached for his.

"Kiss me," she demanded and stopped his roaming mouth with hers.

The kiss was shattering and stormy. It was as though he poured all his needs into the single meeting of lips. It left her breathless, shaken, wanting more. He probed her lip with his teeth until she moaned in drugged excitement. Then he drove deeper, using his tongue to destroy any hold on sanity. Ruth murmured mindlessly, craving for him to touch her.

As if reading her thoughts, he brought his hand to her breast. She shuddered as the rough fabric of her cotton blouse scraped her skin. With his other hand he tugged it from the waistband of her jeans. His fingers snaked up over her ribcage and found her. Together they caught their breath at the contact.

When the phone on his desk began to ring, Nick let out a steady stream of curses. He spun to answer and yanked the receiver from the cradle.

"What is it?"

Ruth let out a long breath and sat. Her knees were trembling.

"I can't see him now." She had heard that sharp, impatient tone before and felt a small tingle of sympathy for the caller. "No, he'll wait. I'm busy, Nadine."

Ruth's brows shot up. No one spoke to Nadine that way. She sighed then and looked up at Nick. No one else was Davidov.

"Yes, I'm aware of that. In twenty minutes, then. No, twenty." He set the phone down with a final click. When he looked back down at Ruth, the annoyance was still in his eyes. "It seems an open wallet requires my attention." He swore and thrust his hands into his pockets. "There are times when this business of money drives me mad. It must be forever coaxed and tugged. It was simple once just to dance. Now it's not enough. They give us little time, Ruth."

"Come and eat," she said, wanting to soothe him. "Twenty minutes is time enough."

"I don't speak of only now!" The anger rose in his voice, and she braced herself for the torrent. "I wanted to be with you last night and all the other nights I slept alone. I need more than this—more than a few moments in the day, a few nights in the week."

"Nick—" she began, but he cut her off.

"I want you to move in with me. To live with me."

Whatever she had been about to say escaped her. He stood over her, furious and demanding. "Move in with you?" she repeated dumbly.

"Yes. Today. Tonight."

Her thoughts were whirling as she stared up at him. "Into your apartment?"

"Yes." Impatient, he pulled her to her feet. "I cannot—

will not—keep going home to empty rooms." His grip was firm on her arms. "I want you there."

"Live with you," Ruth said again, struggling to take it in. "My things…"

"Bring your things." Nick shook her in frustration. "What does it matter?"

Ruth shook her head, lifting a hand to push herself away. "You have to give me time to think."

"Damn it, what need is there to think?" He betrayed the depth of his agitation by swearing in English. She was too confused to notice. She might have been prepared for him to ask her to take such a step, but she hadn't been prepared for him to shout it at her.

"I have a need to think," she shot back. "You're asking me to change my life, give up the only home of my own I've ever had."

"I'm asking you to have a home with me." His fingers dug deeper. "I will not go on stealing little moments of time with you."

"*You* can't, *you* won't! I have the final say in my own life. I won't be pressured this way!"

"Pressured? Hell!" Nick stormed to the window, then back to her. "You speak to me of pressures? Five years, *five years* I've waited for you. I wanted a child and must wait until the child grows to a woman." His English began to elude him.

Ruth's eyes grew enormous. "Are you telling me you felt…had feelings for me since…since the beginning and never told me?"

"What was I to say?" he countered furiously. "You were seventeen."

"I had a right to make my own choice!" She tossed

her hair back and glared at him. "You had no right to make it for me."

"I gave you your choice when the time was right."

"You gave!" she retorted. Indignation nearly choked her. "You're the director of the company, Davidov, not of my life. How dare you presume to make any decisions for me!"

"My life was also involved," he reminded her. His eyes glittered as he spoke. "Or do you forget?"

"You always treated me like a child," she fumed, ignoring his question. "You never considered that between my childhood and dancing, I was grown up before I ever met you. And now you stand there and tell me you kept something from me for years for my own good. *And* you tell me to pack my things and move in with you without giving it a thought."

"I had no idea such a suggestion would offend you," he said coldly.

"Suggestion?" she repeated. "It came out as an order. I won't be *ordered* to live with you."

"Very well, do as you wish." He gave her a long, steady look. "I have an appointment."

Her eyes opened wider in fresh rage as he moved to the door. "I'm taking some time off," she said impulsively.

Nick paused with his hand on the knob and turned to her. "Rehearsals begin again in seven days," he said, deadly calm. "You will be back or you will be fired. I leave the choice to you."

He walked out without bothering to close the door behind him.

Chapter 14

Lindsay hefted Amanda and settled her into the curve of her hip while Justin skidded a car across the wood-planked floor.

"Dinner in ten minutes, young man," she warned, stepping expertly between the wrecked and parked cars. "Go wash your hands."

"They're not dirty." Justin bowed his blond head over a tiny, flashy racer as if to repair the engine.

Lindsay narrowed her eyes while Amanda squirmed for freedom. "Worth might think otherwise," she said. It was her ultimate weapon.

Justin slipped the toy Ferrari into his pocket and got up. With a weighty, world-weary sigh, he walked from the room.

Lindsay smiled after him. Justin had a healthy respect for the fastidious British butler. She listened to the squeak of her son's tennis shoes as he climbed the stairs. He could have used the downstairs bath, but when Justin Bannion was being a martyr, he liked to do it properly.

It amazed Lindsay, when she had time to think of it, that her son was four years old. He had already outgrown the chunky toddler stage and was lean as a whippet. And, she thought, not without pride, he has his mother's hair and eyes. Glancing around the room, she grimaced at the wreckage of cars and small buildings. And his mother's lack of organization, she mused.

"Not like you at all, is he?" She buried her face in her daughter's neck and earned a giggle.

Amanda was dark, the female image of her father. And like Seth, she was meticulous. Armies of dolls were arranged just so in her room. She showed almost a comical knack for neatly stacking her blocks into buildings. Temper perhaps came from both of her parents, as she wasn't too ladylike to chuck a block at her brother if he infringed on her territory.

With a last kiss, Lindsay set Amanda down and began to gather Justin's abandoned traffic jam. She stopped, car in hand, and shot her daughter a look. "Daddy won't like it if I pick these up."

"Justin's sloppy," Amanda stated with sisterly disdain. At two, she had a penchant for picking up telling phrases.

"No argument there," Lindsay agreed and passed a car from hand to hand. "And he certainly has to learn better, but if Worth walks in here…" She let the thought hang, weighing whose disapproval she would rather face. Worth won. Moving quickly, she began scooping up the evidence. "I'll speak to Justin. We won't have to tell Daddy."

"Tell Daddy what?" Seth demanded from the doorway.

"Uh-oh." Lindsay rolled her eyes to the ceiling, then peered over her shoulder. "I thought you were working."

"I was." He took in the tableau quickly. "Covering up for the little devil again, are you?"

"I sent him up to wash his hands." Lindsay pushed the hair out of her eyes and continued to stay on her hands and knees. Amanda walked over to wrap an arm around Seth's leg. Both of them studied her in quiet disapproval. "Oh, please!" She laughed, sitting back on her haunches. "We throw ourselves on the mercy of the court."

"Well." He laid a hand on his daughter's head. "What should the punishment be, Amanda?"

"Can't spank Mama."

"No?" Seth gave Lindsay a wicked grin. Walking over, he pulled her to her feet. "In the interest of justice, I might find it necessary." He gave her a light, teasing kiss.

"Are you open to a bribe?" she murmured.

"Always," he told her as she pressed her mouth more firmly to his.

Justin bounced to the doorway with his freshly scrubbed hands in front of him. He made a face at his parents, then looked down at his sister. "I thought we were going to eat."

An hour later Lindsay rushed down the steps, heading out for her evening ballet class. Spotting another of Justin's cars at the foot of the steps, she picked it up and stuffed it into her bag.

"A life of crime," she muttered and pulled open the front door. "Ruth!" Astonished, she simply stared.

"Hi. Got a room for an escaped dancer and a slightly overweight cat for the weekend?"

"Oh, of course!" She pulled Ruth across the threshold for a huge hug. Nijinsky scrambled from between them, leaped to the floor and stalked away. He wasn't fond of traveling. "It's wonderful to see you. Seth and the children will be so surprised."

Through her first rush of pleasure, Lindsay could feel the hard desperation of Ruth's grip. She drew her away and studied her face. She had no trouble spotting the unhappiness. "Are you all right?"

"Yes." Lindsay's eyes were direct on hers. "No," she admitted. "I need some time."

"All right." She picked up Ruth's bag and closed the door behind them. "Your room's in the same place. Go up and surprise Seth and the children. I'll be back in a couple of hours."

"Thanks."

Lindsay dashed out the door, and Ruth drew a deep breath.

Two days later Ruth sat on the couch, a child on each side of her. She read aloud from one of Justin's books. Nijinsky dozed in a patch of sunlight on the floor. She was feeling more settled.

She should have known that she would find exactly what she had needed at the Cliff House. No questions, no coddling. Lindsay had opened the door, and Ruth had found acceptance and love.

After Ruth had left Nick's office, she'd gone back to her apartment, packed and come directly to Cliff-side. She hadn't even thought about it, but had simply followed instinct. Now, after two days, Ruth knew her instincts had been right. There were times when only family could heal.

"I thought you must have bound and gagged them," Seth commented as he strode into the room. "They're not this quiet when they're asleep."

Ruth laughed. Both children went to climb into Seth's lap the moment he sat down.

"They're angels, Uncle Seth." She watched him wrap his arms around both his children. "You should be ashamed of yourself, blackening their names."

"They don't need my help for that." He tugged Amanda's hair. "Worth announced that there was a half-eaten lollipop in someone's bed this morning."

"I was going to finish it tonight," Justin stated, looking earnestly up at his father. "He didn't throw it away, did he?"

"Afraid so."

"Nuts."

"He had a few choice things to say about the state of the sheets," Seth added mildly.

Justin set his mouth—his mother's mouth—into a pout. "Do I have to 'pologize again?"

"I should think so."

"I wanna watch." Amanda was already scrambling down in anticipation.

"I'm always 'pologizing," Justin said wearily. Ruth watched him troop from the room with Amanda trotting to keep up.

"You know, of course," Ruth began, "that Worth adores them."

"Yes, but he'd hate to know his secret was out." Seth

could hear both sets of feet clattering down the hall toward the kitchen.

"He always awed me." Ruth set the book aside. "All the months I lived with you I never grew completely used to him."

"No one handles him as well as Lindsay does." Seth sat back and let his mind relax. "He's never yet realized he's being handled."

"There's no one like Lindsay," Ruth said.

"No," Seth said in simple agreement. "No one."

"Was it frightening falling in love with someone so—special?"

He could read the question in her eyes and knew what she was thinking. "Loving's always frightening if it's important. Loving someone special only adds to it. Lindsay scared me to death."

"How strange. I always thought of you as invulnerable and fearless."

"Love makes cowards of all of us, Ruth." The memories of his first months with Lindsay, before their marriage, came back to him. "I nearly lost her once. Nothing's ever frightened me more."

"I've watched you for five years." Ruth was frowning in concentration. "Your love's the same as it was in the very beginning."

"No." Seth shook his head. "I love her more, incredibly more. So I have more to lose."

They both heard her burst through the front door. "God save me from mothers who want Pavlova after five lessons!"

"She's home," Seth said mildly.

"Mrs. Fitzwalter," Lindsay began without preamble as she stormed into the room, "wants her Mitzie to take class with Janet Conner. Never mind that Janet has been taking lessons for two years and Mitzie just started two weeks ago." Lindsay plopped into a chair and glared. "Never mind that Janet has talent and Mitzie has lead feet. Mitzie wants to take class with her best friend, and Mrs. Fitzwalter wants to car pool."

"You, of course, explained diplomatically." Seth lifted a brow.

"I was the epitome of diplomacy. I've been taking Worth lessons." She turned to Ruth. "Mitzie is ten pounds overweight and can't manage first position. Janet's been on toe for two months."

"You might find her another car pool," Ruth suggested.

"I did." Lindsay smiled, pleased with herself. The smile faded as she noted the abnormal quiet. "Where are the children?"

"Apologizing," Seth told her.

"Oh, dear, again?" Lindsay sighed and smiled. Rising, she crossed to Seth. "Hi." She bent and kissed him. "Did you solve your cantilever problem?"

"Just about," he told her and brought her back for a more satisfying kiss.

"You're so clever." She sat on the arm of his chair.

"Naturally."

"And you work too hard. Holed up in that office every day, and on Saturday." She slipped her hand into his. "Let's all go for a walk on the beach."

Seth started to agree, then paused. "You and Ruth go. The kids need a nap. I think I'll join them."

Lindsay looked at him in surprise. The last thing Seth would do on a beautiful Saturday afternoon was take a nap. But his message passed to her quickly, and she turned to Ruth with no change in rhythm. "Yes, let's go. I need some air after Mrs. Fitzwalter."

"All right. Do I need a jacket?"

"A light one."

Lindsay looked back down at Seth as Ruth went to fetch one. "Have I told you today how marvelous you are and how I adore you?"

"Not that I recall." He lifted his hand to her hair. "Tell me now."

"You're marvelous and I adore you." She kissed him again before she rose. "I should warn you that Justin informed me yesterday that he was entirely too old for naps."

"We'll discuss it."

"Diplomatically?" she asked, smiling over her shoulder as she walked from the room.

The air smelled of the sea. Ruth had nearly forgotten how clean and sharp the scent was. The beach was long and rocky, with a noisy surf. An occasional leaf found its way down from the grove on the ridge. One scuttled along the sand in front of them. "I've always loved it here." Lindsay stuck her hands into the deep pockets of her jacket.

"I hated it when we first came," Ruth mused, gazing down the stretch of beach as they walked. "The house, the sound, everything."

"Yes, I know."

Ruth cast her a quick look. Yes, she thought, she would have known. "I don't know when I stopped. It seemed I just woke up one day and found I was home. Uncle Seth was so patient."

"He's a patient man." Lindsay laughed. "At times,

infuriatingly so. I rant and rave, and he calmly wins the battle. His control can be frustrating." She studied Ruth's profile. "You're a great deal like him."

"Am I?" Ruth pondered the idea a moment. "I wouldn't have thought myself very controlled lately."

"He has his moments, too." Lindsay reached over to pick up a stone and slipped it into her pocket, a habit she had never broken.

"Lindsay, you've never asked why I came so suddenly or how long I intend to stay."

"It's your home, Ruth. You don't have to explain coming here."

"I told Uncle Seth there was no one else like you."

"Did you?" Lindsay smiled at that and brushed some flying hair from her eyes. "That's the best sort of compliment, I think."

"It's Nick," Ruth said suddenly.

"Yes, I know."

Ruth let out a long breath. "I love him, Lindsay. I'm scared."

"I know the feeling. You've fought, I imagine."

"Yes. Oh, there are so many things." Ruth's voice was suddenly filled with the passion of frustration. "I've tried to work it out in my head these past couple of days, but nothing seems to make sense."

"Being in love never makes sense. That's the first rule." They had come to a clump of rocks, and Lindsay sat.

It was right here, she remembered, that Seth and she had stood that day. She had been in love and frightened because nothing made sense. Ruth had come down from the house with a kitten zipped up in her jacket. She'd been seventeen and cautious about letting anyone get too close. Maybe she's still being cautious, Lindsay thought, looking back at her. "Do you want to talk about it?"

Ruth hesitated only a moment. "Yes, I think I would."

"Then sit, and start at the beginning."

It was so simple once begun. Ruth told her of the suddenness of their coming together after so many years of working side by side. She told her of the shock of learning he loved her and of the frustrations at having no time together. She left nothing out: the scenes with Leah, Nick's quick mood changes, her own uncertainties.

"Then, the day I left, Nadine spoke to me. She wanted me to know that if Nick and I had a break-up and wouldn't work together, she'd have to let me go. I was furious that we couldn't seem to keep what we had between us between us." She stared out toward the sound, feeling impotent with frustration.

"Before I had a chance to simmer down, Nick was demanding that I give up my apartment and move in with him. Just like that," she added, looking back at Lindsay. "Demanding. He was so infuriating, standing there, shouting at me about what *he* wanted. He tossed in that he'd wanted me for five years and had never said a word. I could hardly believe it. The nerve!"

She paused, dealing with a fresh spurt of anger. "I couldn't stand thinking he'd been directing my life. He was unreasonable and becoming more Russian by the minute. I was to pack up my things and move in with him without a moment's thought. He didn't even ask; he was ordering, as though he were staging his latest ballet. No," she corrected herself and rose, no longer able to sit, "he's more human when he's staging. He didn't once ask me what my feelings were. He just threw this at me straight after my little session with Nadine and after the dreadful week of taping."

Ruth ran out of steam all at once and sat back down. "Lindsay, I've never been so confused in my life."

Idly, Lindsay jiggled the stone in her pocket. She had listened throughout Ruth's speech without a single interruption. "Well," she said finally, "I have a firm policy against offering advice." Pausing, she gazed out at the sea. "And policies are made to be broken. How well do you know Nick?"

"Not as well as you do," Ruth said without thinking. "He was in love with you." The words were out before she realized she had thought them. "Oh, Lindsay."

"Oh, indeed." She faced Ruth directly. "When I first joined the company, Nadine was struggling to keep it going. Nick's coming gave it much-needed momentum, but there were internal problems, financial pressures outsiders are rarely aware of. I know you think Nadine was hard—she undoubtedly was—but the company is everything to her. It's easier for me to understand that now with the distance. I didn't always.

"In any case," she continued, "Nick's coming was the turning point. He was very young, thrown into the spotlight in a strange country. He barely spoke coherent English. French, Italian, a bit of German, but he had to learn English from the ground up. Of all people, you should understand what it's like to be in a strange country with strange customs, to be the outsider."

"Yes," Ruth murmured. "Yes, I do."

"Well, then." Lindsay wrapped her arms around her knee. "Try to picture a twenty-year-old who had just made the most important decision of his life. He had left

his country, his friends, his family. Yes, he has family,"
Lindsay said, noting Ruth's surprise. "It wasn't easy for
him, and the first years made him very careful. There
were a lot of people out there who were very eager to
exploit him—his story, his background. He learned to
edit his life. When I met him, he was already Davidov,
a name in capital letters."

She took a moment, watching the surf fly up on
the rocks. "Yes, I was attracted to him, very attracted.
Maybe half in love for a while. It might have been the
same for him. We were dancers and young and ambi-
tious. Maybe if my parents hadn't had the accident,
maybe if I had stayed with the company, something
would have developed between us. I don't know. I met
Seth." Lindsay smiled and glanced back up at the Cliff
House. "What I do know is that whatever Nick and I
might have had, it wouldn't have been the right choice
for either of us. There's no one for me but Seth. Now
or ever."

"Lindsay, I didn't mean to pry." Ruth gestured helplessly.

"You're not prying. We're all bound up in this. That's
why I'm breaking my policy." She paused another moment. "Nick talked to me in those days because he
needed someone. There were very few people he felt
he could trust. He thought he could trust me. If there
are things he hasn't told you, it's simply because it's become a habit of his not to dwell on what he left behind.
Nick is a man who looks ahead. But he feels, Ruth, don't
imagine he doesn't."

"I know he does," Ruth said quietly. "I've only
wanted to share it with him."

"When he's ready, you will." She said it simply.

"Nick made ballet first in his life out of choice or necessity, take your pick. From what you've told me, it appears something else is beginning to take the driver's seat. I imagine it scares him to death."

"Yes." Ruth remembered what her uncle had said to her. "I hadn't thought that he'd feel that way, too."

"When a man, especially a man with a flair for words and staging, asks a woman to live with him so clumsily, I'd guess he was scared right out of his shoes." She smiled a little and touched Ruth's hand. "Now, as for this Leah and the rest of this nonsense about your relationship interfering with your careers or vice versa, you should know better. After five years with the company you should be able to spot basic jealousy when it hits you in the face."

Ruth let out a sigh. "I've always been able to before."

"This time the stakes were higher. Love can cloud the issue." She studied Ruth in silence for a moment. "And how much have you been willing to give him?"

Ruth opened her mouth to speak, then shut it again. "Not enough," she admitted. "I was afraid, too. He's such a strong man, Lindsay. His personality is overwhelming. I didn't want to lose myself." She looked at Lindsay searchingly. "Is that wrong?"

"No. If you were weak and bent under every demand he handed out, he wouldn't be in love with you." She took Ruth's hand and squeezed it. "Nick needs a partner, Ruth, not a fan."

"He can be so arrogant. So impossible."

"Yes, bless him."

Ruth laughed and hugged her. "Lindsay, I needed to come home."

"You've come." Lindsay returned the hug. "Do you love him?"

"Yes. Yes, I love him."

"Then go pack and go after him. Time's too precious. He's in California." She smiled at Ruth's puzzled face. "I called Nadine this morning. I'd already decided to break my policy."

Chapter 15

Nick's feet pounded into the sand. He was on his third mile. The sun was rising slowly, casting rose-gold glints into the ocean. Dawn had been pale and gray when he had started. He had the beach to himself. It was too early for even the most enthusiastic jogger. He liked the lonely stretch of sand turning gold under the sun, the empty cry of gulls over his head and the whooshing sound of the waves beside him.

The only pressures here were the ones he put on his own body. Like dancing, running could be a solitary challenge. And here, too, he could put his mind above the pain. Today, if he ran hard enough, far enough, he might stop thinking of Ruth.

How could he have been so stupid? Nick cursed himself again and increased his pace. *What timing! What style!* He had meant to give her more space, meant to wait until the scene was right. Nothing had come out the way he had intended. Had he actually ordered her to pack? What had possessed him? Anger, frustration, need. Fear. The choreography he had so carefully devised had become stumbling missteps.

He had wanted to ease her into living with him, letting her grow used to the first commitment before he slid her into marriage. He had destroyed it all with temper and arrogance.

Once he had begun, he had been unable to stop himself. And how she had looked at him! First stunned, then furious. How could he have been so clumsy? There had been countless women in his life, and he had never had such trouble telling them what he felt—what he didn't feel. How many languages could he make love in? Why, when it finally mattered, had he struck out like a blundering fool? Yet it had been so with every step in his courtship of Ruth.

Courtship! He berated himself and kept running as the sun grew higher. He set himself a punishing rhythm. What courtship had he given her? He had taken her like a crazed man the first time, and when he had told her he loved her, had there been any finesse? A schoolboy would have shown more care!

Well out at sea a school of dolphins took turns leaping into the air; a beautifully choreographed water ballet. Nick kept running.

She won't be back, he thought grimly. Then in despair—*good God what will I do? Will I bury myself in the company and have nothing else, like poor Nadine? Is this what all the years have been for? Every time I dance, she'll be there, just out of reach. She'll go to an-*

other company, dance with Mitchell or Kirminov. The thought made his blood boil.

I'll drag her back. He pounded on, letting the pain fill him. *She's so young! What right do I have to force her back to me? Could I? It isn't right; a man doesn't drag a woman back when she leaves him. There's the pride. I won't.*

The hell I won't, he thought suddenly and turned back toward the house. He never slackened his pace. *The hell I won't.*

Ruth pulled up in front of the house and sat in the rented car, letting the engine idle. The house was two stories of wind-and salt-weathered cedar and gleaming glass. *Very impressive, Uncle Seth,* she decided, admiring the clean, sharp lines and lavish use of open space he had used in designing this house.

Swallowing, she wondered for the hundredth time how to approach the situation. All the neat little speeches she had rehearsed on the plane seemed hopelessly silly or strained.

"Nick, I thought we should talk," she tried out loud, then laid her forehead on the steering wheel. Brilliant. *Why don't I just use, "Hello, Nick, I was just passing by, thought I'd drop in?" That's original.*

Just do it, she told herself. *Just go up there and knock on the door and let it happen.* Moving quickly, Ruth shut off the engine and slid out of the car. The six steps leading to the front door looked impossibly high. Taking a deep breath, as she had so many other times for a jeté from the wings, she climbed them.

Now, knock, she ordered herself as she stared at the door. *Just lift your hand, close it into a fist and knock.*

It took her a full minute to manage it. She waited, the breath backing up in her lungs. No answer. With more determination she knocked again. And waited.

Unable to bear the suspense any longer, Ruth put her hand on the knob and turned. She almost leaped back when it opened to her touch. The locks and bolts of Manhattan were more familiar.

The living room apparently took up the entire first floor. The back wall was almost completely in glass, featuring a stunning panorama of the Pacific. For a moment Ruth forgot her anxiety. She had seen other buildings of her uncle's design, but this was a masterpiece.

The floor was wood, graced by a few very plain buff-colored rugs. He had placed no paintings on the walls. The ocean was art enough. Trinkets were few, but she lifted an exquisite old brass silent butler that pleased her tremendously. There was a bar with shelves behind it lined with glasses of varying colors and shapes. The sofa was thick and deep and piled with pillows. A gleaming mahogany grand piano stood in the back of the room, its top opened wide. Ruth went to it and lifted a sheet of staff paper.

Musical notes dotted it, with Nick's meticulous hand-writing in the margins. The Russian writing was unintelligible to her, but she began to pick out the melody on the piano.

His new ballet? She listened carefully to the unfamiliar music. With a smile she set the paper back in place. He was amazing, she decided. Davidov had the greatest capacity for work of anyone she had ever known.

But where was he?

Ruth turned to look around the room again. Could he have gone back to New York? Not with the door unlocked and pages of his new ballet still on the piano! She glanced at her watch and suddenly remembered: she was still on East Coast time. Oh, for heaven's sake, she thought as she quickly calculated the time difference. It was early! He was probably still in bed.

Slowly, Ruth walked to the stairs and peered up. *I can't just go up there.* She pressed her lips together. *I could call.* She opened her mouth and shut it again on a sound of annoyance. What could she say? *Yoo-hoo, Nick, time to get up?* She lifted her fingers to her lips to stifle a nervous giggle.

Taking a deep breath, Ruth put her hand on the banister and started to climb.

Nick opened the double glass doors that led from the back deck to the living room. He was breathing hard. His sweat shirt was dampened in a long vee from neck to hem. The exertion had helped. He felt cleaner, clearer. He would go up and have a shower and then work through the day on the new ballet. His plans to go east and drag Ruth back with him were the thoughts of a crazy man.

Halfway into the room, he stopped. The scent of wildflowers overwhelmed him. God! Would he never escape her?

What right had she to do this to him, to haunt him wherever he went? Damn her, he thought furiously. *I've had enough of this!*

Striding to the phone, he lifted it and punched out Ruth's number in New York. Without any idea of what he would say, Nick waited in blind fury for her to answer. With another curse, he hung up again. *Where the devil is she? The company? No.* He shook his head immediately. *Lindsay.* Of course, where else would she go?

Nick picked up the phone again and had pushed four numbers when a sound caught his attention. Frowning, he glanced toward the stairs. Ruth walked down, her own face creased in a frown.

Their eyes met immediately.

"So, there you are," she said and hoped the words didn't sound as foolish as they felt. "I was looking for you."

With infinite care Nick replaced the phone receiver on its cradle. "Yes?"

Though his response was far from gracious, Ruth came down the rest of the steps. "Yes. Your door was unlocked. I hope you don't mind that I just came in."

"No."

She fidgeted nervously, concentrating all her effort into a smile. "I noticed you've started work on a new ballet."

"I've begun, yes." The words were carefully spaced. His eyes never left hers.

Unable to bear the contact, Ruth turned to wander the room. "This is a lovely place. I can see why you come whenever you have the chance. I've always loved the ocean. We stayed in a house on the Pacific once in Japan." She began to ramble on, hardly knowing what she said but needing to fill the space with words. Nick remained silent, studying her back as she stared out to sea.

Realizing his muscles were balled tight, Nick forced them to relax. He hadn't heard a word she had said.

"Do you come to enjoy the view?" he demanded, interrupting her.

Ruth winced, then composed her face before she turned. "I came to see you," she told him. "I have things to say."

"Very well." He gestured with his hand. "Say them."

His unconscious gesture stiffened her spine. "Oh, I intend to. Sit down."

His brow lifted at the order. After a moment he moved to the sofa. "I'm sitting."

"Do you practice being insufferable, Davidov, or is it a natural talent?"

Nick waited a moment, then leaned back against the pillows. "You've traveled three thousand miles to tell me this?"

"And more," Ruth shot back. "I've no intention of being buried by you, professionally or personally. We'll speak of the dancing first."

"By all means." Nick lifted his hands and let them fall. "Please continue."

"I'm a good dancer, and whether you partner me or not, I'll continue to be a good dancer. In the company you can tell me to dance until my feet drop off, and I'll do it. You're the director."

"I'm aware of that."

Ruth glared at him. "But that's where it stops. You don't direct my life. Whatever I do or don't do is my choice and my responsibility. If I choose to take a dozen lovers or live like a hermit, you have nothing whatever to say about it."

"You think not?" His words were cool enough, his position still easy against the pillows, but fury had leaped into his eyes.

"I *know* you." Ruth took another step toward him. "As long as I'm free, until I make a personal commitment, no one has any business interfering with how I live, with what I do. No one questions you, Davidov. You wouldn't permit it. Well, neither will I." She put her hands on her hips. "If you think I'll run along like a good little girl and pack my bags because you tell me to, you're sadly mistaken. I'm not a little girl, and I won't be told what to do. I make my own choices." She walked toward him.

"You always expect everyone to cheerfully do your bidding," she continued, still fuming. "But you'd better prepare yourself for a shock. I've no intention of being your underling. Partners, Davidov, in every sense. And I won't live with you. It's not good enough. If you want me, you'll have to marry me. That's it." Ruth crossed her arms over her chest and waited.

Nick straightened slowly, then, taking another moment, rose. "Is that an ultimatum?"

"You bet it is."

"I see." He studied her consideringly. "It seems you give me no choice. You will wish to be married in New York?"

Ruth opened her mouth, and when there were no words, cleared her throat. "Well, yes—I suppose."

"Did you have in mind a small ceremony or something large?"

With the impetus gone, she stared at him in confusion. "I don't know… I hadn't thought…"

"Well, you can decide on the plane, yes?" He gave her an odd smile. "Shall I make reservations for a flight now?"

"Yes. No," she said when he turned for the phone. Nick tilted his head and waited. "All right, yes, go ahead." Ruth went to the windows again and stared out. *Why*, she asked herself, *does it seem so wrong?*

"Ruth." He waited until she faced him again. "I've told you I love you. I've said the same words to women I don't even remember. Words mean little."

She swallowed and felt the ache begin. The whole expanse of the room separated them.

"I have not shown you, as I wanted to, the way I felt. You make me clumsy." He spread his fingers. "A difficult thing for a dancer to admit. If I were not clumsy, I could tell you that my life is not my life without you. I could tell you that you are the heart of it, the muscle, the bone. I could tell you there is only emptiness and aching without you. I could tell you that to be your partner, your husband, your lover, is what I want more than breath. But..." He shook his head. "You make me clumsy, and I can only tell you that I love you and hope it is enough."

"Nick!" She ran for him, and he caught her before she was halfway across the room.

He held her tightly, just filling himself with the joy of having her in his arms again. "When I saw you walk down the stairs, I thought it was a dream. I thought I had gone mad."

"I thought you'd still be asleep."

"Sleep? I don't think there has been sleep since you left me." He drew her away. "Never again," he said fiercely. "Hate me, shout at me, but don't leave me again." His mouth came down on hers and smothered her promise.

Her answer was as wild and heated as his demand. She tangled her fingers into his hair, pressing him closer, wanting to drown in the current that raged between them. Need soared through her, a raw, urgent hunger that made her mouth grow more desperate under his. Desire came in an avalanche of sensations; his taste, his scent, the thick soft texture of his hair in her hands.

"I love you." Her mouth formed the words but made no sound. "I want you."

She felt him release the zipper at her back and let the dress slip to the floor. Nick let out a low groaning murmur as he stroked his hands down her sides.

"So small, *lyubovnitsa*, I fear always to hurt you."

"I'm a dancer," she reminded him, thrilling to the touch of his hands over the thin silk of her chemise. "Strong as an ox." They lowered to the sofa and lay tangled together. "I was afraid," she murmured, closing her eyes as his hands gently aroused her. "Afraid to trust you, afraid to love you, afraid to lose you."

"Both of us." He pulled her close and just held her. "No more."

Ruth slipped her hand under his shirt to lay it on his heart. *Davidov*, she thought. How many years had she worshipped the legend? Now the man was hers. And she his. She held his heart and was sure of it. Smiling, she pressed her lips to his neck and lingered there.

"Davidov?"

"Mmm?"

"Are you really going to accept that ultimatum?"

His hand reached for her breast. "I've thought about it. It seems for the best. You were very fierce. I think I'll humor you."

"Oh, do you?" Her smile was in her voice.

"Yes, but I will not permit your dozen lovers unless they are all me." He took his mouth on a teasing journey along her jaw line. "I think I should keep you busy enough."

"Maybe," she said and sighed luxuriously as he began to unlace the front of her chemise.

His mouth came to hers and swept her away even as he continued to undress her. "I will be a very jealous husband. Unreasonable, perhaps violent." He lifted his face to smile down at her. "Very hard to live with. Do I still call for the plane?"

Ruth opened her eyes and looked into his. She smiled. "Yes. Tomorrow."

* * * * *